ADA'S
TERRACE

Hull: Love and Romance
in Wartime

Margaret King

Jo Eva, Edited by J & F Kelly
you have experienced
the times and the places
I hope they are happy
memories for you

Best wishes Margaret

Published by
Frismeck Publishing

This novel is entirely a work of fiction
based upon an informed imagination, and except in the case
of historical fact, any resemblance to actual persons
living or dead is purely coincidental.

Acknowledgements

Margaret and Bill King for this wonderful story and for their inspiration, patience, creativity and friendship.

Rex Booth for his invaluable praise and direction with the project, proof reading the whole text and advising with literary contacts, and Mavis for letting Rex give so much of his time to the book.

Jane Hitchin for proof reading the whole book and helping us understand the genre.

Pat Greaken for her patience and kindness while correcting grammatical mistakes and proof reading.

Julie Reay for her proofreading, encouragement and enjoyment of the book.

Barbara Watkinson for reading the book, for her encouragement and interest in the project.

Rowan Paris and Andrew Burgess for their help with cover design, execution, technical support, formatting and uploading to the template.

Alec Gill for helping us with his literary contacts and know how.

Claire Carroll for her wonderful and creative character portraits for the front book cover.

Dorothy and Monica Bohm for allowing us to use Dorothy's wonderful photograph of a mother and child.

James Mitchell at *The Hull Daily Mail* for his kind permission to use the original photo for the back book cover.

Steve Terjeson *at wwii.com* for advising us on the use of the photograph of an unknown soldier in Burma.

Borge Solem from *Skipper Heritage Ships* for his kind permission to use the Riverside Quay Painting.

Paul Jennison for all his practical support and help.

To my beloved Bill,
who believes that every man has a soul,
and that no man is just a number.

Author's Preface

It has been my privilege and pleasure to know several dockers and their families over a number of years. Uncles, fathers, brothers, cousins and grandfathers: being a docker was a family affair. They were a band of hard working men with a wry sense of humour and strong beliefs who worked hard and played hard (as anyone who enjoyed a Saturday night at the dockers' social club will know!) From the day when hundreds of bicycles were the dockers' mode of transport to the night in the club, all has changed now that the dockers' work force has been decimated. In this book I have tried to encapsulate some of the camaraderie and caring that existed. Although it is a work of fiction, as you read it perhaps you may think, 'I knew someone like that,' or 'yes, it was a bit like that!'

Margaret King

Characters

Sam Walters: A docker living at No. 7 Ada's Terrace
Emma Walters: Sam's wife
Billy Walters: Oldest son
George Walters: Second son
Mary Walters: Oldest daughter
Joanie Walters: Youngest daughter
Jack Walters 'Jackie': Youngest son

John Walters: Sam's father at No. 44 Swatman Street
Eliza Walters: 'Nanna Shushkin' Sam's mother
Daisy Walters: Sam's sister

Bert Johnson: Emma's father at *Bann's Farm*, Redtoft
Jane Johnson: Emma's mother
Annie Johnson: Emma's sister

Harry Hawkins: Labourer, neighbour of the Walters'
Lily Hawkins 'Lil': Harry's wife and friend of Emma's
Ivan Hawkins: Harry and Lil's eldest son
Willie Hawkins: Harry and Lil's youngest son
Joy Hawkins: Harry and Lil's daughter
Ronnie and Roy Hawkins: twins

Ada's Terrace: A fictional terrace in Hull

CHAPTER ONE

'Seeya tomorrow Sam!' said Gappy Howles as - with the gummiest smile anyone could imagine - he got on his bike.

Sam grinned back, 'Seeya Gappy! Don't drink too much!'

It was early June in 1935 as Sam Walters, wearing the customary flat peaked cap, came cycling off the Hull docks after a hard day's work and set off, with relief, for his home in Ada's Terrace.

In the uncharacteristic heat wave the East Yorkshire summer sun was still shining like it never would rest, and away from the docks and the main road, Sam cheerfully whistled *The Gypsy Rover* to himself as he wove past the happy boys and girls spilling out from all the little terraces that backed away from every street. Watching the *bains* playing games reminded Sam of his own boys. 'Will our lads become dockers like me?' he wondered, 'Will George or our Jackie?'

Near Sam's home the clothes lines which criss-crossed over the terraces were mostly empty, as yesterday, the traditional Monday washday, had also been a burning scorcher of a day. Sam spoke cheerily to some of the women who were sitting on the window-sills of their houses in the sunshine, watching the children play.

Now rounding the corner of Merton Street, Sam saw his daughter Mary standing on the corner of Ada's Terrace. With the hint of a proud father's smile resting on his features, he pulled up his bike to watch her. She saw him in the same instant and came running to meet him. Affectionately swinging on his arm, her blue eyes joyfully alight in a face that was older than her years she said, 'Come on our Dad, Mam's made you a meat and tattie pie!'

Sam smiled, 'And what have you been doin' today, me lass?'

'Ah, boring, old school. I don't know how our Billy stands it. I wouldn't want to stay in school until I'm sixteen. All that maths and foreign languages, I'm going to leave as soon as I can.'

'And what about being a nurse?' Sam asked, 'I thought that was what you wanted?'

1

Mary shook her head, 'That was weeks ago. I've changed my mind since then. Oh, there's Jean!' she said with a flash of a grin and catching sight of her friend, she dashed off.

Sam pushed open their back gate and parked his bike. 'Ah'm back!' he called, hanging his jacket in the lobby and stepping into the kitchen to kiss Emma, his wife tenderly on the cheek. He felt fortunate to have such an attractive wife and appreciated again her sleek, brown hair in the neat bun, her retroussé nose, brown eyes and warm smile with which she happily greeted him.

Noticing her husband's extra weariness and not wanting to bother him too much, Emma murmured, 'Here you are, love,' and passed him a kettle of hot water which he poured into the bowl in the brownstone sink in the corner.

Grateful, he gave her a frazzled smile as he washed the day's grime from his face, arms and hands. He was starting to relax now that he was home.

As he took off his shirt, Emma could see the angry, red blotches which covered his muscular back, neck and arms from handling the ship's cargo of copra: he was not a complainer, but it was an irritating cargo to work on and the coconut fibres seemed to get everywhere.

Emma went over to tenderly cover his blotches with calamine lotion. It was the only remedy she had for him. 'Did you finish the ship?' she asked.

Sam nodded, 'Aye lass, and thanks for the calamine; I don't think there will be much more work this week.'

Emma put Sam's dinner on the table and as he started to eat he began to feel that his day was definitely getting better. 'Good pie!' he said. 'Where have our lads got themselves to?'

'George has gone fishing down at the pier, Billy's upstairs doing his homework and Mary's keeping an eye on Jackie.'

'Does Joanie think herself above all that?' asked Sam.

'Aye it's hard enough to get her to do *anything*. You'll have to talk to her, Sam. All her head is full of is film stars and how she's going to be one. She's been going on about tap-dancing lessons again and when I said that we couldn't afford it, she flounced off to that drama group at the Methodist Hall.'

'I suppose everyone has their dreams,' Sam remarked.

'And with most people that's just how they stay. Just dreams. Such things won't fill hungry bellies or pay the rent!' retorted Emma.

2

'Well,' said Sam trying to be conciliatory, 'at least we know where she is!' Emma's suspicions were that Joanie was more secretive than she wanted other people to know.

'There's the paper for you to have a look at. I know you like to know what's going on in the world,' said Sam, pulling an evening paper from his jacket pocket and putting it on the table. 'Bob Pearson gave it to me, he only wanted to look at the racing results.'

'Thanks love. I'll just mash this pot of tea for you.' When Emma sat down to look at the paper *The Evening Record* had the banner headlines:

Hitler's New Proposals to the Powers
Mr Baldwin gave an assurance to the House of Commons
No Conscription While Peace Prevails.

'Do you really think, Sam, it will come to war with Germany?'

Sam paused in his eating, 'How should I know? I'm only a docker! But the country couldn't afford another war because we haven't finished paying for the last one yet!'

Just then, Billy, their eldest son, came into the room, 'Oh! There'll be a war all right!' he said. 'This Hitler chap will string them along just to get more time to be fully armed. Mr. Dennison says…'

'Mr Dennison should know better than to fill young lads' heads with all this talk of war,' Emma scolded, 'you are supposed to be learning, not listening to such talk as that.'

'We're taught to think Mam, to use our heads and anyone with half an eye can see…'

'Don't you argue with your mother!' Sam ordered. 'It's all very well to be *thinking* but you need to be treating your parents with due respect - even when you do disagree!'

Billy shrugged and walked to the open door, 'There's John, I'm just going for a yarn,' he called as he went out of their concreted yard.

Sam finished his tea and emptied his pockets carefully, putting most of his change on to the mantelpiece above the *Yorkist* cast-iron kitchen range. He picked up his jacket and said, 'I'll just have a walk to *The Volunteer*.'

3

'Send our Mary and our lad Jackie in, if you see them!' Emma called, as Sam turned out of the terrace and on to Merton Street where the children were playing.

'Your Mam wants you,' he told them.

'Oh, do we have to?' groaned Mary. Her game of hopscotch was at a crucial point.

Sam was unmoved, 'In!' he repeated. 'Your Mam wants you. Come on our Jackie!' Mary knew it was useless to argue and sister and brother together, they went in. The sun had gone down and up from the river a light breeze brought the smell of kippers being smoked in the fish yards.

Having arrived at his favourite haunt, Sam greeted Wally Ingles, landlord of *The Volunteer* pub, 'Ah! It will rain before mornin'.'

'You're right there Sam,' Wally's double chin shook as he nodded his assent, 'What's it to be - the usual?'

'Aye, just a half,' agreed Sam.

Clarry Hughes nodded familiarly to Sam over the top of his paper, 'Looks like the bookies caught a cold over the Derby winner!'

Sam smiled sceptically, 'Aye, Clarry, but they have lots of aspirin to go with it! Them bookies who took your bets are the *only* ones who come out on top. After all, it's them who stay in business and live a life of luxury!'

Clarry had touched on a raw nerve, as Sam's father, John Walters, had been one for having a bet. It irked Sam to remember how much trouble his mother, Eliza, used to have in trying to put food on the table for the family. This was especially so when his father had *invested* his payday wages in betting on his way home. 'Some things you don't forget,' he thought to himself ruefully while remembering that at least it taught him to *invest* in the care of his own family.

Back home in the upstairs bedroom in their little terraced house, young Jackie was already asleep and Mary was lolling complacently in the old wicker-bottomed chair by the window. Joanie was brushing her soft, brown hair in front of the mirror counting the strokes, 'Fifty-eight, fifty-nine, sixty...'

'Why does it have to be a hundred strokes? Why not seventy-eight or ninety-six?' asked Mary.

4

Joanie could not tell her why. 'All the beauty hints in the magazines say *a hundred strokes* - so that's what it's going to be!' replied Joanie firmly.

'Mary asked in puzzlement, 'What did you go to the Methodist Hall for? I just can't stand that Mr Sawdon. He wears funny ties and cracks jokes all the time!'

Joanie did not answer her. Thwarted for now in her desire to learn tap-dancing, she had her own reasons for going to the Methodist Hall drama class and did not want her presently formulating plans to be known or hinted at and not least to family members who could prevent them.

She had decided, no matter what the obstacles, that she was going to act, to dance and sing. More than that Joanie was going to be a *film star*. Methodism? Huh! Her career awaited her, and the meaning of life was only for old people!

None of the other Walters children went to the Methodist Hall drama class that Joanie attended. Neither did they aspire to a life of fame. However, on Sunday mornings, all of the younger Walters children went to the Methodist Sunday School as part of their weekly routine. For Emma, Sunday mornings gave her a chance to get on with the usual Sunday dinner that was the family high spot of the week.

Sunday mornings, for Sam, meant that he was able, while the children were at Sunday School, to fetch the big tin bath off the nail where it hung in the yard, fill it up with lots of lovely, warm water and throw in a handful of soda crystals for his relaxing weekly bath. This was a sluicing routine that was carried out in many a home, so that everyone knew what his neighbour was doing and would not dream of bothering him, even if he did sing in the bath!

The Walters children used to bathe in the kitchen on a Saturday night - a rowdy, noisy, wishy-washy, splashy, scrubby time. But now that they were older Billy, George, Mary and Joanie went to the Public Baths in Rawling Street where there was proper privacy and full-sized *slipper baths* with hot and cold running water, almost unimaginable total luxury!

Up in the airless bedroom which Joanie, Mary and young Jackie shared, the silence had been too long for Mary, 'I asked you what you went to the Methodist Hall for!' she repeated with vehemence.

Joanie's face flushed as she stressed every word of her reply, 'I heard what you said!'

'*I heard what you said,*' Mary mimicked while pulling a face at her sister, but failed to duck quickly enough when Joanie flung her hairbrush at her hitting her on the side of the head.

Enraged, Mary dived across the bed to reach Joanie but only succeeded in accidentally kicking their little brother, Jackie who woke up with a frightened look and a scared howl.

Mary gathered him up in her skinny arms, 'Hush my bain!' she whispered in imitation of her mother, rocking the boy so that he settled back to sleep. 'Look what you made me do!' she grumbled, 'If Mam had heard...' But fortunately for both of them there was no creak on the stairs.

As Mary had hinted, if Emma had cause to come upstairs to investigate there would indeed have been swift justice. Both would have been punished so that the real culprit would undoubtedly get the chastening. Emma often believed that the guilt for these rows was shared equally - as in six of one and half a dozen of the other!

In order to smooth her own ruffled feathers Joanie took a little bottle from her dress pocket and dabbed some of the contents behind her ears; the sweet aroma of bergamot, sandalwood, orange and cedar spread quickly.

'Where did you get that?' demanded Mary.

'Wouldn't you like to know!' she answered tauntingly, 'Joy Hawkins gave it to me.' Joanie was positively smirking now.

Mary was, in turn, horrified, 'Then it was pinched from *Woolworths'* shop! You know her brothers are always *at it* with nicking things, and our Dad said we were not to have anything from off them Hawkins kids.'

Joanie only smiled, 'It's *Phul-Nana* perfume. You just keep quiet and I'll let you have some on Sunday!' Saying no more she slipped the thin, cotton nightie over her head and climbed into bed.

As Sam walked home from the pub, the first spots of rain were beginning to fall. Although it was not yet dark, he had spent up to his limit and it was not his custom to let another man buy his beer if he could not stand a round for those drinking with him. Sam did not want to be thought of as a scrounger.

Walking along the street, he was suddenly accosted by two strangers who leaped out from a dingy doorway, demanding his money and watch.

Avoiding their first blows with a swift dance step, he said 'Oi! Wotcha doin'? You've got the wrong man!'

They rushed at him together from the front shouting, 'We're going to get you!'

Sam's years of physical labour, of lifting and carrying stood him in good stead. He reached out swiftly, grabbed them both by their shirt fronts, lifted them up bodily and twice banged them together forcefully like a pair of cymbals, before dropping them on their backsides on the pavement. They moaned in their unconsciousness but Sam said to them, 'I told you that you'd got the wrong man!'

The two *pedestrian highwaymen* had found to their cost, as other people could have told them, that Sam was no pushover. Brushing himself off, he continued his journey while allowing himself the luxury of a little chortle of merriment and truly giving thanks to the Almighty for his own preservation.

When Sam arrived home to No. 7 Ada's Terrace, pleased to return to what he hoped was normal, calm domesticity, George, his second eldest boy, was quietly and carefully washing himself at the sink.

'Where's our Billy?' Sam wanted to know. Billy had a family obligation to set a good example for his younger brothers and sisters, but lately he had been staying out late.

'Billy will be in soon,' interjected Emma, as she pushed her hair back from her forehead betraying her nervous worry.

Sam looked displeased, 'What on earth does he think he's doing when he has to be at school early tomorrow morning? Huh! My eldest! Getting fancy ideas just because he goes to High School. Aye, I was at work at his age! He may just be getting a taste of my belt if he isn't back soon!'

Sam, with a cup of tea in his hand, had nothing else to do but to wait for Billy's return and contemplate events.

No one could say for a moment that Sam was not proud of Billy as a son, and of the fact that he had actually won a school scholarship with his brains. Without that scholarship there would have been no easy likelihood of Sam and Emma being able to afford to let Billy go to *Wordsworth High*.

Eliza, Sam's mother had insisted that Billy should have his chance in education and paid for all the school things that he needed, but Sam felt that she was trying to control Billy's future, as she had been unable to do with him.

Sam had got his own way about working on the docks like his father, and was proud to do so; he was very happy to belong to the band of men who worked there. As a boy he could not ever imagine doing anything else apart from honest dock labouring. But this had not been a popular idea with his mother, especially when he left school!

She had not wanted him to go on the docks and instead she had spoken to the manager of the *Co-op* food shop where she was a good customer, and arranged for Sam to start work there as a bicycle errand boy.

He had tried very hard to be a good errand boy, but regardless of where he was supposed to be delivering groceries, somehow or other his bike and the groceries seemed to end up unattended by the dock railings where some opportunist without a conscience, would be busy acquiring an unexpected treat for his next meal!

Mr Pawson, the manager could see that his errand boy's heart was not in the job, and then Sam had the difficult job of telling his mother that he had been sacked.

The very next morning, his father with a happy twinkle in his eye, handed Sam a green scarf and told him to put it on. Then Sam had walked proudly along Commercial Road with his father to the docks, in the way that he had always wanted!

'You there with the green muffler!' the foreman had said, and Sam, to the mutters of some of the men who had not been so fortunate, walked up the gangplank amidst dark comments about *left-footer*s getting the jobs!

Sam knew from his father's experience, that it was not an easy job nor was daily work guaranteed. You got to the dock early, and waited there hopefully at the gangplank with all the other casual dockworkers, and if you were fortunate, the foreman would give you the nod and you were employed for the day.

Sam also knew, as did many of his workmates, that in the choice of workers for the day, there was fiddling going on; corruption on the job. It was not unknown for an unscrupulous man to pass the foreman a matchbox; the bribe would be in it, two shillings or half a crown. But that was not true for all the foremen. After all, most of them were straight-dealing and they knew which of the men would give an honest day's work.

Dock workers, known universally as dockers, were a close-knit group of men whose families had lived for generations with loading and offloading cargoes, trimming and ballasting aboard ships, filling dock sheds, carrying boxes, rolling barrels and handling bales.

Fathers, sons, grandfathers, brothers and uncles had all learned their trade and were proud of it. Hundreds of them could be seen at the end of their day, riding home on old bicycles with flat caps on their heads and string tied round their protective, long overcoats. Dockers also had a wry sense of humour that was evident in the nicknames that some of them acquired!

Apart from dock cranes and ship's cranes, lorries, trains and coal chutes, there was not much in the way of machinery that could easily help with dock work. Much dock work involved the personal use of human muscle power and a good repertoire of manual skills, including the use of the humble wheelbarrow!

Within their code of ethics, when Sam was first learning his trade as a young boy, they had expected him to really pull his weight. However, they also did not expect him to lift anything which because of his youth, would have caused him injury. Instead they expected him to look and learn as he worked. Muscle alone was not enough.

'Ah well! All that was in the past,' he thought to himself but he knew that it still rankled with his mother that he had become only a docker; why had he not wanted to become a teacher or a bank manager?

And she had not forgiven him for marrying Emma, 'Marrying below his station. Huh!'

Sam had fallen for Emma while they were both schoolchildren, her loving heart and pretty face had won him. Sam was not the greatest of romantics.

While she was not perfect, he knew that there was something about her that made him want to spend the rest of his days with her.

Sam had tried to tell his mother that Emma's family were just as house-proud as she was. Emma's family, he told her, lived in an old house in the country in the village of Redtoft about five miles east of Hull, on a piece of land from which

9

Emma's father, Bert Johnson, her mother Jane and sister Annie, tried to wrest an honest living.

They were a happy-go-lucky family. It had made no difference that Sam told his mother that they ate proper food. No! Not hedgehogs baked in clay, or stolen poultry. Emma's father genuinely reared his own poultry, grew his own fruit and vegetables and had a pony and pig!

Sadly, old Mrs Walters saw Emma only as a threat; getting herself pregnant so that Sam would be forced to marry her.

Sam's mother had steadfastly refused to go to Sam and Emma's wedding, because in her mind those people were, in social status, nothing removed from gypsies.

All the dreams Sam's mother had cherished, including the idea of Sam as a manager of a *Co-op* shop, with a wife who was a cut above the rest and a new house like the ones they were building on the Ridgeway, had been shattered by a girl with big, brown eyes, and a family that were not even good Catholics!

'Sam,' she thought, 'could have had such a bright future.' And she could not accept it when John Walters, her husband, said, 'Let the lad alone, he has his own life to lead!'

Voices from outside his Ada's Terrace home broke in on Sam's reverie, and told him that Billy was arriving back home. Sam, Emma and George heard his cheery goodnight as he left his friend and came into their little backyard. Moments later, he entered the kitchen and the atmosphere became tense.

'Do you know what time it is?' was Sam's terse greeting.

Billy was quickly on the defensive, 'It's not late!'

'It might not be what your fine school friends call late,' said Sam, 'but I'm a working man and I have to be up in the morning. No fancy suits and nine o'clock starts for me!'

Emma and George held their breath; Emma was silently praying that Billy would not say the wrong thing.

Billy, who was now deeply aware of the tension, licked his lips. Looking to his brother George for moral support he said tentatively, 'Not all the lads have got bank managers for fathers.'

'Billy, I'm not taking any lip from you!' warned Sam. 'George, it's time you were in bed!' Clearly sorry that he was about to miss the rest of the drama, George went slowly up the stairs.

Sam turned again to Billy. 'Where have you been?'

10

'I went with John to *Willis Street School*,' was the reply. 'There was a meeting about a Peace Campaign. Some councillors say, that as our town cannot be identified as having naval, air, or military bases, we don't need to worry about defence plans or precautions, but Mr Percival said we ought to have plans for ambulances and medical aid.'

'Meeting or not, you know what time you should be in.' Sam would not be appeased, 'Now get to bed!'

For a moment it seemed that Billy would argue, but with a shrug of the shoulders, he went upstairs without another word.

Emma sighed an inward and outward sigh of relief and gave thanks to the Almighty that there had been no family explosion over Billy breaking the house rules. In her relief, her thoughts turned to her friend, Mrs Lily Hawkins from No. 11 Ada's Terrace. Lily had said that Billy had *spirit* and she liked a kid with *spirit*.

Privately Emma thought, that with Lily's husband, Harry, her son, Ivan, the twins Ronnie and Roy and Willie and Joy, there was more than enough *spirit* for a dozen such families! 'With all seven of them crowded together into their little house, they do well to survive as well as they do - just like us!' Emma thought to herself.

Mr Harry Hawkins worked as a labourer whenever he could get taken on for work. He was a little shrivelled-up man with red-rimmed eyes. He looked just as if his life's strength had been sapped away by his large, ebullient wife and his noisy, rumbustuous family.

Lily herself was a larger than life character; a true matriarch of the Terrace. She would stand in her doorway, with her knitting needles tucked under her arms and her skilful fingers flying through the woollen yarn as she watched the children play. All the while she would be keeping an eye on everything. Indeed, nothing moved in the terrace that she did not know about, but she was also one of those people known as having *a heart of gold*.

George looked up at his brother as Billy came into the bedroom, 'Pushing your luck with the old man, weren't you?' he asked.

Billy's mouth tightened up in partial agreement, 'Sometimes I wonder if he really knows that there's a world beyond the docks and Merton Street,' was Billy's answer.

'Did you actually go to that meeting?' George wanted to know.

'Yes, and I'm going to another one soon,' was the answer. 'Mr Dennison says it's no use just sitting back and waiting for something to happen.'

'Then I guess he doesn't go fishing!' chuckled George as he rolled over in bed.

CHAPTER TWO

The corner of Ada's Terrace led directly away from Merton Street, as did several other little terraces. It was dark and shady because somehow the sun never adequately reached the rows of houses that stood there modestly back-to-back. Backing on to Ada's Terrace were the houses of Nelson Terrace, and across the bottom of them both, stood the warehouse belonging to *Cantrell's* shop.

In these crowded terraces, privacy was a rare luxury and everybody knew everybody else's affairs and foibles. Just as an elephant could not easily be hidden on a cricket pitch; singing, laughing, shouting and arguing could not easily be hidden from your neighbours. Indeed it was a well-known joke that the walls were so thin that if you opened the oven door, you could reach through and dip your bread in your neighbour's gravy! It was always as well to be able to get on with your neighbours.

It was eleven o'clock at night and all was quiet now except for the occasional wail of a ship's siren or the whistle of a railway steam engine. Most working folk were in their beds, which they would say was *only right and proper* when they had to be up early for work the next day.

The rain that had threatened to fall earlier in the day had not come and the wind had dropped. Once more the air was hot and sticky; if only Ada's Terrace felt cooler!

Downstairs, Sam and Emma lay in their makeshift, patent put-you-up bed, the one which they made up every night in their living room. With only two bedrooms upstairs in the small house, it was the youngsters who slept up there. This, in a well-managed household, was one of the reasons why the boys needed to be in bed when told to be, so that their parents could go to bed at their usual time.

When Sam and Emma settled down for the night, Sam would be settled in to the world of his dreams within five or ten minutes. This night however, was different. As time passed, Emma thought he must be asleep, but then he stirred and spoke, 'Did you see in the paper about Jack Poskwith?' he asked.

Emma whispered, 'No, I didn't get round to reading it, Jackie had torn his trousers so I 'ad them to mend so he's tidy for school tomorrow.'

'Yeh! Jack Poskwith. He got copped. Absolutely red-handed he was; coming off *Corporation Dock* with a shilling's worth of stolen rags!'

'So?' Emma was now intrigued and in the darkness her eyes brightened with interest, 'What happened?' she asked.

'Bound over he was, by the court,' was Sam's reply. 'Sergeant Price spoke up for him, an' he's fair, you know. The Sergeant said that Jack was a good worker, when he can get taken on. He gets but thirty-five bob a week government dole money, and there's three little bains to feed and clothe.'

Emma could not help thinking how hard it was to manage her own budget on what Sam brought home, but suddenly her reverie was interrupted by the sound of glass breaking. 'Did you hear that?' Emma whispered in alarm.

Sam had heard it and, fearless, was out of bed pulling on his trousers and making for the door.

Emma sat up, warning him to be careful.

He stood on the doorstep, eyes and ears straining in the gloom. Windows do not break themselves.

'Tis a fine night, Mr Walters,' came a woman's voice from across the terrace.

'It is that,' agreed Sam. 'I just had to have a breath of air,' he said, as he shut the door and went back to bed.

'What's going on?' asked Emma.

'It's the Hawkins lads,' Sam said, 'they're out on the roof of *Cantrell's* warehouse and old Lil Hawkins is keeping watch. I didn't let on that I'd seen 'em. No doubt tomorrow her pantry will be full. Don't you have anything from her!' he warned.

Emma agreed. If anything went wrong, old Lily Hawkins would be looking round to see just who had shopped her lads. Emma did not want anything to do with that!

Now that there were no more disturbances, Sam turned over in bed.

Emma, letting her fancies fly, said with a yawn, 'A big 'ouse would suit me just fine!'

'Aye, lass, me too!' said Sam, 'but we should be thankful for small mercies. For now let's think: you an' me's married, we've got five kids an' however small the 'ouse, we're all together!'

'You're right Sam, of course,' murmured Emma drowsily before she slept, 'we 'ave to make the most of it.'

The next morning, Sam went out after breakfast to catch the early edition of the *Hull Daily Mail* newspaper before going to work. Apart from worrying rumours of an outbreak of typhoid, Sam found in the letters column some lively discussion about housing: one humourist wrote that there were rules that said every house should be big enough to allow for people to have separate rooms to sleep in; the exception would be for husbands and wives, and also for children under ten, who would be counted as half a child.

'But which half?' Sam wisecracked to himself!

Another letter writer said that bathrooms and indoor lavatories were for moneyed people - nice if you had the money but who would be able to afford the rent!

Sam sighed, looked up to heaven and agreed with the writer.

Although unnoticed by many, the Government's Housing Survey of 1935 had been passed; its aim, to make slum clearance possible and to provide local council housing.

It had all sounded very nice to Emma and Sam when they read about it in the paper, but they could not really see it happening. Naturally, they would have liked more room and more privacy for themselves and their family. Living as they did, they thought that having the two of them and five children in a house with only two bedrooms was approaching lunacy!

The next day, Sam treated Mary and Joanie to the cinema as he always did on Saturdays. Mary had wanted to see a Laurel and Hardy film, but Joanie, who loved to hear good singing, had insisted that they should go and see Grace Moore in *Wings of Song*. And Lily Hawkins gave her daughter, Joy, tuppence to go to the *Rialto* with them.

Along with the feature film was the *Pathé* newsreel in which the big news was all about Amy Johnson, a Hull girl, who had recently become a world famous record-breaking flyer! Mary and Joanie gasped and everyone was excited as they watched the footage of her in her little aeroplane! Joanie felt inspired: if women like Amy Johnson could do heroic things if they put their minds to it, then what could she do?

15

Young Jackie had stayed at home playing in a bath of water in the backyard and had spent his tuppence pocket money on sweets. He had been joined by Willie Hawkins who had been left to his own devices for the day and a grand battle was taking place with their home-made boats and the splashing of water everywhere.

The *Butcher's Arms* pub had gone on a charabanc outing to the seaside at Bridlington and Lily Hawkins, all dolled up, went with them leaving Pop Hawkins to hold the fort, not that any of the children took much notice of him!

Ivan Hawkins, the eldest boy had recently got a job and treated his mum to a permanent wave.

She had come home, in high spirits from the hairdressers with her new perm: her hair was set with deep waves and sausage-like curls and there was no stopping her proclaiming just how good her boys were to her.

After hearing this praise for the umpteenth time, Harry Hawkins felt moved to protest, 'I'm your husband, I work, you know, whenever I can - in fact I give you everything I earn - what more can I do?'

Lil's chuckling answer was swift and to the point, 'Go out and ruddy well earn some more!'

After the films were over, the girls came out of the cinema, blinking into the bright sunshine. They made their way safely across the road to the far side, where a piece of wasteland was piled high with old, wooden fish boxes just waiting to be climbed.

Joanie watched disdainfully as Mary sat on a box and Joy played at *stepping stones*. 'If you aren't careful, you'll stink of fish,' Joanie warned them.

'You're not careful because you already do!' said Joy cheekily. At this Joy and Mary beat a hasty retreat for home with Joanie trailing behind.

Joanie, star-struck as ever, would have liked to have used the boxes as a stage, and to have sung, the way the actress in the film had done.

For the famous actress, the sky had *turned blue* and even the birds had sung along with her. Joanie was sure it could happen like that for her if only she had the chance.

Billy met his friend, John Taylor, after dinner and they walked down to the Railway Dock.

Sitting on a pile of wooden railway sleepers, they skimmed stones across the water.

'So,' said John, clearly annoyed. 'You won't come to the meeting tomorrow afternoon?'

'We always have to go and see my Nanna on Sunday,' Billy replied.

'No one would get me to go and visit family on a Sunday afternoon,' replied John.

'It's alright for you,' Billy told him, 'but it's Nanna who's helped me to go to High School! I have to go and see her and tell her how I'm getting on. Making my report, if you see what I mean. Now she wants to know all about the job I've got.'

'Alright,' agreed John, 'but how about going to the meeting tonight then? After all, one of Oswald Moseley's men is speaking at the *Wilton Rooms*.'

Billy hesitated. If he went home for tea and his parents knew where he meant to go, he would never get out again that night. But, what if he did not go home for tea...?

Ah! Bath night! Back home, Sam was filling the old tin bath for Emma.

She set about bathing young Jackie, in spite of his protests. 'I'm not dirty enough for a bath because I've been playing in water all afternoon!' he complained.

Next, it was Mary and Joanie's turn to wash their hair, then Emma washed hers.

George had been out fishing all day as he usually did when he had enough spare time. He had come home triumphantly carrying a big eel and stopped to talk to the older Hawkins boys who were playing a game of cards on the path outside their house while Joy and Willie raced noisily up and down.

'Where's your Billy?' Roy Hawkins wanted to know, 'I thought he would have been ready for a game.'

'He's out!' was all that George would say, while wondering in his own mind where Billy could have got to.

What was Billy up to? It was a mystery to George. He could not understand why Billy was late into the house on *two nights running.* And George knew that the *old man* was not best pleased whenever Billy did not show up for tea.

Sam had gone off to *The Volunteer* for his half-pint of beer, leaving behind strict instructions that Billy was to have no tea when he did come in and the promise that Sam would personally deal with him when he came home. George thought that the old man was not that bad; perhaps a bit strict if you judged by Hawkins' standards, but then, if they had been Hawkins, they may not have had a dad worth the name.

Ronnie Hawkins took a fag from his pocket and brought George's attention back to the present, 'Want a drag George?' he asked.

Before George could answer, Emma came to the door and beckoned her son to come in. Her hair hung loose after washing, instead of being coiled up in the neat bun that she usually wore. George knew that she wanted him to run an errand for her, after all it was Saturday night.

Emma took out her purse. He had guessed right, 'George, just run up to *Skerrit's* and get us a pennyworth of chips each,' she said.

In the house, Mary and Joanie were sitting on the old couch. This was a gift from Emma's parents' home, and a legacy of a bygone era. It was a horsehair couch and the shiny, black covering stuck to their bare legs in hot weather. Joanie was poring over a copy of *Picture Show* magazine that someone had passed on.

Mary was hemming a piece of material in accordance with Joanie's instructions.

'Head scarves are fashion's new craze...' Joanie read aloud.

Her mother laughed, 'Women have worn scarves and shawls on their heads for donkey's years!'

Joanie felt inspired by the magazine, 'You could hardly call this a shawl, Mam. Look, you can tie it in under the hair at the back, or across the hips for the gypsy look.'

Emma smiled. Helped by Joanie, Mary kept on placidly stitching the hem. Their Mum had found enough material for both girls, but it was Mary doing the work.

George came back from *Skerrit's* with the chips and the inviting smell alone was cause enough for the sewing to be laid aside. Emma took some chips upstairs for Jackie but he was fast asleep, so the chips were put aside to be warmed up in the morning as his special treat.

George looked hopefully at Emma, 'Have a game of cards?'

Emma, pleased to spend time with her children, nodded. 'Alright, what's it to be, *rummy* or *sevens*?' and glancing at the clock, 'Pack up you girls, and off to bed!'

Unusually, George won every game so easily that there was no fun in it. Emma just could not concentrate, listening for every footstep and willing it to be Billy. She knew he must get home before Sam, otherwise, there would be trouble! Meanwhile time hung heavily on her hands.

Across Ada's Terrace, outside the Hawkins' house, two cigarettes glowed unhealthily in the dark. Willie and Joy had grown tired of racing round and had gone indoors. Willie had gone to sleep in the little bed he shared with Joy while Joy began to sift through a pile of old comics and broken toys.

Pop Hawkins was dozing in a chair. He could not go out for a pint for there was no money left. To fund her own outing Lily had *scooped up* all the money that there was to be found.

Ronnie and Roy carried on smoking and shared a bottle of beer.

'Is this *the last*?' Ronnie wanted to know.

Roy nodded and, reading his twin's mind, shook his head. 'Nah. It's just too soon to do old *Cantrell's* warehouse again.'

Their brother Ivan, who worked at a small engineering and boat repair company, had gone to town with one of his workmates, wearing his smartest casual clothes in the hopes of finding some interesting female company. A new milkshake bar had opened and there were sure to be girls there, attracted by the bright glass and chrome interior. It was surely a place to be admired and to be seen in and what young lady would not want to be noticed in such a splendid emporium?

Unbeknownst to any member of the Walters family, Billy and John had gone to the meeting in the *Wilton Rooms*, organised by the loathsome, fascist Brown Shirts. There had been a lot of heckling and catcalling which led to the break out of a free-for-all fight of unusual ferocity.

John had warned Billy not to get involved in any part of the fracas and together they had edged their way towards the door.

Suddenly, an ugly, angry face appeared and demanded, 'Where do you think you're going?' It was one of the fighters,

'Are you one of them Black Shirts?' He hung a dangerous fist under Billy's nose.

Whistles blew and policemen ran into the hall. John and Billy seized the chance to get away from their captor and to slip out of a side door.

'Run!' shouted John, and parting company they made off in different directions.

Puffing, panting and half afraid to hear running footsteps behind him, Billy headed for Merton Street where he almost collided with Ivan Hawkins who was on his way home from the milk bar.

'Where have you been in such a hurry?' Ivan wanted to know from his friend, 'Ya' robbed a bank or something? Ummhh, no, I think not,' he said with an amused twinkle in his eye, 'I know, you've got to get home before your old man!'

Too much out of breath to speak after evading fascist hooligans, Billy nodded vigorously.

Ivan took up his own story while Billy was recovering his breath. Ivan had not quite found the romantic kind of company that he had hoped to meet at the milk bar! Two pretty girls had caught their eyes and he and Jim had sat for a while with them.

In order to impress the young ladies, they had bought fashionably expensive Knickerbocker Glory ice creams for them rather than just buying ordinary milkshakes. The girls, after consuming the ice creams to the accompaniment of their frequent giggles, had gone off to the *Ladies' Room.*

There they had used the opportunity to make their unsignalled departure. Unknown to the boys, next to the toilets there was a back entrance, and the waiter had obligingly let the girls out that way.

Ivan grumbled, 'Them lasses were bloomin' gold-diggers!'

As they both turned into Ada's Terrace, Billy, in his turn, told Ivan about the brutal, fascist Blackshirt meeting. When he got to the part where the hall was being raided by the police, Ivan whistled, 'You'd better tell your old man you've been out with me,' he said, 'you know he won't like the idea of you being chased by Paddy Kelly. Well, goodnight to you. Hope it goes well.'

Billy, with a sigh agreed wholeheartedly.

Emma, still on the alert for Billy's return home, heard a stumbling sound from the passage outside, and sat up suddenly.

Both she and George were straining their ears to know who was going to come in first.

Billy, with his hand on the latch to the Walters' home, fervently hoped that he was home before his Dad.

Opening the door, he was confronted by Emma, 'Where have you been?' she said, her voice shaking with a mixture of fear, anger and relief.

Billy shook the fog of the last half hour from his brain. 'We went to that new milk bar,' he explained, lying through his teeth, 'such a laugh we had, the time just flew by.'

'And your tea is wasted, your Dad said you can go without.'

Billy did not care, and his face showed it.

Emma felt drained and weary with worry, 'Oh, get to bed with you. Your Dad will have something to say to you tomorrow about where you've been and what you've been doing. And give him the truth, mind!'

Fortunately by the time tomorrow evening came, time and the ale had soothed Sam. Wally Ingles had said what *good lads* Billy and George were, and he had asked about Billy's new job. Sam had gone home feeling that he had done a good job in fathering them, but grimly told himself, 'those boys had better not step out of line.'

So it was that the next morning Billy had a long lecture on not coming home for tea, and a terse warning that he was not too old for a taste of Sam's belt.

In the busy port city of Kingston upon Hull there had seemed to be no end to the long, hot summer, and the school term was coming to an end at a time when both Billy and George were leaving school.

Sam, Emma and Sam's mother, Grandma Eliza, went to the school-leaving and prize-giving meeting at *Wordsworth High School.* There, Billy, bursting with pleasure and achievement, received his prizes for mathematics and history.

Eliza looked on proudly, pointedly sitting next to Sam, and having little to say to Emma.

'Do you really like history, all those dates and things that happened so long ago?' Emma asked Billy.

'Why, yes,' he answered. 'By looking at the past, you can sometimes see a pattern of things for the future.'

Eliza snorted. She would not show herself up by asking silly questions.

In the refreshments room, Sam balanced his cup and saucer awkwardly. Unused to wearing a collar and tie he felt very hot and uncomfortable; it was as if he was being strangled. Sam had to acknowledge to himself that he was more at home in the company of other working class families. Nonetheless, he was there with Emma, to show how truly proud they were of their son.

Sam's thoughts wandered to his boat…

He had, as a child, been on a school outing to Whitby and had fallen in love with the open *coble* type fishing boats which were of the traditional *clinker built* design. They were fifteen to thirty feet long, some with inboard motors; but Sam remembered seeing one being rowed out to sea by a grizzled fisherman standing up amidships and pushing the long sweep oars forwards instead of pulling them backwards.

After talking with Brian *Sailor* Hamilton one day on the docks, while they were waiting to unload an incoming tramp steamer, they found that they both had an interest in boats. *Sailor* looked quizzically at Sam and said, 'Are you after finding yourself a coble?'

Sam was surprised at the question. 'Yes, I suppose so, but I imagine they are pretty expensive to buy!'

The older man grinned artfully, 'Well it just so happens that I might have a coble that you can afford!' Sam's eyes grew bright at the thought. The deal that they agreed on meant that Sam would help Brian at weekends to restore *The Lady Julia*, a thirty foot coble, and when that was done *Sailor* would help Sam to restore *The Galilee* a fifteen foot coble, and sell it to him for a much reduced cost.

'Great!' said Sam the newly amateur boat restorer. And so it was done. *The Galilee,* along with many other small boats, made her home in the creek inlet off the River Humber. His eyes glowed with pleasure as he remembered his first excursion, rowing up the river on the incoming tide and then rowing back to the creek on the outgoing tide.

His mother broke in on his reverie. 'I'm so proud of our Billy,' she said, happily basking in the success of her grandson. How she wished that she could have helped him to continue with his education. He could have been anything, perhaps even a doctor. But her own financial resources were getting worn away and after all, Billy's leanings and interests were not in that direction. Billy, like many boys of his age wanted to leave school and to have some money in his pockets. He wanted to have fun!

Sadly, Eliza did not feel quite so proud of George and did not go to his school-leaving event. Steadfastly undeterred, Sam and Emma did go to it. They were just as proud of George and his achievements as they were of Billy. While George's academic achievements were merely ordinary; by contrast, his work from the woodwork class was so good that it was on display and much admired. George's happiness was complete when his prize was a voucher which he could use to spend at a hardware shop that sold tools. He took pleasure in the anticipation and kept mulling over just what he would choose for his prize. Mentally, he spent the voucher in a dozen different ways long before it ever left his hands.

George's ambition for himself was to be, like his father, quick, strong, able, patient and a good example to his fellow workmates.

Back home in Ada's Terrace, Mary and Joanie had been charged with the task of looking after young Jackie, while Sam and Emma attended the prize-givings and school-leavings. Jackie, in turn, had been warned not to be difficult or to play up. Knowing, however, the kinds of mischief that small boys can get up to, Emma, on both formal school occasions was anxious to return home.

She left Sam to walk his mother to the bus stop, after the three of them had been to Billy's school.

'She spoils that child,' said Eliza.

Sam, as usual, tried to pour oil on troubled water, 'He's only a bain, Mam,' he said. 'I bet you were spoiled at his age too!' he said with a cheeky grown-up grin.

Through the hot, summer days that followed the break-up of school for the holidays, not everyone noticed the terrible storm clouds that were brewing over Europe.

However, as he read the evening paper, Billy did feel a shiver of dread, dark apprehension coming over him. There were the reports of those nasty political things happening in Germany: the Jewish butchers' shops attacked with the daubing of black,

Nazi swastikas over their door and windows; the fascist German Brownshirt meetings, the marching and the promotion of sundry violence in different German cities. At the heart of it there was Hitler, strutting the world stage, and causing people to wonder how long peace would last in Europe.

Sam's two oldest lads had no evil plans to take over the world. Billy and George now could look each other in the eye and think of themselves as working men. But, no matter how grown up the lads felt, Sam did not relax his views on what they were allowed to do. He wanted them to grow up right and to be a proper credit to the family.

CHAPTER THREE

When young Jackie and his sisters, Mary and Joanie, came home from Sunday School, the girls were told strictly by Emma not to mess up their dresses.

'Oh, Mam!' moaned Joanie, 'Do you think we're still babies?'

Emma could well have answered her on that one, but she was more than sufficiently occupied in dishing up the family dinner.

Joanie was much more intent on consuming fashion than eating the best meal of the week; the Sunday lunch. She thought it would be lovely if she could own a real Japanese kimono, just like the one she had seen in a magazine. It was a pretty one in pink and green satin. Wrapped up in her own thoughts she could just imagine its silkiness against her skin.

Meanwhile, an exasperated Emma was saying, 'Did you hear me? I said did you want any more gravy?'

Joanie came down to earth with a jolt, accepted the gravy and made sure she did not spill it on herself.

After dinner, the girls had the job of clearing away the dishes and washing them up.

'Your Mam's been busy all morning tidying up and cooking for us all,' Sam reminded them. He wanted to make sure that they did their bit to help her around the house.

Emma dabbed away at a black mark on Jackie's shirt, and determinedly brushed his hair where it stood up defiantly on the crown of his head. Both Mary and Joanie were given strict instructions not to let Jackie get dirty and were sent on their way to visit Sam's mother, Eliza Walters at No. 44 Swatman Street.

As a firm believer in the Victorian motto that children should be seen and not heard, the old lady had earned herself the nickname of Nanna Shushkin by her habit of *shushing* the children into silence whenever they tried to talk in her presence. As it was their own special, private name for their grandma, they made sure that she never got to hear of it.

In Nanna's house the curtains were kept drawn so that the sun did not fade the furnishings. The room felt airless and the childrens' legs stuck uncomfortably to the sofa.

Nanna, who was herself a widow, had a grown-up daughter living at home with her who was, as people said, *tuppence short of a shilling.* Nonetheless, Daisy was a hard worker, whenever she could remember what it was that she was meant to be doing.

To Mrs Walters, Daisy was her cross to bear. Not being greatly familiar with the *Good Book*, she felt that there must have been some unknown sin in her life for which this was to be her punishment.

Daisy was kept close to her mother, who protected her as best she could. She was affectionate with people she knew well, gentle, timid and shy, but also afraid of the boys in the street who shouted out rude names after her, such as *Dotty Daisy* or *Loonie.* To her kind and loving nature, this was deeply offensive. And in order to frighten the unfortunate girl more, those same cruel, unthinking boys were also in the habit of making faces at her, and then running off when Eliza would turn angrily upon them.

People might have wondered just how Eliza Walters managed to keep Daisy and herself, and support Billy through High School, on only the little she received from her widow's pension and from doing the neighbours' washing. For those who had wondered, there was indeed a family mystery!

In earlier times, her husband, John Walters, Sam's father, had been a man who regrettably, loved to have a bet. Wastrel-like, he had loved the thrill of betting so much that Eliza had received very little housekeeping money from him. Indeed, rather than give her money it was more likely that he would feloniously raid her purse in order to pay for his betting.

One day while walking home from work, John had found a wallet, and inside it was a crisp, white, five pound note. Five Pounds! Riches galore! If any man ever thought he had received a gift from heaven it was John Walters.

In the wallet there was just the money. No name to be found. No address to be seen. No chance then of returning it to its rightful owner. In two days' time there was going to be the big horse race: surely it must be a good omen! Here was the money for a big win on the galloping gee-gees! It had to be!

An acquaintance of John's, Fred Rollins did a bit of running for a bookie who took bets for a living at the race course. Without any further hesitation John Walters met up with Fred and put the whole five pounds on a horse called *Easy Money* at odds of ten to one!

'That donkey will never win,' warned Fred. But *Easy Money*, the very horse that was a rank outsider, actually came in first and John held in his hand fifty pounds, more money than he had ever seen at one time! His own little goldmine!

'Keep this quiet!' he warned Fred, while furtively slipping him a fiver to ensure his compliance.

Returning home, it became more obvious to John that his problems had increased. He could not tell Eliza about his winnings because she viewed gambling as the work of the devil and she would instantly tell him that keeping that fiver, without trying to find its rightful owner, was wrong. Furthermore, there was just no place that John could hide those big, white, *tablecloth* five pound notes, where Eliza, his tidy housewife, would not eventually find them. Then he would be in trouble because she would want to know where such a large sum had all come from.

In the end he went out of the house, walked over to the old *Penny Bank* and deposited his winnings there. But he felt as if the counter clerk was peering at him suspiciously and that he should explain himself and his doings. 'My old aunt…' he said, 'died. She used to be a maid in service in India and never spent anything.' Adopting a confidential tone, he told the clerk how he had had a nice windfall and his wife had said that it would be safer in the bank.

The clerk nodded in a bored manner while dealing with the transaction. Privately he wondered to himself how it was that many customers reckoned they had a fortune, without realising that bank tellers handle more money in a day than most people can earn in a lifetime!

However, life for the Walters was always full of surprises and the following day was no different; John Walters, who had never had a day's illness in his life, collapsed and died on his way home from work.

He had not been a great husband, but Eliza had always loved him and so she grieved deeply for him. If Eliza had known of her husband's covert flutter on the horses, she would have felt her views on gambling to be justified, and would have blamed her husband's sad demise on his guilt and worry.

As he went through his father's things, Sam's eyes went wide with surprise when he came across the record of a large sum of money written into his father's bank book.

The discovery of the bank book, hidden away in an old tin box in the upstairs bedroom, took place while Sam was helping his mother with the arrangements for his father's funeral. Along with the bank book were the family's life insurance policies, the payments for which Eliza had struggled to keep up.

Mysteriously, there was no written indication of where John had got the money and the amount had been deposited in one day rather than having been built up over time.

After several visits to the solicitor, as advised by the insurance man, the money came to Eliza. Now Eliza had John's little goldmine!

One night, after John's funeral, Sam was in *The Volunteer,* tucked away in a corner, nursing his half pint glass.

Fred Rollins, who had earlier been waving a five pound note at the bar while buying drinks for himself and his friends, settled down to sup more beer than was good for him. By the time that Fred was feeling very merry, with at least seven pints inside of him, Sam and half the pub were easily able to hear him bring out his best story of the night: how John had found a fiver and turned it into fifty pounds, by betting on a hopeless horse called *Easy Money*! Sam's eyes grew wide as he listened, then swallowing the last sip of his half pint he slipped discreetly out of the door so that Fred would not notice him. Mystery solved!

Family life went on. Eliza had seen in her grandson Billy a chance to mould his life in the way she would have liked with Sam when he was young.

Now sixteen years old, Billy had left school, and was working in an office and there were strong expectations for his future.

'You'll need a suit,' Eliza had said, 'a good, dark blue serge suit will wear well; then you can save up and get yourself another one.'

Billy laughed, 'Gran, I'll have a wardrobe full of suits, and I'll have a car and take you and Daisy for a drive on Sunday afternoons.'

Eliza laughed with him. Picking up her old, black handbag and grandly taking out her purse, she gave him three pounds.

'Get your father to go with you to get the suit and there should be enough for two white shirts as well.'

In truth, Billy was the apple of her eye. The girls she tolerated - well Mary anyway. To her, young Jackie was a typical small boy who would be sure to get into some mischief, and as for George, well, he was not clever like her Billy.

Eliza had sadly missed out, in her childhood, on the experience of being valued equally with other children.

George was younger than his brother Billy and since he had no academic leanings, he was able, at fourteen, to leave school. As he had always been of a practical mind he had been happiest at woodwork classes or at carving and whittling away at a piece of wood. So it was fortunate for him that a good recommendation from his schoolmaster had got him a job, in *Dawson's Woodyard*.

The girls were visiting their Grandma Eliza as usual, and Grandma was boldly on the offensive in promoting Billy's reputation. 'I should hope your George has got a job!' she said.

Joanie was quick to jump to her brother's defence, 'George can do anything he wants to do. Have you not seen, Grandma, all the lovely things he has carved? He just doesn't want to work indoors, shut up in an office, like Billy.'

For Eliza, like the proverbial red rag to a bull or like a match to dry gunpowder, that retort really *did it!* After all, no one was going to decry Billy in her hearing, and the girls were treated to a long tirade on the virtues of their elder brother.

After the tirade had ended, and with inward sighs of relief, the girls heard the Dutch clock on the mantelshelf strike four: it was time to go. Jackie was dragged from the kitchen, protesting that he had not finished his game of *Snakes and Ladders* with Daisy.

On leaving the house and standing together outside in the fresh air, the girls looked at each other, 'Shush!' said Joanie, and all three of the children giggled furiously.

As autumn made its approach, the building work began on the much-talked-about houses on Rotterdam Road.

'Ready for those folk with two-and-a-half children!' laughed Emma.

The men from the council had been round Ada's Terrace with their books and files. They were listing the number of people in each house; looking at the sink in the corner of the kitchen with the cold tap; the outside lavatory; the old coal shed.

Lily Hawkins came to Emma with a letter in her hand, 'We've been given one of them new houses,' she said. 'The old man will have to look sharp and keep on at work if we're going to pay the rent for that.'

'Will you go?' asked Emma.

'Council says we're overcrowded,' said Lil. 'They're talking of pulling these terraces down, and calling them slums. What a blooming cheek!' But aren't you flitting as well, Emma?'

'We haven't heard a thing,' replied Emma, not a little put out. 'I suppose that either the Council thinks we're not overcrowded enough - even though we have as many kids as you - or else they've not got down to the letter *'W'* for Walters in their list!' They both had a rueful chortle over this and gave each other a hug.

Lil said wistfully, 'How I wish you could come and live near us on the new estate.'

The big Hawkins moving day came in November. To move their household contents to their new home in Alfresco Drive, Harry Hawkins borrowed a handcart with its two great steel wheels. Before many journeys had been completed, Harry wearily began to wish that they could afford the use of a lorry as he thought he was a poor substitute for a horse!

Now that the Hawkins family had gone it seemed strangely and depressingly quiet. At the bottom of Ada's Terrace no one went clattering up and down the cobblestone path in the way that the Hawkins lads used to do and there were no welcoming lights glowing in No 11.

In the morning, poor, young Jackie moped about, feeling very disconsolate at losing his good friend, Willie Hawkins. Jackie was learning the meaning of the saying that *a good neighbour departed is a great treasure lost.*

Joanie did not share Jackie's sense of loss over the Hawkins' departure. For Joanie, her greatest ambition in life was to be a performer on the stage with all the lights on her. It was all she wanted.

Mr Sawdon and the Methodist Drama Group were busy rehearsing their Christmas show and for her, this was her big opening opportunity. The Sunday School always did the Nativity play in the week before Christmas. Mr Sawdon was busy coaxing and drilling his little drama group into performing his own special Christmas production. He wanted to do something different and so he worked with them on his own production of *A Yuletide Revue.*

For her part, Joanie never missed a rehearsal. She had roles in two sketches; sang *Poor Little Angeline* in a trio with Betty Blake and Barbara Palmer; and together they tried to dance *The Palais Glide.*

What a pretty scene on the village green
When the prince was wed to Angeline!
Now as his princess, she's a great success.
Poor little Angeline!

Emma, Mary and Jackie came to watch the show and Joanie was praised by the Producer, 'Proper little star you have there!' Mr Sawdon told Emma. That only added fuel to the fire of Joanie's pleading to have dancing lessons, but it was met with the usual refusal from Emma, who always said that they could not afford them.

Joanie went off in a sulk, and moaned to her friends about the unfairness of it.

Jackie pronounced the Christmas show to be, 'Alright!' Much better though, in his estimation, were the mince pies and lemonade which were on offer afterwards, even if the ladies in charge of refreshments had been a little sparing with the lemonade powder!

'This is only the start!' Joanie informed Mary, 'I'll be a star, you'll see.' With a little sigh she intoned, 'I wish our Mam would let me go to dancing lessons...' while visions of herself, dressed as her latest idol, Ginger Rogers, came to mind.

In reply, Mary could not resist passing on the comment, 'Nanna Shushkin says play-acting, and that sort of thing, won't keep you in peanuts, let alone fill your belly.'

'You'll see when I'm rich and famous!' Joanie said as she nodded her head sagely.

That Christmas was, financially, the best one they could ever remember. Billy and George were now both working, and Emma, had managed to save a little bit more in the corner shop Christmas Savings Club.

Sam had also had a good run of work with the new dock and the bigger ships coming to the port of Hull from all over the world.

Emma also had her own little flush of prosperity: her very own windfall. Every Sunday, there was a Fashion Competition in the *News of the World* paper. Surprisingly, though she could never afford to buy much in the shape of fashion-wear, Emma never missed entering it.

In the competition, the reader had to decide which of the outfits (A, B or C etc...) looked the most fashionable. Emma's lines of entry were usually made up of family initials, as she said she did not know much about fashions, and she was often teased by Sam on her hopes of winning.

One week in December she received a letter which in itself was unusual, 'Who could be writing to me?' she wondered.

'Well, you won't know until you open it,' was Mary's advice.

Emma had won a runner-up prize of five whole pounds! She stood, holding the note in her hand, gazing at it with amazement, until George, with a ready grin, suggested that perhaps she might like to frame it!

'Frame it?' she said, 'I'm going to spend it on Christmas!'

That year they had a bigger Christmas tree than ever before, along with special treats and presents that cost a little more than usual. But Joanie still did not get the tap-dancing shoes that she was hankering after.

Christmas was hardly over before the news came that the old King was gravely ill, and before the new year of 1936 was a month old, George V had died. Then was said: *The King is dead, Long Live the King!* The old King had died and the new King had acceded instantly to the throne.

Sadness apart, the loss of the old monarch did not make much difference to the pattern of life in Ada's Terrace, since work went on much the same as usual. The talk in *The Volunteer* was not so much of the new King Edward VIII because after all - what could he do embroiled in scandal with Mrs Wallis Simpson, as he was? When the young girls skipped in the street they added a new rhyme to their usual chant.

Here comes Simpson down the street,
With no stockings on her feet.

Twice she's married, she wants more.
Now she's knocking on Eddie's door.

Lily Hawkins had met up with Emma in the street and invited her to come round one afternoon to view the new Hawkins house and have a cup of tea with her. This she gladly accepted, happy to delight in the modern conveniences of hot running water, an inside toilet and more rooms! Needless to say, they had a *right good gossip.*

After Emma returned home she cooked their evening meal and waited for Sam's arrival. When he arrived back that evening, had eaten and was settled down with a cup of tea, she could not restrain herself a moment longer from telling him her latest news. Looking heavenward, Emma spoke her heart when she said, 'Oh, it's a lovely house that Lily's got, with a bathroom and a hot water tap in the...'

It was not one of Sam's best days for empathizing with his wife's domestic aspirations as he interjected with a critical smile, 'Ah! But are they keeping coal in the bath?' Sadly, Sam had no greatly exalted opinion of the Hawkins' household habits. But in their favour, he had never known them to keep a pony stalled in the bathroom! Not that they would not be tempted if they had a pony...

Unexpectedly nonplussed and with the wind somewhat taken out of her sails, Emma changed the subject and went on to tell him the headlines she had seen on the news stands; namely that foreign envoys were coming to present their credentials to the newly acclaimed King. With a cheeky look on her face, she added, 'Never mind foreign folk coming to present their credentials to the King - Lily's husband Harry has presented his own credentials and now Lily is pregnant!'

Sam roared with laughter at the news and nearly breathed in his cup of tea in the process!

The following week, Emma met Lily at the shop, and invited her back to Ada's Terrace for a cup of tea. Their conversation reverted naturally to the reports in the paper that more midwives were needed because three thousand mothers a year were dying in childbirth. Happily in Hull, a lady doctor had laid the foundation stone for a hospital for women and had given five thousand pounds towards the cost of the building.

'That's it!' said Lily, 'Pity there aren't more lady doctors. They understand women's problems. Not like men. If they had to have babies, the population would go down rapidly! Just imagine if Harry was expecting!'

Emma tried and almost choked on her cup of tea at the thought.

Later that evening, Emma got out her knitting needles and brought out some wool in order to knit a *matinee coat* for the expected Hawkins baby. It caused some consternation.

'Who's it for?' Mary wanted to know.

On hearing that it was for Lily Hawkins, Joanie's only comment was, 'Thank goodness for that!'

'But babies are lovely...' Mary was shocked at her sister's reaction.

'Huh!' said Joanie, not impressed, 'Not if we had to have one in our bedroom!'

There had been no news of Sam and Emma having their chance of leaving Ada's Terrace.

The building of the new council houses seemed somehow to have ground to a halt. Emma said to herself, 'Sometimes, I suppose, you have to be patient with these things. Meanwhile I can daydream...and hope.'

Another Christmas passed and Billy had settled into his work at Roylands' office and was the only youngster there. He was popular with the other members of staff, and worked conscientiously. Mr Roylands senior was over sixty. Mr Tom and Mr John Roylands were in their forties.

It was David Harris who was Billy's immediate senior. Nearly thirty years old, he had a wife, two children and a mortgage on a little house on the west side of town. David Harris enthused warmly about married life, and tried to instruct Billy in the art of saving to buy a house, but Billy was sure he did not want to get tied down just yet.

Joanie had fantasies about what it would be like to be a glamorous secretary at a place like *Roylands*. However, these fantasies would have been quickly dispelled if she had seen Miss Iveson. Miss Iveson was the pleasant but oh-so-correct spinster in her late forties who lived to serve the Mr Roylands' clerical requirements.

Billy had kept in touch with his school friend John. They had attended several more political meetings, and were rather sorry that Sir Oswald Mosley's *British Union of Fascists* had been refused the use of the *City Hall.* Not that the boys embraced the ideals of that company, but a lively meeting with plenty of heckling added a bit of spice to the evening's entertainment.

Of course, the seeds of world turmoil and distress were being sown in fascist movements across the world.

In Germany, May 1st 1937 was scheduled to be a big day. A command had gone out from Hitler's headquarters that the German people should enjoy themselves. There would be marching, singing, dancing, saluting and the beating of drums all through the day.

Herr Hitler was to head a triumphal parade, and children were to be in the *Post Stadium* at four o'clock to hear Hitler and Goebbels speaking. It would be headline news across the world.

To some young people it might have seemed an idyllic situation: seeing all the rosy-cheeked, blonde, young girls; the boys sturdy in their uniforms busy at the Youth Camps - more sinister by far than any Boy Scout camps; little girls in national costumes carrying bunches of flowers, and the *lucky ones* presenting their bunches of flowers to Herr Hitler.

Emma saw it all on the Pathé newsreels at the cinema and the roars of '*Sieg Heil!*' sent shivers running up her spine.

Emma's sister, Annie, had come to sit in with the children at home in Ada's Terrace. Sam was taking Emma out to the pictures for a rare treat and this time they went out to see Fred Astaire and Ginger Rogers in the film: *Shall We Dance?*

At nearly fourteen, some mothers would have considered Mary to be quite old enough to be left in charge of the other children, but Emma knew that sparks could easily fly between the two girls, and she also knew how easily young Jackie could react with his own brand of *playing up.* As a responsible mother, Emma would not have been able to enjoy the film if she had not known that her sister, Annie was there to keep an eye on things. Of course, Annie was a great favourite with the children and loved spending time with them.

Emma often said, 'Our Annie should have had children,' but Annie's young man had not come back from the trenches of the *Great War* and there had been no one else in her life. Annie had a great aptitude for caring work, having nursed their mother through the racking stages of consumption before her death and she was now looking after Bert, their father.

Happily content with their evening out, and hand firmly in hand, Emma and Sam arrived home just before ten o'clock. The starlight had shone on them as they had walked home.

'Oh, it was lovely!' Emma said, bright-eyed and flushed with the excitement of being out with Sam. It had been just the two of them and love was in the air. It was like old times again.

Annie greeted them and noted, with quiet pleasure, their happiness. The girls and Jackie had gone to bed, although Annie had let them stay up later than usual.

Sam, protective of his sister-in-law, waited while Annie put on her coat, ready to walk her back to the bus.

'I've promised Mary some wool,' Annie said, 'she wants to knit a pixie hood.' Although these were the latest fashion, Mary did not want it for herself but she thought it would be nice for the Spanish refugees, some of whom had come to live in Hull. At church the ladies were knitting squares to make blankets for them.

War was coming and everyone had to prepare for it. In the papers it said that gas masks and respirators would be issued to all the people who were employed in the *Air Raid Precautionary Service*, as well as to the *Police* and *Fire Brigade* services.

David Harris had joined the *Territorial Army Reserve* and he tried to interest Billy in it by saying, 'We've got to be ready when this war comes.' Billy agreed that there would be a war, but if there was, he wanted to be in the *Air Force*.

Being lively youngsters, political meetings were not all that Billy and his friend John were interested in. After all, it was not as important as starting courting! They often met two girls at the fashionable Milk Bar.

As yet it had been a friendly foursome but the boys had hopes. Sometimes they went to the pictures, but now Irene and Susan wanted the boys to go to a dance!

Billy was embarrassed, 'I can't dance!'

'Is that all?' Irene wanted to know, 'You'll soon pick it up.'

'Sure thing,' John chimed in, 'it will be a laugh.'

Billy was not so sure he wanted them laughing at him! However, it was finally agreed that they would go to the dance at the *People's Institute* on Thursday night.

George, although Billy's younger brother, had not wasted any time either in courtship activities and already had a steady, attractive girlfriend by the name of Daphne. She served in the canteen at *Dawson's Woodyard* where he now worked. For her part, she collected the customers' cups and plates and then washed up the crockery. All this activity was done in between answering the urgent calls of the canteen women behind the counter calling for 'More cups! More biscuits! More milk!'

Daphne went with George to visit his Grandpa Bert, and was a great favourite with his Aunt Annie. As yet though, George had not taken Daphne home to introduce her to his family. Together, George and Daphne went for walks when it was fine, or played cards with Daphne's brothers.

Billy's attitude to the ladies was of the *love 'em and leave 'em* variety; indeed he sneered that he was not going to get tied down to any girl; he was going to enjoy himself while he was young.

George, however, was more serious and went on in his own amiable, good-natured way.

Like many people, George and Daphne's special treat was a visit to the pictures on a Saturday night. But when, in the *Hull Daily Mail*, there was a report of a sea monster being spotted off the coast of Withernsea, many people were intrigued and George and Daphne were no exception.

At the weekend, they joined the crowd on the platform at *Paragon Railway Station* waiting for the train to take them to the seaside for *monster spotting.*

To the railway employees such a crowd was quite a surprise. They would not normally have expected quite so many people in the two weeks before the Whitsun holiday.

It was a gloriously hot day and so it was very natural for George and Daphne to be picnicking on the sand with a pile of sandwiches which Daphne's mother had thoughtfully made for them.

On such a beautiful day, they did not bother whether there was a sea monster or not, because they had for company the sun, the sea and each other.

All around them, children were digging in the sand, paddling in the sea or racing madly around while kicking spurts of sand over anyone who happened to be in the way.

Sam said the sea monster was a ploy of the shopkeepers in Withernsea to get more people there! But two weeks later, most of the revellers were glad that they had gone when they did: the Whitsun holiday weekend was thoroughly wet through - from Friday until Tuesday.

In this poor weather the seaside beach was deserted and the unobserved pennants and bunting outside the deserted cafés and ice cream parlours were left flapping dismally in the cold, seaside wind.

Had anyone turned up they would not have been in any mood for finding a sea monster!

CHAPTER FOUR

The constitutional crisis had struck both the nation and the Empire with grief, pain and distress but it came as no surprise when King Edward VIII finally made up his mind and left the thousand year old throne behind to be with *the lady that he could not live without.*

The fact that he had previously been connected with so many women and that his latest woman had managed to shuffle off two previous husbands before him, in a country where British law only supported divorce on the grounds of adultery did not make the King and Mrs Simpson the country's most popular choice for the roles of King and Queen!

It was generally felt that such airy ways of life were for film stars and the like, ordinary people just got on with living. What else could you do? If you made a mistake in your choice of partner your parents were very likely to say, 'You've made your bed. Now you'll have to lie on it!'

After the scandal and Edward's abdication, it was only natural that the people's attention, and affection, were drawn to the shy, dutiful, stuttering man who would be their new King George V1; to his wife Queen Elizabeth, and to the two little princesses, Elizabeth and Margaret.

The late King George V had celebrated his reign of twenty-five years on the throne with the 1935 Silver Jubilee and memories of the enthusiastic celebrations and Jubilee street parties fired people up to plan again for great celebrations.

Emma, herself, remembered the great and joyous party that they had in Ada's Terrace in those Silver Jubilee times. She knew and felt that the Coronation fever had begun to burn in the hearts of many people as they looked forward to George V's second son being crowned as the new King.

So, now with this great national event coming up, Emma wanted to experience it with those who enjoyed the previous Ada's Terrace royal celebration. But would it be the same without Lily Hawkins and her family there? Lil would have wanted her to enjoy the day for all it was worth, so together with Hilda Brown from No. 4, Emma began to collect sixpence a week from all the Ada's Terrace inhabitants, putting it into the bank towards the great day of the Coronation. It was true that even sixpence a week was hard for some people to find. Certainly, Emma could count herself fortunate with three wages coming into the household and she knew that she would help the others out where she could.

Sadly, many people were not able to find work so easily. Emma had read in the evening paper about the case of a woman who had taken a baby's empty pram from outside a house. 'Poor soul!' sighed Emma.

Sam wrinkled his left cheek and said, 'I remember we were really hard up when you were having the bains, but you didn't steal.'

'I know,' Emma sighed, 'this poor lass had three bains, no food in the house, and her husband had been out of work for six years. I know she did wrong, but your heart does go out to people in a desperate plight.'

Sam grimaced, 'Aye lass, but sometimes you've got to suffer to be doing right!'

Along with the low state of the British economy, there were reports in the paper of pilfering on the docks. The *London and North Eastern Railway Police* had said that a vacuum cleaner brush had been stolen. When the story was read out in *The Volunteer* it gave rise to some wry humour, 'It ain't no use looking for it in our houses,' was the general sentiment, 'because the likes of us don't have vacuum cleaners, we have wives!'

Mary's time at school was drawing to an end and she was really looking forward to getting a job and earning her own money. She was due to start work soon at *Walpole's* factory.

In her spare time, as usual, Mary sewed. Since all the family had been issued with gas masks in case of war and poison gas attacks, she was sewing cases for the gas masks. She wanted everybody to be ready in case the worst came to the worst.

The dreadful *Spanish Civil War* was raging and both the Fascists and the Republicans were responsible for callous massacres of Spanish civilians. Even in their visits to the cinema, Mary and Joanie could not escape seeing there on the screen, the impending threat of wars and rumours of wars.

In their naivety, Mary and Joanie only thought of war as two rows of soldiers fighting against each other on a tidy battlefield. Consequently, they were really horrified at the filmed news reports and scenes of dead bodies on the streets of Madrid.

The two girls could not understand that parents would send their children away from a war zone and remain behind themselves. Puzzled and hurt, they watched the sad scenes of Basque refugee children in Spain, fleeing from that war zone without their parents. The girls fought to understand this merciful and mass evacuation of children brought into a safe zone by train and walking from the railway station with their faces solemn, distraught and tear-stained.

Joanie and Mary sighed with relief as they saw *The Sisters of Mercy* taking them to their convent where in time they would be accepted as part of the community. Somehow, shockingly, it seemed likely that such evacuations of bewildered children, with parcel labels to identify them, could actually happen in England.

In order to take their minds off the dismal international goings on, Sam asked George if he wanted to go and see the five-masted jackass barque that had just arrived at the docks.

Sam, of course, went to examine the ship because anything that sailed or steamed across the sea was like a magnet to him. George went because this unusual sailing ship had brought a large cargo of wood, and because - well - in the docks and on the sea, large sailing ships were becoming scarcer. George wanted to know why it was called a *jackass barque.*

Sam said, 'I suppose you could say it's like a mule. A mule, being part horse and part donkey is neither nowt nor summat - but it is a mighty fine pack-animal!'

The jackass barque was unusual in that it was set up like a cross between a square-rigged sailing ship and a fore-and-aft rigged schooner; usually they would have at least three masts, but five masts, well that was something worth seeing!

A docker's work takes place on or around the dockside, loading or unloading the ship's cargo. Alternatively, his work may take place on, around or within a ship's hold. Cranes, winches, cargoes and holds all go towards making a dangerous working environment. Sam and his friends had seen too many accidents not to care about these things.

So when the following week, there was a report about ship safety matters in the paper the men in *The Volunteer* crowded around as Sam read aloud:

> *The ship's master of the Corona has been fined for not providing a safe means of access to his ship's holds and because the back shafts of the winches were not securely fenced.*

It also seemed that the *Corona's* captain had not cared enough to prevent the ship's exhaust steam from obscuring the work on board the ship.

Sam remarked that the court fine of forty-four pounds for maritime negligence and the warning to the ship's master that a further offence would render him inoperable, seemed fair under the circumstances. For if a docker could not see where he was going, he could fall down twenty or more feet into the ship's hold and serious accidents were well known to happen.

The Mount Atlas, was the biggest timber ship that had ever been in the dock. When she arrived, she brought in a full load: two thousand seven hundred and seventeen standards of timber. Jock Sprain had been elated to get a job as part of the *Mount Atlas* unloading team. The ship was easily carrying enough to provide the dockers with good steady work for at least a couple of weeks and when he heard the news Jock felt arithmetically inspired and worked that sum out on the back of an envelope with a pencil, as being:

> *One London Standard of timber = 270 cubic feet*
> *270 cubic feet x 2,717 standards = 733,590 cubic feet of solid wood.*

'Phew - that's an awful lot of wood!' he said.

However, the next morning while working on the dock, one of the slings of timber that was hanging from the moving crane fell, catching Jock on the side of the head, and knocking him unconscious.

He was rushed by ambulance to the *Infirmary* where he was joined by Dot, his wife, while Emma sat with the three Sprain children.

When the usual conclave met in *The Volunteer* at the end of the working day, their mood was sober and subdued. They all knew the risks, and it could have happened to any one of them. This time it had happened to Jock Sprain but the lesson had to be the avoiding of it happening to anyone.

Sam felt the downcast mood, finished his beer and went home thoughtfully.

He was asleep in his chair when Emma arrived back at Ada's Terrace at two o'clock in the morning.

He knew his wife well enough not to have to ask any questions as Emma turned a tear-stained face to him, 'Oh Sam, Jock's gone.'

Sam put his arms around her, there were no words sufficient. They put out the lights and went to bed. It would be a short night and, except for Jock, the work would go on as usual in the morning.

Emma's two boys were both doing well at work. Billy was settled well into his work at the Roylands' office and George was well established in his work at the woodyard. He never shirked the difficult jobs and his calm, friendly manner meant he was well liked by his workmates. He also liked football and was always ready for a sociable kick-about at lunchtime.

More than just being popular and successful in their work, Emma wanted her boys to look smart. To that end, out of the money Billy and George gave her for their upkeep each week, she paid a few shillings to the *Mutuality* man. When they had saved enough the boys could use the *Mutuality Savings Club* cheques for clothes. Billy got his second suit and George got a sports jacket and flannels. Emma positively beamed with happiness to see her boys looking so well-dressed.

The Hawkins boys were also working. Ronnie Hawkins worked at *Martin's Bakery* and was home earlier than most because of the very early start to his day. Simply put, it was his job to get to the bakery first, see to the ovens and make sure that they were fully ready for the bakers' use. Getting up early never bothered Ronnie Hawkins because he never bothered going to bed! Now and then he would have an afternoon nap and then get up when other folks were going to bed.

As Lily Hawkins was the least enthusiastic of cooks, her cooking of meals was more or less non-existent. As a result in their home it was a case of every man for himself! Ronnie would go to the fish and chip shop or else send Willie out for the fish and chips. This diet gave Ronnie's face a somewhat pasty look, so he was given the name of *Dough-buns*.

Roy, by contrast did not have a regular job but made himself useful at the market by getting there early in the morning and always being ready to help the stallholders, running errands for them, and doing all their fetching and carrying, earning him enough to keep both himself happy and to pay his mother for her housekeeping.

Ronnie's perks were stale buns and bread from work, while Roy brought home spotted fruit and vegetables.

Lily had never before been so well off, and more happiness was about to come her way!

Emma answered a knock at the door one day to find Harry Hawkins there, twisting his cap in his hands.

'Come in Harry,' Emma invited in neighbourly fashion, 'it's a long time since we saw you last!'

'Aye, it's Lily,' he stammered. 'The baby's come now. It's a little lass. Lily would take it kindly if you would come and see her.'

Emma gladly agreed to visit the next day. Mary was quite put out that her Mum would not take her along to see the baby as well, but Emma knew that Lily would want to pass on all the details of the birth. It would not bother Lily that Mary was there, but Emma felt that there was plenty of time before Mary needed to know all the intimate details that Lily would want to relate.

Emma went alone, listened to Lily's tales, and joyfully nursed the baby who looked just like a miniature version of Lily herself. Mum and daughter were obviously happy.

Lily said Joy had been a good girl. She had run all the way to get Mrs Bowles, the midwife to come over and then was so helpful in fetching and carrying for her. The newborn baby was to be named Shirley, which was Joy's choice of name.

Speaking of tiny, little Shirley, Emma told Sam that night, 'She's a lovely bain.'

Sam listened and shook his head, 'Poor kid, and being born into what may become wartime! It sometimes makes you wonder if it's right to bring a child into the world, the way things are, but then again,' he said, 'the fact is, life must go on!'

Emma smiled at Sam and said, 'I think you've said that before!'

To which he replied humorously and in a thoughtful fashion, 'Aye, lass. That's 'cos its right!' and he gave her a big grin.

Having poured a cup of tea for them both, she told him that Lily was upset as Ivan had been to sign up for the Navy and was now waiting to be called up.

'I thought he had a job?' Sam queried.

'Oh yes, but if there's going to be a war, Ivan wants to be in the Navy. Family tradition, y'know. Lily's father was a proper naval man and Ivan wants to be like his Granddad.'

So much happened in those threatening months; the world was poised over the abyss of a terrible war, yet at times, everything went on in the same old way and seemed normal, except that as an early prototype, on the corner of Merton Street and Ada's Terrace, the council had built an air raid shelter.

Although originally the door was locked, it was not long before someone found out how to get into it and so it became the haunt of courting couples and the odd tramp.

As war-awareness increased, the people who had money and a big enough garden, began to plan and eventually to build their own *Anderson bomb shelters*: as the prospect of war grew even grimmer, many people stocked their shelters with bunks, matches, torches, batteries and candles. So it was not surprising that there was a shortage of candles.

Mary was becoming well-established at *Walpole's* factory in Hull. Certainly, she was shy and unsure of what she should do when she started work there, but the kind-hearted women in the production room soon took her under their wing. It also helped that Mary was a polite and willing worker, always ready to fetch and carry.

It was not long before one of the young lads from the works named Robert began walking her home. He had trained as a gas fitter and used his skills in the factory.

Joanie turned up her nose at the news, 'You don't want to get tied down!' she cautioned her sister. And with a look of horror and disbelief she said, 'Do you really want to get tied down like our Mam?'

Such a comment was like a red rag to a bull and Mary coloured up with disdain, 'There's nothing wrong with our Mam and Dad!' she said and an awkward silence ensued.

Joanie tossed her head and thought to herself, 'If housework and babies are all that Mary wants, she can keep them. She's welcome to them, but I want excitement! Yes!' she thought, 'I want more from life, I want excitement, travel, lovely clothes and jewels.' She daydreamed on.

Mary abruptly broke in on her thoughts, 'What about love? What if you fell for a young man?'

Joanie sneered, 'He would have to have plenty of money!'

Mary looked sadly at her sister; she certainly had some strange ideas.

The women at work all took an interest in Mary's love life, giving her advice on her relationship with Robert, often in terms that Emma would not have used, but all well-meant, and so Mary kept young Robert Stavin in check. 'Save it for the honeymoon!' she said to him.

Joanie ran errands for *Cantrell's* shop, dusted shelves, swept floors and earned some pocket money. Work of this kind was a necessary evil as far as Joanie was concerned. Much of what she earned went on nail varnish, *Californian Poppy* perfume and *Velouty Dixor* makeup from *Woolworths*, but as this rough shop work was only a stepping stone for her ambitions, she fell to anxiously studying her hands and nails for signs of wear and tear.

Emma was well known to her family and friends as a big-hearted woman. Not surprisingly then, she had been disturbed by the reports in the papers that some families in Germany were sending their children to Britain because of the appalling treatment of Jewish people in Germany. Emma prayed fervently that Hitler would never take over the British mainland, because if he did, he might be equally merciless with his British opponents.

The proverbial feeling of a *calm before a storm* was lived out in the routine of work, shopping and having a pint at the local, but all the time across the country there was that certain feeling of waiting and waiting for something really dreadful to happen.

The Prime Minister, Mr Chamberlain, had been to Germany for what seemed to be a successful meeting with Herr Hitler. During the newsreels at the cinema, the audience cheered as they saw him return triumphantly from the meeting waving a piece of paper saying that there would be peace in our time.

Christmas came and went; this year, perhaps not with the less clouded happiness of last year, but who knew what next year could yet bring?

Lily Hawkins visited Emma in Ada's Terrace with Joy, Willie and baby Shirley, knowing full well that they would be invited to stay for tea. Ivan had gone to join his training ship and Lily was missing his financial contribution to the housekeeping.

For both Sam and Emma, as for Harry and Lily, it was going to be an emotionally draining experience for them as their respective children left home, but even more so as the threat of war moved nearer to them all.

In spite of all the news, both local and foreign, Emma and Sam were totally unprepared for the day when Billy came home to tell them that he had enlisted in the *Royal Air Force*. His mother was beyond distraught and shed many tears as she went through his wardrobe, washing his clothes and making them all look presentable.

'You don't have to bother, Mam,' he said, 'I'll be all kitted out when I get my uniform.'

There was enough time for him to give his notice in to Mr Roylands. 'Seems like I will be losing all my staff,' said Mr Roylands as he shook hands and wished Billy, 'All the Best!'

Billy's friend, David Harris was in the *Territorial Army Reserve*. He knew that if there was a serious military emergency he would be called on first to be a full-time soldier.

Very soon, Billy in his turn received his instructions to report to the air force base at Cardington. He was excited, but the excitement was somewhat clouded by the thought of how his family members would take it. 'Now to say goodbye to Nanna Shushkin,' he thought.

When he went to see her, she was shattered, seeing all her hopes for Billy's safety and prosperity dashed, rather like her hopes for Sam.

For Billy there was just enough time for a farewell night out with the lads and a drink at *The Volunteer* with his Dad.

In the pub, Sam struggled with a welter of mixed feelings. On the one hand, he felt such pride in Billy, his eldest son, for going into the *Royal Air Force* at a time of potential conflict for the country. Yet, on the other hand, he was struggling with a feeling that he should be giving Billy advice about duty and danger, but not knowing quite what to say. Sam took his courage into his hands, drew Billy's attention with a gesture, and looked him straight in the eye, 'Son,' he said, 'I've got some advice for you: fly right and do your best. We're all going to be very proud of you.' Father and son hugged as if they might not see each other for a long time.

Billy's friend John was puzzling things over as he walked home from the pub. Why did Billy need to go and join up voluntarily? Why go early into the forces when there was no call-up? But Billy had said he wanted to choose which branch of the armed forces he would go into and if he were to be a conscript, he could not choose. John, sitting at his breakfast the next day, thought that there was still much fun to be found as a civilian!

Billy was now part way through his training course at *R.A.F. Cardington* and George was happily working at the woodyard and spending his evenings with Daphne.

On the 2nd of September 1939 the hot weather broke. As they lay in bed, Sam and Emma listened to the growling of thunder echoing across the heavens. It was so hot and humid that Emma longed to throw the covers back, yet the vivid flashes of lightning made her want to bury her head in them. Presently the jug and bowl on the wash stand rattled with the ferocity of the storm.

To keep herself occupied, Emma got up and wandered upstairs into the girls' room. There, Mary and Joanie were awake but Jackie carried on sleeping through the thunderstorm.

For Joanie, it was a bone of contention with her parents that Jackie still shared the room with his sisters when he could have slept in Billy's bed, but Emma felt that Billy's room was the only living connection she had with her eldest son now that he had taken on the perils of the skies.

The next morning was fresh after the rain, but no one felt like doing anything; everyone was waiting for the Prime

Minister's speech at eleven o'clock, the most important speech of his life.

Not everyone could afford a radio but Mr Gorsedale at No. 3 Ada's Terrace had a wireless. Generously he turned it up loud and opened the window so that the grown-ups could listen to the speech.

The tones of Mr Chamberlain were heard announcing that no assurance had been received from Herr Hitler that Poland would not be invaded, '*and that consequently this country is at war with Germany.*'

The unearthly wail of the air raid siren rent the air, a dog started howling, a little girl from down the terrace screamed.

Jackie turned to Emma, 'Are the Germans coming, Mam?' he asked.

Emma bewildered, looked questioningly at Sam, over Jackie's head. In her heart, she was asking, 'What will happen in the weeks and the months ahead? What will happen to our country and to our family?'

Sam sighed heavily, 'Aye, lad,' he said. 'If the other countries that they fought are anything to go by, then they want to be coming here. And if they try to come, they'll have a right, royal fight on their hands. You mark my words!'

At first, things in Ada's Terrace went on in much the same way as before. The *Phoney War* had begun and things seemed to drift along very much as usual.

Children who had been evacuated to another part of the country at the start of the war, began drifting home. And Jackie, who had gone to stay for safety at *Bann's Farm* with his Aunt Annie and Grandpa Bert in Redtoft, came home and returned to his school.

Billy wrote enthusiastically from Cardington about his life and training in the *Air Force*. He came home on leave at Christmas, looking so smart in his uniform that Nanna Shushkin almost forgave him for enlisting!

When Lily Hawkins saw him she pronounced him a real *Bobby Dazzler,* and reckoned he would not be short of girlfriends. In this she was not wrong.

Billy had finished his initial training and was now learning the intricacies and technicalities of being a pilot. Dashing and devil-may-care in his demeanour, he had many girlfriends, but as yet his motto was *love them and leave them!* He was not dashing into marriage!

Ivan Hawkins had been home on leave too, looking outstandingly smart in his naval uniform. He had treated his Dad Harry, to a drink in *The Volunteer* and his Mum, Lil was not going to miss out on that either, for in her eyes her daughter Joy was quite old enough to look after baby Shirley, and if she had any worries about it the *Missus* from next door would come in.

It was a great night for Ivan and his parents at *The Volunteer* and was full of fun and frolic for all the crowd, enhanced by the imminence of war. Sam who had called in for his usual half-pint of beer, told all the happenings to Emma when he went home. Music was all a-plenty. Sooty Martin had brought his *squeeze box* and Pete Newton played the piano. Since Harry was not a great dancer Lily had trawled the bar for a partner, picked up her skirts and danced merrily to her heart's content.

The war moved inexorably onwards and on foreign shores Britain was fighting a desperate battle with little cause for dancing.

George had been to have his medical examination and subsequently had been passed *A1* - as fit for military service. Nonetheless, for Emma, it was still a heart-stopping moment when she picked up the brown envelope from the doormat. Written on it were the words *On His Majesty's Service.* George's call-up papers had arrived.

Carefully she placed the letter on the mantelpiece and when George came in and saw it he went pale. It was a shock for him too. He had to report for army training within ten days' time.

Men were called up into the Forces in their age groups and Mary's young man, Robert, would normally have been called up at this time; but he was a gas fitter, and at *Walpole's* the gas fitters were a *reserved occupation,* and so he remained behind.

Training for George began with a train journey from Hull's *Paragon station* to *Beverley Station* which was only eight miles away; he had been issued with a pass, and instructions to arrive at the *East Yorkshire Regimental Barracks* at no later than eight o'clock in the morning.

Not wishing to be late, he took a 6.30 a.m. train and when he arrived at Beverley he took care to ask directions of a passing pedestrian.

When he arrived the camp was busy, but along with other early arrivers he had his first experience of a cooked Army breakfast.

After documentation procedures and the allocation of a place in one of the barrack huts, George and his fellow recruits were allowed *settling in time.*

The following day, the culture shock began for them all with the issue of both clothing and kit, followed by dental checks, medical checks and an array of vaccinations. None of them felt at all ready for war over the next two days, while recovering from the gruesome effects of the hypodermics' assaults.

The Sergeant Major, on the morning of the third day lined them all up on the parade ground and addressed them in a mighty voice which made George, who was only six feet away, wince.

'ATTENTION! Now you 'orrible little monkeys! You are a real, ragbag bunch if ever I saw one, but we are going to make proper soldiers of you yet! We are going ter make you fit enough to carry a horse for a hundred miles. Stand still when I am talking to yer! You are going to get so smartened up on the parade ground that your mothers will hardly recognise you. Trenches you are going to dig; rifles and Bren guns you are going to fire and bayonets you are going to learn to use. Your proper training starts NOW!'

Learn they did. Exaggeration apart, the Sergeant Major kept to his word and became duly proud of them as real soldiers.

Daphne was inconsolable as all their plans for happiness would have to be put on hold. Feelings of terror filled her nights as she thought of the scenes she had witnessed at the cinema.

That weekend Sam and Emma invited Daphne to tea. Having young brothers herself she was soon a favourite with Jackie; she laughed and joked with him and Mary too became a close friend.

But Joanie remained aloof and looked down her nose at Daphne, 'Fame before family,' she told herself.

As Jackie was sent to wash himself that teatime, he protested at the threat of too much soap and water, 'I *am* clean!' he said. And with impeccable logic, 'How can I not be when I've been to see Nanna Shushkin?'

Mary and Joanie were no longer under obligation to do the dutiful Sunday afternoon visit. Nevertheless, Mary's love and respect for her Grandma Eliza had grown over time and she often walked round there with Jackie and sometimes went during the week to visit the old lady when Robert, her boyfriend, was at a rugby match. She had even done some ironing for her when she had had a heavy cold.

Nanna's eyes were the critical eyes of a perfectionist but secretly she enjoyed instructing Mary, who took it in a good-natured way.

'It's a pity that *flibbertigibbet* sister of yours hasn't a bit more sense about her, like you!' she grumbled to Mary.

The *flibbertigibbet* sister, Joanie, had signed up as a messenger girl at the *Air Raid Precautions* headquarters. It was based in a room in the Methodist Chapel, which was very handy for her.

Rooms at the Chapel were rented out and there was also a dancing class held there. Now that Joanie was working at *Woolworths* she was able to pay to have her own dancing lessons. This was, in Emma's eyes a sad waste of money. Mr Stank and his wife Phyllis both ran the classes; Mr Vernon played the piano; and together they drilled the older girls into a troupe.

At the end of the Thursday night class, Mr Vernon asked Joanie and some of the other girls to stay behind. 'I've got bookings for you,' he told them, 'as *Vernon's Variety Sparklers*. The pay is good and lodgings are found for us in the towns that we visit. When you get older,' he continued, his eyes growing brighter, 'you will probably be able to go into the *Entertainments National Service Association* which will keep you out of working in dirty munitions factories or joining the Forces. Go home and talk to your parents about it as you'll need their permission to come on the tour. I know it's short notice but we go in a week's time!'

'My Mam will never let me go,' sighed Gladys Cunningham, but Mr Vernon had already realized that.

'What about you Joanie?' he asked encouragingly, 'I'd say there's definitely a future for you on the stage.'

'I'll talk to my parents,' promised Joanie knowing that Sam and Emma would never agree. But Joanie was scheming to go anyway. It was not likely that Emma would get to hear of it as she did not move in the same circles as the other girls' mothers. Joanie only hoped that none of the other girls' fathers frequented *The Volunteer* or were likely to talk widely about the project.

At work Joanie bought some writing paper and worked on forging the letter purporting to be from Emma to Mr Vernon, giving their permission for Joanie to go with the concert party.

Joanie did not dare let *Woolworths* know that she was leaving their employment even though it would lose her the week's earnings. Handing in her notice to *Woolworths* was too risky as Emma often came into the shop and was friendly with several of the women. She did not want to be found out that way.

In response to the delivered parental consent Mr Vernon instructed the girls to be at *Hull Paragon Station* on Sunday morning, 'We're going on the 11.15 a.m. train. Our first engagement is in Darlington.'

Joanie went to extraordinary lengths to keep her departure plans secret so that no one at home found out about them. It was difficult for her to pack her clothes without being noticed, and she got over the problem by taking only a few things at a time to Barbara's house.

Barbara was one of the girls in the troupe befriended by Joanie: she had more freedom and laxity in her home life than was quite good for her. Emma was rather annoyed that Barbara Palmer and Joanie often borrowed each other's clothes as she thought that Barbara's choice of clothes was decidedly vulgar, to the point of being trashy.

Joanie wanted to be at the station to catch the train on time without leaving any tell-tale clues behind. No one was going to stop her being one of *Vernon's Variety Sparklers* and so she began secretly plotting in her mind. Emma would be cooking the Sunday dinner; Sam always went out for his Sunday pint; that left Mary, who if all went well would take Jackie to Nanna Shushkin's.

Joanie considered herself fortunate with how things turned out because Mary did take Jackie for the visit to Nanna's and from there they were going on to a display and a picnic being held by Mary's workplace.

In the end, it was surprisingly easy although Joanie was the only one with no one to see her off at the station. The thought made her sad, but as the train picked up speed she hardened herself. The lying was getting easier. 'My Nanna's ill,' she had told Mr Vernon, 'my Mam and Dad couldn't very well leave her but they didn't want me to miss my chance and they know Mrs Vernon will look after us.' And so fired with ambition, excitement, guilt and not a little trepidation, Joanie's career as a wartime entertainer began.

The letter that she left behind in the bedroom disquieted her a little when she thought of Emma reading it, 'But that's just life,' she thought carelessly, 'and mine's just beginning!'

Even the rather dingy troupe lodgings in a back street behind the station - that was permanently haunted by the smell of cabbage - did not dampen her enthusiasm. 'Joanie Walters,' she said to herself, 'you are on the way up!'

That name, *Joanie Walters* would have to go for a start. She would choose one that looked good on billboards and she eventually fell asleep trying to dream one up.

Meanwhile, back in Ada's Terrace, for Emma it was like having a death in the family.

With Joanie, her fifteen and a half year old daughter gone like the wind itself, she sat without consolation, her face drenched in tears with the parting letter like a suicidal note in her hand, seeing only Joanie's laughing face dancing round the room in the way she used to do. 'Dear Joanie. All the time she knew exactly what she was going to do, yet she lived a lie with us. I feel betrayed. Betrayed by the child of my own womb!'

'Don't cry Mam,' said Mary who was also crying. It was Mary who had found the letter when she came home from the picnic:

Dear Mam and Dad,
I've got my chance to go on the stage.
Like I told you, I'm going to be a star.
Don't worry about me.
Love, Joanie.

Sam went to see Mr Sawdon at the Methodist Chapel but he could not help directly. The people from the dance class only hired the room. They had pinned a note to the door saying that classes were cancelled and had gone away owing a month's rent.

Sam was in detective mode looking for his errant daughter; he spent the rest of the afternoon and evening just trying to find any friends of Joanie's but found that he did not know them.

In his frustration and anger he turned on his daughter Mary, 'Surely you know who she went round with? She must have spoken to you about her friends?' But Joanie never had and although she and Mary were sisters, they had never been close in the *sharing secrets* kind of way.

Mary wept, not so much just because Joanie had gone but more because her parents were upset. Billy and George had left home and now Joanie had gone also. Mary mourned the old way of life that once had seemed so safe and secure. Now all had changed.

Sam, still in detective mode spent long hours tramping the streets trying to find his daughter but to no avail. He went to the *Paragon* train station which was full of steam engines chuffing and hissing, locomotives at the ready, and carriages thronged with people leaving from the many platforms. There were servicemen going back to camp after a week's leave and families with children who had been evacuated and had come home for the weekend.

Sam spoke to the policeman on duty at the station but he could not help, 'I'd be hard put to it to sort anyone out in this crowd,' he said.

The answer from the ticket office was the same. The clerk could not remember any young woman of Joanie's description buying a ticket, 'In any case,' he told Sam, 'I didn't come on shift until the late afternoon.' But the staff did not know that Mr Vernon had purchased all the tickets in a block so the booking clerk would not have seen Joanie at all.

Tense and worried for their daughter, Sam and Emma sat up all night hoping against hope that Joanie would come home.

Mary lay awake, missing Joanie and conscious of the empty space beside her.

The next day the women at work commented on Mary's pale face and red-rimmed eyes, 'That Robert hasn't put you in the club?' they teased.

Mary blushingly denied the remarks and the question.

Christmas came and went and George came home on *embarkation leave*. As well as spending time with Daphne,

George had time to meet up with Robert, who listened to his tales of army training with avid fascination. Robert was eager to defend his country, but his job had prevented him from leaving. So at the end of the week and upon discussion with his family, he gave in his notice at *Walpole's* and went along to sign up.

After some weeks, he received his call-up papers and was preparing now to go into the Army.

On the day of departure, Mary went with him to the station to see him off. She was distraught at the thought of the dangers he was going to be trained for, but she admired his courage. At the station platform, she tried hard to restrain her tears.

'No need to cry!' he said, 'I'll be home on leave in a month or two.' He kissed and hugged her and whispered heartfelt words of love. Then he waved to her and was gone.

Walking home alone, Mary felt as if there was suddenly a great big hole inside her heart. Bravely, she resolved upon joining the war effort herself. 'If it's good enough for Robert, it will be good enough for me,' she said.

When Robert had first started walking her home from work, Joanie, quite unfairly had not been impressed with him at all. 'Too ordinary, for the likes of me!' she had said tossing her head. 'He's a real stick in the mud. You mark my words, Mary. I'll bet he hasn't got a romantic bone in his body!' But Mary had known differently and kept hidden away from Joanie the silver heart-shaped locket that Robert had given her.

Meanwhile, she continued to visit Nanna Shushkin; helping the old lady by taking her some fresh vegetables and sometimes a few fresh eggs from Grandpa Bert's farm.

A few weeks later, while Robert was still away training, a letter arrived for Mary. It was not one of the longed-for ones from Robert, but a letter from the *Ministry of Labour* responding to her enquiry about war work, and directing her to a munitions factory near Birmingham. She was billeted with Mr and Mrs Murgatroyd, a kind-hearted couple who very quickly began to look on her affectionately as a daughter and one whom they could trust.

Other female volunteers at the factory invited her to join them on nights out and urged her to change her lodgings for greater freedom, 'You don't want to stay at home moping! That fellow of yours will be out having a drink or going to dances,' they said.

But Mary knew that she could trust Robert and she saved the money she earned for their home when the war was over. She sat in at night with Mrs Murgatroyd, as company for that good lady when Mr Murgatroyd had to go out on fire watch.

'I can go out with an easy mind,' Mr Murgatroyd told Mary, 'knowing that you are here.'

The two ladies passed the time in knitting, often in the air raid shelter as the time ran on. Mary also made good use of the time in the long evenings to write to Robert and to Emma.

It was another Christmas before Mary was able to go home for a couple of days, even though work at the munitions factory never actually stopped. She visited her Grandpa Bert, Aunt Annie, Nanna Shushkin and Aunt Daisy. She took Jackie to the cinema and saw a big change in him from the young boy she had left at home. 'How you've grown!' she said proudly.

Back at the munitions factory near Birmingham notices had gone up in the canteen to say that the popular *B.B.C.* radio programme, *Workers' Playtime*, would be broadcast from there on the following Wednesday lunchtime.

Someone had sarcastically scrawled underneath: *This broadcast by kind permission of Adolf Hitler and the Luftwaffe.* However, the munitions work and the *Workers' Playtime* concert went on without any interruption from nasty Nazi visitors!

On the day of the concert Mary was glad to be present and she settled back comfortably into her seat. A few minutes into the show she suddenly sat upright in shock: there in front of her was Joanie, as large as life, singing on the stage in the chorus line - but there was no mention of her name on the programme!

Mary hardly heard the comedian's saucy jokes as blindly she staggered out to the canteen.

'Was it something I said?' called the comedian to gales of laughter as Mary left crimson-faced. Swiftly she knocked at the backstage door.

'Looking for someone dearie?' asked a heavily made-up blonde woman who came to the door.

'I want to see Joanie Walters!' Mary stammered.

The blonde woman frowned, 'No one of that name here.'

'It's alright Iris, I'll see to it,' came a familiar voice as Joanie came up behind her - and Mary just had to hug her.

'I never thought I'd see you here in a Birmingham factory,' said Joanie.

Mary's strong feelings came to the fore, 'I volunteered for work and was sent here! I didn't run away from home like you upsetting our Mam and Dad!' Mary's face was flushed with purple and her tone was bitter.'

'Just as I might have been,' Joanie rejoined, 'but I had the chance to make something of myself. I'm with this concert party now. This is my war work.'

'You're still the same selfish cow that you always were.' Mary was really worked up now. 'You can believe that I shall tell our Mam so too when I write.'

'Tell her what you like,' retorted Joanie, 'Saint Mary rides again. You never change do you?'

The blonde woman approached and laid a hand on Joanie's shoulder, 'Serena, how nice for you to see a friend but we have to go now.'

'She's no friend of mine!' answered Mary, and through angry tears she watched them walk away from her.

'Fancy our Mary meeting up with Joanie like that!' commented Sam as he read her letter. 'Got herself a posh name as well, *Serena Waters*.'

'There'll be *troubled waters* if she dares to show herself round here after all she put us through!' Emma would not be pacified.

Sam knew in his heart that if Joanie wanted to come home, Emma would not turn her away. But it did not seem likely that Joanie would make that move. Mary had got no address for Joanie and had no idea where the concert party was headed for next.

The air raids over Hull became more intense and almost every morning an announcement came over the radio, '*This is the BBC. Here is the news. German raiders have attacked a north east town.*'

Sam and Emma knew their north-eastern town was under the deadly rain of German bombs and together they decided it might be best for Jackie to go and live with Bert and Annie in Redtoft. Night after night the sky was lit up with gunfire flashes and searchlights while the earth echoed and shook with exploding bombs. The city was not a safe place.

With great courage Emma stayed on with Sam at Ada's Terrace but most nights were spent in the shelter at the corner of Merton Street. It was particularly bad in the month of May when going to bed began to seem like a thing of the past. Even the customers at *The Volunteer* seemed subdued. Sam was on fire watch and it was his turn to be on duty with Boggy Snell.

For once it had been a reasonably quiet night. With the arrival of daylight, the men had come down from the roof of a tall insurance building to make their way home ready for the day's work. Suddenly the air raid sirens wailed and before the noise had died away they could hear the dreaded drone of the German bomber aircraft engines.

'Get your running shoes on Sam!' shouted Boggy and in that instant they heard the whistle of bombs and threw themselves under an army lorry that was parked nearby. The ground heaved and debris rained down around them. They looked at each other pale-faced with shock; they were still alive and could hardly believe it.

Emma had been just about to leave the shelter when the air raid siren went off, and together with most of the other people she turned round and went straight back into the shelter.

When the *All Clear* siren sounded at last, she made her way back home to Ada's Terrace. There she found Sam and clung madly to him; thankful that they both had survived.

'Now lass, why not go and stay with Annie and Bert at *Bann's Farm* tonight? You could see our Jackie and get a better night's rest,' Sam tried to persuade her.

Emma reluctantly agreed to go. Although she felt that her place was with Sam, her wish to see their son Jackie was strong also.

At twelve years old, Jackie was now a tall, thin lad. He was greatly attached to his grandfather. He loved fetching and carrying for him while Bert pottered around the smallholding where he grew his vegetables. The old man was feeling his age and, being rather forgetful, he appreciated the young lad's help.

Back in the skies over Hull, the Germans had taken to dropping phosphorus incendiary bombs in order to destroy houses and warehouses. Even out as far as *Bann's Farm*, the night sky was lit up with the disastrous flare of the city's fires, so that Emma did not quite get that hoped-for, good night's rest.

Bert and Jackie patrolled up and down outside the residence, ever on the alert for stray missiles while, in sympathy, the pony stamped restlessly in the stable.

It was the aim of the *German High Command*, by means of *Luftwaffe* bombing raids, to prevent food and other desperately-needed supplies from getting through to Britain by sea. As Hull was rated as a major shipping port, it had also received the infliction of *shock and awe* bombings on civilians which, in the case of other countries, had caused them to surrender.

Emma made her way home the next morning and miraculously found a bus had arrived at the stop. It had not got far inside the city boundary before it halted. 'Can't go no further!' said the conductor, 'Look!' and there in front of them was a big bomb crater in the road with water clearly gushing from a broken mains water supply pipe.

Wearily the passengers got off. Most of them had been out of the city to stay overnight with relatives or friends in the hope of getting a few hours of sleep on a makeshift bed.

Sadly, Emma learned that, in the previous day's raid, a number of people had been trapped in the ruins of some big offices. Rescuers had worked through the night until they were satisfied there were no survivors, and as it seemed impossible to recover the bodies, their graves were where they lay buried.

It had been the worst night's bombing that Hull had endured for some time. Across the city, fires still burned fiercely, but still dauntless, the city struggled to its feet and went about its business.

Emma began to make her way through the rubble-strewn streets picking her way carefully wherever she could find a navigable path.

At Bercom Street fire engines were busy at the remains of a burning building, fire hoses snaking everywhere.

'Where are you going, love?' asked a homely-sounding policeman as he made his way over to Emma.

'Ada's Terrace,' Emma told him.

He thought for a minute, 'I think the best way for you is to go down Rymer Street and Wickham Road then back along Derby Road and you should be able to get on to Merton Street from there. There are a lot of fires this way, an unexploded bomb on Fawcett Street and a landmine has hit Passmore Road.'

Thanking him, Emma began the long walk home. Along the route a *Salvation Army* mobile van was busy serving mugs of tea to the salvage and rescue workers and a sad-faced woman pressed a mug into Emma's hands, 'Here, have this love. It'll take you a while to get home.'

Grateful for and heartened by the tea, Emma finally turned into Ada's Terrace. The air was thick with dust and the acrid smell of burning buildings. With a sensation almost of disbelief, she saw it was still standing. With a sigh of relief, she went to let herself in knowing that Sam would probably be at work but was surprised to find the door unlocked. 'What does it matter,' she said to herself, 'if Jerry the German wanted to be in he'd have blown the place up anyway,' and she felt a desire to laugh hysterically.

Then she noticed a kitbag standing in the corner and, half in disbelief, she mounted the stairs to find her darling son Billy in bed in his old room!

He sat up half-awake as Emma sat on the bed hugging him with tears running down her face.

'Give over Mam!' he protested, 'You'll soak me vest!'

Shakily Emma got to her feet saying that if there was any milk in the house she would make a brew, and went downstairs to put the kettle on.

Emma could see the change in Billy; the boy who had gone away had returned a man. He had been in air battles, had seen other men shot down and had tried to shoot other men down and he had seen the burned bodies of friends tenderly removed from the wreckage of their planes which had become their coffins.

'Have you seen your Dad yet?' she called.

'Yes, I got home yesterday but it was a rough night Mam, with all the bombing. They came for Dad at three o'clock in the morning because of the fires on the ships and in the warehouses. I wanted to help but Dad told me to stay here and get some rest.'

'How long have you got son?' Emma asked.

'Seven days,' Billy told her, 'and I've got leave because I'm being posted to another station and I'm going to Nottingham on Monday.'

'But that's not seven days,' Emma protested.

'No, I know. But you see Mam, I've got a girl. Her name's Jenny. She's sweet and funny. She's in the *W.A.A.F* and she's on leave too. She lives in Nottingham so I'm going to see her and perhaps meet her family. The next time we're on leave I'll bring her home to meet you.'

'What's she like?' Emma wanted to know, intrigued.

'Oh, you'll like her Mam. She's little, dark-haired, pretty and full of fun.'

'Alright,' Emma laughed, 'I get the picture!' Although outwardly she laughed and chatted with Billy, inwardly her emotions surged, 'Who was this chit of a girl who was taking Billy away from them on his precious leave? Would she expect Billy to up sticks and live in Nottingham after the war?'

Billy was eager for news of the family and Emma showed him the letter from George that had arrived three weeks ago.

Billy chuckled as he read about George and his mates having a kick-about with a football in the North African desert. 'That's our George,' he said, 'always loved his soccer!'

When he heard of Mary's encounter with Joanie he whistled through his teeth. 'She always said she was going on the stage,' he mused, 'some things don't change.'

'It would be nice to think that they didn't,' said Emma, 'but the war has changed the lives of so many people, that things may never be the same again.' Emma made them both a sandwich and Billy decided to go and see his Nanna Shushkin and Aunt Daisy.

CHAPTER FIVE

It is strange the way that peacetime attempts to make a liar out of wartime.

The Great War of 1914-1918 was viciously real to the many that lived through it. However for many of those who were born in Hull in the following two decades, *the Great War* was *a thing of the past and nothing to do with now.*

For such people to be told that the Germans had in that conflict flown many sorties over Hull, terrified its citizens, bombed the city twelve times and in one raid alone with high explosives and incendiaries, destroyed forty shops and houses as well as killing twenty-four people - well, they would have been incredulous!

Billy boldly set out to see Nanna, albeit rather slowly but it was not his fault. In this *Second World War* conflict, the face of the City of Hull had been seriously altered by enemy bombing. Gaping holes now yawned where once had stood rows of settled terraced houses.

The Germans were better at it this time, not bringing the old slow *Zeppelins* over but rather using numerous and faster aeroplane bombers, dealing out terror, death and destruction in industrial quantities.

In a flight of fancy Billy thought he could hear the echoes of children's voices long ago as they played outside or the voices of their mothers calling them in.

Some places where he had played as a youngster had become almost unrecognisable and some of the streets that he had known like the back of his hand were now fields of rubble and broken bricks, as if they had never had any human value or meaning.

Feeling degraded as a person by this war on civilians, he was forced to look out over a dire vista such as he had not seen and could not have imagined before. He was horrified and in the pit of his stomach he had a bad feeling. He was no coward but he was not unmoved by the evidence of freshly destroyed lives and homes in his city.

It was a relief for him therefore when he bumped into Barry Robinson, an old school friend who was serving in the *Navy* and was home on leave.

Barry was in a good mood, 'How about meeting me tonight for a pint?' he asked Billy, 'Two other old mates will be there, it'll be great!'

Billy thought for a moment. Would Sam expect him to go out to the pub with him later? 'No,' he thought, 'Sam would say, *Go out and have a good night, son*,' and if he was not working or on fire watch, his Dad might join them anyway.

Billy decided to meet his friends in the famous *Bluebell* public house in the centre of town. It was a favourite rendezvous for the sailors, in proof of which the *Bluebell's* walls were decorated with the ribbons from many sailors' caps, proudly proclaiming the names of the ships on which they served.

With a cheerful wave and a 'Seeya later!' Billy left his friend and made his way up to his Nanna's house. That good lady had no idea that her grandson was home but when she saw who was knocking on her door, tears filled her eyes. Not that she shed tears easily, she looked on that as a sign of weakness but the tears flowed anyway!

His Aunt Daisy hung on to Billy's arm with great affection until Eliza dispatched her to make a pot of tea. It was something she was proud to demonstrate that she could do.

'The air raids over Hull have been bad, Nanna,' Billy said, 'do you go to the shelter?'

Eliza shook her head, 'Daisy's frightened of being shut in the shelter so we go under the stairs, see?' and she showed Billy how she had dragged the rocking chair into the space with a pouffe for Daisy. 'I make a flask of tea so it's all ready if we have to go in there. It's our little place under the stairs!'

'Well, Nanna,' Billy said affectionately with a bright grin, 'you just take care!' Billy hugged her and Daisy before leaving.

Nanna, reluctant to part with him for a moment wanted to know all about Jenny.

'You would like her, Nanna!' Billy promised.

But Eliza was not so sure. It was doubtful if any girl would be good enough for her grandson.

He promised to come and see her again before going off to Nottingham. Billy looked at his watch, he would have to step along quickly if he was to get home and then go out again with his friends. He had only gone two streets when the sirens wailed and almost at once came the throb of enemy aircraft engines.

Already an air raid warden was shepherding people into the safety of a nearby shelter. 'Come along son,' he said to Billy, who acknowledging the warden's authority went into the shelter too.

The ground shook and shrapnel rained down as the bombs exploded. As raids go, it was short and sharp - not nice. Soon the planes had gone and relieved people were preparing to make their way out of the shelter.

'Looks like Swatman Street caught it badly,' observed the warden who was the first to emerge.

Billy gasped and his heart seemed to leap into his throat - that was Nanna's street! He started to push his way out.

'Where do you think you're going?' queried the warden.

'It's my Grandma, she lives in Swatman Street,' he replied.

The warden's tone changed, and he said with compassion, 'You'd better hurry and see if the old lady is alright. I'll come along with you.' The two set out together and breaking into a run, Billy kept going until he had rounded the corner which led to the top of Swatman Street where he stopped short, as if he had been punched in the chest. Where Nanna's house and her neighbours' houses had been, there was now a gaping, smoking ruin. Already rescue workers and people were gathering around.

'Does anyone know if there were people in these houses?' shouted the Head Warden.

'My Nanna and Aunt Daisy lived in No. 44,' he shouted back, 'they used to shelter under the stairs,' Billy's voice although he was trying to be calm, sounded hoarse.

'Well that's where we'll start,' the Warden decided.

The work was slow and arduous, moving piece by piece the rubble, wood, glass and debris. The hours passed and Billy's heart raced. Mugs of tea were pushed into the rescuers' grimy hands. Only stopping for a quick gulp of hot tea, they worked on, fuelled by the need to find and rescue his two family members, to find someone alive and something to give them hope.

Dark clouds of night had spread their fingers across the sky when there was a shout, 'I think I've found where the stairs were!' Their ears straining for the slightest sound, they all stood silent and listened. Hearing a faint cry they worked on with renewed vigour, needing only a chance.

By digging and lifting some of the bigger pieces of rubble and stopping to listen, they were able to pinpoint more accurately the direction of the sounds.

'There's someone here!' called one of the workers.

Gently they lifted the pieces of debris out of the way until gradually a human figure began to emerge in front of them. Eliza Walters his Nanna was pulled from the wreckage alive but bloodstained and covered in dirt and soot.

Billy hugged her before she was put, protesting into a waiting ambulance. 'It's alright Nanna,' Billy told her joyfully, 'we'll find Daisy,' and he turned back to carry on with the search.

The salvage worker held his hand up for silence.

Two soldiers who were passing by stopped to help, 'I'm sure I heard something,' one of them said, 'it came from down there,' pointing to a hole in the rubble with a beam lying across it and more debris resting on top of that.

'I'll go,' volunteered Billy, 'she won't be so frightened if she sees me.' Armed with a torch Billy crawled into the hole and began tunnelling his way through. 'I can see her!' he shouted to the waiting rescuers.

The sound of shifting debris from further up the mound sent showers of dust and mortar cascading over them and then, with a shattering roar, the whole mass of masonry upon which they stood, shifted and resettled in a cloud of dust and soot, knocking them off their feet.

The beam and the hole underneath it vanished under tons of detritus.

'Blasted Germans!' one of the soldiers railed aloud as tears rolled down his face. His mate put an arm round his shoulders, too choked with emotion to speak.

They returned to digging but they knew in their hearts that the chance of finding anyone alive now was small. Mercifully there were no more raids that night. The work continued on until finding two bruised and broken bodies, they tenderly lifted them out of the ruins, took off their hats and bowed their heads in prayer. Two very precious, very dear lives had been snuffed out.

After going to the shops Emma Walters finally got home feeling unaccountably depressed. The butcher was only able to sell her some mutton rib bones but with some of Bert's vegetables and some dumplings she could make a passable stew. 'Billy's taking his time,' she thought, 'but he's probably met up with friends.'

When she heard footsteps outside the house it was Sam and not Billy who came in, dog-tired, face blackened and eyes red-rimmed from smoke, sweat and dust.

As he washed, Sam told her a little of his day: the struggle to try and salvage some of the goods from the burning warehouses; the ships in the docks burning, exploding and sinking and the policemen who were needed on duty to prevent looting.

No. 23 shed which had held sacks of sugar had gone up in flames completely. Sam felt that he would never be rid of the acrid smell and taste in his throat and nostrils. He did not know what was in shed No. 19 but the army lads were seeing to it and no one else was allowed near; he did know that two of the soldiers on duty there had been badly burned.

'Billy's doing well in the *Air Force*,' said Sam, 'it might be that he'll be posted up this way and then we can see more of him. Anything from George yet?' he asked looking across to the mantelpiece where any post might have been.

'Nothing from George, but Billy's new girlfriend, Jenny lives in Nottingham,' Emma said pointedly, 'and that's a long way away.'

Hardly had Sam finished tea when the air raid sirens sounded again and they both had to make their way to the shelter.

'Looks like we're in for another night of it,' remarked Sam inside the shelter. 'I expect Billy will stay on at Mam's, or he might have met up with some of his old pals. He'll know where to find us.'

The bombing raids went on all night, and Sam and Emma's ears rang from the closeness of the blasts. Several people were crying and they all felt stunned and exhausted.

When they emerged from the shelter into the strong sunlight they did not know what they would find.

'Now, lass,' said Sam, 'Thank God we're alive but do we have a home to go to?'

A house at the bottom of Merton Street was leaning at a crazy angle and two others smouldered nearby. As they turned towards Ada's Terrace, Emma could see that the bomb blast had blown their front door open and some of their windows had gone but their house was still there! The blasts had deposited soot, dust and glass everywhere.

'We still have a home to go to!' said Emma. They smiled with weary relief. Sam put the kettle on while Emma tried to clean up. 'It'll have to be dried milk in your tea, there's a tin in the cupboard,' she said.

'The windows will need boarding up,' said Sam looking round thoughtfully and assessing the situation. 'Look, love, why not go and stay with Annie and your father?'

'You know you have to stay here for your dock work!' was Emma's strong protest, 'My place is with you!'

It was true that Sam could not really leave the docks. He was an irreplaceable and highly experienced docker. He had a deep knowledge and understanding of the docks and all their services. He was truly a docker as he had always been from his first day on site only now he was no *left-footer*. He had to stay.

Outside the house there were footsteps and voices. Sam, expecting it to be his workmates, went to the door.

Gravely, Sergeant Rawlings introduced both himself and a warden. 'Mr Walters? Does your mother live at 44 Swatman Street? I'm sorry to have to tell you that your mother is in hospital, not badly hurt I'm pleased to say, but very shaken up.'

Stunned, Sam replied, 'What about Daisy?

Embarrassed, the warden shook his head, 'I'm sorry,' he said, finding it hard to speak.

'You'd better both come in,' Sam said guessing that they had been on duty all night, 'we've just made a pot of tea.'

They thanked him. It was true, they had been on duty all night and these calls were the most difficult ones to make. Taking a deep breath and clearing his throat the Policeman said, 'Do you...do you have a son in the *Air Force* presently home on leave?'

Emma in the kitchen, gripped the table as the room seemed to heave and spin round her. She heard the warden tell them how Billy had burrowed into the bomb-damaged house to find Daisy and how the debris had collapsed on top of him.

Emma listened to the words but could not believe they were meant for her. Her Billy was dead? What was it that she had said to him yesterday? *This war will change people's lives for ever.* But she had not expected this.

Sam stood up and went into the kitchen, 'Will you...will you be alright, lass?' he asked her, 'Sergeant Rawlings wants me to go to the mortuary at eleven o'clock tonight. There's certificates and things to see to.'

She nodded numbly, 'I'll be alright Sam,' she said, tears beginning to roll down her face, 'I'll write to Mary. Surely they'll let her come home?'

The kind Policeman asked if Emma would like anyone to talk to. If Lily Hawkins had still lived in Ada's Terrace she would have told her, but she could think of no one else she wanted for company.

Sam patted her shoulder, 'We'll have to go and see Mother in hospital this afternoon. Then we must tell Annie, Bert and Jackie.'

In her grief Emma wondered how you tell a young lad like Jackie that his much beloved older brother would not be coming home.

At the mortuary, Sam had one of the most harrowing experiences of his life, as he identified both his son Billy and his sister Daisy. Billy's injuries were such that his face was not badly marked and Sam was glad, as Emma was insistent that she must see her son. Poor Daisy was another matter.

Emma wrote her letter to Mary. Then seeing again Billy's kitbag still in the corner, she picked it up and hugged it. Only yesterday he was alive and telling her about Jenny and she had been worried that a girlfriend would take him away from them. 'Oh Billy, Billy!' she wept. 'You could have married a girl from Timbuctoo if only you could be alive again.'

Sam made enquiries about compassionate leave for George, but the army authorities were not hopeful. He was a long way away and the funeral, which was only a few days away, would be over long before he could get home.

In the afternoon they went to see Eliza in hospital. Her head and hands were bandaged and she sat staring into space looking suddenly so much older and very frail.

Sister Kennet took Emma's arm, answering her unspoken question about Eliza, 'Yes, she knows about her daughter and grandson. Father Goldsworthy came to see her on a pastoral visit this morning. You can take her home now. She needs to be with the people she loves.'

Emma sighed wondering how on earth she could look after her mother-in-law back home in Ada's Terrace with its broken windows and door.

It was Sam who, wisely, took the matter out of her hands by suggesting that Eliza should stay with Annie and Bert. Reassuring Sister Kennet that they would make arrangements and be back for Eliza later, they left.

Sam got on his bike and went to see Annie and Bert. Jackie was out with friends. They were devastated by the news of Daisy and Billy's death and at a loss to know how they were going to break the news to Jackie. Sam tentatively broached the matter of a place for Eliza.

'Of course Eliza must come here!' said Annie, wondering at the same time how well the old lady would fit in, 'We'll make her comfortable.'

When Eliza arrived at *Bann's Farm* later that day, she did not seem to notice where she was. The ladies of the local *Women's Royal Voluntary Service* had fitted her out with some clothes and Sam had got a taxi to take them there. Eliza was still in shock. She just sat in the chair with a blank look on her face rocking herself back and forth. For so many years Eliza had looked after Daisy and fretted over what would become of her, if she, Eliza, died first. But now it had all gone.

The worry and the burden had certainly been lifted but in its place was a dark, blank emptiness. Her beloved Billy had gone too. All the hopes and dreams that she had cherished for life after the war seemed as if they were nothing now, but Father Goldsworthy had said to her that she needed to find a new sense of purpose for her own life, as well as being grateful for the lives that she had loved and lost.

Emma in her own grief scarcely knew one day from the next. The air raids went on and the funerals were planned for Daisy and Billy. Sam quietly took Emma to say her mortuary farewells; she was shaken by the occasion but later felt relieved that she had done so.

One grey morning Daisy was laid to rest. Father Goldsworthy conducted the service and mercifully, there were no bombings.

Emma thought how very tired the old priest looked; his cassock and surplice gave the impression that they had been slept in.

Billy's funeral was set for the next afternoon. Four young airmen came from his station to act as pall-bearers; the *Union Jack* fluttered over his coffin in the light breeze and the *R.A.F.* Padre took the service as he had known Billy and recognised his talent. In his eulogy, the Padre offered words of comfort:

> Billy loved his Nanna and his Auntie Daisy. He did all he possibly could to rescue them. He died a hero's death. How do we know that? We know that because the *Good Book* says:
>
> 'Greater love has no man than this, that a man lay down his life for his friends.'
>
> Billy laid down his life for his Aunt Daisy and we can all learn something good, from a caring heart that is unselfish.

After the funeral service and with the help of Annie, Emma managed to clean and tidy the house in Ada's Terrace, bake some buns, set out a cake and make a few sandwiches for the mourners.

Mary was home for the week. It was such a relief and so good to have her there! She was an older, thinner Mary but still their very own daughter of whom they were very proud.

Of Joanie they had no word nor any idea of where she was. Jackie watched everything that went on, a child who was growing up fast.

Nervous at the funeral, Jackie looked round the cemetery with tear-filled eyes. His Aunt Annie, unfamiliar-looking in her best coat tenderly put her arm round him. His Nanna was placed between his Mam and Dad who were gently supporting her. He had known grief over the loss of a pet animal before but at the funeral Jackie was fully facing his own grief over his family members.

'How can it be,' he felt, 'that everything's going on like nothing has happened? Don't they know that my big brother has died?' Jackie, in despair thought that maybe people did not care

71

that the worst thing in the world had happened to him: that his big brother had died and that his own heart was breaking.

At last they turned away and the little party went home to Ada's Terrace. Where else was there to go?

But before long they were back again in the shelter as the enemy bombers began their nightly raids. Unused to the town, Jackie was petrified. Emma rejoiced in noticing that Eliza had a kindly arm around Jackie's shoulder and was talking quietly to him.

A few weeks later at Ada's Terrace Mary had a letter to say that Robert was coming home on leave, probably embarkation leave. Everybody was guessing where Robert and his new squaddie mates were going, but actually nobody knew.

In the letter, Robert, though no great artist, had drawn a cartoon of himself down on one knee putting a ring on Mary's finger and asking her to marry him. At the end of the letter Robert, confident of her agreement, asked Mary to see about a Special Licence so they could get married straight away.

Mary said to her Mum, 'Somehow knowing the grief that we all share over Billy's death, it seems selfish and wrong to be planning a wedding at a time like this.'

Nonetheless, Emma reassured her, 'Life is worthwhile and must go on, love. Billy would have wanted you to be happy. Didn't he always say: *Live for the day?* He would have been the first to congratulate you on getting engaged and married.'

So in the few days she had left at home she and Emma went shopping. Wartime austerity meant that wedding clothes were simple and practical, so Mary bought a dusky pink wedding suit for the occasion. Noting Mary's concern, Eliza also insisted on putting ten pounds in her hand along with clothing coupons for her wedding clothes.

Mary returned to her factory work in Birmingham on the Sunday, hugging her parents at the station. Emma was tearful as the events of the past two weeks washed over her.

'Don't worry lass,' Sam told Mary, 'you know I'll see your mother alright.'

And Mary knew that he would be true to his word. In her heart she hoped and prayed fervently for her marriage to Robert to be at least as strong as her own parents' marriage. After all they had set her a good example!

CHAPTER SIX

The air raids over Hull seemed to increase in both frequency and ferocity. It became hard to remember a time when Hull was not being bombed by the German foe. Civilian businesses, civilian homes and civilian families were being burnt and blown to pieces with an extraordinary callousness. Emma could imagine the *Heinkel* bomber pilots saying, 'After all, when you're bombing from ten thousand feet, you can't hear people screaming…'

Tiredness was something that Sam often found himself fighting. Night or day, he was having to deal with emergencies on the docks and also in the town as a volunteer fire watcher. Emma wondered if he was not overdoing things…

Coming home one very windy night, he had seen a house that had two incendiaries dropped on it. Besides rescuing the occupants, within a few minutes, before anyone could do anything about it, ten houses on the same street were ablaze. This was proof that, even with diligent fire watchers on duty, not every building could be saved. Sam had thought about it and concluded that doing something to help was far better than to do nothing and he was a volunteer because he knew how he would feel if it happened in Ada's Terrace.

Saint Columba's church, led by the Reverend Maurice Morley was a lovely church with a lively congregation and Mary had always planned to get married there. But only two weeks before the wedding, phosphorous incendiary bombs and high explosives rained down upon it and the church building was burned to a shell.

Mary, although very upset was determined that her wedding day would not be spoiled, 'I'd marry him in an outhouse if I had to!' she said defiantly and, 'The church hall will be good enough for me!'

The bridegroom-to-be, Private Robert Stavin arrived safely home in Hull on ten days' leave shortly before the wedding. He brought his parents, John and Sarah Stavin to introduce them to Mary's parents.

Robert looked like a different man from the one who had left Mary only a short time before. Muscles had grown as a result of his army training and his puppy fat had vanished. He looked tall and impressive in his uniform, and Mary fell head over heels in love with him all over again! More importantly though, she knew he was a steady character and that he loved her truly.

The two mothers got on well straight away, and over a cup of tea were soon planning the best wedding they could under the circumstances. In this they were aided by Sarah's youngest son, David Stavin, who worked in *The Home and Colonial* Stores in Hull and who was kindly able to procure the little extras that would help to make a happy wedding feast.

Sam took John Stavin to *The Volunteer* where having just had a delivery of beer, they were able to drink a toast to the bride and bridegroom. As the evening progressed, the two fathers got on very well, finding that they had many mutual acquaintances, including John's Uncle Peter, who also worked on the docks.

Walking back to Ada's Terrace Sam remarked, 'I'm glad there were no raids tonight.'

'That's right but it does feel like there might be a storm brewing,' replied John.

'Ah, you can always smell the fish docks if it's going to rain!' chuckled Sam, as smells of the fish dock wafted across the city.

George's girlfriend, Daphne was delighted to find that she was going to be one of the bridesmaids. She was a *land army* girl now and was based on a farm just a few miles out of town. She had found it natural to keep in touch with Emma and Sam but her working hours were long and the labour was hard. She preferred the open-air life and felt fitter for it.

It was a hard experience for many people to be kept long out of touch with their loved ones by the terrible chaos of war. Daphne had suffered just like Sam and Emma. None of them had heard from George for several weeks, not that the army post was exactly swift from soldiers abroad.

In fact, training completed, George had been allocated to the *Rifle Brigade* and after embarkation leave, soon found himself on a troopship heading for Egypt.

Like many another soldier, George had never been outside of his own country. To travel so far and to see the sights and sounds of the Middle East was a baffling experience for him. Fancy having sunshine all day long! 'It's gonna take me a bit of a while to get used to!' he said to himself.

It was the first week in March 1941 and he had arrived in Tobruk. As he was supposed to be in the *Rifles*, he was not quite sure why he had arrived in Libya and not in Egypt but he was going to enjoy himself and not worry overmuch if the authorities had lost his postal address!

In the few *shore leave* days that he was granted, after he settled into his new quarters in the barracks, he decided to do some exploring. In so doing, he was offered - for a price - camel rides, squirmy octopus to eat, and men's daughters! George quickly learned not to walk around the city on his own and that if he carried one of the locally made short swordsticks under his arm, when he was out walking in the *kasbah*, he would not be treated with disrespect.

George was given three days' training in desert warfare and found himself hurriedly attached to the *King's Own Royal Regiment (Lancaster)* because big events were stirring. Rommel and the *Afrika Corps* arrived and besieged the port city. With this, George had his first experiences of real warfare there and witnessed the *thunder and lightning* tactics of the German army.

In the front line he remembered what he had been taught: 'Let the tanks cross our front lines, so that they can be shot up by our twenty-five pounders - and then stand firm and shoot up their infantry!'

The German infantry attacked with a will, not expecting resistance following the tank charge. Then it was their turn to be shocked as the defending British, Australian and New Zealand soldiers returned fire and followed up with bayonet charges.

After several such charges with his new comrades in arms, George came under submachine fire and felt the two bullets striking his chest and arm before he passed out.

When he came to his senses he could feel the swaying of the stretcher and the pain from his wounds. Two stretcher bearers had waited twenty minutes in a trench while under heavy fire in order to rescue him. He passed out completely and a day and a half later he woke up in the field hospital with his wounds dressed and a blessedly heavy dose of morphine running through his bloodstream. Unknown to him, he had been operated on by a very fine surgeon and had some very fine stitches to prove it - along with a big plaster cast!

The Padre came to his bedside to chat and said, 'I can tell that you aren't dying, so you'll not need to have the last rites! But is there anything that I can do for you?'

Aware that having his right side in plaster would do nothing for his letter writing skills, George asked for help in writing a letter to Daphne.

Smiling, the Padre reached into his briefcase, produced a pen and writing materials and skilfully took dictation from George. Before going off to ensure that the letter was despatched, he said, 'I believe you may get repatriated somewhere at the beginning of next month so - God bless you - and stay alive ready for the boat home!'

George thanked him and tried to get comfortable in bed before the next volley of shells came over.

Sure enough, on the 5th of May 1941, feeling foolish and guilty because he was being invalided out of the war zone so quickly, he was placed onboard a *Tobruk Ferry Service* supply vessel on the dangerously contested so-called suicide run which would take him back to Britain and a better chance of recovery.

One morning, pedalling as if she wanted to be a cycling champion, Daphne arrived at Ada's Terrace almost throwing her bike against the wall as she screeched to a halt.

'Where's the fire, lass?' chuckled Sam.

'It's George!' she gasped holding out the letter, 'The Padre says that he's going to be on his way back to England. He's coming home!'

Sam could hardly believe what he was hearing and called Emma who took the letter with shaking hands, 'He's been wounded,' she said and burst into tears. When she had recovered she read on. George, although now in a war zone hospital, was being transferred to an army hospital in England, and could be home by next week. They all talked and laughed at once, faces bright and shining with joy.

'He could be here for the wedding,' thought Emma joyfully as she put the kettle on.

When the news was sent to *Bann's Farm*, Eliza sat quietly rocking in her chair, pleased that George was safe, but - oh - how her heart ached for Billy.

When the middle of the week arrived, George, the wounded warrior, arrived home in Ada's Terrace looking thinner but tanned.

Both his arm and chest were heavily bandaged and he was under orders to report daily to have his dressings changed, but nothing could keep the smile off his face. 'It's great to be home,' he said, 'much better than being shot at!'

The wedding morning came up bright and sunny. Tired from the previous week's bombing but happy, the family prepared themselves for the day's marital celebrations.

The church hall smelled of smoke and soot, the pianist played: *Here Comes The Bride* and Sam, the proud father, led Mary down the aisle to where Robert, and the Minister were waiting:

> Wilt thou, Robert Stavin, have this woman to
> thy wedded wife, to live together according to the law
> of God in the holy estate of matrimony? Wilt thou love
> her, comfort her, honour and keep her; and, forsaking
> all other, keep thee only unto her, so long as you both
> shall live?

Robert looked into the eyes that he loved so much. Speaking with happy conviction and passion, he said, 'I will!'

Mary, eyes shining with joy, spoke out her devotion, 'I will!'

After the giving and exchanging of rings, the Reverend Maurice Morley joined their hands together and sandwiching them both between his own hands, spoke up with ringing tones:

> Forasmuch as Robert Stavin and Mary Walters have
> consented together in holy wedlock, and have witnessed
> the same before God and this company, and thereto
> have pledged their troth either to other, and have
> declared the same by giving and receiving of a ring,
> and by joining of hands; I pronounce that they be Man
> and Wife together in the Name of the Father and of the

Son and of the Holy Ghost. Those whom God hath joined together let no man put asunder.

There was much wiping of eyes and blowing of noses and a gentle outburst of joy within those assembled there. When the service was over, the bride and groom processed down the aisle, bathed in bliss, approval and happiness.

On the way out of the church, George offered his good arm to Eliza to lean on, and thankfully, she took it. Eliza stood straight-backed and nearly dry-eyed as both Sam and Emma mopped up their tears, while smiling at the same time. And George gave thanks that there had been no air raids that day.

Back home at Ada's Terrace, everyone enjoyed a wartime *wedding breakfast*. Jackie's eyes grew wide with amazement at the food and its plentifulness, 'Corrhh!' was all he could say, between one mouthful and the next.

Wedding toasts and speeches over, the light was beginning to fade when the newly-weds Mr and Mrs Stavin were ready to leave. With confetti in their hair and the shouts of well-wishers in their ears, they left to spend the night of their honeymoon at Robert's Auntie Maisie's home in the village of Westrae north-west of Manchester. And on the first full day of their married life, they hoped to go to the seaside at Blackpool and visit some of Robert's relations there before spending the rest of the week just being together, as honeymooners do.

After the meal's conclusion, and the newly-weds had gone, the wedding celebrations began in earnest and there were more surprises in store for Jackie. He had never seen the grown-ups letting down their hair like this: the relief that the wedding had gone off well without the hitch of sirens and bombs, had left them all feeling relaxed and mellow. This feeling was plentifully aided by Bert's home-brewed beer while Sooty Martin played some very lively tunes on the squeeze box and Lil Hawkins and some of the others danced their feet off.

'Give us a song, Bert!' clamoured one of the guests.

Bert demurred, 'I said I wouldn't sing until our boys were safely home.' But he gave in and sang *My Grandfather's Clock* and *The Farmer's Boy* to much applause from the gathering, and even Eliza joined in the chorus.

Robert's Uncle Stanley sang a rather bawdy song that Jackie did not fully understand, but stored it all up so that he could remember to tell his friends, and the party went on until late into the night and was unanimously acclaimed as *a good do*.

Sam and Emma had the rare luxury of sleeping in their bed that night and George saw Daphne home.

'Those two will be next!' Sam forecast.

Back in Ada's Terrace while Sam was at work, Emma found that she had to spend most of the day in the air raid shelter. It certainly was not her favourite occupation but it was far better than not surviving.

Sam was kept busy working on the docks but he often had to take cover, and the fire boat was kept dangerously occupied as bombs fell down among the ships.

At the end of another day, Sam made his weary way home. How much longer would the bombardment go on for? How much more killing and pounding could people take?

There was still much work to be done on the ship in the dock, but Harry Hawkins had not turned in for work that day and Sam puzzled over whether he was ill or not. Certainly he had had a real skinful of drink at Robert and Mary's wedding but he should have got over it by now.

Just then, a voice called out, 'Mr Walters?'

As Sam looked up, he saw standing by the gate a young man in naval uniform who grinned and stepped forward to shake his hand.

'Why Ivan Hawkins! As I live and breathe…' said Sam shaking him by the hand, but he was startled and really *cut to the quick* to see tears beginning to well up in the young man's red-rimmed eyes.

Haltingly, Ivan told his story. Lily and Harry Hawkins had both been in the shelter with little Shirley and the young couple from next door. Without warning, the air raid shelter had received a direct hit from a large five hundred pound bomb and all in it had died instantly. Ivan, in returning home on leave, had unwittingly walked in on his own family's tragedy.

With his face as white as a sheet, Ivan clearly was in deep shock at the loss of his parents and little sister and Sam barely knew what to say or do. However he ushered him into the house and not long after, Emma came home to hear the sad news.

Her complexion turned pale and all Emma could do was to let him cry on her shoulder along with her own tears, and while making the tea, listen to the story again, as often as he needed to tell it.

Emma was badly shaken too, more than she wanted to admit. It was hard to believe that laughing, devil-may-care Lil was gone; the friend and neighbour of so many years, no longer available for Emma to celebrate with her in the good times, or commiserate with her in the bad times.

While Sam, Emma and Ivan were sitting in the bomb shelter that night, Emma found herself repeatedly going over and over those dire events.

'Maybe I should go and pay my respects to Lily,' she had tentatively suggested, 'after all I'd like to say goodbye to my old friend.'

This was gently but strongly discouraged by both Ivan and Sam, whose eyes had gone wide at the very thought of it.

Ivan, brave as he was, knew that although Lil's head was there with a strangely peaceful look on her face, there was very little else left of her.

Wisely, Sam said to Emma, 'Remember her as she was at the wedding.'

In her grief, Emma remembered that Harry and young Shirley were gone too, and Emma wept especially for the little girl who would never grow up.

Ivan was given the hospitality of their home and they did all they could to help him make the funeral arrangements. It was so personally difficult to think of making the funeral arrangements but fortunately, they found a funeral director who helped them through the practicalities of it all.

Ronnie and Roy Hawkins, who were both in the *Catering Corps,* were able to get compassionate leave. Fortunately, they were stationed in England at the time, but they did not eat for twenty-four hours after hearing the sad news.

Lily Hawkins had allowed Willie to be evacuated to a kindly couple in Scotland. When they had heard of the disaster, they said at once said that Willie could live with them for as long as he liked. Ivan had met the couple when his ship had put into a Scottish port and, in their usual, kind fashion, they had made him most welcome.

Willie was greatly attached to the man of the house, and was frequently willing to help him in the garden. He had made real friends there and his skinny frame had filled out. Although he did not seem to be fretting for his old home, the kindly foster mother had made sure he had written to Lil each Sunday. No one could easily have known how much those letters from Willie had meant to Lil. Perhaps she had seemed brash on the outside, but, without doubt she had deeply loved her children.

Joy Hawkins also came home and stayed with the Walters. It was, to say the least, a bit of a squeeze in the little terraced house, but they were glad of the closeness and Emma found Joy's presence a comfort.

The Hawkins' house had been badly damaged. They tried to salvage what they could and dispose of the rest.

All of them had had their horizons greatly widened by the war and Joy was quite definite that she, for one, would not be coming back to the North again. She was engaged to a soldier whose home was in London, so - were they spared - that was where they would be setting up home after the war.

After Lil's funeral, when everyone had gone, Emma felt empty and flat. There was plenty of the usual routine shopping, cleaning and cooking to be done but, somehow, with the loss of the Hawkins family, something of the sparkle seemed to have gone out of life. Yet, over time, the sparkle insistently returned.

Sometimes she thought of her errant daughter, Joanie. Where was she? What was she doing?

Soon afterwards, a letter came from Mary. She wrote regularly, knowing how much the loss of her old friend and neighbour had affected her mother. Emma sat down and read the letter twice, tears of joy running down her face. Mary was in the early stages of pregnancy and Sam and Emma were going to become grandparents for the first time! Emma wished that she could have gone to Lily with the news. They would have sorted through knitting patterns together and decided which little outfits to make. 'Well, I could still do that,' Emma said to herself, as she dived into the cupboard under the stairs where she kept the box of patterns. 'Oh Sam! Hurry home so that I can tell you about our first grandchild!

There she was sitting on the floor with knitting patterns scattered around her, when there was a knock at the door: it was to herald yet another turning point in the Walters' lives.

Stiffly, Emma got up and opened the door. A pretty dark-haired girl whose face was vaguely familiar was standing there, her coat taut across her swelling stomach.

'Mrs Walters?' she asked hesitantly.

Emma nodded, trying desperately to remember where she had seen this young woman before. She had been with the group of airmen who had come to Billy's funeral.

'You'd better come in!' Emma said, holding the door open.

The young woman swallowed nervously, 'I'm Jenny. Did Billy tell you about me?'

In a flash, Emma remembered - the girl from Nottingham. Billy was going to go there on his leave, but he had...

Jenny nervously followed Emma indoors.

Emma was also nervous. To create a distraction she waved a hand at the patterns spread on the floor, 'Excuse the mess, our Mary is going to have a baby. I was just looking at patterns. Sit yourself down, love. I'll put the kettle on for us.'

As Emma came back from the kitchen, Jenny was wiping her eyes.

'Yes, she would be upset,' Emma thought, knowing that she still often shed tears herself; it only needed the sight of a tall, young man in air force uniform to bring it all back. 'The kettle won't take long to boil,' she said, 'at least we've got a gas supply today. Had you known our Billy long?'

'About six months,' Jenny was twisting her handkerchief nervously, 'we were both stationed at Cardington. I'm still there.'

The silence hung heavily between them, then the kettle whistled and Emma darted into the kitchen, glad of the diversion. She brought the tea through and passed a cup to Jenny.

'Have you...' they both started to talk at once, and laughed anxiously together.

Jenny began, 'I was going to ask if you have heard from George. Billy told me all about his brothers and sisters.'

Emma flushed with pride, 'Oh yes, George is home on sick leave, he's gone to have his dressing changed, he'll be home soon, you might see him.'

'And Mary's going to have a baby?' Jenny asked.

'Yes, it's early days yet, but I can't wait to get started on the little bain's clothes.'

'At least hers will be wanted,' Jenny ended with a sob.

'Are you...' Emma let the question hang between them. Jenny nodded, 'I get my discharge next week, but I can't go home. My Dad says I've disgraced the family and he won't have me around.'

'What will you do, lass?'

'I don't know. There are homes for girls like me and they will arrange for the baby to be adopted. But I don't want that, I want to keep my baby. It's all I've got left of Billy.' And the tears that were never far away ran unchecked down Jenny's face.

Emma was not far from tears herself, 'Isn't there anywhere you can go?'

'No, I would have gone to my Gran's, but she's quite poorly and my Mam says it would be too much for her.'

Emma wondered how Jenny's mother could bear to see her daughter turned away, but it seemed that Jenny's father, whose word was law, simply *wanted* to reject her. But where was the graciousness in that? Emma thought long and hard as she sipped her tea. This was Billy's child, bone of his bone, flesh of his flesh. How could she turn Jenny away? A germ of an idea formed in her mind, but first she needed to talk to Sam.

Jenny finished her tea and stood up, 'I have to go, there's a train at four from *Paragon Station* and I need to be back on the base by eight, tonight.'

'When do you get discharged?'

'Next week, probably Tuesday.'

'I was going to say, come here and we'll see what we can do to help.'

Jenny's eyes widened and her face brightened, 'Oh, I will! Billy said that his Dad...'

'Yes, we need to have a talk, me and Sam. But will you come next week?'

Jenny gratefully said that she would.

Emma sat still on the stool for a long time after Jenny had gone. Her thoughts were with Billy and this girl of his. He had always laughed and said he would not be getting tied down, but that had been before he met Jenny and his life had changed. Emma vividly remembered the pride he had shown when he had told her about Jenny; the confidence with which he was able to meet Jenny's parents; the boy becoming a man.

Emma knew about the development of the *Spitfire* and the heroic pilots fighting in the *Battle of Britain*.

Billy would have lived their kind of life; dashing to his plane, soaring and diving in the sky; nights spent in the officers' mess or at the local pub; singing and joking, living each day as if it would be their last - and sometimes it was. Billy, spending evenings with Jenny and making plans for when the war was over. *After the war* would have seemed far away to them then, so they lived for the day. But Billy did not die there living the hectic life, he came home and died a hero's death. And Emma wept for the loss of her eldest boy and all that might have been for him.

As she dried her eyes again, she thought of Jenny and the new life that she carried in her womb and with determination in her heart she said, 'We can do something!'

CHAPTER SEVEN

Emma sat thoughtfully in front of her mirror, pushed her hair back from her face and sighed. She normally wore it in a bun, but should it be? 'Hair!' she said, 'Hmmph!' She could get it cut, she supposed, but she had always worn her hair long and not least because her beloved Sam seemed to like it that way.

Still, everything seemed to be changing now, perhaps it was time for her to change the style of her hair. After all she was going to be a grandmother twice over and she was not that old. There was a hairdresser near where Annie and Bert lived. 'Maybe I could try and get an appointment there and spend the day with Annie, Bert, Eliza and Jackie,' she thought to herself, 'it must be two weeks since I last saw young Jackie.'

The clicking of the back gate brought Emma back to the present as Sam and George came in.

'What did the doctor have to say?' Emma asked George.

'Ah, the wound, it's all healed nicely,' George told her, 'though I have to go back to Beverley and see the army medic there. If he passes me as fit I'll be on my way back to camp.'

Emma sighed, it would all begin again: the worrying, the waiting; the hoping for a letter; dreading the fatal knock on the door from the telegram boy bearing the worst news.

'Are you seeing Daphne tonight?' Sam asked George.

George grimaced ruefully, 'No they're very busy on the farm with the harvest, so she won't be home at the weekend.'

'I'm surprised you two haven't named the date yet!' Sam remarked.

George stiffened. Sam had obviously touched on a raw nerve.

'It's not that easy. I did suggest it, but Daphne wants to wait until this dratted war is over, or at least until things are looking brighter.'

'I suppose she has a point,' mused Emma doubtfully.

'You would have been counting on a new outfit, Emma, if there was a wedding in sight!' said Sam.

Emma pursed her lips and shook her head, while not rising to Sam's gentle teasing. Sam gave up for the time being. He would get to the bottom of it, it was not like Emma to be moody.

After tea, father and son went out for a walk together. Wally Ingles had not received his quota of beer at *The Volunteer*, so they walked further afield. The summer night was warm; the moon was floating among the clouds and it was a pleasant night for a stroll. As they approached Tanning Street they could hear the hum of voices emanating from the open door of *The Prince Albert* pub, and the tapping sound of darts either hitting the board or dropping on the floor. They went in to sample the hospitality.

'Two pints please, landlord!' Sam requested as he leaned on the bar.

The surly landlord looked them up and down, and turned his gaze directly on to George, who was not in his uniform, 'I only serve young men if they're in the Forces!' he said.

Sam gasped and was ready to give the man a piece of his mind, but George took his arm, 'Let it go Dad, there won't always be a war on.' And so they walked out and returned home.

Later that night they all sat round the table with their fish and chip supper. Leaning back, George stretched his legs and yawned, 'I think I'll be hitting the hay.'

'Well you might get a couple of hours shut-eye before the German fireworks get started again,' said Sam, 'but it's a bomber's moon.'

George, remembering his experience of the *Siege of Tobruk* gave a humorous glance, said goodnight and stumped up the stairs to the little bedroom.

Downstairs, his parents went through their usual routine of setting up their bed. When they were settled, Sam turned to Emma, 'Now what's the matter lass? Are you frettin' over our George going back?'

Emma shook her head, 'Of course I don't want him to go back but that's not the only thing on my mind.' She told Sam about Jenny's visit and her expectant bump.

'Aye lass, it's a rum do!' Sam agreed. 'Do you really think this girl's on the level, after all, it could be anyone's babe?'

Emma was quick to disagree. She believed the girl was genuine because Billy had told her about Jenny, and the way he had spoken about her showed that he thought she was someone special.

'You mean that you want the lass to come here to live?' Sam was incredulous, he would never understand women. But Emma had no doubts. She had barely thought of anything else since her meeting with Jenny that morning.

'And what about our Mary?' Sam asked. 'She might want to have her baby here?'

'Of course she can come here, where else would she go? We'll manage.'

The question of Jenny hung heavily between them as Sam stretched out on the bed and fell into an uneasy sleep.

Sam woke later to see Emma standing by the window, 'Is it a raid?' he asked.

Emma shook her head, 'It's thundering,' she said.

Sam raised himself up on his arm. 'Did it wake you up?'

But Emma had not been able to sleep. Her talk with Jenny had been playing continually over and over again in her mind. Jenny's tear-stained face floated before her eyes. And then there was Mary, so full of joy, looking forward to her own baby. Emma was longing to see her. 'It's Jenny and the baby,' she said.

Sam joined her at the window and put his arm round her. With his voice low and positive, he said, 'If it really means that much to you to have that lass here, well…it's up to you.'

Emma nodded and hugged him tight. 'You're a good husband. I really, really do want Jenny to come and have her baby here and stay with us for as long as she wants. We may be a bit crowded, but that'll be nothing. The house is empty now, compared with when we had all the family at home.'

Not having been to the smallholding for a while, a few days later Emma went to see her father and sister over in *Bann's Farm*.

Eliza was there in the garden picking some runner beans. She had settled in with Annie and liked nothing more than spending time in the garden with Bert.

He scratched his head and pushed his battered, old trilby to one side, 'The old lady takes over!' he said ruefully, yet inwardly he was pleased with the interest that Eliza showed, 'We'll make a farmer of her yet!'

On hearing that Eliza grunted, 'There's a good crop of plums,' she told Emma, 'I said to Annie we should bottle some and make some jam.'

Annie patted the old lady's shoulder, 'We'll see.'

It had not been easy at first, for any of them. Eliza's pride would not let her be dependent on these people who were no kin of hers. Added to that, she was grieving for both Billy and Daisy.

Skilfully, Jackie with his jet-black hair, his farm-developed physique and growing height, helped to bridge the gap between Eliza and the rest of them with a game of cards - he had them all sitting round to play *rummy* at night. They loved the feeling of fun and togetherness that it gave them.

Jackie also was the one who took Eliza to see the hens and the pig. Annie's kind understanding had also helped. Once Eliza had thought of the family as *these people*, but now they were friends, almost like family.

Rather like having a holiday, Emma knew she was happier for being there with them, if only for a few hours. She took the opportunity to walk into the village and make an appointment to get her hair trimmed for the following week. Now was the time for a change. 'My hair in a bun?' she thought to herself, 'No - goodbye to the bun!' She knew that getting it trimmed would be a new venture for her.

On her return to the smallholding, Emma sat out in the garden with Eliza and Annie. As Annie poured tea from the big brown pot, she had a gentle, quizzical expression on her face. 'What's troubling you, lass?' she asked Emma, 'For I can see that something is.'

Emma started to tell her, but once she started, the floodgates opened and the words and the tears just tumbled out of their own accord.

When Emma told them of Jenny's visit, Eliza asked, 'Can you be sure that this is Billy's child, that the lass isn't just saying that, and trying to see where she can find a home?'

Emma shook her head and told them of the photo that Jenny had shown her. It was one that she had not seen before - of two young people in air force uniform; a laughing, happy couple who looked so right together, and there, on the back, in Billy's own handwriting, were the words: *Together forever.*

Eliza spoke for them all when she said, 'You can't turn Billy's child away.'

And Emma knew again that what she meant to do was right.

She returned home and had tea ready for Sam when he got in. He was tired but listened eagerly to Emma's news of how Eliza was coping with a new way of life.

'How's Jackie?' Sam wanted to know, 'Is he going to school?' Other children who had not been evacuated were missing school because of the air raids and were running rather wild. Emma was able to allay his fears on that score. Annie, Bert and Eliza made sure that Jackie went to school.

'And how's me Mam?' queried Sam.

Emma laughed, 'Oh, she's fine. A real country woman stringing beans, feeding hens, wanting to bottle fruit and make jam.'

Sam said, 'I could have guessed. Whatever me Mam does, it just has to be her best. If it's washing her sheets, they have to be whiter than anyone else's - nothing else will do - and so it's the same in her country life!'

Then Emma told Sam of Eliza's and Annie's reaction to the news of Jenny's visit.

'So they also think we should take her in?' Sam rubbed his chin thoughtfully. 'Well, I think it's up to you lass, with all the extra work, and the sharing of your home.'

All that had occurred to Emma, but now her mind was made up, and as Sam said, 'It could have happened to one of our own.' As for Billy, Emma was sure he would have wanted to marry Jenny if he had known about the baby. Thoughts went buzzing round and round in Emma's head but she knew that what she was set on - accepting Jenny and the forthcoming baby into the family household - was the right thing to do. Of that she was sure.

George returned to the base at Beverley, was passed as fit for active duty, and came home for a weekend, telling them all that he thought it would not be long before he was sent abroad again.

George's heart was in the *Western Desert Campaign* and he felt disabled because he could not talk about it safely before it was all over: *LOOSE LIPS SINK SHIPS* and *CARELESS TALK COSTS LIVES*, the government slogans clearly said.

Daphne, with less enthusiasm than before, came over to see George before he left. She had been shocked to hear just how close he had been to dying and did not know how to react to it.

When Emma told Daphne the news about Jenny, she was surprised at the girl's scornful response.

'You'd think Jenny's family would have had more sense than to treat her so badly. Anybody can make mistakes!' she said.

Emma felt shocked, regardless of Jenny's family's attitude. This was an unknown and different side to Daphne that she had not seen before.

The next week, Emma managed to get over to see Annie and the rest of the family and have a very happy day with them. Jackie came bouncing in from school, happy to tell Emma that the older children including himself, could have two weeks off school to help with the potato harvest in the autumn.

The schoolmaster, Mr Harding was not at all in favour of his pupils being let loose, because they were the very ones who needed teaching the most.

But someone at the back of the class muttered, 'There is a war on!' although no one would admit to the remark when invited to do so!

Emma went home to Ada's Terrace with her bags well loaded with food. A lettuce here, some potatoes there, a supply of Bert's beans and the blackberries that they had picked that afternoon.

As she came to her own back gate in the Terrace, she was aware of voices from within the house. Perhaps George had got a few hours leave - and she went in ready to welcome him - but stopped short in the doorway as Sam and the visitor turned round.

It was Jenny. In his hospitable way, Sam had made a pot of tea and Jenny was sitting by the hearth. Sam got up as Emma came into the room: the air was electric with tension and their visitor looked nervously at Emma.

'You did say,' Jenny faltered, 'to come back and see you when I was discharged.'

'And,' in a voice sounding large in the small house, Sam assured her, 'you did right!'

Emma smiled at Sam, hung her jacket up and went over to Jenny, 'You can stay with us love, if you like. It's not grand, but it is home and you are welcome.'

Jenny's face crumpled as she fumbled in her pocket for a handkerchief. 'I don't know what to say…' she sobbed.

'Well, that's settled then!' said Sam, while Emma put her arms round the girl saying, 'It's what Billy would have wanted.'

Jenny had a small case and a couple of bags with her, the sum total of her belongings.

'You can have the girls' room for now,' Emma said. 'If Mary comes home to have her baby, we may have to do a switch round. I'll leave the little room for George, at the moment.'

And so Jenny settled in, but not into the girls' room that night, for, as on so many nights, the air raid sirens sounded, and they all spent the night in the bomb shelter.

A few days later, Emma and Sam took Jenny to meet Annie, Bert, Eliza and Jackie. Eliza sat back in the old rocking chair watching and listening and saying little. That worried Emma. Did Eliza regret saying that they should help Jenny? She voiced her fears to Annie.

'Goodness no!' Annie laughed. 'That's the last thing on Eliza's mind. She's just thinking of where she can get some wool to crochet shawls for the two babies.'

That information eased Emma's mind considerably, and Jenny's too when Emma told her. Jenny's relieved smile seemed to light up the whole room as she confessed, 'I was afraid that Nanna Shushkin didn't like me!'

'Nor would she if she heard you call her that!' chuckled Emma. It seemed that Billy had told Jenny all about his family, even the children's secret name for Eliza - who did manage to get some wool, and so was happily employed in making those baby shawls.

George had been sent overseas again and so the letters from him were few and far between. Sadly, Daphne's visits to Emma began to dwindle. If she visited Ada's Terrace, the visit became uncomfortable, as she made no secret of her resentment of Jenny.

The nights were drawing in. The air had that smell of damp earth and wet, mouldy leaves that speaks of the approach of autumn. There was misty rain at night and misty rain in the morning. Trees, bushes and trolley bus wires dripped continually. As people crossed the road, the tramlines underfoot were noticeably wet and slippery. So much of the city was laid waste from the bombing, yet it was the proud boast of local commerce that Hitler had not succeeded in closing them down.

Emma wondered how she would cope with only two months in which to prepare for Christmas. All the family were due to go over to *Bann's Farm* on Christmas Day. Bert was planning to kill the pig that he shared in the *Pig Club*.

Emma wanted to do her part for the Christmas festivities by gathering in any appropriate supplies that she could get hold of. She plunged into a foray of queuing and shopping; whenever there was a whisper of supplies in a shop, she made her way there.

Jenny, who had not an ounce of laziness in her body, was proving to be a godsend in the way that she was able to team up with Emma in domestic things. If one of them was out queuing for supplies, the other would be seeing to the housework.

A sharp, bright day in Ada's Terrace had seen Emma's line of new nappies strung out in the wind.

'I see you've got your flags out!' quipped Sam when he came home for dinner. Emma missed Lily Hawkins more than ever. Oh, how they would have planned together and knitted for those babies!

One great disappointment for Ada's Terrace and for Emma in particular, was that Mary was not coming home for the birth of her baby. She was going to stay with Robert's Aunt Maisie and this pleased Robert well enough. His natural feeling was that whenever the bombers were coming over, the countryside was a much safer place.

Mary's baby was due in January and Jenny's baby in February. A new year with two new babies to be welcomed into the family, and what sort of world were they coming into? One, perhaps, of bombs, fire and destruction? The war could not go on for ever and the babies themselves were a ray of hope for the future.

George had returned to North Africa to rejoin the Forces there. This time the Army *knew his postal address* and placed him with the *2nd Battalion of the Rifle Brigade*.

In the earlier part of the Western Desert war under General Wavell, the Allied forces had smashed the *Italian Tenth Army* and put a stop to their invasion of Egypt. However, progress had not been continued, and at Hitler's instigation, Rommel and the *Afrika Korps* had entered the conflict.

Rommel had become accustomed to defeating the Allies in the desert, but when it came to the vital supply port of Tobruk, he made serious mistakes by expecting to take the port from the Allies in a single day and arriving without even having a map of the defences which surrounded the city.

Fortunately for the Allies, General Leslie Morshead, in charge of the fortress, was no pushover. Instead, the city, though under siege for some months and frequently attacked, was not taken while under his care.

Having the advantage of a deep and sheltered harbour, Tobruk was vital as a supply base for the Allies. If Rommel could have taken it when the siege began, then he would not have had to bring his supplies along hundreds of miles of desert roads.

Fortunately for George, he was not inside the fortress of Tobruk - he was part of the *Eighth Army* which was there to liberate it. Those inside Tobruk would try to break out of the siege and join up with the *Eighth Army* so that supplies would thus be available to the Allies. For George, the high spot of the week was the news that a concert party was coming to entertain them.

On the night of the concert, the troops gathered round a makeshift stage with a truck alongside for a dressing room. The comedian with his string of jokes had them all laughing; the impersonator with his thumbnail sketches of Hitler and Rommel drew light-hearted, raucous booing. His turn ended with cheers and applause. Then a slender, young woman with shining, brown hair stepped on to the stage. Wearing a revealing, blue dress, she sang for the men all the favourite songs of the moment. It almost would not have mattered if she could not sing a note because she had come to entertain them. Because she had come, they mattered and their cares were forgotten. When she danced, and she danced so well, there were whistles and wild applause.

George could only stare wide-eyed at the girl he knew so well, 'Joanie!' he gasped.

'Nah!' said his mate, ''Er name's Serena Waters. It says so in the programme.'

George insisted incredulously, 'It *is* my sister Joanie!'

'Ah! They all say that,' smirked one of the guards. 'Anything to get near the girls!' But as George joined the crowd of men thronging the dressing room truck, Joanie saw him. She pointed him out to the officer standing beside her, and George was propelled over to the tailboard.

'Joanie!' he gasped, grasping her hand.

Joanie hugged him, 'I never thought I'd see you again, let alone here!'

George was serious, 'Mam took it hard when you left.'

'I know and I'm sorry, but I had to get away, and I'm getting somewhere now, doing what I wanted.'

'Yes,' George admitted, 'you put on a good show.'

'How is everyone?' Joanie wanted to know. 'Our Mary, Billy, Jackie, Dad, and Nanna Shushkin and Daisy, are they all alright?'

George took a deep breath, 'Billy's dead. He died trying to rescue Daisy when their house was bombed, and she died too.'

Joanie sat hunched up looking small and vulnerable; the brightness was draining away from her.

George sought for words, 'Mary and Robert got wed, she's having a bain.'

'Oh!' said Joanie with a slightly scornful smile, 'That will suit Mary, she was always one for the bains.' The officer coughed discreetly.

'I have to go,' Joanie said as she hugged George. 'Are you and Daphne…?'

'Oh yes!' George laughed. 'But she says she won't get married until the war's over.'

The driver came round to Joanie, 'Sorry to hurry you, Miss, but *His Nibs* is getting impatient. We have to go.'

Joanie nodded across to the officer, 'Be right with you Charles.'

After kissing George to a chorus of wolf whistles from the soldiers, she got into the truck's cab, while waving to George as they drove off.

'Ruddy officers get all the cushy jobs!' griped one soldier.

'Was that really your sister?' George's mates wanted to know. Other lads, red-faced and enthusiastic, declared that

Joanie was a real cracker, and wanted to know if George had any pin-up photos to hand round.

Later, head resting on his arms, George lay on his camp bed with thoughts swirling round in his head. How Joanie had changed! The slip of a girl he used to know was now a lovely, young woman in her own right. He picked up his writing pad to write home:

Dear Dad and Mam,
You'll never guess who I've just seen...!

For herself, Joanie was really quiet as they drove away to an airstrip. It was as if the whole family had reached out and touched her, and for a moment, her self-imposed isolation was gone.

'You alright sweetheart?' the officer asked.

Joanie dabbed at her eyes. 'I didn't know my brother had been killed.'

Charles put his arm round her, 'I'm so sorry,' he said. 'What you need is someone older to look after you.'

Joanie shot him a glare, moved away from him and shook her head emphatically, 'No thank you! I'm looking out for myself. I'm going to the top. I've got an audience with Michael De Witt when we get back.'

Charles whistled, 'Flying high. Well, good luck anyway!' he said ruefully. All the while, he was thinking to himself that *Concert Party Joanie* would probably do well to get a part in a second-rate pantomime or musical - if she was lucky. Not that he cared too much. After all, there were plenty of girls about who knew how to be grateful.

Joanie stared ahead as the truck sped on its way. She had met men like Charles before; men who thought that their rank would sway the girls.

At the North African front line, the *nightly illuminations* began. German tracer bullets raced across the sky, followed by the crump of exploding shells which, landing nearby, shook the ground.

George was due to be on watch in four hours and so he tried to snatch some sleep. His final waking thoughts were of a young, dearly loved sister whom he had lost and then rediscovered in a desert battle zone. And his dreams were blessed by the memory of a brown-haired girl in a blue dress who had grown up and found her own niche in the world. There in his dreams, a radiant Joanie was holding out her arms to the troops, laughing, singing and being loved by an applauding audience.

CHAPTER EIGHT

Early in the North African morning, a number of eagles soared with pleasure in a light breeze at a thousand feet. Down below and breakfasted, George's platoon eagerly made a push forwards which took the enemy completely by surprise and brought about the capture of eighteen inexperienced Italian soldiers who were sitting comfortably around a small cooking fire and drinking *vino*, as if they were having a garden party. None of them were near any weapons and when one made a dash for a rifle, a burst of machine-gun fire at his feet discouraged him from being a dead hero.

Fortunately, in the push forwards, no platoon members were seriously injured and the prisoners who were largely raw recruits, gave useful information when they were interrogated by the army intelligence unit.

George's mate was jealous of the captured soldiers, 'Them *Eyeties* have got it made,' he jeered, 'they're out of it now. Nobody will be shooting at them everyday! As like as not, they'll get sent back to England and spend the rest of the war at work on our farms. Nice work for some!'

Back home in England, Daphne would have expressed a different opinion. She and her companion land girls did not think it so nice when they themselves had to put up with Italian prisoners of war working on *their* farm. Not that they had ever seen any Italians before, but prisoners of war were to be regarded, by the land girls, as being a potentially serious threat to their safety and well-being.

British soldiers brought the prisoners in each day and also kept guard over them while they worked. They seemed a loud, uncouth, raggle-taggle bunch of men, whistling and calling to the land girls as if they were sheepdogs.

The guards responded with a surly, 'Shut up!' or, 'Get on with your work!'

But not all of the prisoners were entirely uncouth. One of the prisoners was clever with his hands and had carved a *pecking hen* game: a square game board had a little hen in each corner and cords leading to a weight underneath. When the weight was swung each chicken in turn would dip its head as if it was pecking. One of the land girls wanted the toy for her younger brother and she successfully bartered for it with a packet of cigarettes.

Daphne, watchful and wary, became conscious that one prisoner was watching her with interest as she worked. He was a small, swarthy man with a mop of dark, curly hair, chocolate brown eyes and a winning smile. That he was handsome in his way was in no doubt, as far as she was concerned. She knew the other prisoners called him Alberto and she saw that he tried to work in the fields as near to her as possible. Daphne felt cautiously puzzled - and interested.

One day the land girls and the prisoner party were again out in the fields hoeing beet, when the steel head of Daphne's hoe became loose and flew off the handle.

Meaning no harm, Alberto picked up the hoe head and used a stone to knock it back on again. Daphne cautiously smiled, thanked him, and returned to hoeing the weeds out of the row.

Just then one of the guards shouted at Alberto, 'Get your filthy self away from our girls!'

Daphne had actually received a letter from George only that morning. He was still *banging away* about them getting married when he came home again.

But somehow Daphne did not want to get married. Not yet. Not to George. She wanted some excitement in her life. Was it boredom, curiosity or fear, or was it just loneliness that she felt? An old quotation sprang into mind: *hope deferred maketh the heart sick.* Was it that?

Daphne and George had been going out together since she was fourteen, and what else did she know? What she did know now was that there was a whole world out there and she wanted to be part of it. Marriage? Well, perhaps later.

It was the strangest thing, but George had mentioned in his letter that his company had captured some Italian prisoners who were in a hurry to surrender. How odd it would be if Alberto had been one of those captured by George.

'Coming for a drink tonight?' asked one of the land girls.

Daphne nodded. Her written reply to George could wait.

In Ada's Terrace, Emma too received a letter from George and read it as if she hoped that the writing would leap off the page and imprint itself on her heart.

George had been in battle and - *thank God* - George was safe! What a surprise that he had seen their Joanie in Africa of all places, entertaining the troops! George had written glowingly of how beautiful Joanie was, what a star performer she was and how sad she had been to hear of the loss of Billy and Daisy.

'Has anyone seen Daphne recently?' he wanted to know, his tone of disappointment, obvious, 'I haven't heard from her in a while…'

Later that month, Emma, Sam, Jenny, Eliza, Annie and Bert all gathered at *Bann's Farm* for the Christmas Day celebrations.

Eliza, with fingers flying through her wool, was crocheting another shawl, this time for Jenny's baby.

When told of Joanie's concert in the desert, Eliza said with emphasis, 'It's a pity that Joanie hasn't anything better to do than traipse around after soldiers.' But George had said that the girl could really sing, and Eliza hugged that bit of information to herself.

It was so pleasant to be indoors, warm and comfortable as they sat down together around the big dining table. The ordinary midday meal had been transformed into a Christmas feast. The piece of prime pork for Christmas dinner had been done to a turn and Bert had excelled himself, providing all kinds of vegetables from the smallholding. He had been up to the loft where the trays of lovely eating apples were stored so that he could choose the best and the sweetest to hand round.

As the proud father of Jackie, Sam had managed to get a second-hand bicycle for his growing son. Firstly he had spent hours overhauling it. Then after painting it up, he sneaked it into the village and presented it to him after dinner. Jackie was so happy with this splendid Christmas present that he spent the next two hours just riding it about the village! With the onset of dusk, the precious bike was locked away in the shed.

Now the family sat round the fire, the oil lamp casting shadows on the ceiling and the blackout shutters put firmly in their place to keep out the gloom.

Jenny and Bert were engaged in the complex card game of *cribbage*. Her considerate nature had helped her to become a favourite with Bert, and he had taught her how to play.

Emma leaned back in her chair. With all the preparations for Christmas and the broken hours of sleep from spending nights in the air raid shelter instead of resting comfortably in her own bed - Lord - was she tired! 'It's so good to be able to relax for a few hours away from home,' she said.

Annie leaned over and patted her hand, 'I'll make a pot of tea. No, don't you get up,' she said as Emma got to her feet. Annie, with the wisdom of three centuries of British tea-making behind her said kindly, 'It only takes one to make a pot of tea!'

Sam and Jackie were engrossed in the father and son project of constructing a model of a ship. On the little side table a newspaper had been spread which was supposed to catch all the bits and the shavings. 'Well lad,' said Sam, 'you're doin' so well we'll be done in no time flat! It's teamwork that does it! Did I tell you that *Sailor* Hamilton has found us a nice set of second-hand sails for the *Galilee?*' This was news to Jackie. 'They're in need of a bit of stitchery,' Sam continued, 'but in about two weeks' time they'll be ready. You can come and help us try them out.' Jackie's face was a picture of happiness and trepidation. He knew how to do a bit of rowing but sailing was different. 'Don't look so worried, lad!' Sam smiled, 'We'll make a day of it together with Gappy Howles and *Sailor* Hamilton too.' The trepidation faded as Jackie looked forward to learning to sail, as part of a full crew.

At six o'clock, Bert turned the wireless on to hear the *B.B.C.* news. The Western world was still reeling from the savage Japanese attack on American soil at *Pearl Harbour* earlier in the month. Then Singapore, Britain's great stronghold in South East Asia, had been bombed, and now tonight they heard that Hong Kong, another of Britain's prize possessions, had surrendered to the Japanese. Bert turned the wireless off feeling decidedly depressed but knowing that the fortunes of war could still change for the better.

Spirits were somewhat lifted when Annie brought in the family's meal: a dish of pork and pickle sandwiches followed by a fruit jelly.

'Cor!' said Jackie in amazement and, 'Corrhh!' again when Emma brought out the Christmas cake. She had made the body

100

of the cake with gorgeous dried fruit, the marzipan was made with semolina and almond essence and she had topped it all with a precious bar of chocolate, melted and spread over the top.

'If there wasn't a war on, I would have said that this is one of the best Christmases I've ever had,' said Jenny. Billy's family had graciously taken her in, accepted her just for being herself and now she loved them in return and looked on them as her own.

Jenny's childhood had been blighted with a father who was more domineering than loving, and a mother who was just too crushed and weak to stand up to him with conviction. 'You mustn't upset your father!' was a frequent cry that came from her mother's lips.

Later, when Jenny joined the *W.A.A.F.* she had found a new kind of freedom - and then she had met Billy. 'If only he could be here now,' she thought. Soon she would have his baby and she would make sure that the little one knew all about its father.

It frightened her at times that she found it hard to picture Billy's face. Then she would get out the photograph and take a hard look at it. What did she see? The laughing young man was almost a stranger, but his legacy of life was growing inside her.

After their tea, Jackie got the dice and tokens to set up on the *Ludo* game board and Emma and Annie agreed to play.

'Will you play Nanna?' said Jackie looking hopefully at Eliza.

'Aye alright, but mind, no cheating!' Memory took Eliza back to a playful Sunday afternoon when Jackie and Daisy had been arguing over another board game of *Snakes and Ladders.*

Eliza gave herself a mental shake; those days were past and Daisy was at peace. Poor Daisy, the bombing had terrified her and, for some reason, she would not go in the shelter. Well she was out of it now, but Eliza did miss her dreadfully.

With a glint in her eye, the old lady took her place at the table, 'I'll play if I can have the blue counters!' she said.

A little later, Bert went outside to do the rounds of the stable, pigsty and henhouse and Sam went with him, their cigarettes glowing in the dark. The rain had given up now and thin clouds were racing across the sky in the grip of a fresh wind.

Having satisfied themselves that all was well with the livestock, the two men were glad to get back indoors. As they warmed themselves by the fire they listened to a service of Christmas carols on the wireless. Sam, Emma and Jenny were staying overnight at the smallholding. It was a bit of a squeeze all told, but with a little shuffling around everyone had a place to sleep that night.

The next day, Sam cycled back home to Ada's Terrace, to check on the house. Emma and Jenny were spending another day with Annie, and on his way back to them, Sam decided to call at *The Volunteer*.

'Mornin' Sam!' Wally greeted him. 'What'll you have?'

'That rather depends on what you've got!' laughed Sam.

'I'll get these!' a tall sailor said as he got up from a seat in the corner.

Sam turned to see who was speaking, 'Why, Ivan Hawkins as I live and breathe!' he said, grinning and clapping the young man on the back. 'What brings you here?'

Ivan paid for their beers and they sat down. 'I had a few days' leave,' he explained with a cheerful grin, 'I've been doin' the rounds, so to speak. First I went up to Scotland to see Willie, then I went to see Joy in Birmingham. It was grand to be able to see them. Then I thought - why not go home? Only it isn't quite home anymore.'

Sam drew thoughtfully on his pint, 'We've been at Annie and Bert's place over Christmas. Aye, and we had a good time and good food!'

'How are they doing?' Ivan wanted to know. Many times he had been there with Billy.

'Oh, they're fine,' Sam grinned reassuringly, 'we've got Jenny, Billy's girlfriend living with us now; she's having his bain.'

'That's tough isn't it?' said Ivan.

'Well, she's a nice, little lass and very caring,' Sam went on, 'and no doubt they would have got wed if Billy...' Overcome by emotion, he could say no more about it. Having paused, he went on, 'Anyway, she's such good company for Emma, what with Mary being away and Jackie living over with Annie and Bert.'

Then Sam, as the idea took hold of him said, 'Why don't you come back to Annie and Bert's with me now? We could get a taxi.'

Ivan, moved by such understated kindness demurred, 'Do you...do you think they'd mind?'

Sam was emphatic, 'Emma *would mind* if I didn't take you back with me, and so would Annie and Bert. Why, you're almost family, lad!' And so when Sam went back, Ivan went with him.

Emma and Annie made much of Ivan as they welcomed him, and Eliza warmed to the young sailor who had been Billy's friend. Jenny listened intently as Ivan joyously recounted some of the times that he and Billy had shared, and she found herself crying with laughter at their madcap escapades.

'Now now lass,' Annie said to her, 'don't get all het up.' However, the tears and laughter for Jenny were a much-needed kind of release after all the tensions of the past few months.

'I should go and have a rest if I were you,' Emma kindly advised and Jenny did so. Somehow, lying down on the little bed and going over in her mind all the things that she had heard about Billy - well it did something good for her. She fell asleep contentedly, with tears on her cheek.

Jackie sat as close to Ivan as he could get, revelling in the stories of Billy when he was younger, and the pranks that Ivan and Billy had got up to together. When Ivan told Sam and Bert about some of the trips he had made in the Navy, Jackie was enthralled. He had always wanted to be a *Royal Air Force* pilot like Billy, but the Navy life sounded exciting as well.

Jackie was also eager for news of his old friend, Willie, who had been evacuated to live with a young couple in Scotland. Willie had grown tall, Ivan said, and helped out now on the farm. He even had a girlfriend.

Emma sat listening and watching. She was just content to hear some of the tales that she had heard before. She felt sad too that her old friend, Lily Hawkins, had never lived to see what a smart, lovely young man her son, Ivan Hawkins, had grown into. She shed tears for her lost friend.

The afternoon began to draw in while Annie made a pot of tea and brought out the remains of the magnificent Christmas cake. Everyone approved of the plan that Emma and Jenny should stay with them for one more night.

As the season of goodwill, Christmas had touched them all in different ways: Eliza was feeling at peace as the music of the well-loved carols washed over her, Emma was filled with the excitement of two brand new, little lives to come in the months ahead, and Annie was just enjoying having friends and family round her - truly thankful they were all alive.

Christmas had been a mixture of emotions and renewed meetings but now they had to face a new year, and whatever trials or blessings it might bring.

Sam had to go back to Ada's Terrace, as he was due to be on fire watch that night, and Ivan, having been invited to join him, travelled with him. As they set off, they were hoping to thumb a lift on a lorry that was going back to town, and in that they were fortunate.

The next day, while Sam was at work, Emma and Jenny caught the bus back to Ada's Terrace. It had been a quiet night and Sam had even managed to doze a little at the depot where he was on duty. Ivan was still at the house in Ada's Terrace when Emma and Jenny arrived.

Emma was ready to make a pot of tea but Ivan, in gentlemanly fashion, insisted that she sit down while he put the kettle on.

'When do you go back to your ship?' Emma asked.

'I'm sorry to say it'll be the day after tomorrow. Doubtless, *The Admiralty* will send us somewhere that's particularly cold and wet!' he said.

On the morning of Ivan's return to his ship, after breakfast, Sam, Jenny, Emma and Ivan made slightly embarrassed conversation in the kitchen. Amongst them there was somehow a feeling of the importance of Ivan being able to spend time with them.

'Do you hear from Ronnie and Roy?' Emma asked.

Ivan said that they were not much good at letter writing, 'Roy might even be hitched by now. No doubt we'll all catch up with each other one day.'

They had been such a close family, Emma mused, that you might have thought they would keep in touch with each other. Lil had always been the lynch-pin of the family, but the war had blown them apart, like so many families. Well, that was war for you.

Ivan said his farewells to Sam and Emma. Then it was time for Ivan to say goodbye to Jenny. She was peeling potatoes. He stood in the doorway, hat in hand, feeling awkward, 'Will you write to me, Jenny?' he asked hesitantly. 'Young Willie writes to me sometimes and my sister Joy, but it's always nice to get mail.'

Jenny agreed, 'Yes, I can write and let you know how Sam and Emma are getting on!'

He smiled at her and thanked her, 'I'd best get off to Aunt Queenie's. Goodbye for now, Jenny!' Then, with a wave, he was out of the door and on his way.

Later that morning, over a cup of tea before going out, Emma thought about the family and how the children were not great letter writers. She knew that Mary wrote to George. Then there was Joanie who did not write to anyone and nobody knew, seemingly, how to write to her. If it had not been for the war, would Joanie have upped and gone like that? Perhaps she might have done because she was always star-struck and wartime made it that much easier for her.

Emma, with her coat on ready to go to the shops, did not want Jenny to risk having a fall in the icy weather, so Emma braved the weather alone.

Everywhere was quiet around Ada's Terrace, with that rather flat feeling that sometimes follows Christmas. The old year was dying and its days were now at their shortest.

In the street a few schoolchildren were scraping up frost from garden walls, or anywhere, just to make up the semblance of a snowball. School was closed for the week, and some of the children who had been evacuated had come home for Christmas.

With all her errands done, Emma hurried home. She did not like leaving Jenny alone for long. True, the baby was not due until February, but the girl was looking peaky with dark circles under her eyes.

As well as bearing the baby, Jenny was grieving for the loss of her family as well as the loss of Billy. She needed to have a sense of direction about her future and did not want to be an unnecessary burden to other people.

Of course the experience of becoming a mum for the first time would not be quite the same for Jenny as having the support of her own family, but Emma knew she and Sam would do their best to look after her.

Emma reached round for the sneck that opened the back gate and went into the house. Hanging up her coat and going to warm her hands at the fire, she said to Jenny, '*Rawdon's* had some meat offal today so I bought some liver and we've got a couple of onions. So that will take care of tea tonight!'

Sam's day at work had been very busy and when he got home he was very thankful after his meal to be able to doze in the chair by the fire. He stayed there in his favourite spot until Jenny decided to go upstairs for an early night. Sam and Emma made their preparations and put out their bed downstairs for a good night's sleep. Thank Heaven! For once the sirens did not sound that night.

On New Year's Eve, with some bottles of home brew that Bert had sent over, Sam, Emma, and Jenny saw the New Year in around the fire. When the clock showed just after midnight Sam opened the front door; all was quiet.

'It doesn't seem like New Year without the church bells ringing,' Emma said. But other neighbouring families had also come out across Ada's Terrace. They greeted each other with, 'Happy New Year, a better one - please God - with an end to the war in sight!'

Emma felt glad to be a part of the little community; she remembered the old days when Lil would have come out laughing and singing, drawing them all in a circle to sing *Auld Lang Syne,* going in and out of every house with a lump of coal for luck and a nip of something to keep out the cold. They went back indoors and Sam made sure that the blackout shutters were secure before they went to bed.

At three o'clock in the morning, the air raid sirens dutifully wailed their warning. By the time they got back from the shelter, it was five o'clock, still dark and a clear, starry night.

Sam carefully raked the ashes out of the kitchen fire. Emma sent Jenny upstairs, saying that she would bring her up a hot water bottle and a cup of tea. Jenny's teeth were chattering with cold and since coal was in such short supply, Emma did not want to light the fire just yet.

While waiting for the kettle to boil on the gas stove, Emma was so cold that she kept her coat on. She set about filling the old stone hot-water bottle and wrapping it in a towel, so it did

106

not burn Jenny. When she took it upstairs to her, the girl was crying with cold and exhaustion.

'Aw, lass, don't take on so!' Emma felt tears rushing to her eyes at Jenny's distress.

'I'm sorry,' sniffed Jenny, 'it's just that you're so kind to me.'

Emma patted Jenny's hand, 'Try to get some rest, lass, you'll need all your strength.' She tucked the covers round Jenny and went downstairs.

Sam had refilled the kettle for a flask of tea and Emma made him his sandwiches to take to work, grateful for the piece of leftover pork that Annie had given her.

From next door came the sound of the fire being raked out as their neighbours prepared for the day ahead. Thin walls! It was New Year's Day.

Emma sometimes felt guilty that she did not get over to see Annie and the rest of her family at *Bann's Farm* as often as she would like, but it was not easy for Jenny pregnant as she was, to make the journey or to stand around waiting. Indeed after an air raid, bomb craters in the road could cause route diversions which could mean the bus might not arrive at all! Emma might be gone all day and she was not happy to leave Jenny alone like that.

Emma remembered that when Jenny had come to stay with them, she had written to her parents to let them know where she was, but there had never been any reply. 'It'll be my Dad, I suppose,' she had told Emma, 'he'll have told Mam that she's not to write to me, and Mam has to do as she's told.'

'Well!' thought Emma, 'There's no doubt that Sam would have been badly disappointed if Mary had gone down the same road as Jenny. But he would never have turned Mary away.' She thought of how deeply upset Sam had been at Joanie's unannounced departure and how long he had searched for his errant daughter. If she had wanted to come home, the way would have been clear for her to do so. She would have been welcomed with open arms. 'But,' thought Emma emphatically, 'if Jenny's family won't forgive her and stand by her in her need, there's one family in Ada's Terrace that will!'

CHAPTER NINE

It was the second week in January when the telegram came to Ada's Terrace. It was strange how the arrival of a telegram or the reading of a telegram could make people's hearts pound madly. It nearly always announced big, dramatic personal news, and often the worst news.

Jenny answered the telegram man's knock at the door, 'Mam!' she quavered when she saw the distinctive, yellow telegram envelope.

Emma rushed to the door and felt her heart leap and turn over as she held the telegram in her hand, 'Not George, surely not George?' She opened the envelope and the letters of the telegram were swiftly smudged with tears, as relief and joy washed over her - news of Mary! *Baby boy born today stop mother and baby both well stop.*

Emma clung to Jenny, both laughing and crying at the same time.

When Sam came home and heard the good news, he reckoned that, 'Enough tears have been shed to bathe Mary's baby in and a dozen besides!'

It had been previously arranged that when Mary's baby arrived, Emma would go to spend some time with Mary at Aunt Maisie's home near Manchester, and Jenny would go to stay with Annie and Bert at *Bann's Farm.* Naturally now, Emma just could not wait to see her grandson, and she sent a happy reply telegram to let them know of her imminent arrival.

Sam was able to take Jenny over to the farmhouse by taxi before he went to work. However, Jenny did not feel at all well but was determined not to upset Emma's visit to Mary. After all, her baby was not due for another month.

When they arrived, Jenny was made very welcome and was fussed over greatly.

'Ah,' said Bert, 'it will be grand to have another hand at a game of *cribbage*!'

Annie and Eliza both noticed Jenny's pallor and soon settled her in the easy chair by the fire with a cup of tea. Jackie took her little case up to the room that was normally his; he would make do with a shakedown for a couple of nights.

It was a heavenly two days that Emma spent at Westrae. Mary was amazingly well and the birth had been just as easy as such a thing could be. The baby looked like a miniature version of Mary, having a tuft of soft, brown hair but also Robert's determined chin. The precious baby shawl, which Eliza had crocheted for the newest member of the Stavin clan, had been entrusted to Emma's care, carefully packed and taken to Mary and was much admired.

Auntie Maisie, out of kindness, would scarcely allow Emma to do anything to assist her, saying that Emma should enjoy the time she had with Mary and her grandson. Emma gratefully allowed herself to be persuaded.

In due course, a happy letter came from Robert who was thrilled at the arrival of his son.

For Emma it was so pleasant to sit by Mary's bed in the wicker chair and nurse the baby. The war seemed to recede there in the peace of the village of Westrae. But after two days Emma began to fret at leaving Sam. She missed him terribly and was ready to go home.

Back at *Bann's Farm*, Eliza and Annie chatted away, happily surmising how pleased Emma would be to see Mary and the baby. Jenny felt so tired and heavy she found herself dozing fitfully. Annie and Eliza decided not to wake her up for lunch, it would be easy enough to make her something to eat when she had rested.

In the afternoon, Jenny felt a sharp pain that was so sudden that it startled her into wakefulness, 'Owhh!' she cried out.

Annie left the ironing and hurried over to Jenny, 'What is it, lass?'

Jenny felt both worried and foolish for crying out and tried to make light of it.

Annie and Eliza exchanged worried looks over Jenny's head, 'Can I get you anything, Jenny?' Eliza asked.

'A drink of water, please,' said Jenny getting up to fetch it, but Eliza would hear none of it and made her sit down.

'There's nothing wrong with my old legs,' commented Annie and trotted into the kitchen to fetch the water.

Within half an hour, another spasm of pain racked Jenny.

Annie was decidedly worried by now. 'I'm going to get the village nurse to come and have a look at you,' she said, and she gave Jackie a note to take to Nurse Gibson.

A little later, Jackie returned, saying there was a notice on the door showing that the Nurse was out on a call, so he had put Annie's note through the letter box.

Annie wondered how long they would have to wait. The lack of contact details gave her some hope that the Nurse would be back soon.

The next half hour brought more pain to Jenny; she walked up and down the room to see if that would help, 'Maybe it's just cramp,' she said, without conviction.

Fortunately Nurse Gibson came just after six o'clock and went straight upstairs to examine Jenny, while Annie and Eliza waited anxiously downstairs. 'Well,' she said, 'it could be the onset of labour, although the baby ain't due for another month, and is breeched at the moment. Let Jenny walk about and do what she feels comfortable with. I'll come back about nine o'clock to see how she is.'

After the Nurse had gone, Annie said anxiously, 'All the baby things are at Ada's Terrace. We've got nothing here.'

But Eliza remembered that Nurse Gibson had a fund of baby clothes collected for emergencies, and went to find some old, still useable sheets in the dresser.

Jenny came down and sat by the fire, 'It could be a false alarm,' she tried to convince herself.

Bert had come in from his livestock rounds and Eliza had got the tea. Jenny only wanted a cup of tea. The pains were still coming at half-hourly intervals and as the evening wore on, her back ached so much that neither sitting nor standing brought any relief.

When Nurse Gibson returned and went upstairs to see her, she did not think there was much change, but indicated that Jenny was definitely in labour. 'Get as much rest as you can,' she advised her, 'it will be a long time yet and you'll need all your strength.' This advice was repeated to Annie and Eliza downstairs. She had seen births like this before; quite in contrast to Martha Hobson whom she had attended that very afternoon; with her it was like shelling peas; it had been her fourth baby and all with different fathers! 'What about Jenny's husband?' the Nurse asked.

Annie told her that Billy had been killed.

Nurse Gibson shook her head saying, 'I reckon it makes so much difference to a girl to show the father his baby and it gives the girl the will to go through with it, so to speak.' Then saying that she would see them in the morning, she left instructions for them to call her if there was any change.

Annie stood by the gate after Nurse Gibson had cycled off into the night.

An approaching rustle on the path and the smell of cigarette smoke announced Bert's arrival, 'You're troubled, girl?'

'Aye, I'm not exactly used to babies coming. I worry that everything will be alright, as you might expect.'

'You'll manage,' said Bert with a comforting arm round his daughter's shoulder.

As they went in, Jenny had her coat on ready to go down the yard to the *privy* armed with a torch, and Annie helped her down the path. The night was cold and damp. No stars flickered and no moon flitted between the clouds. Shivering, Annie and Jenny began to make their way back to the house.

Nearby someone on the low road was drunkenly making their way homewards singing: *South of the Border down Mexico Way* loudly and terribly out of tune!

They both began giggling spontaneously and as it continued, Annie said, 'It won't feel like Mexico Way, for him, if he takes the wrong turn and falls into Burton's pond!'

This made Jenny laugh, ending in a gasp of pain.

Having returned indoors, they did their best to settle down for the night.

Annie slept fitfully in the *Lloyd Loom* chair in Jenny's room saying, 'I'll be here if you need me.'

Jenny was restless as the labour pains kept on coming and her back ached even more. At four o'clock in the morning, Annie made them both a cup of tea.

Eliza who had slept with one ear open, heard the movement and came through.

'No!' said Annie, answering the unspoken question, 'Nothing's happening.'

Eliza offered to sit with Jenny so that Annie could get some rest. Annie agreed although she did not feel much like sleeping.

Annie managed to doze and woke up with a start at half past seven in the morning to the sound of Bert raking out the ashes in the fireplace downstairs. The house was coming to life.

As she walked down the stairs, she could hear Jackie talking to the old man, 'Can I stay off school today?' he asked Bert with an eager face, 'I can run errands for you, and fetch the Nurse.'

Annie intervened and quickly decided against that. 'School will be the best place for you, Jackie lad. There are some things that lads of your age do not need to know about just now.'

Amidst all the drama and excitement, Jackie was quite put out that his offers of help were refused, but Annie was adamant and when he appealed to Eliza, she fully backed Annie's decision.

Disappointed as he was, Jackie consoled himself with a hearty breakfast before setting off for school. Living in the country had opened his eyes to many things. Jackie had been the one who found out where Trixie the cat had gone to have her kittens and there was all the circle of life with the other animals.

It was a dull, dark morning and barely light at nine o'clock. There were heavy clouds in the sky and the threat of rain when Nurse Gibson arrived to see her patient. She observed that things were progressing slowly and promised that she would call back later.

For Jenny, her condition made the day seem nearly endless: the uncertainty was nagging at her; the pains were stronger and the backache was unrelenting. There was no relief from the aches and pains when she tried walking up and down, or sitting, or lying down. By mid-afternoon the spasms were running into each other and becoming more intense.

On her latest visit Nurse Gibson put the covers back over Jenny, and beckoned to Annie to come out of the room. 'The baby is still a breech presentation so I'm going to send for Doctor Brown,' she said. 'This has gone on long enough and the poor girl is so weary.' So saying, Nurse Gibson went off to ring for the Doctor.

In deep sympathy with their friend, Annie and Eliza sat with Jenny and shared something of her pain. Eliza mopped Jenny's forehead and Annie held the hands that intensely gripped hers with every new pain.

For all of them, it seemed like an eternity before the doctor came. While he examined Jenny, Annie and Eliza huddled together outside on the upstairs landing. Annie only left to fetch the water or anything else that the Nurse requested. When the Nurse appeared, as she did from time to time, Annie asked her anxiously, 'Is everything alright?'

'It will be,' was the answer. 'Doctor is just going to make a little cut and then it will all be over.' Nurse Gibson returned to the room.

Outside, Annie and Eliza could hardly allow themselves to breathe because of their mounting tension. They could hear Jenny crying - then came a thin hiccoughing wail, 'Wahhh! Waaaah!' - the baby was crying, and so were Annie and Eliza.

Nurse Gibson poked her head round the door with a big grin, 'It's a boy! Can we have some more hot water, and I'm sure Jenny would like a cup of tea.'

Eliza and Annie, drunk with euphoric happiness, hardly knowing what they were doing, padded off to the kitchen to lay out a tray with the best tray cloth and best china because this was an occasion!

Annie, in taking the hot water up, was allowed a glimpse of a red-faced baby. Following shortly after, Eliza too was able to have a quick look at the wonder of a new little person embarking on life. Eliza and Annie took the opportunity to seek out the port wine and raise their glasses in a toast to the new mother and baby. Bert joined them and they celebrated together.

As they do at times, the baby continued protesting at his entry into the world. For Jenny herself, there was the ordeal of having some stitches put in but at least the anxious uncertainty was over and the household could marvel at how such a little scrap could make so much noise!

The *babby,* though washed and dressed in the tiniest of the clothes that Nurse Gibson could find in her store, still looked somewhat lost inside of them. He weighed 4lb 12 oz and was a long baby. He would be tall like Billy, Eliza joyfully predicted.

Dr Brown had packed his doctor's bag and had long gone on his way. Nurse Gibson settled Jenny down to sleep and gladly accepted a glass of port before she went.

Annie went upstairs to see Jenny, 'We'll take baby out of the room if he doesn't settle,' she said. Jenny protested at this, but the strain of the last two days, coupled with the injection that the Doctor had given her made her sleep through the night.

When she did wake up, it was still dark outside and the baby was crying in Annie's arms and waiting for his mother. At the sound of him Jenny felt a rush of *colostrum* milk to her breasts. Annie brought him to Jenny who was anxious to feed him. At first his little button of a nose got in the way and he snuffled into Jenny's breast, wailing in frustration. Then suddenly he latched on and sucked greedily, quickly becoming tired and falling asleep contentedly.

The busy morning continued for Annie and Eliza as they prepared breakfast for Jenny and sent a reluctant Jackie off to school. Meanwhile Bert got on with the everyday chores of feeding the hens, the milk goats and the other livestock.

When Mrs Briggs, from down the lane, knocked and came in, Annie had just lit the fire under the copper cauldron so that the water would be ready for washing the clothes.

Mrs Briggs had heard about the baby. With her cheery smile she looked at Annie and said, 'I haven't come to hold you up, but Nurse said you weren't prepared for the baby, so I've brought this baby talc and soap.' Practical kindness like this melted Jenny's heart. And so it was that several times that morning there was a knock at the door and neighbours brought little gifts for the baby.

'But they don't even know me,' marvelled Jenny.

'People round here are like that,' said Eliza, remembering the many kindnesses she had received from the people of Redtoft. When her house was bombed and she had no more possessions than the clothes she was wearing, the villagers had loved and helped her too.

'What a surprise Emma will get when she comes to collect me today,' Jenny said to Annie, excited at the thought.

'Emma?' queried Annie, 'Good heavens, she's coming today!' In all the excitement and bustle, Annie had forgotten that Emma had arranged to come to *Bann's Farm* and collect Jenny that day.

Later in the morning, Nurse Gibson came to see her charges, 'Have you thought of a name for the baby yet?' she asked Jenny. Jenny had some ideas but wanted to discuss it with Emma. Annie and Eliza came into the room to see the baby have his first bath.

'Now, young lady, you get plenty of rest. When this little man sleeps, you must do the same. And you Annie, you've been up half the night and you're not as young as you used to be.'

So saying, Nurse Gibson went off on her rounds with the promise that she would be back again in the afternoon.

Walking up to the house, Emma was surprised to see that Annie had a line of washing billowing in the wind. By contrast to yesterday, it was a bright day but there was such a keen wind that it would make anyone's eyes water! As she went up the path, Emma thought she heard a baby cry, 'It must be the wind in the trees,' she thought to herself. But on opening the kitchen door, she heard the sound again - it *was* a baby's cry.

Annie had heard Emma come in and was there to meet her.

'I thought I heard a baby cry!' said Emma. Then, looking at Annie's face she said, 'Oh no! not Jenny?'

Annie laughingly assured her, 'Yes it *is* Jenny. She's had a lovely little boy, small of course since he was early, but Nurse Gibson said that with careful mothering he would be fine!'

'Well, I never!' Emma's face broke into a broad grin and she could hardly wait to get her coat off before going upstairs to see Jenny. What a difference those few days had made! Jenny was no longer the pallid-faced girl who had been driven off to Bert's in a taxi. True, there were still dark circles under her eyes, but now those eyes were bright and her cheeks were flushed. Emma hugged her as she heard all about the events of the last two days. 'Seems he couldn't wait to get here,' she remarked, 'wrong way round an' all!'

Emma held the new arrival and marvelled at the existence of his tiny being. 'He's got Billy's chin,' she said as tears momentarily bubbled to the surface at the thought of the father this baby would never know, 'and he's so handsome!'

Dr Brown called in and pronounced that all was well with mother and baby. 'I won't need to come again unless Nurse Gibson feels it's necessary. By the way Mrs Walters, I hear that you've had the good fortune to have had *two* grandchildren come into the world in one week! Heartiest congratulations to you!' and with a cheery smile and a wave he was gone.

Emma's face flushed with happiness and she thanked God for her double blessings.

CHAPTER TEN

The day at *Bann's Farm* passed in a whirl and a flurry of activity. When the washing was dry, Emma got on with the ironing and made Annie sit down, for a while at least. As part of the celebrations, Bert had killed a chicken which he plucked and dressed to make a nourishing broth for Jenny. The lass would need building up, especially if she was going to continue feeding the baby herself.

The little 'un was needing a lot of attention. He would feed for a little time then fall asleep only to be crying again an hour later. As a first-time mother this routine was leaving Jenny tired and sore.

'Keep her quiet,' instructed Nurse Gibson that afternoon, concerned at Jenny's flushed cheeks, 'just yourselves here and no visitors.'

Emma had arranged to go back home to Ada's Terrace that evening. When he got in from work, Sam would be expecting them, but not with a baby! Emma decided that she would return to the farmhouse the following day with some things for Jenny and the baby.

Sam was already home when Emma walked in, 'On your own lass?' he asked. 'Well, I don't blame Jenny for stopping on with Annie. Jenny's a grand lass who's got guts and I can see why Billy thought so much of her. At least at Bert's she'll get to sleep in a bed for a few nights without having to go to the shelter.'

'That, she will...' Emma began with a laugh that changed to tears of happiness.

'Now now!' Sam said, putting a comforting arm around her shoulders.

It's Jenny!' cried Emma, 'She's had the baby, a little boy, Sam - you're a Granddad again!'

'Well that's good, isn't it!' he said with a chuckle, and then wide-eyed he asked, 'They're both alright, aren't they?'

Emma nodded trying to dab her eyes at the same time, 'It's also this business of seeing the baby and realising that Billy won't ever be here to see him growing up.'

Sam hugged her tight, 'I know love, I know.'

'I'll have to go back tomorrow to help Annie and your Mam. It's a lot for them to cope with, you know.'

Sam was pleased at this; their available family members were closer than ever: with Billy gone, George missing and Joanie - Heaven knows where - they needed each other more than ever before.

The bus eventually arrived in the village and the new grandma found that Nurse Gibson had already visited Jenny and the baby that morning. Annie, looking a little harassed, was busy preparing dinner and Eliza was struggling with the washing. Bert was sitting comfortably by the fire and nursing the baby who was dozing in his arms, whilst making the soft, snuffling noises that newborn babes make.

'He smiled!' said Bert.

'He's got wind!' was Eliza's remark.

Emma laughed, 'Between the two of you, that baby will be well spoilt.' Emma took over the washing from Eliza, 'Let me help you out. You sit down Mam!' and Eliza was glad to do so although she would not have admitted it, and only sat down under protest. Emma was surprised that she had called her mother-in-law *'Mam'* and astonished that Eliza had accepted it without a murmur, 'What a difference a baby can make!' she thought to herself.

Later Emma took a dinner tray up to Jenny and sat with her for a while. Of course they had no cot for the baby but Annie, ever resourceful, had lined her big washing basket with blankets and so the baby was very cosy in there.

Emma touched the tiny hand and marvelled as the little fingers curled round her own, 'Have you thought of a name for him?' she asked Jenny.

Jenny hesitated, 'I expect you think I should name him Billy,' she said, 'but there can only be one Billy for me and that's the baby's dad.'

Emma felt rather put out at this as Billy was the obvious choice in her mind, 'You must name him as you see fit,' she answered huffily.

Speaking from the heart Jenny said, 'When we were at Cardington, Billy had a friend named Derek who he was very close to. I think he would have liked for baby to be named after his friend.'

'Well, Derek it is then,' said Emma.

'Derek William,' said Jenny firmly. Was this to be the first of many times when she must stand her ground?

'That's a nice name,' was Annie's reaction, Bert nodded and Eliza said nothing, but was pleased that William had been included in honour of Billy.

Perhaps because of being born prematurely, little Derek had a bout of jaundice and was very fretful. Since it was a liver problem, Nurse Gibson said that he should be given plenty of boiled water, as much as they could get him to take.

Jenny was tired, she was not allowed to get up yet and her stitches hurt no matter which way she tried to position herself in bed. But happily, each new day was one more on the road to recovery.

Sam went to Wally Ingles' pub on the Friday night for the express purpose of *wetting the baby's head* over a pint of beer. He came over to Bert's at the weekend to see his new grandson and with a doting look in his eyes pronounced him to be a *grand little chap* and swept him up high in the air. 'You're a proper Yorkshire lad - born, bred and buttered - an' don't you forget it!' he said with a big, grandfatherly smile.

In his usual manner, Sam spent the greater part of the day helping Bert with the tasks around the smallholding and the outhouses. Over the years he had learnt a lot from him about how to run a small subsistence farm. It was while they were feeding the chickens together that Sam was surprised to notice that Bert's skin was almost translucent; he also looked older and less certain in his movements. Sam wondered, as he must be getting on in years, if he had any plans for retirement and mused that he did not know how old Bert was, but as a smallholder what knowledge and breadth of experience he had gathered with his years! He was quietly respected, not only by his own family but also by the whole village.

It was late in April before Jenny and little Derek came back to Ada's Terrace. In the Walters' home, Billy's old room had now been transformed into Jenny and Derek's room and Emma was so looking forward to having them there. It was so nice to see that the prematurely-born baby Derek was slowly gaining weight. He was a difficult baby to feed and although Jenny had tried to persevere with him he was now being bottle-fed.

At Bert's place, Annie and Eliza had been so good and helpful, but sometimes Jenny had wished that she had more time alone with her baby; now back in Ada's Terrace, Emma, the practised mother was always there with advice, and occasionally making Jenny feel somehow rather more inadequate than was comfortable for her. Indeed there were times when it felt as if Emma was trying to take over the mothering, and at that point Jenny just had to put her foot down. But when she did, she did it graciously.

For hundreds of years there had been a traditional ceremony of celebration for the birth of a child and for the deliverance of the mother from the dangers of child-birth. Eliza knew all about this ceremony of *churching* and quite naturally wanted to play her part in it. She it was who insisted that Jenny be churched as a way of giving thanks to God. 'My Gran wouldn't have me in the house until I had been churched and had the baby christened,' Eliza told Jenny. 'Things have to be celebrated and done properly!'

So Eliza arranged with the vicar for Jenny, Emma along with another young mother from the village to visit the *Redtoft Village Church* one pleasant afternoon. In his naturally cheery manner, the Reverend Rothery warmly welcomed the four ladies. Together, in the traditional way they gave thanks in prayer for the safe delivery of their babies:

> O Almighty God, we give thee humble thanks for that thou hast vouchsafed to deliver these women thy servants from the great pain and peril of childbirth; Grant, we beseech thee, most merciful Father, that they, through thy help, may both faithfully live and walk according to thy will, in this life present; and also be partakers of everlasting glory in the life to come; through Jesus Christ our Lord. Amen.

Eliza, remembering the recent difficult events for Jenny and Derek, liked the Vicar's reading from the Psalms:

> Thou hast delivered my soul from death:
> mine eyes from tears, and my feet from falling.

Afterwards over a cup of tea, Jenny felt that the memory of Billy was very close to her; as she brushed away a tear the priest patted her shoulder, 'Most people find it a very moving service,' he said, 'were you thinking of having the baby christened?'

Jenny had considered it positively but thought that Emma might like little Derek to be christened in Hull at *Saint Columba's*, the church where Billy's funeral had been. But Emma agreed that it would be nice for the service to be in the *Redtoft Village Church*, especially as Derek had been born in the village, and so the christening was arranged for Easter Sunday, and afterwards the two ladies happily made their way home to Ada's Terrace.

Unbeknownst to Emma and Jenny, Ivan Hawkins was just finishing his Arctic voyage, and arrived back in Hull on leave, a few days before the christening.

He had written to Jenny several times, in a way as a letter to them all, and she had written back. However, unfortunately because Ivan had been on a convoy to Murmansk he had not received her last letter. This meant that he did not know about little Derek's early arrival and so when he arrived at Ada's Terrace, he had a wonderful surprise waiting for him!

Ivan was made so very welcome and after tea, and his first introduction to the new baby, Jenny had a few quiet words with Emma, who nodded and said, 'A good idea.' So, Jenny asked Ivan, as Billy's friend, to be Derek's godfather.

Ivan - with a big grin - readily agreed and on the day of the christening dressed in his best uniform, he joined the family round the font.

Both Ivan and Jenny were moved by the baptismal reading from Mark's Gospel:

> And they brought young children to him, that he should touch them: and his disciples rebuked them that brought them. But when Jesus saw it, he was much displeased, and said unto them, 'Suffer the little children to come unto me, and forbid them not: for of such is the kingdom of God. Verily I say unto you, whosoever shall

120

not receive the kingdom of God as a little child, he shall not enter therein.' And he took them up in his arms, put his hands upon them and blessed them.

Little Derek behaved very well, and when it was over they all walked back to Bert's. In advance a nice tea had been prepared for them; Emma had done her part in this and fortunately had managed to get hold of some tinned fruit to bring to the feast.

Liking his food as Jackie did, the tea added greatly to his enjoyment of the day's celebration. Ivan had brought some sweets and *Horlicks* tablets for him, which greatly pleased Jackie, who was also hoping to hear some real-life tales of *U-boats* and destroyers; but Ivan only wanted to put that behind him. War, he knew personally, had its grim side.

After a communal effort to wash and dry the pots, Sam, Jenny, Ivan and baby Derek got ready for the journey back to Ada's Terrace courtesy of a local taxi. On their return, Sam raked the fire into life and Emma soon made a pot of tea, and then it was time for Derek's feed.

Sam and Ivan walked to *The Volunteer* and were warmly welcomed by Wally Ingles and as there were a few other servicemen home on leave, it was a jolly evening.

The following day was bright and sunny with a contrasting cold, raw east wind.

When Ivan came to the Terrace, in time for dinner, he also brought a gift - in the shape of a fresh bunch of daffodils.

They all ate dinner and spoke well of the rabbit pie that Emma had so expertly cooked and after dinner, they settled down to listen to the *B.B.C.* radio news.

Everyone was in a relaxed mood and enjoying being in good company, when Ivan suddenly turned to Jenny and asked the courageous question, 'Would you like to go to the pictures?'

Taken by surprise Jenny looked at Emma, not knowing what to say. Emma, smiling, said that she should go: the outing would be good for her and she would be glad to look after Derek. Emma there and then could have destroyed Ivan's hopes, but she did not and neither did Jenny, who was happily flushed.

When Jenny and Ivan went to the picture house on their first date, it was full of servicemen: groups of the lads out together, others home on leave, and some with wives or girlfriends.

The curtain came up on a light Hollywood romance. It featured glamour girls, and the Hollywood beauties were so much appreciated by the servicemen, that they greeted the ladies with loud wolf whistles and shouts of *Hubba Hubba!*

On this particular evening the Pathé newsreel focussed on *Soldiers In The Desert,* which prompted Ivan to ask Jenny if they had any news of George. Jenny was able to murmur in his ear that they had heard from George, but strangely he had not heard anything from Daphne since Christmas.

When the film came to an end and the credits rolled, the house lights went on, and as they made their way out through the crowd and on to the street, Ivan and Jenny began to feel the beginnings of closeness between them. It was a dark night; the moon was past its fullness. and they were glad of the torch.

As Jenny thanked Ivan for the night out, Ivan asked, 'If you would like, we could go out again next time I'm on leave.' He knew in his heart it was a crucial question which ran the risk of her saying, 'I don't think so,' and crushing his hopes of romance.

Instead Jenny said, 'Oh yes!' with quiet determination. Although there was no telling when his next leave would be; a gentle romance had begun. She knew that Ivan was a man to be trusted. To Jenny this was no one-time date and Ivan, sharing the same feeling, knew that he could breathe again! Ivan was in love. All he had to do now was to survive his marine adventures and come home safely again!

Recollecting himself, Ivan chatted with Jenny about the film and continued walking contentedly towards Ada's Terrace. Merton Street still had plenty of bricks and rubble scattered about for them to pick their way through, until they arrived outside the back door at Ada's Terrace.

'Will you come in?' Jenny invited.

'Aye, I'll say goodbye to Emma and Sam. Auntie Queenie likes me to spend the last day of my leave with her. We're the last links of our family now.' Ivan hesitated, knowing the uncertainty of war: he felt a strong urge to kiss Jenny, but perhaps it was too soon. They could be friends for a while, and on his return, they would both find the stronger feelings they had for each other.

When they opened the door, the warmth of the room hit them and as Jenny had suspected, Emma had Derek comfortably sitting on her knee. 'He's had his bottle, I was just going to put him to bed,' Emma said smiling.

Beaming, Ivan told them how they had enjoyed their evening, said his goodbyes and was ready to leave.

'God bless you love!' Emma tearfully hugged and kissed him.

Sam shook his hand heartily saying, 'Take care lad, there's always a place for you here you know.'

Jenny looked him straight in the eyes, gave him a smile that lit up the room and said, 'Thank you for a lovely evening - and I really enjoyed your company!'

He thanked her warmly. Then, at the last moment, in an emotional whirlwind of happiness and a feeling of some shyness, Ivan touched Jenny's hand, patted her shoulder - and was gone into the night.

Emma's heart rejoiced at the signs of a beautiful relationship developing between Ivan and Jenny. But now her heart was heavy over another matter.

Only that night, Emma had set herself to write to their son George. However, as the words would not come as easily as usual, the task of writing it was laborious as well as painful.

She so hated having to tell him the sad news - *that there had been no news of Daphne*. 'There must be some explanation,' she thought, and again racked her brains to find something - indeed anything at all - that would have caused Daphne to take offence and so cut off all communication with George and the family.

A little while later and far away from Ada's Terrace, George read his mother's letter in Northern Africa, on desert ground, while sitting by a tank and trying to find a bit of shade from the burning sun. Just touching the tank could mean getting a burnt hand and frying eggs on it was a real possibility.

Hitler, having stomped through Europe, needed to be stopped from taking over North Africa, Egypt, the Suez Canal and the oilfields beyond. 'We're here to stop him,' George said to himself, 'and we will!'

George, eager to absorb the news from home, read his mother's description of baby Derek's christening, 'Ivan's on leave. Huh! lucky devil!' he thought to himself, but there was no news of Daphne. This was like getting a burnt hand, only worse. A number of George's mates had been getting a *Dear John* letter and George, pondering to himself said under his breath, 'At least they have certainty but I haven't. I just have the dismissal by silence. We had a long courtship but now nothing!'

The other thing that Emma did say in the letter which disturbed George was that Bert was looking and feeling his age. 'Poor old chap. How old will he be now?' thought George. Grandpa Bert had been a good friend to George, indeed to them all, and George decided that he must write to him.

'Tea up!' said one of his mates handing George a mug of tea.

'Thank God for that cuppa!' he thought to himself, even though the sand somehow managed to get in everywhere and in the desert, water supplies were scarce and brackish. The diet always seemed to be the same limited kind of something-out-of-a-tin, like corned beef, with no fruit or vegetables, and there was no shortage of flies, fleas and rats.

'What's to do?' George asked his mate Jimmy.

'Sarge says we're making a push tonight to the Ridge,' he pointed into the distance. 'Intelligence says there's only a handful of *Eyeties* guarding it.'

Hours passed; preparations were made and tension grew. After the sun went down, there was no moon to show up their movements, nor was there any moonlight to see the enemy by.

Now full of battle anticipation and excitement, George's unit made for the Ridge which was just a vague smudge in the distance.

Within a hundred yards of it, machine gun fire broke the silence and *Very Lights* lit up the sky - they had walked into an ambush!

Within the hour, the survivors had been captured by a whole troop of Italian soldiers. Ignominiously they were rounded up and placed under close surveillance by armed guards.

'You see doctor tomorrow,' said one of their captors, as an orderly gave the Sergeant an injection.

'It's that ruddy Abdul!' spluttered the Sergeant who had taken a bullet in his arm. Abdul had been their guide but had unaccountably vanished. Nonetheless, George was furious, not only at being captured but also at the dismally stupid *intelligence* on which the British assault had been based.

'Ruddy, blasted natives!' the Sergeant exclaimed, continuing, 'Listen to this! When we were stationed in Buq Buq, there was this Arab who came staggering up to the gate. The guards stopped him as he was leaving the camp, and when they looked under his nightshirt - would you believe it - he only had a blacksmith's anvil strapped to his waist and hanging down between his legs! Them lot would pinch anything they would!' The others nodded in amused agreement, but none of them could tell a story that could top the tale of the anvil.

The early morning found them on the move, not as free serving soldiers but as captured prisoners of war who were marched off under Italian command and ignominiously shoved back behind the Italian lines. Fortunately for the Sergeant, he had his arm further attended to there in the field hospital.

But behind the lines the day passed slowly, there seemed to be no plans to get them away to a prisoner of war camp and they remained helpless with nothing that they could do.

On the farm in England, where Daphne was working, the Italian prisoners of war might have seemed to have things slightly better, despite having to work.

Daphne, feeling more sociable, had got used to seeing Alberto on the farm and had been able to exchange a few words with him.

At Christmas, she and one or two of the other girls had asked if they could give the prisoners a parcel, and in the end were given grudging permission.

'I just hope someone, somewhere, will do the same for our boys,' one of the girls said.

Daphne was not so altruistic. No longer under parental scrutiny and living away from home for the first time, she was feeling an unparalleled freedom to do and say more or less what she wanted. George was not there. 'Why should I care?' she said to herself. She had strange stirrings inside of her and she wanted to get to know Alberto better. She was fascinated by his dark good looks and - forgetful of George - felt strongly drawn to him but not in a tea-party manner.

One of the prisoners had shown the girls a snapshot of a young woman with two children, 'Mia bambinos!' he said proudly, but with sadness in his face. It seemed that Alberto was not married; the only photo which he carried was of an elderly couple that Daphne took to be his parents.

Alberto had given Daphne a bar of chocolate when he received his *Red Cross* parcel. Their hands had touched and it had been like an electric shock going through her.

She could not bring herself to write to George as if nothing had happened and she had put off going to see Sam and Emma Walters. She just could not face George's parents and maybe not herself either. Her feelings for George were not the same anymore and although she tried to hide her guilt and niggling doubts, she knew that Emma was sharp enough to see through any subterfuge.

Back in Ada's Terrace Emma had no real idea of what Daphne was thinking. Instead, the dreaded telegram boy had arrived at the Walters' door. Hastily she wrenched open the telegram; Emma felt a deep shiver of horror and dread when she saw the *War Office* communication informing her that George had been posted as *Missing In Action*.

'Posted as Missing!' she exclaimed, 'Is he wounded? Is he dead?' What could have happened? Fearful of either she was both tearful and sleepless.

Sam, who quietly had his own pain, tried to keep a hopeful outlook for Emma's sake but inwardly he feared the worst. They had already lost one son, and were they yet to lose another? Other people had. How many, many times had father and son shared their companionable walks round the docks and by the woodyards? And would there be no more? Ever?

Seeking to cheer Emma up, Sam suggested that she should go to visit Mary and see little David. Emma was doubtful about going and it took a little persuading for her to see that Sam would not starve and that Jenny would be able to cope.

Jenny felt strongly for Sam and Emma in their anxiety and suffering and knew that she would do all that was in her power to help them through this bad time. Oh! Emma had been so kind to Jenny, but as grateful as Jenny was, she also remained forceful in giving her opinion on matters of how her son Derek should be brought up, how he should be fed and the details of his bedtime routines. Often in learning Ada's Terrace diplomacy, Jenny also had to learn to restrain her tongue in order to graciously keep the peace. She could not escape the fact that she owed Emma and Sam a debt of gratitude, love and respect: when nobody else would have done they had taken her into their hearts, and when she had nowhere else to go, they had invited her into their home.

Finally after much cajoling, Emma agreed to go and visit Mary and little David. After all, Robert's Aunt Maisie had always earnestly assured her that she was welcome to visit at any time and Mary would be delighted at the thought of spending time with her mother.

When Emma finally arrived in the village of Westrae north-west of Manchester, there was a joyous and affectionate welcome awaiting her. Naturally in the circumstances, George was never far from their thoughts or conversation. Mary was fortunate in having recently heard from Robert who had also been posted to North Africa, but he knew nothing of George's unit. That desert was a big place and the chances of the two men meeting up were not strong.

David was a happy baby who cooed and gurgled just like babies do. Emma, joyfully, spent many happy hours nursing and playing with him or going out and about with Mary, pushing David's pram through unbombed, leafy lanes. After a couple of nights of undisturbed sleep, Emma felt much more able to cope with life. Declaring herself anxious to see how Sam was faring, and sure in her mind that Jenny would not be able to manage, farewells were said, and she set off on the journey home to Hull.

There were however delays in Manchester because of German air raids, and Emma found herself in an underground shelter by the station during just such a raid. Sitting there on a bench, she suddenly became aware of the tall soldier sitting next to her who was saying something. 'Have some candy Ma'am, it's good for the nerves.'

After some hesitation Emma accepted; she had heard that the American forces were in England but this was her first meeting with any and indeed her very first encounter with an American!

'I take my hat off to you people,' the G.I. went on, 'I can't imagine my folks living like this.' Another soldier was talking to a solemn-faced little girl who refused his offer of chewing gum. In the end her mother took it for her. Emma had read that the

U.S. forces were brash and super-confident, but these two were sympathetic and friendly.

The *All Clear* siren sounded and the people in the shelter departed their different ways. Emma bent down to pick up her case but it was taken from her by the same soldier with a cheerful, 'I'll take that for you, Ma'am!'

Emma demurred, but was met with a bright and breezy, 'It's no trouble,' so she had to accept gratefully.

'Where are you going?' the young man asked and upon hearing that she was going to Hull, he found a porter and enquired of him which platform the Hull train would go from. It turned out to be Platform Three but there were delays on the line. Reaching the train, Emma was courteously helped into the carriage and had her case handed to her by the soldier.

'I hope you have a safe journey,' her helper said before walking away to join his mate at the end of the platform. There he turned to give her a cheery wave.

'What an extraordinarily helpful young man!' Emma said to herself.

The railway journey home was long and tiresome. The train stopped several times and trundled along slowly because of enemy air raids. The carriage was full of servicemen and women and the air was heavy with cigarette smoke.

Arriving back at Kingston upon Hull's *Paragon Station*, Emma was fortunate to get a bus home. There had been a vicious air raid on the city earlier, and rubble and destruction were everywhere. It was like the almost unrecognisable face of a drunk who had been in one fight too many: broken-nosed, teeth missing and two eyes swollen shut. The usual landmarks of the city were either scandalously defaced or completely missing. Considering the destruction it was an absolute wonder that the buses were still running.

Sam was already home when Emma arrived in Ada's Terrace. The docks had become busier again now that war supplies were coming in, and the loss of some of the dock men to the armed forces was keenly felt. Only the previous day there had been a bombing raid which was aimed, by the Germans at disrupting supplies. It had resulted in such terrible damage to the rails that it made them look like part of a bad-tempered child's train set and the main roads of the city had been seriously damaged too.

Shocking damage had been done to the dockside warehouses: No. 23 shed had caught it on *Alexandra Dock*, No. 14 warehouse, and also Hedon Road Stables. The men had worked long hours to try and salvage what cargo goods they could while the fire boat had bravely fought fires aboard two vessels in the dock.

But weary Sam did not want to talk about that, he wanted to hear about Emma's visit and how little David was progressing. He listened as Emma told him about the air raid delays on the way home, and meeting the U.S. soldiers.

'And look!' she said, 'They even gave me a packet of cigs for you.'

Sam laughed, 'American cigarettes, eh? Oh well, I can give 'em a try. I hope I don't cough me lungs up!'

Jenny, with little Derek sitting on her knee, was so very pleased to see Emma back, safe, rested and well. She could barely wait to hear all Emma's news of Mary, and how David was progressing. Amazingly, when Emma had entered the house, little Derek had recognised his Granny and held out his tiny arms so that he could be picked up and cuddled by her. The little household was restored to normality and happiness came with it.

CHAPTER ELEVEN

When Annie got up on that singular May morning, Bert was sitting slumped in his chair by the hearth. Of course, there was nothing unusual about finding him in his favourite place: Bert often found it hard to sleep and sitting in his chair gave him ease when his bed would not suffice and with his farming duties he was often up early. But, on this occasion, just one look told Annie that his body was there, but Bert, the father she had known and loved, had gone.

Annie, despite her great grief and shock, held it all in for Jackie's sake. Annie, the practical daughter tenderly wrapped a rug round Bert and when Jackie came downstairs, told him that his Granddad was poorly and sent the lad to Emma with a note.

A little while after Jackie left the house, Eliza awoke to hear strange wailing sounds downstairs and got up to find Annie crying disconsolately in the kitchen with her apron covering her face.

Confronted herself with the evidence of Bert's passing, Eliza comforted Annie, 'It's how he would have wanted to go, just to slip away with no fuss,' but then Eliza also burst into tears for the man who had given her a home when she had no home, and they wept together.

Sam had gone out of the yard on his way to work and was halfway up Merton Street when he saw Jackie wave and whiz passed him. So unusual was the event that Sam turned round and came in to see what strange news Jackie had brought.

His sudden appearance and unhappy countenance at their door gave Emma and Jenny a surprise. In his pocket he was carrying a message from Annie, 'Granddad's not well!' he said, catching his breath and passing the envelope to Emma.

Aware of the tension of the moment, Jenny kindly asked Jackie if he had had any breakfast, and taking him into the kitchen, made him a cup of cocoa with eggs and bacon.

A sense of dire foreboding clutched at Emma's heart as she opened the note and read it. As Sam arrived at the door, she passed him the note and slipped out of the back. Sam swiftly read it and hearing her crying, went to comfort his distraught wife. When she had recovered herself, she said to Sam, 'Jackie had better stay here today. Jenny will need help with the shopping and will be glad of his company. I must go to Redtoft to be with Annie and Eliza.'

In the kitchen, Jackie protested to Jenny, 'I ought to go back; I can run errands for Auntie Annie and help with Granddad Bert's work.'

It fell to Emma to tell the growing lad the sad truth that his Grandpa Bert had gone.

'Why?' he cried. She sat in the kitchen with her arms round Jackie's shoulders as she cried with him. And it felt that, along with his tears, his boyhood was slipping away from him; his Granddad had gone and nothing could ever be the same again.

When Emma arrived at *Bann's Farm* later that morning, she found Annie crying in the kitchen while washing the plates and dishes. Annie dried her hands and Emma gave her a big hug. They talked between tears and remembered their many good times with their father.

Emma hugged and kissed her father for one last time before the undertaker made his preliminary visit, so that Bert was resting in his coffin in the front parlour.

While Annie and Emma talked, Eliza gently washed Bert's face and hands. The white, blue-veined hands were now still. There was to be no more of him rolling his smokes, or as she particularly remembered him, sitting in his chair cuddling a shawl-wrapped Derek.

The next few days passed as if in a hazy and uncomfortable dream. The household tasks were done as usual; the pigs, hens, goats and pony were fed and watered. Kind friends in the village came to pay their respects. Bert had been well-liked and there were many useful offers of help for the grieving family.

The funeral was held on a Thursday morning. It was a bright day at the end of May. As Bert was laid to rest in the village churchyard, a ship's siren wailed from across the river, and Annie dropped a bunch of Bert's roses into the grave. Across the fields a cuckoo was calling and blackbirds sang in their hedges.

Jenny had stayed behind at the house with a neighbour from down the lane, ready to make the tea when the mourners returned.

'Will you be able to manage?' Sam asked Annie as they sat together at the meal.

'Oh yes,' Annie told him, 'Eliza is such a help and good company too. Mr Brabham at *Home Farm* has offered to help us with any painting, decorating and house repairs that might be needed. And he's bought the pony and the pigs as well, at a good price, which helps with the funeral expenses and such like.'

In his will Bert had left the house and land to Annie, which was only fair as she had done a lot of the farm work and had looked after him all these years.

Emma was to have the Dutch wall clock that had been her mother's and to Sam went Bert's watch with gold waistcoat chain and *albert*. Sam told Jackie, 'You'll have this when you grow up.'

Bert's pewter tankard was also set aside - for George - with the thought uppermost - if he comes back.

Since the telegram which had relayed the news that George was missing, there had been no word about what had happened to him, but not all missing soldiers are dead soldiers!

George and his fellow British captives in North Africa were still very much alive behind the Italian lines. Their captors would have liked to be rid of them, because it was Italian rations that were used to feed the prisoners while they themselves were being harassed by the increasing presence of the British *Air Force*. George knew there would be an *R.A.F.* attack soon but when would it come? Like loyal supporters at a football match, George and his mates cheered on the Allied planes whenever they made their raids even though they were in considerable danger themselves.

Being a prisoner of war for George, was an experience that was worse than if he had been back in a woodyard in Hull being confronted by his boss shouting, 'You are sacked! Get out of here ya little maggot. You are useless!'

It was humiliating enough for him to be ambushed, but to be outwitted in battle and rounded up like a straying sheep was worse. All the Allied soldiers had a responsibility to escape whenever possible and to survive. However, the strong likelihood was that attempting to escape through the blistering heat of the desert would be an ignominious invitation to a lost death by heatstroke. Surely survival would be a blessing, he felt, 'but how depressing to have to spend years in an Italian prisoner of war camp. After all, the only Italian word I know is *espresso!*'

George determined in the long night hours that he would survive to the utmost of his ability, whatever it was that captivity and the war could throw at him. He knew that he greatly wanted to return to the frontline of battle, but meanwhile he was patiently going to make the most of every day.

George had shared some of his food ration with Achmed, one of the many, young native boys who hung around the camp and ran errands for the Italians.

Achmed was an expert scrounger who in turn had snaffled a tiny penknife from one of the unwary guards and given it to George. The young English soldier, remembering his own skills, managed to find a piece of scrap wood and with his penknife he carved a tiny, recognisable horse which he gave to his new-found friend.

The Italian soldiers encouraged the children - none less than the evil Major Oloroso who had an ugly penchant for young boys.

'Keep away from him!' George had warned Achmed but the boy only laughed and slipped George a cigarette.

'I know heem and what he iz - no good!'

Later that day Achmed came round again. With a sly, hinting grin he said, 'My little sister, she love that horse!'

George promised that if Achmed could get the wood, he would carve a doll for his sister.

It was no trouble for the young boy to get a piece of wood. He pointed to one of the Italian guards, 'Roberto, you make for heem a horse?'

George nodded his agreement. He was particularly interested in finding out how vigilant the guards were and if they were open to bartering things.

Roberto turned a blind eye to the bits and pieces that Achmed and his friends brought to George and his mates. And Achmed's sister got her beautifully carved doll. For George, whittling and carving wood was much more fun than just sitting and waiting for the next air raid!

Back in Ada's Terrace, Emma had a strange feeling that somewhere their son was still alive.

The postman came one morning after they had got back from another night in the shelter with an official *On His Majesty's Service* envelope for Emma. Despite her fears, there was no bad news this time.

She was requested by the *Ministry of Labour* to go for an interview at the *Labour Exchange* with a view to doing war work. The war was to be won, not just on the battlefield but in British aeroplane and ammunition factories, as well. Now all women between eighteen and fifty-one were subject to some form of conscription. Emma had some previous experience of work in a shop before she married Sam, but did not think that she was equipped for many other jobs.

The lady from the *Labour Exchange* who interviewed her asked artful but seemingly random questions about such things as: Sam's work, Jackie's whereabouts, schooling and so on. Finally Emma was directed to work at *Sweetings'* store in Hull, where she had a successful interview with Mr Ward, the Manager and it was agreed that she would work there in the mornings.

Most of the staff were older women like Emma, but not all. Other additions to the staff included Mr Everett, an elderly man in charge of the bacon machine and the provision counter, and a couple of young girls not long out of school.

Emma was set to work with two other ladies in the back room, making up orders for their subsequent delivery. The two other ladies were Barbara Anderson, whose husband was a prisoner in the Far East, and the unfortunately named Doris Whenn, whose husband was a River Humber pilot.

Sweetings' store, which had a good reputation, delivered its goods weekly to many of the small villages round about. The customary system was to deliver one order to the customer and to receive the following week's order at the same time. Because of the rationing, many of the orders were small, and there was a shortage of such things as cocoa, candles and matches. These items were allocated on a rota system by the store, which meant that no one went without these supplies for too long.

Mr Wright the delivery man did very well for himself by making sure that the country folk got things like shell grit for their egg-laying hens. Consequently, because of their kind appreciation, he himself was never short of an egg, fresh vegetables, or even a nice, harvest rabbit!

To be fair, if things were good, he would habitually hand on some of these treats to the others in the shop, who, in turn, were always grateful.

For Emma, the advantage of working in the shop, was that she got to meet a wider range of people and, truth to tell, the money that she earned at the store did not hurt her at all!

So Emma settled into the routine of shop work in the mornings, and housework and preparing Sam's dinner in the afternoons. Meanwhile Jenny helped with the house as much as she could whilst dodging into the air raid shelter when it was necessary.

Sweetings' shop had the benefit of a big cellar which was used as a safe shelter for the staff along with any customers who were caught out during an air raid; and air raids generally happened all too often.

There were other staff benefits to be had with working at the shop. Mr Everett was good at seeing that the ladies on the staff had the chance of a bacon hock, whenever there was one available - and good eating too!

While weighing them up, there was a temptation to indulge in *forbidden fruits* following a delivery of dried peaches, apricots and prunes! On one notable occasion, the two younger girls were gruesomely sick from eating too much of the very fruit they were supposed to be packing!

When they returned to work, sounding much quieter than usual, looking very pale-faced and sickly, Doris Whenn confronted them. She had suffered being the butt of many cruel jokes and nicknames - '*Say When, When's Day'* - and so on from the young girls. 'I hear that you've been stuffing yourselves with peaches, apricots and prunes instead of working. You two are real *palefaces!* I think I'm seeing something of divine justice here!' she said with humorous satisfaction. 'If I ever hear any more *When* jokes from you ever again, I will remind you *Palefaces* of this day! It serves you right! So there!'

Of course, Emma found the extra money useful in her budgeting and even managed to *put some money by*. Her thoughts turned to, '...When this war is over and new housing is being built, surely we'll be able to move...although it will take a lot of new houses to replace all those bombed buildings…' She sighed when she thought of Lil Hawkins, who had been so proud of her new council house. It would be so nice to have a house with a garden for young Derek to play in, but then again, would Jenny and little Derek still be living with them? One thing was sure, Jenny's parents did not know for a moment what happiness they were missing.

Emma had received a letter from Annie and Eliza who were planning to come to do some shopping in Hull on the Friday. They enquired, as Emma was due for some time off, whether she would be able to spend the day with them. A ladies' day outing? Emma revelled in the idea. Yes!

Emma loved to think of her family when she was not over-occupied. She thought of Jackie, her youngest, who was working on a nearby farm during the summer holidays. Not only was he revelling in the work and starting to look as brown as a berry but in another year he would be leaving school and looking for work. Mr Brabham, the farmer, had made it clear that there would be a job for him if he was interested. His schooling had been interrupted with the war and like George, he had sadly not passed the scholarship exams, but the lad seemed happy *on the land* and that was what mattered.

Emma remembered that in one of Ivan's letters to Jenny, he had said that young Willie Walters was also being drawn to life *on the land* in Scotland; how strange that the two boys, once such close friends and now so far apart, were following the same paths.

Emma yawned; there had been very little sleep for them again last night.

The day for the shopping trip was blessedly hot and sunny. Annie and Eliza caught the early bus, and before ten o'clock, were having a pleasant morning cup of tea with Emma.

'Biscuits!' said Annie, as Emma passed the plate of custard creams.

'What a treat! said Eliza, 'I don't think our shop man is as fair as Emma's Manager. I could do with more!'

On this occasion, Eliza was wearing her best, navy-coloured straw hat and her flowered, navy crepe dress, and during the bus ride, the cheerful conductor had commented approvingly on it, 'Who got you ready, Ma - *Elsie Battle*?!'

Eliza had sniffed. *Elsie Battle's* was a well-known dress shop and of course she would have been so proud to have had a dress from there. However, like so many shops, it had suffered in the bombing and the price too may have been rather more than Eliza would have liked to pay. After all, *apples may grow on trees but pound notes do not!*

The trio of ladies made their way to the *Co-operative Store*. They had been saving their clothing coupons for just such a shopping trip. It was here that Annie bought some pillowcases and Eliza some underwear. And in the same shop Emma bought herself a pretty, blue-checked dress for sixty shillings and eleven coupons, and also some vests for Jackie, to keep him warm in the winter. Altogether, the shopping day passed without any untoward incidents and the only things flying overhead were the pigeons and not the *Heinkel* bombers! The trio of shoppers stopped in Whitefriargate for a welcome cup of tea at the delightful *Kardomah* café.

'So much has changed!' sighed Annie, 'There's some streets I wouldn't have recognised.' It was true the bombing had altered the face of Hull, as it had in many towns and cities. It was now like watching the face of a familiar loved one being eaten away by pockmarks. But life still went on and it just made Annie's day when they joined a queue, to be rewarded with being able to buy half a pound of biscuits. Rare luxury!

For Annie, if you saw a queue, you joined it, often not knowing what you were queuing for, but you joined because most things that you would need were scarce. Pulling out the prized packet, just to admire it, Annie extolled its contents joyfully, 'Ah, Biscuits! Jackie will think this is a real treat,' she said.

Immediately Emma felt a stab of envy; as Jackie's mother she felt that she herself should be looking after Jackie. But then, giving herself a mental shake she realised that she should be grateful that Jackie was growing up safely in the country, and she knew that he loved the country life.

When they got back to Ada's Terrace, they found that Jenny had put the kettle on and the tea was ready; Sam too was home early. He kissed his sister-in-law Annie, and Eliza his mother warmly and wanted to know how they were coping with their recent loss.

Eliza had bought a romper suit for Derek to wear and a rattle for him to play with and Jenny was delighted, 'Would you like the coupons, Grandma?'

'No thank you!' Eliza said with an emphatic chortle, 'I have plenty enough for what I need but thank you anyway.'

Emma had thoughtfully bought Jenny a blouse and a new cloth cap for Sam; so what with opening the parcels and trying things on, the evening meal became rather rushed as Annie and Eliza had to catch their bus home to Redtoft.

After tea, Emma and Sam walked to the bus stop and saw them safely off. Strolling back they saw a group of boys playing around the Fire Brigade static water tank at the top of Merton Street. The boys were daring each other to get in and have a swim, but fortunately the tank had a fence of barbed wire round it, and the wardens, at their wartime post, kept a stern eye on them.

'I know we both miss Jackie,' said Sam, 'but I think he's better off away from all this. Emma sighed and nodded as arm in arm they turned into Ada's Terrace.

Emma helped Jenny with the washing-up, while Sam bounced Derek on his knee. The little lad was getting more like Billy every day and Eliza had remarked on it too. How Sam and Emma would miss the little boy if Jenny moved away. Not that she had shown any sign of wanting to do so, but the girl needed a life of her own.

Having Jenny around, particularly after losing Billy, had been a blessing for Emma. Now if it had not been for Jenny and the baby, with the uncertainty over George, her burdens would have lain more heavily on her.

So settling down for a quiet evening, Sam switched on the wireless. It was time for the famous comedy show: *It's That Man Again!* better known as *I.T.M.A.*

Twisting the tuning dial, he grimaced at coming across the syrupy tones of *Lord Haw-Haw* with his much hated and infamous *call-sign*, *'Jairmany calling, Jairmany calling...'*

Turning the dial again Sam found dance music, foreign chatter and then the right station for *I.T.M.A.* Emma heard the *I.T.M.A.* cleaner, Mrs Mopp, utter her usual catchphrase, *'Can I do you now, Sir?'* and knew that the girls from the shop, if they were listening, might be giggling. But nonetheless, Doris would suffer no teasing tomorrow. Emma knew that they were not bad girls, just giggly, daft and girlish, while being expected to *grow up before their time* because their young lives were being spoiled by the horrors of war. But they *had* deserved the telling off that they got!

Emma felt relieved that Mary was safe with baby David, and - please God - Robert would be spared to come home and see his little boy grow up. And what of Joanie? She did not know where she was or even if she was alive…

The wireless programme continued to chatter away in the background as Emma's thoughts rambled on until, piercing the cocoon she had wrapped round herself, the radio host announced, '…*and our guest artiste for tonight is Serena Waters!*' Emma jumped up, eyes wide and mouth dropping open, 'That's our Joanie!' she said, while Jenny and Sam listened in shocked disbelief.

The *German High Command* was eager for the *Afrika Corps* to advance eastward from Libya in order to capture Egypt, the Suez Canal and to take the vital Persian oilfields.

While Britain was slipping into autumn, George and his fellow captives in the desert, suffered the burning heat of the day and the extreme cold of the nights. 'Deserts! Who'd 'ave 'em?' they said. George had an additional reason for agreeing with these sentiments, having been stung on the foot by a large scorpion.

The British prisoners had continued to be shunted around since the First Battle of *El Alamein* some months previously and George and his company had ended up near Tel-el-Eisa, close to the Mediterranean Sea. 'Alright for trains to be shunted from place to place, but no good for us!' George muttered to himself. There were days when his anger at P.O.W. incarceration led to bouts of depression but he would turn his mind to woodcarving and patiently watching for a way to safely escape.

The *German Afrika Corps* expeditionary force under the leadership of Rommel had been halted and now it seemed that they could be beaten by the Allied forces. Prisoners of war have special concerns, not the least of which is that of not getting caught like the meat in a sandwich between two opposing armies in action - in this case between the Axis and the Allied forces. George surmised that perhaps now they would be shipped to Italy, but the strength of the Allied bombing attacks on German and Italian shipping, fortunately, made such movements impossible.

Lieutenant-General Montgomery had been installed as the Commander of the *Eighth Army* expeditionary force in North Africa by Prime Minister Churchill in place of General Auchinleck. The men of the Allied *Eighth Army* were war-weary but Monty had given his troops a pep talk, stressing the weakness of the enemy, while being certain that a long battle would ensue. As a leader of inspirational force, he was like a breath of fresh air for the previously dispirited troops. His men could see that victory over the German and Italian Axis forces was possible.

Then one night at half past ten, a barrage of more than half a million artillery shells began and the full might of the Allied force was unleashed.

Two German tankers were sunk at sea by bombers, so the Axis fuel supply was cut, and the German and Italian predicament became acute. Tanks without fuel cannot retreat or advance! In the face of heavy fighting, the German withdrawal began.

Rationing at the camp where George and his fellow prisoners were held became even tighter and so did their belts! At first they could hear the sound of gunfire in the distance; as morning followed morning it got louder and the guards were very nervous, until one morning, as dawn broke, the rising sun showed that the prisoners in the compound were completely alone. The Italian enemy troops had fled and George and his mates were no longer prisoners.

Achmed and his young friends came into the camp and the freed men decided to hoist a white flag and await their release. They did not have to wait long: armoured cars from the Allied advance party soon trundled into the camp to find the Italian enemy gone and a group of hungry Englishmen waiting to greet them. Cigarettes were handed around, tea was brewed and every former prisoner sighed with relief and thankfulness!

'It's the best drink I've had in ages!' said one.

For George, there was a chance to walk to the edge of the camp and to appreciate the beauty of the surrounding desert. Standing on a little mound, he was able to see the waves of desert sand retreating into the far distance and the last, shimmering heat mirages of the afternoon. High above him a lone eagle was playfully circling around on a thermal up-current of air, and he felt its freedom and the beginning of his own.

Shortly after, as he returned to the centre of the camp, the main body of Allied troops arrived and George with his fellow freed-prisoners were ferried behind Allied lines for debriefing.

'Reckon you'll get a spot of leave after this,' one of them said to George - and he was right.

George and his fellow ex-*P.O.W.*'s were nearly starving and dehydrated, while many of them had collected a number of ailments in their captivity. To their relief, courtesy of the *Royal Navy*, only a week later the freed prisoners were on board a supply ship bound for England.

Not only was George now able to write home, but Emma and Sam also received official notification that George - a ***missing in action*** soldier - was now alive and freed! Whatever else happened in the run-up to Christmas, this was going to make it a Christmas to be remembered!

When *slimmer than usual* George finally arrived in England, he was held in a camp on the South coast waiting for medical checks and documentation. Emma wrote to tell him all the family news: about Bert's death, little David crawling, young Derek who was so like his father, but of Daphne, she had no news to pass on.

What she did not know was that George had received a *Dear John* letter from Daphne, one that had been following him round for some time and had finally caught up with him. He had taken the news philosophically. She had not told him who the new man in her life was and fortunately for his temper, George had no idea that his rival in love was an Italian prisoner of war.

After the shortage of water in the desert, for George it was sheer luxury to be able to have a bath and take a shower. His green, red and yellow boils - resulting from malnutrition and germ-laden drinking water - were treated. He could not fully shake off that feeling of being a prisoner of war until at last he was given that precious leave to go home.

Arriving at *Charing Cross station* in London, he got directions to *Kings Cross*, but an air raid warning compelled him to join the people at *Leicester Square* who streamed into the deep underground station for safety. Pleased as he was for his own safety and for those around him, he was shocked to find that for so many people, underground stations had become a communal second home. Disused lines had been boarded over to make floor space, and while children slept, grown-ups talked, played cards, celebrated a birthday, started a new family or had a sing-song.

At last the *All Clear* siren sounded and George was able to continue his journey to *Kings Cross*. He was shocked at the great bomb damage which he saw in London. 'How the Germans must hate us!' he thought to himself as he made ready to board the train north on the journey home.

As night fell, the train began to lull him with its song, *diddly-dee diddly-dum, diddly-dee diddly-dum,* as it took him ever nearer to home. In the light of the *blue bulb*, the carriage looked chokingly thick with cigarette smoke.

'Where are we?' asked a sailor who had woken up as the train ground to a halt.

'Grantham, I think,' said another, and the sailor relaxed back into sleep. At last the train reached Doncaster where George found he would have to wait until five o'clock in the morning for the milk train to take him onwards to Hull. He did not care - he was going home! He felt so light-hearted he could almost have walked it - but there again - perhaps not! The desert and captivity could knock some of the stuffing out of a man.

Back in Ada's Terrace, Emma was up, dressed, raking out the hearth and laying the coal fire ready for Jenny and Derek when they got up. Sam was having breakfast and Emma also was about to go to work when someone rattled at the door. Sam went, thinking it would be one of his workmates; it sounded as if the docks had maybe caught it again last night and goodness knows where the dockers would be needed today. He opened the door and saw a tall soldier.

'Hello, Dad!' said a familiar voice.

'It's George!' he shouted to Emma, as repeatedly shaking his son's hand and patting his shoulder again and again, he drew George into the kitchen. Emma was swiftly there, tears of love and relief streaming down her face. George was soon ensconced by the fire with a familiar mug of tea in his hand. Emma just wanted to look at him. Yes he was thinner and his skin had a yellow tinge, but - it was George, and he was home!

Jenny and Derek came downstairs and George held out his arms to his little nephew who viewed his new uncle with suspicion.

'He's all wet,' laughed Jenny, 'let me change him first.' So Jenny made the bain comfortable before passing a reluctant Derek over to his Uncle George.

Emma remembered that she had to go to work but once there, it seemed as if the morning would never end before she could go home and be part of her own personal, family reunion. Of course the good news of George's homecoming was told and retold in detail to her workmates and although she could not disguise her own immense joy, she felt a deep pity for Barbara whose last news of her husband was that he was in a Japanese prisoner of war camp.

'Does your George like dancing?' the two young girls wanted to know, 'There's a good band on at *The Palais* tonight!'

At last Emma was able to get away from work and make her way home. At the butcher's shop she was able to get two sheep hearts to stuff and roast and there was a jar of Annie's bottled plums for dessert. Her feet fairly flew as she ran down Merton Street to the Terrace but only Jenny and Derek were in, as George had gone to see Daphne's mother.

George had always got on well with Daphne's mother and he had also been good friends with Daphne's brothers who were both now in the Navy.

Daphne's mother was plainly embarrassed by her daughter's behaviour, 'I'm so sorry, George,' she said candidly, 'Daphne's a fool! Though I'm her mother I still say she's a fool - taking up with a prisoner.'

George who had only just learned of Daphne's preference, did not have a very good opinion of Italians already, having been their prisoner, but to learn that Daphne was enamoured with one was like rubbing salt into the wound. Pulling himself together however, he consoled the tearful woman, 'Never mind, Ma! Things will sort themselves out somehow,' but unfortunately not for him and Daphne.

That night Emma went to *The Volunteer* with Sam and George. This was unusual for her but George had said that he wanted Emma to come, and so it was that Wally Ingles greeted her, 'Not often we see you in here, Mrs Walters.'

They decided to sit in the corner and as Wally had received his delivery of beer, Sam and George were in happy receipt of the landlord's bounty. George insisted that Emma should have her favourite drink, a port and lemon.

'Seems like Christmas has come already!' she said, knowing that her Christmas present - from above - had come early. With George's safe return, already her cup of happiness was full. With Emma between Sam and George, arms linked, they went home from *The Volunteer* that night laughing with joy and deep-seated merriment. The wanderer had returned!

Jenny was waiting up for them and they all sat and chatted for another hour before going to bed.

George announced his intention of going to see Annie and Eliza and young Jackie the next day and as it was Emma's day off she said she would like to go with him; everyone had happy dreams that night.

CHAPTER TWELVE

When mother and son arrived at *Bann's Farm* the next day, Annie threw her arms around her nephew.

Grandma Eliza seemed a bit shy and reserved until George put his arms round her and gave her a resounding kiss. She blushed like a schoolgirl to be so much loved by her grandson, 'Get away with you!' she said.

Sooner or later, all eyes turned to Bert's cold pipe still in its place on the mantelpiece and to his empty chair by the fire.

Annie noticed that George's eyes were clouding over with remembered grief as he gazed at the empty chair. 'It wouldn't be home without it there to remind me of him,' she said as tears filled her eyes.

Later, when Jackie came in from school and saw George, he wept for joy and hugged him like he would never let him go. But Emma, realising the time, was feeling the urgency of catching the bus home; so arrangements were made for Emma, Sam, George, Jenny and Derek to return to *Bann's Farm* on Sunday for a family day.

'I've got a chicken that'll be just right for Sunday dinner,' Annie promised and Jackie, who was beside himself with joy to have his older brother home, begged, 'Please can we go fishing?'

Emma and George caught the bus home. So much had changed since George had last seen the town. Whole streets had disappeared and - like Nanna Shushkin's house - a way of life had gone completely.

The days flew by and suddenly Christmas was only a week away; somehow the festive season had crept up on them again and the countdown was on to get things prepared.

Mary, unable to be with them, had sent Emma a framed photograph of David which was generally admired and stood proudly in the place of honour on the sideboard. This year - mercifully - George was at home with them. Nonetheless, there were a further two absentee places: one for Billy and one for Joanie.

'Goodness knows where Joanie is now,' Emma said to herself. She had told George about hearing Joanie on the wireless programme and George had related again how Joanie had entertained them so superbly with the concert party in the desert.

'Joanie looked great!' George told Emma, 'She has grown into a real pretty girl,' and of course the make-up and the clothes all added to the glamour. But from Joanie herself there had been no word - not even a Christmas card.

Ivan Hawkins had joined them last year for Christmas but this year he was far away on naval convoy duty in a supply convoy in the bitterest weather in far northern seas under wartime conditions. But he wrote to Jenny, who always related his news to Emma and Sam.

Last Christmas had been the first without Billy, and this year it would be the first for the son that he had never known.

Thoughtfully, George had obtained some wood and finding his tools still on the rack in the shed, had set about making a push-along truck for each of the babies. He wanted to celebrate Derek and David's first Christmas in the way he knew best.

Jenny had sent a photo of Derek to her parents but there had been no acknowledgement until one morning when the postman brought a parcel. Inside was a little baby's jacket, a golliwog and a note for Jenny. It said:

Don't write back to thank me.
These are for Derek with love.

The note made Jenny's heart ache for her mother and she shed a few tears, 'It's my Dad,' she cried, 'if he knew Mam had been in touch with me, he would go mad.'

Emma felt sorry for the sad woman who could not see or acknowledge her own grandson, or even talk about him. Steeped as he was in a form of religion that was seriously short of grace, forgiveness and redemption, Jenny's father was unbending. In his eyes Jenny had sinned, so by not recognising his own part in Isaiah's dictum: *All we like sheep have gone astray*, he no longer had a daughter.

The week before Christmas the weather was unfavourable for bombers so Ada's Terrace enjoyed a few, quiet nights although one lone plane did manage to sneak in at teatime and unleash a stick of bombs on the city.

Sweetings' store where Emma worked, suffered blast damage; but business went on as usual because of the season. There was a rush of work for the shop's staff, as housewives desperately went from one shop to another in search of any little extras that would make it feel a little bit more like Christmas.

People managed to be so ingenious! It was truly surprising what people could fashion from bits and pieces and so nothing was thrown away that might come in handy. Jenny received one such present from one of the girls she was with in the *R.A.F.* camp. It was a beautifully-made spray of leaves and flowers that was cleverly fashioned from wire and cellophane sweet wrappings. She pinned it on her coat where it looked lovely and was rightly much admired.

She remembered all the girls back at the camp; many of them would have been posted on to different places by now, so it would not have been the same as when she was there - but it was so nice of them to keep in touch.

When the English winter weather - grey and damp - invaded Hull and Ada's Terrace on Christmas morning, it did not perturb the Terrace's inhabitants one bit. Instead as they listened to the early morning carol service on the wireless, sang the Christmas carols and unwrapped the presents which they had received from one another, it was as if the sun had shone for them and for a little while they could forget the war.

Emma loved a good read and fortunately George had managed to get her a copy of *Gone With the Wind*.

Annie, Eliza and Jackie came over for the day. A friend of Sam's had sold him a rabbit which Emma was roasting in the oven, with a feeling of happy contentment. With some dried fruit, she had also managed to make a Christmas pudding of sorts.

Although they missed Bert because it was their first Christmas without him, it was nonetheless a happy day of celebration.

George missed Daphne and had not got over their parting. As he sat quietly watching Jenny playing with little Derek, he knew that there must be happiness for him *somewhere.*

Eliza, compassionately, had been watching George. Leaning over to him she tapped his knee, 'Don't fret lad, there's as good fish in the sea as ever came out of it. That lass doesn't know what she's missing!'

George was startled out of his reverie, he had not realised that Grandma Eliza was so astute. He gave a rueful smile and in his heart he appreciated Eliza's consideration of him. He knew Eliza had been close to Billy, but now he felt her care for him and the others, too.

Sam's rabbit was judged a great success and Jackie said the pudding was *perfect*, in which opinion he was aided by finding in his portion a silver threepenny piece.

After dinner, Jackie sat talking with George, who wisely brought up the subject of his leaving school the following year. 'What will you do?' he asked his younger brother.

'Mr Brabham has promised me a job on *Home Farm*,' he told George, 'it's only fair that I stay with Nanna Eliza and Aunt Annie; I'm the man of the house now!'

Emma heard this and the words wrenched at her heart. Jackie was her baby and here he was talking about being the man of the house!

Together they drank a toast: *To Absent Friends;* Sam produced some bottles of beer, Annie had brought the very last of Bert's home brew, and Emma went to get the bottle of port from the sideboard. Sam poured Jackie a small glass of ale and when Emma was about to protest Sam winked at her, 'Tis best he does his drinking at home as yet,' he said.

The rain had cleared itself away and evening clouds were gathering as Emma closed the blackout curtains and got the tea ready. It had been such a lovely day with all the family together again. But George's leave must come to an end and who knew when they would be together again?

There was a concert on the Forces Programme and they settled down to listen to it. As Vera Lynn's voice flooded the room, Emma thought of Joanie. Where was she? What sort of Christmas was she having? If Emma could but have seen Joanie for a moment or two, she would have known that, in the girl's own words, she was having *a fantastic time.*

Somewhere in the country, Joanie's concert party had been entertaining the troops right up until Christmas Eve when they had all streamed into the village pub. Bob Compass, the producer, director and manager of their group had got talking to an American officer.

'What are you doing tomorrow?' the officer had asked.

Bob had replied that they would probably be travelling, as they had to get up north for their next concert venue.

The American chewed disgustingly on his cigar, 'Say - could you folks do us a favour?'

It appeared that the entertainers who should have come to their camp had not been able to. The officer suggested that he could fix them up with food and billets, and in return the concert party could entertain his men the next day.

Bob put the suggestion to the party who were in agreement and they all spent the night in the U.S. camp.

Joanie and one of the other girls shared a room, 'Better than our usual digs,' she said.

On Christmas Day they had a sumptuous dinner in their honour. There had been presents from the Americans: gifts of silk stockings, chocolates, even perfume! Music was playing and some of the girls were dancing and later the concert party would do their turn in entertaining.

Right now though, Joanie was sitting in a comfy chair with a Staff Sergeant in close attendance fetching her a drink and lighting her cigarette. 'Like to dance?' he suggested.

Stretching her long legs, Joanie got to her feet and before long they had the floor to themselves surrounded by appreciative people who were madly cheering and clapping. No, Emma need not have wondered about Joanie, she was having a great time.

Back in Ada's Terrace, at the family dinner, the toast had been: *To absent loved ones*, including Joanie; but here in the camp as the servicemen raised their glasses, Joanie had only brief thoughts about home.

Were they still safe and living in Ada's Terrace? She had heard that Hull had been quite badly bombed. Billy had been killed, how the family would miss him, and George, was he still in the desert, she wondered? Surely they would miss her too she supposed, but, well, she was having a good time - and she was getting somewhere - like she always said she would. She really must write to them sometime, but not today; today - she was having too much fun.

149

That night as she took her place on the stage and sang, she knew that she had never performed better. It had been such a lovely day, the presents, the food, the wine and the company. When she came on stage, and now as she was singing, she could feel they were with her swept along with the words and music. Oh these people knew how to enjoy themselves and they liked her, she just knew it!

'That was great, Miss!' declared an airman after the concert. 'See here,' he gave her a card, 'I'm an agent for revue and theatrical people; after the war, get in touch and I'll fix you up with some dates.'

Joanie gave him a pleased look and tucked the card into her purse. 'You never know after the war: Hollywood, a film career…' She could see it all now.

And so the Walters ended their Christmas holiday in different ways; Emma and Sam with the family round them, listening to the news and a programme of requests and messages from servicemen at home and abroad, and Joanie: with a cheering crowd of American servicemen who were also far from home. For many it was a day of memories and reading letters over again just to feel close to their loved ones.

Slushy snow covered the ground for the next few days leaving boots and shoes whitened with salty marks. Before they knew it, Emma and Sam were back at work and the old year was fading into memory.

On the farm, Daphne helped to open up a clamp of swedes for fodder for the animals. Alberto, meanwhile was busy along with some of the men who were mucking out the stockyard. The guards had more respect for these Italian prisoners who had actually volunteered to work and were beginning to get used to them, knowing that they were not violent and were not about to run away: however, the guards were there just in case.

As Daphne found it easier to spend time with Alberto, they would sit together in their dinner break. The soldiers had got used to it, though that was not to say they liked the situation. Had they known about George, they would have liked it even less. But amidst the muck and mess, a romance blossomed.

Daphne's mother had told her about George's visit. Daphne had tossed her head; she felt that she had been tied down in that relationship for too long. It had lacked all the romance and the excitement that she felt was humming between her and Alberto.

Not surprisingly, the last day of the old year was cold and rainy. People in Hull went about huddled in their raincoats. Everything was soaked: gloves, scarves and umbrellas.

Emma was glad to get off the bus at Merton Street to make her way home so that she could be dry again. Remembering her own blessings - two grand-bains and George alive - a little shudder of pure joy rippled through her that the rain could not take away.

Jenny had been washing Derek's clothes and nappies and now they were hanging on the fireguard. Sitting there on the hearthrug Derek was playing happily with the bag of pegs.

'We shouldn't have worried about getting toys for him at Christmas,' laughed Jenny, 'the pegs are still his favourite.' Working together happily, Jenny and Emma were intent on preparing the evening meal. George had gone out for a walk to see if any old friends were home on leave.

Sam came in soaking wet, 'Wetter than a pint of water!' he said of himself. After hanging up his wet clothes in the lobby, he held out his hands to feel the warmth of the fire.

Emma made a pot of tea for the adults. They sipped the brew happily in the firelight just before Emma drew the blackout curtains. 'No use advertising your whereabouts to them German bombers coming over!' she thought to herself.

They settled round the table for their teatime meal; the wireless was switched on for the six o'clock news, and George arrived in time to take his place at the table with them. Emma had been able to get a nice piece of haddock to eat; fish was not rationed but you could never be sure of finding it in the shops, as many of the British trawlers had been requisitioned for minesweeping duties or ran the risk of being shot at.

Tonight they had fried fish. This was greatly enjoyed, not only by the adults but also by little Derek who was having his fish mashed up with potato, and spooned into his willing mouth by Jenny.

'That's good for your brains,' laughed George, 'or that's what your Granddad used to tell us.'

After listening to the New Year's Eve *B.B.C.* news, Sam and George got ready to go to *The Volunteer*. They invited Emma to go with them but pleading tiredness, she urged Jenny to go, saying the change would do her good. Derek was fast asleep and Emma would look after him, so Jenny put on her coat and went with Sam and George.

Pushing open the door of the pub, they were met with an almost solid wall of stinging cigarette smoke and the smell of beer. A seat was found for Jenny while Sam and George stood at the bar which was packed like a newly-discovered goldmine. They passed a drink over to Jenny who was soon chatting to the girl sitting next to her.

People had crowded together in preparation for saying goodbye to the Old Year and for welcoming in the New Year. In wartime they naturally hoped that the new year would only be better than the one they had just lived through. The feeling of the celebrating crowd was much along the lines of: *Surely things must get better soon?*

Sam, George and Jenny made sure that they set off home in good time to see the New Year in with Emma.

The rain had stopped now, but in the light of the torch that Sam carried, the half-broken pavements glistened and his anger and annoyance came to the fore. 'Bloomin' bricks and rubble! Why, before the war I could easily have walked home blindfolded. My feet knew the way. But it ain't like that anymore. We'll catch up with Hitler and then he'll know about it!'

Three nights later on the 3rd of January at two o'clock in the morning, the awful air raid sirens wailed their warning once again. From the one-mile-wide River Humber, a boat hooted mournfully, searchlights criss-crossed the sky and people began to make for the air raid shelters.

Sam and George took some cushions and pillows into the shelter; it seemed that *Jerry the blasted German* was beginning the year as he meant to go on.

It was four o'clock in the morning when the *All Clear* siren went off and they made their way back home in the dark. Evident across the city was the glare from the many fires lit by those vicious, phosphorous incendiary bombs. For Sam, George, Emma and Jenny, their hearts were struck with pain at the sight of so many houses destroyed and people made homeless.

Emma quickly heated a bottle for Derek's cot. When in bed herself, she felt she would never be warm again. Sam put his arms around her and was soon asleep. For Emma, lying there thinking about the many fires in the city, sleep just would not come.

A few days later George received his papers recalling him back to service. First he went to *Beverley Barracks* for a medical to ascertain whether he was fit. He still had pain in the old wound in his arm but the doctor cheerfully informed him that it would be with him for life and he was passed as fit for duty. Returning to Hull, he stayed the night with his parents before leaving to rejoin his new regiment in the morning.

Sam said his farewells before going off to work. Following a hearty breakfast, George kissed Emma and Jenny goodbye, and left Ada's Terrace to report to an army unit in the north.

While he waited at the station, he gladly bought a cup of tea from the *Women's Royal Voluntary Service* trolley, whose members did so much to help others throughout the war while often in danger themselves.

The train came and the carriages and corridors were packed with servicemen and women and their kitbags. One desperate army corporal, to the amusement of many, tried to use the toilet but found that even that seat had been taken by a *Wren* which resulted in a shuffle round so that the lad could make use of it - accompanied by plenty of ribald comments!

Back at Ada's Terrace, it seemed to Sam and Emma that it was strange to be without the cheerful presence of George.

He was now back in barracks, kitted out with a new uniform and wrote to let them know how he was doing. He said that hopefully, he might get a spot of leave before going off to unknown parts.

David's birthday was fast approaching and so Emma went to visit Aunt Maisie and Mary in the country and to take little David's presents. It was bitterly cold on the journey, but for Emma, it was well worth the discomfort just to see her baby grandson, who was almost walking, and to spend some time with her daughter. Together they walked into the village, with David snugly wrapped in his pram, while frost gleamed and glinted on the grass and hedgerows.

Robert's aunt was a kindly soul who had a fund of country sayings for every occurrence. She said to Emma, 'You should have brought Jenny and her little one.' But travelling was not easy and certainly not with a baby, and Derek was not the kind of placid baby who would be happy to sit still; he would have been grizzling to get on to the carriage floor. Emma smiled at the thought knowing that her two grandsons were so dissimilar.

Mary was naturally eager for all the news of home and family. 'Does our Jackie really leave school this year?' She had missed so much of her young brother's childhood.

Then there was the business of Daphne jilting George and all on account of an Italian prisoner, it was said. What on earth did she think she was doing? Mary was incensed that anyone could treat good-natured George like that. And how about George - how had he taken it - was he alright?

Unfortunately, Mary had been unable to come through for Grandpa Bert's funeral, something which had caused her much sorrow at the time but Aunt Maisie would not have been able to cope with David by herself. Furthermore, it would not have been right to take David into the danger of a city that was being bombed so often; Robert would certainly have been most unhappy about that.

The weekend passed so quickly. There were presents for David: from Eliza - a money box with some money in it; from Annie - a knitted rabbit and a romper suit; from George - a wooden horse to pull along; and from Jenny and Derek - some wooden bricks.

Robert had been home for Christmas and Mary had hopes of seeing him again soon, but he was now training in Scotland and on the shoulder of his battledress he wore the word *Commando*.

He did not talk about what he was doing. Strangely, during the first two days of his Christmas leave, he had slept all the time as the aftermath of pills administered to keep him awake for his unusually long periods of duty.

The *Commandos'* highly secretive work involved making lightning raids on enemy coasts under the cover of darkness; the covert landing of seaborne supplies of arms and ammunition for the continental resistance fighters; and the blowing up of enemy ships in their harbours by the discreet use of magnetic limpet mines.

On one raid, somehow the enemy had been tipped off. German soldiers were secretly waiting in ambush for the *Commandos* and a tense fire-fight began followed by extremely fierce hand-to-hand fighting, where the *Fairbairn Sykes Commando Knife* proved very effective.

Robert's troop had been ordered to fall back to the little boats that they used. Heroically, Robert had thrown his wounded comrade, Leonard, over his shoulder to carry him to safety. In the process, while turning to avoid his comrade being skewered, Robert had himself been bayoneted in his knee. The German soldier died when Robert shot him with his *.45 Webley Pistol.*

For this act of courage in rescuing a fellow soldier in combat, he was officially commended, although it was something that he did not readily talk about. However, when talking with her Mum, Mary had let slip the story about Robert rescuing Leonard and Emma knew that her son-in-law was indeed a good soldier and a true hero.

As usual, all too soon Emma's visit was over, and she prepared for the journey back home. It had been really lovely to have a couple of peaceful nights, to talk to Mary and to play with little David, but she missed Sam so much and worried about him.

Emma knew that Jenny was a great help; she would make sure there was a meal for Sam when he came in, but it was not easy for her to shop and queue with young Derek to care for, especially if there were air raids.

The journey home was uneventful, no air raids, no American soldiers to give her a hand. How were the family faring back home, she wondered?

CHAPTER THIRTEEN

Back home once more in No. 7 Ada's Terrace, Emma got a rapturous welcome from Derek who had missed his Nanna. Jenny was also pleased to have her back.

Sam was not yet in from work but the pans for dinner were merrily bubbling away on the stove. Jenny had been finding life that bit harder with having to look after Derek as well as doing the housework. But somehow she had managed it.

With a cup of tea in her hand, Emma sat down to tell Jenny all the news about Mary and little David.

Jenny also had some news for Emma. While she had been away, Derek had taken his first steps alone and was now showing Emma that he could walk. Stubby little legs wide apart, he managed - one - two - three steps - before sitting down with a bump and chortling!

'Good job he's well padded!' laughed Jenny.

Jenny was laughing rather more these days, Emma thought; and thank goodness for that, the lass had seen enough dark days in her short life, that was for sure!

Then Sam came in and hugged Emma, and Derek - finding that he was not the centre of attention - stood up and clung to Sam's legs.

'He'll be *as black as the ace of spades*,' began Sam who had been working on a coal boat, but once washed and out of his working gear, he sat with Derek on his knee. Then the news from Mary all had to be repeated again.

It was a happy household that sat round the table that night.

Jenny had received a letter from Ivan Hawkins that morning, though nobody knew when it had been posted.

It was quite a surprise then, when on opening the door in answer to a knock, Jenny found Ivan standing there as large as life, just as if he himself had been sent in the post!

'Come in lad!' said Sam who had got up from his chair to see who the caller was. Emma welcomed him too with a happy hug and it did not seem strange for Jenny to be hugged as well - Ivan did not complain at all!

Ivan had the blessing of seven days of leave and he was staying at his aunt's house. He did not stay late as he knew that Sam would have to be up early in the morning for work and Aunt Queenie also did not keep late hours. But he was more than content to be able to spend the evening with them and as Sam had some beer in the kitchen, he and Ivan had a drink, along with Emma and Jenny.

As Ivan was on the point of leaving he turned to Jenny, 'Will you come to the pictures with me tomorrow night?' he asked gently.

Jenny looked searchingly at Emma who, blessedly, was quick to offer to look after Derek, saying that it would do Jenny good to get out. So it was arranged that Ivan should come for Jenny the next night, and because of that, two young hearts took on a faster beat!

Later on, Sam remarked that it looked as if Ivan had taken a shine to their Jenny.

'Only,' said Emma, 'she isn't quite our Jenny and there might come a day when she wants to move on.'

They were both silent then, realising how much Jenny had come to mean to them and how much they enjoyed her company and quiet ways, to say nothing of what a big part Derek played in their lives.

Sleep was elusive for both of them and when it did come, Emma was troubled by strange dreams. Dreams of little Derek crying and holding out his arms to her while she was unable to pick him up.

At work the next day, Emma was able to tell Barbara and Doris a little about her visit to Mary, but then Mr Ward decided that Emma should get used to counter work.

It was a change seeing so many different people. However with the checking of coupons and ration books, there were times when she really had to keep her wits about her.

Since the shop sold shampoo, Emma thoughtfully bought some for Jenny's special occasion, the date with Ivan, knowing that she would be eager to give her hair a good wash before going out looking her best.

That evening, when it was time for Jenny to leave for the cinema, and perhaps to compensate for her brief absence from her son, she kept on fussing over Derek. That Jenny was happy but nervous was obvious to Emma. To get in at the picture house in good time and find good seats, Ivan and Jenny's departure had to be soon. Ivan waited patiently, twirling his sailor's cap in his hands, then plonking it on the baby's head. Derek obviously thought it was a great game and snatched it off.

'I think you had better get going,' Emma told them, 'or you won't be there for the start of the programme.' At last they set off and as the door closed behind them, Emma started getting Derek ready for bed.

When they arrived, the cinema was packed, as before, with servicemen, servicewomen and civilians trying to forget the worries of the day. First, the curtain went up on the short film and the news.

The main film was: *The Road to Singapore*. Bob Hope and Bing Crosby soon had the audience laughing with their jokes and quips. Dorothy Lamour was looking gloriously glamorous in her trademark sarong and getting plenty of wolf whistles at any sign of romance with her leading men.

Just when it was getting interesting, the screen went blank - to be followed by a notice directing everyone to go to the shelter.

'Oh no,' gasped Jenny, 'I must go home.' But at the exits, air raid wardens and policemen were shepherding everyone into the air raid shelter. Already overhead, the drone of enemy planes could be heard; ground-based anti-aircraft guns were firing to protect the city and searchlights were sweeping their beams of light across the sky to illuminate the bombers.

Jenny and Ivan had scarcely got down into the air raid shelter when the first bombs exploded, sending shrapnel rattling down.

'Oh, I shouldn't have left Derek,' sobbed Jenny in near hysteria, and Ivan did his best to comfort her, saying that Derek would be safe with Emma and Sam.

Bombs continued to rain down - certainly not a time to be outside on the street - then a really close and heavy explosion made the dim light in the shelter go out amid screams and shouts.

'You're alright!' the warden reassured them and everyone who had a torch switched it on. Dust, dust and more dust always accompanied the nearness of these explosions. Now the choking dust filled the air as Ivan held Jenny tight.

'No use crying girl,' said a fatalistic old man, 'if it's got your number on - that's it.'

At this, Jenny was unable to wait any longer and tried to make her way to the entrance with Ivan catching at her arm. The warden at the entrance was impassive, firmly insisting that no one could go outside.

The bombers' raid seemed to Jenny to be never-ending. Why, oh why had she agreed to come out and leave Derek?

Another warden ran up to the doorway where the buckets of sand were kept behind the blast wall. 'Damned incendiaries now!' he said and grabbing the bucket, he ran off.

At long last the raid was over and the *All Clear* siren sounded. Relief! Blinking and stretching, the people began to leave the shelter and make their way back out into the world outside.

Across the street the picture house was a smoking ruin and parts of it were blazing brightly.

'Oh my Goodness!' Ivan thought, 'That really was a near one…'

'Don't hang about!' a policeman warned them. 'Jerry's lit all these fires as *markers for other bombers*.'

With Ivan's arm tight round Jenny, they set out for home. Ivan tried to cheer her up but all she wanted to do was to run home, while being truly afraid of what she might find there.

At the corner of John Street, fires blazed and hoses from the fire engines snaked across the road.

'Sorry! Can't go down there mate!' said one fireman, 'It's not safe. Too many fires and the gas main is dicey.'

Ivan and Jenny stopped to catch their breath and tried to get their bearings; shadowy figures moved around directing the hoses from the fire engines.

'Get the Rescue Squad over here!' he heard someone say and knew that there were people trapped. He could help, but first he must get Jenny home.

'We'll have to try and get round by Whittle Street,' Ivan said, helping Jenny over bricks and rubble. At last they reached Merton Street. Here it was quiet, although two streets away, fires blazed. Jenny started to run until she had rounded the corner into Ada's Terrace. The house was quiet and dark and Jenny's panic rose.

'They've probably decided to stay in the shelter,' Ivan tried to calm her, so they turned back to Merton Street and the shelter and - Ivan was right!

There, in the shelter, Derek was sleeping safely; Emma and Sam had decided not to disturb him. Crying happy tears of relief and gratitude, Jenny's face told its own story as she took Derek from Emma's arms. She gave Ivan a look of relief and gratitude such as he could never, never forget.

Several other people had also wisely stayed in the shelter; it just seemed as if it was going to be one of those nights with more raids to come.

Sam volunteered to return home to fetch a flask of cocoa to comfort and warm them. Ivan also took his leave of them, and Jenny seemed to be too distracted to reply or notice when he said that he would see her the following day.

Ivan felt a pang when she did not respond. Walking with Sam to the Terrace, Ivan told him how upset Jenny had been by the bombing.

'Poor lass!' said Sam, 'Life hasn't been easy for her, and the thought of losing Derek as well...' he left the sentence unfinished.

Ivan nodded and told Sam of his intention of checking up on Aunt Queenie and then returning to help out with the rescue work.

True to expectations there were more raids that night and a pall of smoke and dust hung over the city.

At work the next day, Emma found more dust and dirt to clear up than usual, while Mr Ward put up a courageous notice saying *Business As Usual*.

While Emma was working, the same question that had troubled her through the night still vexed her. She could see that Ivan had feelings for Jenny but she could only guess at how Jenny felt. She was not one for showing her emotions.

Last night had been really different in that respect. Jenny, being caught out in a heavy air raid away from baby Derek, had been frantic with worry, irrationally promising herself that she would never leave her baby again. By contrast, Sam and Emma had tried to point out that, even if she had been there, no one could have taken more care of Derek than they had.

If Ivan wanted to marry Jenny and Jenny agreed, would that be an end to the special bond she and Sam shared with their grandson? With this concern at heart, there seemed to be no immediate answer to the questions in Emma's head.

Emma had already left for work when Ivan arrived at Ada's Terrace that morning. Jenny was playing with Derek on the floor and Ivan soon got down on his hands and knees and was playing too, building a tower of bricks for Derek to knock down - which he did with gurgles of pleasure.

In those moments, Jenny felt a warm surge of love in her heart towards Ivan that was stronger than anything that she had ever known before. Wanting to go to the shops, Jenny set about dressing Derek for the outdoors and putting him in his pram. Ivan - on tenterhooks to know how their relationship was faring after the horror of the previous night's bombing - offered to walk with her and help with the shopping. When Jenny happily agreed, the pang that Ivan had felt the night before vanished and was replaced by an abounding joy, and it felt like they were a real family as they made their way out of Ada's Terrace and down Merton Street.

Merton Street, historically, had been a street lined with shops selling *useful supplies* for the fishermen's voyages. Straw palliases, humorously nicknamed *donkey's breakfasts*, used to hang in the shop doorways there.

When the fishermen came home from sea, they would often dispose of their old straw mattresses by *chucking them away* overboard into the docks. So, after a long voyage, as the legend had it, the fish dock was left full of abandoned floating straw beds!

While some such Merton Street shops still survived, the sad gaps left by the bombing and other shops that were just too damaged to carry on, told their own story of a dying fisherman heritage.

Ivan, Jenny and Derek turned into Whittle Street and Jenny bought the vegetables. Ivan took the bag from Jenny to put into the bottom of the pram, when a large turnip rolled out and, laughing, they both bumped heads as they bent down to reach for it. Ivan held on to Jenny's arm. 'Marry me, Jenny,' he said.

Startled, the smile went from Jenny's lips, as her thoughts turned to Emma - and what she might think.

'Oh, forget what I said. I know I'm rushing things and you probably don't feel the same way about me.'

Jenny took a deep breath, 'I do think a lot of you Ivan, but I don't know how Emma would feel about it. She might not want me and Derek to go on living there.'

Ivan flushed, 'It may seem a bit soon to be thinking of getting wed, but I know how I feel about you and the little lad. I just want to take care of you both.'

Together, they walked on with Ivan pushing the pram and Jenny holding closely on to his arm.

And that was how Sam saw them as he cycled home for his lunch, 'So, that's how the land lies!' he said to himself. 'Well, Ivan's a nice enough lad, we've known him all his life. And as for Jenny...but will Emma take it well...?'

That night as they all sat by the fire, Ivan self-consciously cleared his throat. 'Mr Walters, Mrs Walters...'

Sam smiled because he could guess what was coming next, 'Getting our full titles are we? You've known us long enough to call us Emma and Sam!'

Ivan slipped his hand into Jenny's as she sat beside him, 'I've asked Jenny to marry me,' he blurted out.

Emma's hand stopped with the needle poised over the sock she was darning.

Sam got up, clapped Ivan on the back and kissed Jenny, saying how pleased he was for them. Emma felt as if she had been turned to stone as she murmured something in the way of congratulations, but could not have told you what she had said.

Jenny put her arms round Emma, 'I'd like to stay on with you,' she said, 'we won't be getting married for a while yet and even when we do, Derek will still be close to you, the only Nanna he has ever known.'

At this it was Emma's turn to weep as a wave of relief swept over her, 'And there's a home for you here lass, as long as you want it,' she said kindly.

'A celebration is definitely called for!' pronounced Sam, and he raked the bottle of vintage port, left over from the previous Christmas, out of the sideboard. So they drank to the young couple's happiness.

As she got ready for bed that night Emma looked at Billy's picture: the same smiling face with the same bright eyes, he would never change. She hugged the frame close to her.

Sam took it from her hands, placing it back on the dressing table. 'Billy would have approved,' he said and Emma nodded. Sam too gazed at the picture of a face caught in time. He would never grow old: always their memories of him would be of a young, happy, devil-may-care lad, but with another side to him that only Jenny had known.

They put out the light but it was a long time before they fell asleep - and what a blessing - there were no raids that night.

Ivan had two more days' leave and so he took Jenny and Derek to meet his Aunt Queenie who made them very welcome.

'I'm so glad that he has you lass, he has been so alone,' his aunt said with conviction.

That afternoon Ivan took Jenny to buy an engagement ring; it was a single stone of zircon set in a plain band of gold and was Jenny's choice; there had been no time for rings with Billy.

Ivan said they must not be afraid to talk of Billy since they had been friends, and little Derek must know about his father, a Dad to be proud of. Jenny was touched by his thoughtfulness.

The following day, Ivan went back to his ship and life settled back into a routine again, for Emma, Sam and Jenny.

The British and American forces were now wreaking revenge on Germany with huge bombing raids, although this did not altogether stop the German planes from making their raids on Britain.

At the docks, despite the air raid sirens wailing their alarm, Sam was kept busy shifting goods, because more shipping and therefore more cargo was getting through, danger or no danger.

Everyone knew that German *U-Boats* had been exacting a terrible toll on British shipping, but now it seemed as if the tide of sea warfare was turning a little for the better and to Sam's relief they had men from the *American Pioneer Corps* working on the docks to help keep supplies moving.

One particular June morning, Emma had finished her shift at *Sweetings'* and was making her way to the butcher's shop to try and get something for the evening meal, when the air raid sirens began their unearthly wail and almost at once the anti-aircraft guns started firing as the droning of enemy aircraft sounded overhead.

'Come on love!' said the butcher as he shepherded Emma and two other customers who were in the shop through the back and into the shelter.

With unbelievable power, the ground shook with explosion after explosion, and the raid just seemed to go on and on and on.

One of the women burst into uncontrollable sobs over her child at school, 'They'll have them in the shelter for sure,' she sniffed, 'he'll be safe enough until this is over - but he'll be so frightened! A really bad bombing raid upsets him for days.'

Emma nodded understandingly but her thoughts turned to Sam as a large explosion shook the shelter and the planes droned overhead. What was he doing? Would he be taking cover? Fortunately there were air raid shelters for the workers on the dock and Emma prayed fervently that Sam would be safe.

Once the *All Clear* siren sounded, Emma thanked the butcher for his help and made her way home to Ada's Terrace. She tried to get a meal ready for Sam but when she went to light the oven, there was no gas, leaving her thinking that one of the main pipelines might have been hit by the bombing. Emma had an oil stove put by for just such emergencies and very fortunately, a drop of paraffin, so she was able to put a pan on to warm up.

When Sam finally came in she clung to him, 'Thank God you're alright!' she said, breathing a deeper than usual sigh of relief.

'Yes, I'm alright and thank goodness you are too!' he said, hugging her to him.

Sitting down, they were having a cup of tea when the air raid siren went off again. Making sure that everything was switched off, they made their way to the shelter together, where they encountered their neighbours and old Mrs Beecham and her friends who had quite a tale to tell.

The previous month, Tom Beecham had taken their dog out to the playing fields when a lone *Messerschmitt* fighter plane had flown in at low level with its machine guns blazing. To save his life, her husband had sheltered under a tree and had not been hit, although little spurts of earth had flown up as the bullets hit the ground. Now early this morning, she reported, a stray bomb had blown the tree up, 'Aye, they meant to have it!' she said nodding sagely.

'Ah well,' put in her friend, 'if it hasn't got your number on it, you're alright.'

'Jerry's made an early start today though,' moaned Mrs Beecham, 'it's me birthday and we was going for a drink at *The Volunteer*.'

'Never mind Ma,' said the warden and he got the adults to join with the children in singing *Happy Birthday* to her.

Later, as the *All Clear* sounded, some of the people gathered themselves together to go home, while others said that it wasn't worth it and they might as well stay where they were.

Sam and Emma decided to go home, 'I need my bed!' said Sam. He had had so many broken nights, but had to keep going into work as usual. Across to the east of them a big fire was blazing and fire engines were dashing along the road.

Unfortunately they did not have much rest in bed because at two o'clock in the morning the air raid alert went again, and so they trailed back to the shelter, where they remained until five o'clock.

When Sam and Emma came blinking out of the air raid shelter in the early brightness of a summer morning, there was a pall of smoke hanging over the city - yet the birds were still singing.

Emma hugged Sam and made her way home. Sam set off for work, facing the grim possibility of unknown detours because of streets blocked by rubble, unexploded bombs, burst water and gas mains or bomb craters.

As it happened his route took him past *The Volunteer*, but unusually at the entrance to Whittle Street there was a barrier across the street with a warden standing guard. 'You can't go down there mate!' the warden shouted. Gritting his teeth, Sam could see the roof of *The Volunteer* had been bomb-blasted clear of slates and the windows were blank, empty spaces. Swinging from the chimney, hanging by its parachute, was a large, powerful landmine, capable of destroying half a street. Fleetingly, Sam thought of Mrs Beecham, the old lady in the shelter who had been on her way to *The Volunteer* to celebrate her birthday when the raid began. Her birthday present had been that of escaping alive!

Looking at the battered remains of his favourite public house, Sam felt a chill run down his spine as he asked the warden if he knew where Wally and May might be.

'They're in hospital mate,' the warden told him. 'Most of *The Volunteer's* customers were in the pub's cellar like sensible folks. Mr and Mrs Ingles were just ushering the last ones in but some of them wouldn't hurry and they were both still at the top of the steps to the shelter when the bombs fell. Both of 'em got caught in the blast. Go and see 'em for yerself and tell 'em 'Hello' and 'Get Well!' from Charlie!'

Worried for Sam and the dangers he faced, Emma sighed as she arrived back in Ada's Terrace and looked round her home. She was fortunate, she supposed, that she still had a home. True, just now there was soot everywhere which had been shaken down by the explosions, but she still had a home! Living in bloomin' Kingston *bombed-by-the-Germans* upon Hull, it could have been so very different. Coming from the bottom of her heart up into the heavens, the honest words passed her lips, 'Thank you for our survival!'

Wearily she began to clear up the soot, wondering if she should bother to go into work that day. 'Never mind,' she thought, 'it's only for the morning and today's half-day closing anyway,' so she got herself ready and left for the shop.

Bomb craters in the road meant that her bus had to take another route so she was late, but Mr Ward was very pleased to see her, clapping her on the back. 'It's good to see you're alright,' he said.

When the time came to shut up shop, Emma put on her coat with relief and set out for home. The day had lived up to the morning's promise and was warm and sunny, 'I might even get some washing done!' Emma said brightly to herself.

When Sam came in that evening, he told her what he had discovered about Wally and May; that they were in the *Infirmary* hospital. After tea, putting on his best flat cap, he and Emma set off to visit the friendly landlord and his wife.

Arriving first at the Ladies' Ward, they found May in bed bandaged up round her chest and legs and in some pain. She was still in shock and kept living over and over again the previous night's events. 'It's that Barney Tomlinson! He's as daft as a

166

brush!' she explained, 'Afraid to leave his beer, he wanted to stay there and drink up as if nothing could hurt him! If it weren't for him we would have been safe in the cellar with everyone else! But then they had to dig us out and so much stuff had fallen on top of us that those in the cellar couldn't get out until it was moved.' May wept and Emma lent her a hankie; she listened intently while struggling with her own feelings as May went on, 'We've lost the pub and I don't know what we'll do. I'm glad I haven't got any kids.' Then remembering Emma's family, she said, 'Sorry love, but you'll know what a worry that is.' Emma nodded understandingly and gave her the flowers that she had brought before going with Sam to see Wally in the men's ward. He was also heavily bandaged round his legs, feet, ribs and head and in pain from his shrapnel injuries but glad of the tablets which helped him to bear it better.

'Come again!' he entreated Emma and Sam before they left, 'it's good to see you.'

Outside the *Infirmary*, it was Emma's turn to weep on Sam's shoulder for Wally and May's distresses. Then, arm in arm and grateful that their friends did not get caught in the full blast of the bomb, Sam and Emma walked on home.

Some streets were still criss-crossed with fire hoses. At the corner of one road there were barriers with the *Unexploded Bomb U.X.B.* sign on them.

It was a lovely night; without saying anything, they walked up the road as far as *Saint Columba's* church and gazed at the ruins. So many memories lay there, theirs among them.

'I wonder if they will ever build it again?' said Emma.

Sam squeezed her hand and they turned to walk home. Surprisingly, the fish and chip shop on the corner of Merton Street was open, so they took some home for supper, and enjoyed the crisp batter and fragrant smell of hot vinegar.

CHAPTER FOURTEEN

Fortunately, America joined the Allies in late 1941. Before this time, many British people had never ever seen or met or talked to any American people.

Now however, hundreds and thousands of American military personnel were arriving in the United Kingdom as part of the Allied war effort. Suddenly Americans were not just people who were only seen in Hollywood productions!

The British people were urged by the Government to make the incoming American servicemen and women feel welcome, and indeed to invite them to their homes at the weekend.

Sam, during his lunch break, met up with a young American serviceman who was working in the same area on the docks.

Introducing himself politely, the serviceman said, 'My name's Joseph Ganton, but you can call me Joe if you like, everybody does!'

They struck up an easy-going rapport which enabled them to exchange views on the differences and similarities between their countries and how the war affected them.

Back at home Emma wondered how long the war would continue; she felt ground down by the business of staying alive day after day and felt at that moment how much she would have liked to talk to her good friend, Lil. She would have told her how much she missed their conversations, friendship and camaraderie, 'With good friends, you can face the worst with courage,' she thought.

After a little more time getting acquainted with his new American friend, Sam graciously invited him to their home on the following Sunday.

When Emma heard about Sam's invitation, she was pleased at the thought of welcoming a friendly, new face to the Terrace but worried about what they could give their guest to eat.

'You shouldn't worry lass!' Sam said, 'Americans are like any one else.'

But Emma had heard stories of how well supplied these soldiers were, and decided to obtain all of their meat ration in one joint. 'How very small it looks on a plate,' she thought. She planned to pad it out with vegetables, followed by a nice bramble and apple pie, with the apples and cauliflower from *Bann's Farm* which Jackie would bring over for them.

Emma was cooking dinner when Jackie arrived with the vegetables. He was given a prompt invitation to stay.

Sam left to collect Joe in town, and soon extra footsteps heralded their guest's arrival.

'We're 'ere!' called Sam, as he ushered his guest inside. Sam, very broad-shouldered and of medium height, was no midget - he was well-known for his ability to pick up and carry a twenty stone bag of grain in each hand - but the tall young man had to duck down when he came through the doorway.

Emma looked up at their guest while Sam made the introductions. As Joe shook her hand, recognition dawned in his blue eyes, 'The lady on the train!' he said smiling.

Emma laughed, 'Is it really you?'

Sam was puzzled, 'How do you two know each other?'

Emma explained, 'Don't you remember Sam? I told you about the young man who helped me with my case at Manchester!'

'Sure is a small world!' agreed Joe. Like most Americans, Joe had been told about the rationing and how poorly off the British people were for food in general. Consequently he had brought with him gifts of butter, sugar, chocolates, bottles of American beer, chewing gum and candy! All these gifts were gratefully received with true wonder and admiration by the whole family and it was a very happy party that sat round the table that day. Joe was full of praise for the meal, especially the Yorkshire pudding and he generously included Jackie in his conversation.

After Emma had cleared the table and washed up, they all sat around chatting over cups of tea until late in the afternoon. When it began to get dark at around four o'clock, Jackie got up to leave as he had to cycle home. When he arrived back at *Bann's Farm,* he was full of the news about the day and Derek clung to his legs demanding attention while Annie, Eliza and Jenny listened eagerly. 'That Joe's a real nice chap,' he told them, 'I know Dad likes him.'

'I suppose he would,' Eliza put in tartly, 'with him bringing back cigarettes and beer and presents.'

'Oh no!' Jackie protested, desiring to defend the generous American, 'He's a really good sort.'

Back at Ada's Terrace, Joe was getting ready to leave and go back to camp. Emma shook his hand and found herself, without any prior discussion with Sam, inviting Joe to come again. There was a flicker in Joe's eyes for a moment that Emma did not understand.

'I'd like that Ma'am, very much,' he said, 'but would it be alright to bring my buddy with me? He works in the stores so he doesn't get to meet folks so much.'

Sam said that of course he could bring his friend and they would be welcome any time. Hospitably, he walked his guest down Merton Street to the bus stop, so that he would not get lost or bombed.

Both Sam and Emma were quiet that evening, both thinking in their own way of their visitor and the conversational topics of the afternoon. Sam dozed by the fire and gradually, the paper which he had been reading fell from his grasp. Emma picked it up pleased to have her first real chance of a good read that day. She took a particular interest in the articles on health and beauty; she knew she was not getting any younger and felt that the lack of sleep and constant stress had all begun to take their toll on her looks. Sam often told her he loved her and she was pretty enough for him, but she still felt in need of his further reassurance. But with being so busy at the docks, just surviving could seem overwhelming at times, let alone finding time and energy for romance.

After seeing Joe on his way Sam had locked up as usual, so when without any warning the letter box rattled loudly, a startled Emma went to the door and asked softly, 'Who's there?'

'It's me!' said a voice.

Straight away she recognised it as belonging to George! Quickly she unbolted the door to be greeted by her dear son. With one arm round his mother he swiftly dropped his kitbag to the floor and hugged her properly. Meanwhile, Sam was rousing himself from sleep and when George came into the room, he grasped his son's hand with pleasure and delight. What joy for them!

Emma pulled up a chair to the fire for George, 'Tea?' she enquired, while going to put the kettle on.

'Or maybe a bottle of beer?' suggested Sam with a grin. George opted for the beer.

'Cigarettes too?' said Sam offering the packet to George. 'I know it sounds like a silly question since you've only just arrived, but how long is your leave this time?'

'Embarkation leave; I've got the dreaded seven days' embarkation leave.

'Do you know where you'll be going?' they asked him.

George said there were rumours going round the camp that they were getting issued with tropical kit, so it might be somewhere warm! 'Right time of year,' continued George, 'no slushing around for us in ice and snow!'

Father, mother and grown-up son sat talking until late into the night. Sam said that he had better get some rest before work in the morning, while George declared that he could sleep on a clothes line.

Once in the bed in the front room, Emma was tired but did not sleep well. She lay there listening to Sam's heavy breathing, and the bed in the upstairs room rattling, as George turned over. What a day it had been!

The next morning Emma went off to work, leaving George asleep in bed. 'He must be really tired,' she thought.

When she got home in the afternoon her son was sorting through his fishing gear, 'I may try my luck at a bit of fishing tomorrow,' he said. 'Are Jenny and Derek still staying with Annie and Eliza?'

Emma confirmed that they were, and asked George if he would like to come with her to visit them on her day off.

'Of course!' he said with a grin.

When Emma woke up on the morning of her day off, it was a golden day with not a cloud in the sky and she greeted it with elation.

Joyfully, and as arranged, she and George made the bus journey to *Bann's Farm*. Truth to tell, Emma still had not quite got used to being a grandma and was looking forward to getting her boisterous welcome from Derek.

On the journey there, Emma noticed that in the fields the farmworkers had already started bringing in the wheat harvest. She spotted Jackie there, and with gratification, noted that he was enjoying being in the thick of the action. He was driving the big horses. Working outside had broadened his frame and with his eager, brown eyes, ready smile, tanned face and square jaw he was very nearly a man.

He had a role at *Bann's Farm* now in looking out for the welfare of his Aunt Annie and Grandma Eliza. Jenny was like an older sister and little Derek like his younger brother, the boy was fast becoming a man; but Emma still saw her little boy.

Arriving at the farmhouse, it gave her much pleasure to see Jenny and Derek, Annie and Eliza, and they in turn were delighted to see both their visitors and to sit them down with a strong cup of tea.

Later that afternoon, while George chatted to Annie and Eliza, Emma took the opportunity to go with Jenny and Derek to take a bottle of tea and some shortcake to Jackie who was still out working on the neighbouring farm.

The big *Clydesdale* horse that pulled the crop cutter and binder stood snorting in the shade and stamping its feet. Jackie wanted his little nephew Derek, to love the horses as much as he did. So with a swoop, he picked him up and held him high to the horse's head. Derek was terrified of a monstrous animal that might eat him and clung tightly to Jackie.

'Oh, get on with yer, no need to be afraid!' said Jackie as he finished his *fourses*, 'He's not a dragon yu' know!'

When it was time for Emma and George to get on the bus home to Ada's Terrace, Jenny and Derek, who were staying on a little longer at *Bann's Farm,* walked to the bus stop with them.

George turned to Jenny, 'I hear you and Ivan are going to get wed! I'm happy for you! Ivan's a good chap. He'll do right by you and the nipper.'

Jenny nodded her gratitude, 'I'm sorry things didn't work out for you and Daphne,' she said.

George was silent for a moment. 'It was for the best I suppose.' What he did not tell her was that he had seen Daphne's brother who had told him the news that Daphne was pregnant! Some things he considered were perhaps better left unsaid.

As the bus trundled away from the village, Emma and George enjoyed the tranquillity and peace of the countryside, and almost forgot that there was a war on! That is, until they arrived back in Kingston upon Hull where the war was all too evident.

Emma thought that if her Great-Aunt Betty had been told in her day, that such devastating things as Emma was now seeing would happen in Britain, she would scarcely have believed it. 'Such things,' thought Emma, 'would have been deeply offensive to her imagination and she would have had more than a thing or two to say about it all!'

When they arrived back home at Ada's Terrace, Sam greeted Emma with a loving kiss and George with a slap on the back and laughingly pulled out a packet of chewing gum from his pocket.

'What's that?' George asked.

'Well, you see it's from the *Yanks*. They gimme it. We've got a labour force of five hundred *Yanks*!' replied Sam. 'In fact there's so many of their supplies coming in now that their army's going to handle it - but don't worry - I ain't out of a job, there's still plenty for us dockers to do!'

For the family, the days flew by and the week passed all too quickly. George managed to go fishing a couple of times and at the end of his leave returned back to camp.

Amazingly, because rumours are not always true, he and his troop were indeed issued with tropical kit. On a crisp morning in November they embarked on a troop ship; there would be no Christmas home leave for them this year.

What George did not know was that ironically, Ivan was on the escort ship conducting George's ship safely back to war! Without knowing it and without being able to meet, the two friends were together in the same convoy!

Christmas Day that year was a lively affair. Jenny and Derek were living back home at No. 7 Ada's Terrace and Jackie cycled over to join in the fun. The American guests, Joe and his buddy Len, had managed to rustle up a magnificent, fully cooked Christmas turkey! Everyone's eyes grew wide with surprise.

'We hope we did the right thing in bringing it?' they said modestly.

Emma had used her position at *Sweetings'* store over the year to buy the ingredients for a Christmas pudding which everyone felt was a grand success. Indeed, the residents of No. 7 lived on the benefits of that meal for more than a week!

The *B.B.C.* radio was switched on after the meal and nobody wanted to do much for some time after.

Jackie noticed that Len had less hair than Joe and was older and quieter. Little Derek had taken to him and sat on his knee, quite happy in his company.

Later when Emma was washing up the dishes and Jenny was putting Derek to bed, Joe came through to the kitchen and began to help dry up the pots.

'It's alright,' Emma protested, 'I can manage!'

With an impudent look in his eye Joe said, 'I think we've known each other for long enough Mrs Walters and it really makes me feel at home to be in the kitchen with you.'

As the host, Sam knew that a game of cards can sometimes help the quieter people in a party to come out of themselves and relate to the others, and so he was engaged in a game of *Beggar My Neighbour* with Jackie and Len and did not notice the exclusive interaction between Emma and Joe.

'Aren't you going to join in with them?' Emma asked Joe.

'Oh no, I'm happy to sit here with you,' was his answer.

After Len and Joe left that evening, the rest of the little party sat round the fire talking.

'Len was good with our Derek,' remarked Jenny, 'is he married?'

'Yes,' said Sam.

'And Joe?'

Sam was not sure, 'I asked him once, and he said *sort of* whatever that might mean,' he said wrinkling his nose.

'He seems a nice man, don't you think, Mam?' Jenny asked. Emma nodded.

'They really seem to appreciate coming here,' said Sam, 'it must be hard for them being so far away from home.'

'Our George is a soldier away from home and I doubt if he's been invited out and made welcome - wherever he is!' replied Emma sharply.

Sam and Jenny were silent. Jenny thought it was most unlike Emma to be snappy, especially with Sam. But maybe she was missing her sister Annie this Christmas, as Eliza was getting increasingly frail and Annie had thought it best if they stayed at *Bann's Farm* for the celebrations this year.

For a few months, Joe was a frequent visitor to Ada's Terrace, often coming on his own if Len was on duty and Sam was at work. He was remarkably easy to talk to and always made a point of seeking Emma out for a chat.

In her understanding, Americans were easy-going and forthcoming in their conversation and so Emma allowed social and conversational boundaries to be ignored in a way that she would not have done among English people; somehow the boundaries of propriety were slowly sandpapered away by such an easy familiarity.

On one occasion, when Emma put some plates on the table Joe went to help her and as his hand brushed against hers, Emma felt as if she had received an electric shock. She looked at Joe and knew - without any words being passed between them - that he had felt it too. The thrill of it made her not want to question it but to live only for the moment and be damned to all else. Quickly she emptied the washing-up bowl, finished putting things away and went back into the living room with Joe following close behind her, as if it was his right. A shudder ran through her - a frisson of foreboding and excitement.

She knew that Sam cared deeply for her, but it was not romance with a capital *'R'*; the kind of *sweep-you-off-your-feet* experience. Emma had only ever had one boyfriend in her life, Sam. And although she had some understanding of how women thought, her understanding of mens' thinking by comparison was quite small.

One blustery afternoon in March, Emma was more surprised than would be expected of a woman of her years, to find that as she left the shop, Joe was waiting.

He had asked her once where she worked, but naively, she had not realised that he had wanted to meet her for *herself.* As this realisation of 'wantedness' dawned on her, it was so attractive that when he asked, 'Come and have a coffee with me!' she felt that the word *'No'* could not pass her lips.

Joe took her arm and led her into a nearby café. They sat down by the window which was steamed up with the warmth and fleeting sensuality of the immediate moment.

Emma for a few seconds wondered, 'Why does it not feel like this with Sam?' and then dismissed the thought. In the café with Joe, she felt like they were in a warm, little world that was

175

just theirs. Outside the weather was cold, raw and uninviting. Joe took her hand and stroked her wrist, watching her face with a smile. Emma suddenly felt as though she mattered to someone in a new way and that perhaps if she ignored her conscience, she might have some happiness.

After a brief chat she said hurriedly, 'I'll have to go; I'm taking the food in for tea.' She stood up and gathered her shopping together, 'Jenny and Derek will be waiting.'

'Lucky them!' was Joe's reply, and taking Emma by surprise, he pulled her close to him and kissed her.

A very startled Emma pulled away from him and almost without saying 'Goodbye!' ran down the street, heart beating wildly and face blushing hotly. A fierce battle was being fought within her being, between the flush of desire, the excitement of the moment and the fear of being discovered.

The next day Joe was there again, and this seemed to set the pattern of her days. To Emma, Joe was like her knight in armour who had come from a far land to rescue her from feeling lonely and neglected. She felt that as long as she did not have to think about the meaning of love, romance, marriage and faithfulness, then Joe and the feeling of wantedness would always be waiting for her at the café.

Jenny found that Emma was frequently out until quite late in the afternoon although she finished work at lunchtime. Not that Jenny minded as she cheerfully prepared whatever was at hand for their evening meal and she could have Derek in the routine that she wanted.

But one day, for the first time on leaving work, Emma found that there was no Joe there, waiting for her. She scanned the street for a sight of that tall figure in the smart uniform that was so different from the British soldiers' rough khaki. He was not there, and there were only the usual women shoppers engaged in the search for food to feed their families.

Like that day, there were a couple of occasions when Joe was called out on duty at short notice and did not come. Emma was surprised to find that she felt such keen disappointment at his absence, yet on the days when they did meet in the café, she was half dreading that she would be discovered, either by her fellow shoppers or else by someone who knew her.

One day in April, a letter came from May Ingles, former landlady of *The Volunteer,* asking if they would visit her husband Wally, who was still in the hospital rehabilitation unit recovering from the bomb blast.

Emma and Sam went to visit him that evening. He was feeling a lot better physically but was decidedly depressed because of the loss of his business. '*The Volunteer* is beyond repair and is going to be pulled down!' he said dolefully, 'Twenty-five years and what have I got to show for it?'

Emma and Sam did their best to keep him cheerful, 'Maybe the brewery will let you rent another pub,' they suggested hopefully before they left.

As dusk gathered itself, they walked home from the hospital. With the loss of their local pub, the central place for community solidarity, talking over gossip, grievances and celebrating good news, it seemed that another whole part of their lives had come to an end.

While Sam took Wally's news more philosophically, Emma inwardly raged at Wally's loss, their own loss, the city's losses and the war not being won yet. Fortunately *The Red Lion* pub was open, and Sam, sensing that Emma was brooding, suggested they stop in for a sup.

On the *Red Lion's* wall in the snug area, there were a number of brass and copper ornaments. Sam thought back through the years. When he was a youngster, he often used to help his Mum, Eliza, by feeding the fire under the copper cauldron. It made him feel content that she trusted him with this important task of heating the water for the washing of their clothes. He recalled the brick-layered base that the cauldron nestled in; the stove pipe letting the smoke out through the roof and the wooden lid cover that prevented him from getting splashed by the boiling water.

Sam reminisced about growing up with his Mum and Dad and the good times they had had together.

'Do you remember the strange dream Mam had about the washing in the copper?' he asked Emma, who shook her head. 'She dreamed that she put the washing into the old copper boiler in the corner, but when she went to get it out, the copper was empty and bottomless. Now when Herbert Bingham and his brother cleared the bombsite where Mam's house used to be, guess what they found?

'What?' asked Emma, intrigued.

'They found seven wells!'

'So it's no wonder she dreamed of having a bottomless copper and losing the washing!' said Emma chuckling. She went on to tell Sam how she had noticed that on her visits to *Bann's Farm*, Eliza was visibly aging, but despite her frailty still insisted on doing her share of the chores.

'That's Mam for you!' said Sam.

Unfortunately for Sam, the excessive demands of wartime dock work on time and energy; the continual loss of sleep from air raids and fire-watching, along with a certain amount of taking the marriage happiness for granted, had not helped the Walters to be as happy as when they first made their marriage vows.

Wives are protected by the vigilant love of their husbands through all the changing scenes of life. But sadly, while Sam's love for Emma did not fade, his vigilance dozed off instead of remaining on duty.

Despite his good-humoured ways, Sam did not notice much difference in Emma's behaviour. He was as busy as ever at work as the dockers attempted to keep goods moving in and out of the docks and clear up after the destruction of the air raids; and by the time he returned home in the evenings, Emma was always present, as if nothing out of the ordinary had happened in the routine of her day.

So it was that as time went by, Jenny saw and noted a new and unusual kind of sparkle in Emma who, when going to work, took more than usual care with her dress and make-up.

For Joe and Emma, their meetings had become an enduring pattern of things. As the days blossomed into spring, they took to boldly strolling into a little park nearby, instead of always sitting in the café.

One day Emma came home and said that she had an announcement to make. She wanted to have a permanent wave set in her hair.

Sam was not over-enthusiastic, 'Are you sure this is what you really want?' he asked. 'Your hair has always looked so lovely.'

'That style is old-fashioned and it makes me look old!' retorted Emma loudly.

Jenny heard again that unusual sharpness in Emma's voice. Sam winced inwardly at her harshness over both her own looks and her rejection of his preferences; he said no more.

'Hey!' said Joe admiringly, when he saw the new hairstyle, 'You look lovely Em.' She blushed as she realised that he was the only one who called her that and she did not stop him because it made her feel special. Joe felt that he could soon make a further move in their relationship and if he was posted away afterwards - so what?

It happened that one late autumn afternoon, Jenny decided to take Derek out for a walk. Strapping him into his pushchair, she promised the little lad a treat, 'We'll go and meet Nanna!'

They were still a little distance from the shop when Jenny saw Emma coming out of the shop. She was about to wave, when suddenly, out of nowhere, Joe boldly stepped up to Emma and kissed her cheek as if he was accustomed to it, and walked off with his arm around her!

Shocked to the core, Jenny turned round and walked back the way she had come. 'We'll go to the swings,' she said to Derek. Then, after the swings, she made sure that she was home before Emma with the kettle on and everything in its place, leaving no clue to the afternoon's excursion with Derek.

When Emma arrived home she said brightly, 'Everywhere in town's so busy with people trying to shop between the raids, I'm not late am I?'

Taking a deep breath and looking her straight in the face, Jenny replied, 'We came to meet you, but you were otherwise engaged!'

'Oh!' said Emma, taken aback, 'I ran into Joe.'

Jenny was stern, 'It seems to me that you've been doing a lot of running into Joe. Does Sam know about it?'

Emma's face coloured up furiously, 'It's none of your business!' she snapped.

'It is when it affects someone like Sam,' Jenny retorted quickly, 'he's only ever been kind to me and Derek, letting us stay here.'

'Well, just keep that buttoned up if you want to carry on living here!' Emma snapped furiously, 'I only have to say to Sam that I want you out, and that would be that.'

'I think that you should keep away from Joe,' replied Jenny bravely, 'one good turn deserves another - not that I like deceiving Sam, he's a good man, honest and kind - so you finish with Joe and nothing more will be said.'

Shocked at being found out and worse still, having to face her own conscience, Emma spluttered, 'Don't think for a minute that you can threaten me!' All the while she was just beginning to experience in her own heart a serious niggle of doubt about Joe.

To Emma, Joe had been her strong, young and handsome fantasy man: the man who was *sort of* married, and therefore desirable to women, who made her feel wanted and needed; who made no great demands on her and could come and go as the occasion pleased him.

Later, sitting by the fireside with a warm brew of tea, Emma looked into the friendly flames and thought harder and clearer than she had done for some time.

'What kind of man is Joe?' she said to herself. 'If he could leave his *sort-of-wife* for me, how would I know he wouldn't leave me for someone else?' And she knew how Sam would feel about her betrayal. As she was trying to think through how well Joe's character measured up, without any conscious trying on her part, an old, familiar quotation crept into her memory: *even mine own familiar friend, in whom I trusted, which did eat of my bread, hath lifted up his heel against me.*

Sam had received Joe into their home as a bona fide friend, had trusted him and fed him at the family meal table. Suddenly Emma felt a shudder of horror. It was true that she had been flattered by Joe's attention, but she began to feel now that she should not hurt Sam.

The next afternoon, Joe, with a devil-may-care smile, was waiting outside the café as usual. Autumn was progressing into an early winter and rain was lashing against the window of the café. It all felt so bleak and empty, 'Just like I feel inside,' Emma thought to herself. But contrary to their previous meetings, she stayed outside the café, in the rain.

'Joe,' she said. 'I can't see you anymore. I'm at fault myself for being thoughtless and brainless with regard to you and it is going to stop now. It has taken me long enough to realise it, but I need a husband called Sam, not a boyfriend called Joe.'

Joe's open, cheery face clouded over. This time Emma saw it clearly and understood, there was a flicker on his face of something that was not love and not generosity but thwarted possession.

He sighed, 'I knew it was too good to last. I've seen the way Sam looks at you, and I envy him.' So saying, he tore a leaf out of a pocket book, and writing an address and an army number down on it, he gave it to Emma.

Inwardly, Joe felt that he had lost an easy conquest and was riddled with anger and confusion, 'Don't these British women understand that a good time is all that matters?'

Outwardly he said, 'I won't trouble you again. I shall put in for a transfer to another camp and will be gone in a few days. I love you Emma - too much to cause you any trouble! Sam is a lucky man and I hope he knows it! But if you do change your mind, you can get in touch with me at this address.'

Emma was near to tears; she felt angry and foolish. This man said he did not want to cause her any trouble, and trouble there was and more trouble there could easily be, because she was attracted to him and he knew it.

The rain had not abated. He kissed her unresponsive cheek, and walked away, soon to be lost from sight. With the heaviness of her foolishness and irresponsibility inside her, Emma made her way home in the rain, near to tears.

With every step that brought her closer to Ada's Terrace, she set her heart on not only being faithful to Sam for the rest of her days but also on finding good opportunities to make their marriage stronger.

Len continued to visit them while merely commenting that Joe had been posted away, and that was that. There were, inevitably, thoughts in Emma's mind as to what might have been but she had at last found out what kind of man Joe was and that *wandering by the way* was a dangerous and worthless folly.

She reminded herself that she had to be true to herself and to Sam, the good man that she had freely chosen to marry.

CHAPTER FIFTEEN

Extraordinarily for late January, amidst what normally would have been winter weather, the sun shone warmly on Ada's Terrace, as little Derek had his second, raucous birthday.

Emma's eldest daughter, Mary and her soldier husband, Robert, came through for a few days, to stay with his parents while he was on leave. They had brought young David along with them and Sarah, the doting Grandma Stavin was only too happy to look after him. So the happy, younger couple spent several blissfully carefree days together while they had the chance.

Wartime holidays were not only scarce but precious. For Robert's brigade, there was not only a feeling of an intense *busyness* amongst the officers but there was amongst the men a sense of *something in the wind,* which left him sure that perhaps it would be a long time before his next home leave.

Ivan also came home on leave - and Jenny's heart leaped for joy! During the time that Ivan spent with her, Jenny, like wartime soldiers' ladies often do, felt the exceptionality of it all; and all too soon it was time for him to leave her again.

When his departure time came, Jenny clung to Ivan in love, concern, happiness and fear.

'Will he go away and not return from battle?' she wondered. Despite her fears, in that moment she felt that she truly loved him.

'Time and tide wait for no man,' said Ivan, 'don't worry lass, I'll be back, and then we can plan that wedding.' In departing he gave her a cheery wave, turned, and did not look back; there are times when a man has to go to war.

Although life went on as usual for Jenny, she had a strange feeling of tension, as if waiting for something momentous to happen.

On the morning of June 6th 1944, she was listening to the radio when the announcer gave the news of the Allied invasion of France. The liberation of Nazi-held Europe had actually begun! Jenny felt sure that somewhere in the naval support of the landings in Normandy, in the thick of it all, her Ivan was surely there. Just as similarly Mary also knew with an inner certainty that as a soldier and as a *Commando*, her Robert was also there.

Even with the Normandy landings, things did not happen easily or all at once as in the way of fairy stories. War is not beautiful and the blood and abundant death are not beautiful either. There was hard and bitter fighting with terrible losses on both sides of the battle, but if Britain and the Continent were ever to be safe from slavery and tyranny, Hitler had to be defeated at all costs.

Just at the time when people might have guessed that the German *Luftwaffe* was very busy trying to keep the skies clear of Allied planes over their own country, Hitler unleashed his secret weapon: the jet-propelled *V-1* flying bomb. This pilot-less missile with short, stubby wings was quickly christened the buzz bomb or doodlebug by the long-suffering people of Britain, who stoically faced this new hazard.

Not too far away from Ada's Terrace, there was a shop where a little crowd of staff and customers huddled in the doorway as the dreaded *V-1* machine passed overhead. It was almost out of sight when the engine stopped, ready for descent. The silence of the plummeting doodlebug seemed to last forever, and then came the ground-shattering explosion and in the busy city of Hull, the crowd knew that somebody's loved ones may well just have died in the explosion.

People thought, without justifying it, that in a way you could understand the thinking of the *Luftwaffe* airmen who bombed your towns and cities. They wanted their country to defeat your country, just as they had done with other countries. They had not been beaten before and did not expect to be beaten by your country. They hated you, and you in turn, hated them back.

To the Germans, they themselves felt they were the superior race and the British were the inferior race, so it was obviously natural that they should win. Killing an inferior race was not felt to be wrong because it was only the survival of the fittest, and that was what evolution was all about. So for the Germans, the British were the hated enemy whose cities and civilian population had to be bombed into submission. That way the *Third Reich* could expand into new territory.

However to the residents of Ada's Terrace, this buzz bomb business was obscene; there was no courage in it. It was merely a thoughtless, deadly machine, without feelings, sent on a mindless mission to kill and spread terror before it could be shot down from the skies. And shooting it down was not an easy thing to do. The instantly recognisable *'putt putt putt'* sound of the wretched doodlebugs was heard by day and by night. When one doodlebug landed in a field, not far from *Bann's Farm*, the blast smashed windows, shook tiles from the roof, and caused the timbers in the roof to bend!

Young people of Jackie's age had a great interest in the bomb fragments, which they collected, and some had even collected live bombs! Others had tried to open live bombs by hitting their outer casings with hammers! With this particular doodlebug blast, Jackie had cycled up to see it and to get as close to it as he was allowed by the guards at the bomb site.

Emma thought often about Jackie and what would happen to him in the future; after all, he was coming up to sixteen now. When the invasion of France by the Allies began, Emma's first thought was that the war might soon be over and then Jackie would not have to take part in it. If the war carried on for much longer, he would certainly be recruited into the services. He himself however, was not afraid. He knew that he would be called up for military service as soon as he was old enough and thought that he might go into the *Air Force*, just as his brother Billy had done.

When Japan attacked Manchuria, the Pacific islands, Burma, Mongolia and China their intention was to conquer all of East Asia and India; and when they threatened India and Burma - part of the British colonies - Great Britain was forced not only to protect her own local interests but also the lives of those who lived within her empire. George was in Burma and letters arriving in Ada's Terrace from him were woefully infrequent.

The war in the Far East seemed to George and his company to be interminably slow. This was especially so in the monsoon rainy season when the managing of patrols and transportation were exceedingly difficult. Even the crossing of normally tame rivers could very easily become a life and death struggle.

With Britain fighting on many fronts, the desperate guerilla war being fought in Burma against the Japanese forces, was terribly short of troops and equipment. Supplies were dropped by parachute behind enemy lines, but the sense of isolation and hopelessness among the soldiers was terrible and although news filtered through to them about the progress of the war in Europe, it seemed to them that they were largely the *Forgotten Army.*

Back in England, Emma and Sam could only grasp at the scraps of news that they heard from the radio, and pray for their son's safety.

In France there had been fierce fighting over a small village which stood at a vital crossroads. In the conflict, under fierce machine gun and enemy artillery fire, Robert was badly wounded. With the help of three of his comrades, he was enabled to withdraw from the line of fire and get help in the field hospital. From there he was repatriated to England and spent a long and initially painful time in convalescing.

When the time came for his medical examination, the doctors felt that he had not sufficiently recovered from his shrapnel wound to be sent back to the fighting. Much to his and Mary's relief, he was placed on office duties in Hull. Strangely enough, considering the housing shortage, he was able to get a *billet* in a house in Ada's Terrace and whenever he was on leave, he went to stay in Westrae with his new family which helped him greatly in his recuperation.

At first, Robert's son, young David, was wary of this stranger who shared his mother's bed, a privilege he had assumed was his. Gradually though, he accepted the new situation. He had a Dad!

But there was disappointment for Emma because Mary was not going to be moving back to live in Hull. She liked the fresh air and community spirit of rural village life, as did Robert. Aunt Maisie was so keen to help them make the transition that she was willing to invest in a business with them, and they were thinking of taking on the running of the village shop.

The optimists in some newspaper columns, when they learned of the vast military resources that were put into the June 1944 invasion of the Normandy beaches, had wanted to predict that the war would be over by Christmas. But this was not to be.

Worse even than the *V-1* buzz bombs were the *V-2* rockets. They delivered 2,200 lbs of explosives to their target and now

Hitler unleashed them on England. With the *V-1's*, you could at least hear them coming, but the *V-2* rockets came without any warning, were silent and could not be shot down.

London and the South East of the country were particularly within the range of these terrible weapons and the loss of life and the loss of property were cruelly high. There was a price to be paid for being even a non-combatant civilian in wartime.

People lived through another year of daily reports on the various battlefronts. The Allies had the bitter setback at *Arnhem* in September 1944 where so many gallant men were lost. But the ocean tide of war seemed, however slowly, to be turning in favour of the Allies and the frequency of the air raids on the Home Front were blessedly decreasing.

Another Christmas came and went. Derek was now an incessant chatterer: having spent so much time in grown-up company he had soon lost his babyish ways and language, and was growing into a bright little boy.

In Ada's Terrace, Sam and Emma had heard from G.I. Joe's buddy, Len, who was with a supply unit in France, but from Joe himself nothing was heard. This of course puzzled Sam who in an injured tone said, 'You would have thought he might keep in touch…'

Emma murmured something about mail not always being reliable and nothing more was said. With so many people, military personnel as well as civilians, being haphazardly thrown together and thrown apart by the war, it was remarkable that so many liaisons and friendships lasted at all.

What Sam did not know was that when she had seen Joe for the very last time, he had given her his contact details and Emma had gone home and given them to the fire: she wanted nothing more to do with him ever again.

Ivan came home on leave and together with Jenny and Derek spent halcyon days. Ivan's ship was having a refit, and so it looked likely that he would have another period of leave before his ship sailed for foreign parts. With much excited discussion and anticipation, plans went ahead for their wedding.

Taking into consideration the destruction to property from the bombing, Ivan thought it best to get settled somewhere quickly in case there was a housing shortage, and as No. 9 Ada's Terrace was about to be vacated they were able to rent it. Emma was hugely relieved and pleased that when they were married, the two newly-weds would only be two doors away.

From George there was still but little news: all that the family knew was that he was in the Far East. In fact, George, as part of the *Fourteenth Army,* had been sent to defend the vast Burmese frontier against the Japanese.

Allocated to reconnaissance and sabotage, George's platoon carried out forays into the countryside, monitoring a settlement of Japanese troops who had taken over a village a few miles up river. The occupants of this village had either fled or been killed by the enemy.

The Japanese, knowing that there were British troops in the area, had their own Intelligence Units trying to track them down. Wisely, George and his soldiers decided not to stay in the villages and put the lives of the village population at risk.

Conditions were extremely testing in the Burmese jungle as the troops faced difficult terrain, illness, terrible roads and continual harassment from enemy soldiers. In this desperate fight, their allies were the heroic, local Burmese people who risked their lives to help them with food, supplies and local knowledge.

Any Burmese suspected of helping the British was in great danger, and could suffer torture and death at the hands of the Japanese; yet they did their best to help the soldiers, knowing that they were there to fight for their freedom.

One such native was Boon Phi. He had a characteristic small white scar above his left eye. He volunteered to show the soldiers how to track the enemy in difficult conditions. Under his guidance, George and his unit crawled on their stomachs through the jungle - hour after hour - moving quietly so that they could outwit the Japanese marksmen waiting above them in the trees.

George, two comrades and Boon Phi, on one patrol, were dangerously cut off from the rest of their party. Crouching in a ditch, they could hear the sound of nearby Japanese soldiers wading through the swamps and calling to each other. There the little party escaped discovery by remaining quiet and still despite the leeches fastening on to their legs.

Shortly after, the villagers were working in the paddy fields when the Japanese raided the village and began searching the long hut for hidden food supplies and signs of collaboration with the British. In their frustrated fury, they beat the two old women who were preparing the meal for the rest of the community. Because of that Boon Phi made only sporadic return trips to the village and did not dare stay there for long anymore.

Over time, as Boon Phi's tracking and jungle navigation skills became more evident among the soldiers on patrol, the men found it hard to understand why he never joined them when they swam in one of the jungle pools and preferred to roll up separately from them when it was his rest period.

There was a lot of teasing but George seeing the young man was embarrassed, defended him, 'We're in a foreign country,' he told his men, 'what might seem alright for us, could be taboo for them.'

Some days later, on his rest break George heard the village children laughing and splashing in a jungle pool and sat down to watch them play. Suddenly he saw the familiar white scar and dark eyes. The sight stopped him in his tracks.

Now it appeared to George that Boon Phi was not the boy he purported to be. Gone was the all-covering cap and camouflage kit, and in its place, a headful of shining, black hair hung down a light-brown back. Boon Phi was a lovely young woman.

George's head went into a spin...but suddenly it all began to make sense; the differences, the embarrassment, the awkwardness... To hide herself away from the depredations of the Japanese soldiers, Boon Phi had dressed as a boy!

In a flash, seeing George, a horrified Boon Phi was rushing towards the bank to don her camouflage.

George, giving her a decent interval to dress, tried to reassure her that he would keep her secret.

She searched his face to see if he was telling the truth and was satisfied, 'I live in danger,' she said simply, 'I need you to keep my secret.'

George learned that Boon Phi had been widowed when her husband, like all the Burmese village men folk, had been herded off to labour for the Japanese. In this slavery, while barely managing to exist on the meagre rice rations that their captors reluctantly gave them, they were put to extreme exertions: hacking paths through the jungle, building roads and railways.

The Japanese seemed conscienceless in the way they treated the Burmese as if they were less than animals and not human beings. Consequently, they suffered from untended fevers, malaria and infections and when they could not work, they often were beaten and left to die where they fell.

Nor were the men the only ones to be humiliated and put to slavery, as many of the women and girls were used as sex slaves in the Japanese *comfort stations*, and never seen again.

Right then and there, George determined that he would do everything in his power to protect Boon Phi from such a fate. He really felt for her situation and the daily life-and-death struggle that she faced - and even more so after he learned that she had a son, Kau Li.

There was not much opportunity for romance but something more than camaraderie grew between them. Boon Phi found herself relying on George and in his leisure moments he often found himself thinking about a brown face with a small white scar and a better world for them both to live in.

One morning in the spring when Emma was out at work, a local reporter paid a visit to Ada's Terrace. Jenny spotted him from the window and answered the door saying that Emma would be home later.

Emma had not been home long before the caller with his notebook was back again, announcing himself as a reporter, 'I understand that you have a daughter called Serena Waters?'

Emma's heart beat faster; had something happened to Joanie?

Before she could answer, the man continued, 'Of course Serena Waters is her stage name but to you and your family she is Joan Walters, I understand?'

Emma agreed that this was so, all the time wondering and dreading what was coming next. To her, it felt a little like receiving one of those telegrams in the moment before it is opened.

To her immense relief and astonishment, the reporter informed her that Joanie was going to appear in a revue at *The Tivoli Theatre* in Hull, where *Old Mother Riley* was to top the bill! And fortunately Joanie was not at the bottom of the programme either!

Emma rallied herself; the reporter wanted to take a photograph of her which would be put in the paper, but she would not allow it. After a brief chat, the reporter left. What Emma did not know until later, was that he had taken pictures of the outside of the house and, based on them, was already planning a story celebrating: *A Local Girl Makes Good!*

Emma could hardly wait to tell Sam of the reporter's visit. And what a surprise they had when on the very next day they saw the evening paper: it showed a photograph of their house in Ada's Terrace, of their Joanie, and a big write-up of the story of her career and rise to fame!

Although the show was due to open the following week, they still had no word from Joanie herself and Emma hoped against hope that Joanie would come home and stay for that week. To that end, she busied herself with cleaning and preparing Joanie's old room.

Sam eyed the preparations with concern and became tight-lipped when he saw how Emma's expectations had been raised; he would have a few words to say to that young lady if she should come round.

The days passed until Sunday night when there was a knock at the door and, resplendent in a fur coat, there stood Joanie at their front door!

'Hello Mam, Hello Dad!' she greeted them as if she had not been away for the past six years! Emma shed tears while she put the kettle on. Sam, who had rehearsed the hard words that he would say, found that they just would not come. Joanie prattled away while walking round the room and picking up a photo of David.

'Who's this - is it really Mary's little boy?' And George - did they know that she and George had met up in the desert?

'Your old room is ready for you,' Emma said hopefully.

Joanie hesitated before saying in an offhand manner, 'Oh, I won't be staying with you. Digs have already been arranged for all the cast. I've brought you some tickets for the first performance tomorrow night; we can meet after that.' With that, Joanie left in a cloud of expensive perfume. Emma as a mother, felt cast aside like an old leather handbag.

Sam was not at all sure that he wanted to go to see the show, and felt that it was not really his kind of thing. However, he was persuaded by seeing just how much it meant to Emma.

Afterwards, he had to admit that it was a good show and that Joanie's singing was really well-received.

When the show was over, she came and took them backstage and introduced them to the other members of the cast. To Emma, who was slightly awestruck by the whole idea of show business, the backstage area was definitely less glamorous than she had previously imagined. Wires and cables seemed to trail everywhere and it smelt hot and dusty.

Joanie led the way to the bar and ordered a whisky for Sam although he would rather have had a beer, and a port and lemon for Emma. The conversation between them was desultory, mainly about Joanie's career and travels.

Apparently, on this tour, the show was only playing in Hull for a week after which they would travel to Leeds before going further north. Joanie also hoped that they would eventually play in London too.

Wondering at Joanie's apparent detachment from them, Sam and Emma said their farewells to her as best they could. When they arrived home, feeling more than slightly stunned from the evening's experience, they sat up talking late into the night, if only to recover from the encountering of Joanie's alien theatrical world and alien theatrical ways.

Sam thought it was a very false world, with *Darling* this, and *Darling* that; it all seemed so tinselly and insincere to him. Neither he nor Emma felt comfortable in the presence of the artistes and Emma felt embarrassed by the scanty clothes that some of the girls had run around in. Worse than all this, where was their little Joanie? What had they done to cause her to treat them more like distant cousins than parents? The anguish lessened slightly over the week but did not disappear entirely. To her credit and during that week, Joanie visited twice and then she was gone again. She lived in a different world to her parents; that world of mere appearance where her Mum and Dad would never feel completely at ease.

Back at work at *Sweetings'*, Emma had to answer all sorts of questions about the show, the clothes Joanie wore and the stage costumes of the chorus girls.

Joanie had said quite calmly, that she would not be breaking her tour to attend Jenny and Ivan's wedding. She had already met Jenny and Derek, but little children and domesticity were not really on her wavelength.

191

The rejection did not bother Jenny at all but she noted the hurt and disappointment that Joanie's staying away had caused her mother and felt sorry for Emma.

Jenny had already moved into No. 9 Ada's Terrace with little Derek, and Emma was grateful that they were so near.

Sam said laughingly, 'The path between the two houses will soon be worn away!'

Emma and Jenny had both had their differences. Emma accepted and took Jenny in for Billy's sake; then she loved Jenny for baby Derek's sake; finally she loved Jenny as a daughter, for her own sake. With the blessing of this growing family bond between them, Emma knew that Jenny would never want to stop her from seeing her grandson.

And Jenny knew that Emma had kept her part of their bargain too: she was no longer seeing Joe; he was out of the picture completely.

Somehow, all this living together and working together through all their difficulties had made for a more trusting relationship, which was all to the good because not long after moving to No. 9, Jenny heard word that Ivan would be coming home on leave and their plans for the wedding could begin.

CHAPTER SIXTEEN

Ivan and Jenny's wedding was planned for April 10th 1945. Jenny, after being disowned by her whole family, did not have to puzzle long over who should give her away. After consulting Ivan, they talked to the man who was the most qualified for the job.

Jenny said to Sam, 'You've been like a father to me ever since I arrived. Please be a father to me again and give me away at the church tomorrow!'

Sam with a firmly quavering voice said, 'It will be my honour...' and he reached for his large handkerchief and dabbed his eyes with it.

The next day was a blustery wedding day with showers, but the sun shone on the bride who looked so very pretty, wearing a neat, navy suit and pretty, pink blouse, with tiny, pink flowers on the small, navy pillbox hat and veil.

Ivan and Don, his friend and best man, were both resplendent in their naval uniforms with white ribbons in their collar fronts.

Derek in his blue romper suit *uniform*, was an imp fired up with all the excitement, taking nearly all of Emma's time and attention to hold on to him.

It was a small, unpretentious and precious wedding party that arrived at *Saint Columba's* church hall at three o'clock that afternoon. The wedding guests included: Robert who had been granted leave until nine o'clock the following day, Mary with little David, Ivan's Aunt Queenie, Annie, Eliza and Jackie.

Sam did his part in walking Jenny down the central aisle of the church hall and gave her away like he was the proudest father in all of Yorkshire.

The church piano was played splendidly and the choir sang like there were a few angels singing along with them.

After the happy couple said 'I do!' and were pronounced *man and wife* by the Reverend Maurice Morley, the little party returned to Ada's Terrace where Emma and Annie had prepared sandwiches and cake.

Emma had been able to buy a few little edible extras from work and store them away for the occasion, and Annie had brought eggs and chickens.

Friends and one-time regulars from *The Volunteer* came round, as well as neighbours bringing a bottle that they had saved for just such an occasion, all of them welcoming the chance for a bit of jollity.

The men stood smoking and coughing outside the door, while taking the opportunity to talk about something other than clothes, styles, fashions, or how to feed a hungry family on rations. After all - that was for the lasses!

Like a mouse being chased with a broom, Derek ran from one person to another, becoming more and more excited by the minute until he finally fell asleep on Eliza's knee and was carried off to bed.

The blackout curtains were drawn and the younger ones sat on the floor. Someone said, 'Give us a song, Geordie,' and Geordie gleefully did. It seemed that nearly everyone had an entertaining party piece which they wanted to perform. Napper Floyd played the spoons, Froggy Benson told jokes which, when repeated later in the cold light of day, did not sound nearly so funny as on the previous night when they were all convulsed with laughter. It seemed as if *all* the inhabitants of Ada's Terrace had packed themselves into Emma's house, and together they rejoiced rightly and royally on behalf of the newly weds.

Midnight had passed when the party broke up amidst much laughter and jokery, as Ivan, with a big smile on his face, carried Jenny over the threshold to No. 9 Ada's Terrace for the first time. Then came the sound of doors being closed all round the Terrace as everyone went home to bed. Emma made a final pot of tea and sat around with Annie, Jackie and Eliza, savouring the delights of the day.

Back in the jungle, George preferred not to dwell too much on the damp conditions, the dysentery, leeches, ticks, thorns and sores, and the scariness of some of his comrades!

Only the previous week, he had been temporarily unnerved by the *Gurkhas* who approached him asking for payment in return for producing, right there in front of them, the heads of Japanese soldiers.

More shockingly yet, he had woken up one morning to find an enormous constrictor snake wrapped around him. Unable to move, except for one free arm, he shouted urgently for help. In seconds, Boon Phi rushed into the clearing and at risk to herself, handed him the gun to shoot it before it could tighten up its coils and kill him. The men were happy to eat fresh meat that night - snake meat and lots of it!

George had heard from another group with a field radio, that British paratroops had landed somewhere south of Rangoon and were now engaged in the fight against the last pockets of enemy resistance. So it was greeted with dismay when they found that five of their own men had contracted jungle fever. With the sick soldiers alternately shivering, shouting and muttering incoherently, they could not move quietly at all. Desperate to not endanger the others and to make sure his sick men were looked after, George left them behind under the watchful eye of Boon Phi, before joining two *British Army* contingents up river to destroy the Japanese encampment there.

Moving quietly and cautiously through the jungle in case of suicidal snipers hidden in the trees, it was not long before they came across a bedraggled looking troop of Japanese soldiers carrying a white flag.

'Be careful lads!' George warned his men as they surrounded the troop, 'Watch out for knives or daggers; they aren't allowed to surrender, it isn't honourable!'

Every man had his finger on the trigger, but to their relief, no skirmishes occurred, as knives and swords were surrendered quietly. George looked intently at the Japanese officer standing at the head of his men. Immediately he recognised the face behind the glasses and the scar across the cheek, as the despicable Captain Sakamoto who was well known for his regime of sadism, and the brutality he inflicted.

Suddenly, the small Japanese officer started laughing at him. George raised his rifle quickly as the Japanese man continued to laugh and speak in Japanese.

'He deserves to die!' he thought. George felt his fingers tighten on the trigger as the smiling face of Sakamoto goaded him on.

'Not that way George!' the warning sound of his second in command, brought George back to his senses.

Taking a deep breath, he ordered his second to line the prisoners up ready for the march ahead, and as he did so, the smile faded from the Japanese captain's face.

Suddenly, Sakamoto, with lightning speed snatched back his sword and turning it to himself, plunged it into his own body. The ignominious self-murder was over in a flash and the body was thrown under a bush. A senior officer acquired a thousand year old Japanese sword as a trophy of war, and God only knew if Sakamoto's conscience had pronounced him guilty of so very much villainy.

The British troops continued on with their captives to a rendezvous in a clearing further north, where they were relieved of their prisoners.

The next day, having received permission to be able to pick up their sick comrades by night, George's squad returned to their own hideout in the stifling heat. The degree of humidity was unbearably high and their damp clothes clung to them.

Not finding their comrades where they had left them, they began casting around for tracks. The footprints headed in the direction of Boon Phi's village and were clearly more than those of the sick men they had left behind. The journey required them to make a very cautious detour around the village in case of any active Japanese presence.

The soldiers laid low under the cover of darkness and the jungle. Nothing was moving in the village. George and the men waited cautiously aware that this could be a trap set for them.

All night they waited as insects buzzed and unseen things rustled in the undergrowth. Birds hooted weirdly and chuckled in unearthly cacophony. Silently and patiently, they watched and waited until the darkness began to recede with the approach of day.

In the village all was quiet; very quiet. Finally they could make out some sort of structure in front of the long hut. The troop made their way quietly around the outskirts of the village until they could just make out the outline of a gallows.

Before it got really light, they crept up and found six human bodies hanging from it. Approaching, George could see that the bodies hanging from it were horribly slashed, bruised, burned and disfigured. Visual identification was difficult. Five of the bodies were the missing soldiers of their company. That much they could tell from their uniforms but they were otherwise almost unrecognisable because of the Japanese torture methods.

Fortunately for the patrol, though not for their comrades, they knew that, raving with fever, they had been too ill to have said much that would have compromised their mission.

The other on the gallows was smaller and slighter and had long hair and a blood-stained white scar. It was the mutilated body of Boon Phi. Grief, loss and anguish tore swiftly and deeply at George.

He turned away and was physically sick, as were some of the others. He only prayed that Boon Phi had died before her captors had discovered that she was a young woman.

Quietly the patrol made their way round the long hut, all was silent. It was the odious silence of death. When they looked inside the hut, it was a further scene of carnage. All the women and children of the village had been murdered. But then came a rustle of something or someone in the corner. The noise caused the patrol to swing round, rifles at the ready... It was the sound of one of the old women who was still alive.

With great care, they propped her up and gave her a drink from their canteens. She tried to speak. It was obvious that she was dying from her wounds and they recognised the name *Sakamoto,* before she fell back where she lay.

George ordered his men to cut down the bodies and lay them in the long hut. He longed to bury them or at least burn the hut, but he knew that it was far too dangerous. Murderers, even in Japanese uniform, do revisit the scenes of their crimes and there was no wisdom in lingering there for a moment longer while there was still a war to be won.

At the edge of the clearing and just for a moment, George looked back. All was quiet and peaceful. With heavy hearts, the little company made their way to the next settlement where they were greeted with soldierly warmth and comradely relief by others from their own battalion. They shared what little rations and water they had and made contact with Headquarters by means of a scratchy radio.

Encouraged by the contact, they continued on, encountering three more villages which had also been laid waste and the inhabitants murdered. Despite the atrocities, the patrol did not give up on its duties until later that week when they were taken by truck to Rangoon: there all was hustle and bustle, documentation and debriefing. And finally, they all got their long-awaited bath.

George lay back in the water and felt the last months drain away with the sweat and grime. Tears began to roll down his face and into the water as he thought of Boon Phi and the future they had dreamed of. He knew he would never go back to that little village. Even if he could find it, Boon Phi had died at the hands of their enemies - and with her went his dreams of love and romance - but not his hopes.

Back in England, the war was over! In the streets, cries were heard, 'We're safe, we're safe! No more bombing. We aren't going to die. Our men will be coming home! The war is over!'

There was dancing in the streets: people sang the popular song: *Doing the Lambeth Walk* and joyous parties were everywhere. The celebrations were well deserved and Hitler's attempt to subjugate Britain and the world were over for ever.

After those wonderful, rapturous first days of euphoria, gradually everything began to settle down to normality. Peace came like a benevolent anti-climax, rather like walking into the strength of a gale and then feeling it stopping suddenly. The work, the rationing all went on as before, but at least the air raids had ceased.

Emma listened with interest to the two young girls at work describing their part in the celebrations. On the 8th May 1945, they both had a whale of a time celebrating *Victory in Europe Day (V.E. Day)*. They had gone out together to see a naval vessel which was moored in the dock and having joined the queue of visitors, were all agog to look around the ship and spy out any nice, young sailors.

Sandra had ironed a sailor's collar for him and the girls had been much admired in their turn! After this they had taken part in the night's victory celebrations; walking round the streets; visiting the parties where everyone was welcome; joining in the dancing; and viewing the many *V.E. Day* bonfires that blazed around the city. But these fires were so very different from the fire raining from the skies during the bombing raids on Hull; these fires were fires of joyful celebration.

Sam was at work, and, for the dockers, life went on much the same as usual. There was work to be done. They had people who were depending on them to move cargoes and the dockers could do their own celebrating later.

However, listening to a *B.B.C.* radio broadcast one evening, Sam had heard a speaker in a discussion programme say something that stuck in his mind: *It is a strange thing that people can push themselves to extraordinary limits in a crisis and yet when the crisis is over, they become like an unstrung bow.*

For Sam, there had been massive demands on his time, sleep, skills, energy, physical strength, commitment, relationships and everything about him - because of the war, his work and his volunteering as a fire watcher. Now the war was over, he knew that he desperately needed to recover and resupply his own inward resources. As he had told Emma, a week into the post-war peace, 'I am going to recover from this war, even if it busts me!' As part of his solemn commitment, Sam used up some of his hard-earned savings to get his beloved boat *Galilee* set up with a small but powerful inboard motor. He made a mental note to spend a whole day, taking his coble under power, to explore the River Hull as his own personal way of celebrating the transition from war to peace. It did something for him that the beauty of the river and the surrounding countryside did not disappointment him.

Back at work, Sam and his fellow dockers were grateful that at least there was no more debris to shift from the bombing raids and there were no more ships sunk in the docks where they were working. That there had been dock labour reform was a cause for celebration as well. It had been a big change for the better. No more was there the uncertainty of the casual labour system, under which Sam had worked when he became a docker.

The National Dock Labour Corporation had come into being in 1943: now all the dock workers were *N.D.L.C.* registered and received their own record book. Their book was stamped each time they turned up for work at the call stand. If there was no work, they were guaranteed five shillings for every stamp, although, if there was work, mainly piecework, they could earn more money. This new system meant that there was a steady pool of labour available and that the more experienced dockers were not lost from the work force.

It was all progress and a far cry from waiting at the end of the gangplank in the hope of working and earning that day. Sam, like many others, often wondered what their fathers would have made of it. They would have thought they were *in clover*.

One of the biggest post-war events that happened in July of that year was the General Election. Throughout the war years a coalition government had run the country under the Conservative Prime Minister, Winston Churchill. Winston had been a hugely inspiring leader in wartime and he rather expected to win the next election because of his wartime popularity.

Such suspense! All the ballot boxes were sealed up for three weeks to allow for the postal votes of overseas servicemen and women to be collected. But on the 25th of July 1945 the result was known. Labour had won and people wanted social reform.

There were so many things to put right, not least the housing situation; in Hull alone, ninety-five per cent of the housing stock had been either damaged or destroyed. Nationwide, it was not so surprising that there was a general shortage of materials for patching up homes or building them.

Families that had moved out of town to escape the bombing were coming back and, quite naturally, wives were anxious to have a home ready for their husbands to return to.

Then there were those in the Services whose relations petitioned anyone who had anything to do with housing to find them a home and relations who had boarded homeless members of their family were now desperate to have their homes to themselves once more. All the houses in Ada's Terrace were occupied now with some new families as well as the long-standing ones.

Jenny, Ivan and little Derek were also settled into their family life at No. 9. Emma liked nothing more than to take young Derek with her on her visits to *Bann's Farm*.

Eliza enjoyed these visits, never failing to comment on *how like our Billy,* the little lad was. He would be starting school after Easter. How quickly the years had passed!

It was as if the ghost of Lily Hawkins still haunted Emma, so often she thought of her. Even though Lily and family had moved away before the war began, they had kept in touch until the unthinkable had happened and Lily Hawkins, Harry and little Shirley had passed away.

Meanwhile, on the Home Front, it seemed that everything was still rationed and very severely so. It drove people to question, 'Who won the war anyway?' The implication was that peacetime should bring peace and prosperity, not hardship.

The people of Britain and Germany were faced with the drastic need for the rebuilding of towns and cities, while, at the same time, facing an uncommon shortage of all the materials that were required for such undertakings.

Produced mainly in factories, which previously in wartime, had been manufacturing tanks and armaments, *prefabs*, or single storey prefabricated buildings, began to appear as an aid to overcoming the housing shortage. Largely made out of moulded, concrete slabs, these prefab parts were subsequently erected on site. This particular format for the swift construction of buildings and residences, proved to be quite popular.

The new government of Prime Minister Clement Attlee had a lot to work on. *The Beveridge Report* had come out in 1942 but now after the finish of the Second World War its recommendations for a Welfare State had to be implemented.

Sir William Beveridge addressed the matter of post-war financial benefits for the unemployed and other matters when he said:

> *Social insurance fully developed may provide income security; it is an attack upon Want. But Want is one only of five giants on the road of reconstruction and in some ways the easiest to attack. The others are Disease, Ignorance, Squalor and Idleness.*

The success of the Social Security scheme was to be augmented by the introduction of the *Family Allowance* and the free *National Health Service*. School education became free of charge, along with free spectacles, free false teeth and dental treatment! As for being paid for the children you had, that was the stuff dreams were made of! It all seemed too good to be true!

Sadly, for some unfortunate wives whom Emma knew of, there were mean husbands who actually deducted, as if it was their own pocket money, the child allowance money from their wife's housekeeping money.

So the year of 1945 drew to a close, and if Christmas was still a time of austerity and scarcities, at least the war was over, and surely 1946 would be better?

With some sadness, the time came when Emma found herself surplus to requirements at *Sweetings'*. Peacetime meant that former employees could return from the war to claim their old jobs. Two soldiers returned to do just that.

Sam was on a good assured income in his dock work and liked to think of himself as the main breadwinner.

So Emma, having brought up children and being a proud housewife, enjoyed having some pleasurable time on her hands: there were still many good things to do with her life.

Emma and Sam had heard from George who was still in Burma. He had suffered a nasty bout of dysentery, but was hoping desperately to be home before the summer. A lot of the soldiers who had been in the Far East still considered themselves to have been the *Forgotten Army*. Indeed, a group of servicemen, in despair at ever getting home, had actually mutinied.

In Rangoon, George and the rest of his troop were going through the waiting period of adjustment back to civilian life and to richer food than they had enjoyed for some time.

There were unpleasant blood tests to be administered for insect or water-borne diseases. But worst of all were the ugly nightmares that haunted the soldiers who had seen so much horror and destruction - and sometimes their cries could be heard in the night.

When George was unable to sleep, he looked at the little photo of Sam and Emma that he carried in his wallet. Since he had been back in camp, he had received a letter from home, and - old news or not - by the time it reached him he was just so pleased to have had a letter from home! It told him of Joanie's visit and her appearance in the show in Hull, and of Sam and Emma being in the audience.

So often in his mind, George had remembered Joanie on the make-shift stage in the desert. Where was she now, he wondered?

CHAPTER SEVENTEEN

To Joanie, when she looked back on it, it all seemed so long ago now: catching the train out of Hull *Paragon Station*, going off with the dance troupe and the stomach-churning days which followed it.

At the time of her running away from home, so many questions flooded her mind. Was she doing the right thing? What if it went wrong? Would her Dad come looking for her? She knew in her heart that stern as he was at times, he loved her enough to try very hard to find her.

The truth was that Joanie had covered her tracks very well. Her father had no idea where to start; even his very best efforts could not reveal where she had gone to. Her secrecy and her deception were like Arctic snow covering her footprints completely.

To Joanie, her home was not the place for her to bring her friends. After all, they were the kind of people that her family would label as *toffee-nosed*. Although Mary was her sister, Joanie did not confide in her since she knew that Mary would sneer at her ambitions. In Joanie's eyes, ambition was so much more important than relationships; this was a view which was confirmed in her by the shallow books that she read. They seemed to emphasize that only the outward show of things really mattered. Consequently, she thought that good looks, pretty clothes and good stage performances could give her the good times that she craved, the applause that she wanted and indeed, the world itself.

Joanie's first theatre performance was exactly the start that she wanted with all eyes on her - there she was on the stage in a spangled costume dancing amidst the audience's applause.

Mr Vernon was a hard taskmaster, keeping them at rehearsals every day and drilling them like a Company Sergeant Major. He had strict rules about what time the girls should be in, and they even had to ask his permission to go out at all.

As rehearsals progressed Joanie also noticed that certain girls seemed to be in special favour. First it was Barbara who had the solo spot and then it was Sylvia. What was their secret? Joanie felt that she could dance as well as either of them and that her voice was better too.

She shared a room with Barbara who occasionally came in very late. But when Joanie enquired whether her friend had not been in trouble with Mr Vernon, Barbara just tapped her nose, meaning for her to mind her own business. 'You're such an innocent,' she said mocking Joanie, 'if you were nice to Mr Vernon, you might get to lead the chorus.'

Joanie, though very naive compared with some of the girls, already had her suspicions as to what being nice to Mr Vernon meant as he had patted her bottom when she and the girls were pushing by him to get on stage. Later on, he had put his arm round her in a way that was not paternal. 'Think of me as a kind of extra father,' he had said in his oily manner, 'I'll take care of you!'

Incautiously, Joanie dismissed these warning lights, along with the whispered stories of the casting couch and other vicissitudes of offstage life as being exaggerated and not worth listening to. She felt strongly that she was meant for stardom, fame and fortune; that was her goal and she felt sure she could achieve it.

It was very rare for Joanie's troupe to stay, as they toured, for more than a week in any one place, and so they had very little time to see very much of any town that they visited; this was no sightseeing holiday! Going from town to town, there was the constant rush of the train journeys; *living out of a suitcase* they called it.

Any ideas of romance, with bedazzled young men waiting at the stage door were speedily sidelined: the busyness of rehearsals and shows occupied most of their waking hours. Joanie also reminded herself she was not going to get caught up in the marriage trap. After all, what sort of life did her mother have? Not exciting!

One night after a show in Rochester, Barbara told Joanie she was going out to get some fish and chips. So Joanie pottered about in the bedroom in her favourite silk kimono, washing her hair, creaming her face and keeping to her own strict beauty regime. As she lolled on her bed reading a magazine, the door opened. Not looking up, she said, 'I bet you didn't bring me any chips, Barbara!'

The voice that answered was not Barbara's but Stanley Vernon's.

'I've got something *betterer* than chips…' he said as - with a face flushed with drink - he lurched into the room carrying a bottle of port and two glasses. He kicked the door shut behind him as Joanie raised herself up, now on the defensive.

Feeling like a rabbit being eyed by a stoat at close quarters, Joanie said in a husky voice, 'Barbara will be back very soon.'

Stanley Vernon laughed a less than sober laugh, 'Not if she knows what's good for her, but Joanie, it's time we got to know each other better and we'll see if you're ready for promotion in the troupe.' He poured two glasses of cheap port, which Joanie did not particularly like. 'Come on, drink up,' her mentor urged, 'there's plenty more in the bottle.' Joanie took a small sip and shuddered. 'That's better. Now what would you say if I gave you a solo spot in the second chorus?'

'Thank you…' muttered Joanie.

'Well, I should hope so!' he said while topping up his glass. 'Come on, drink up, you're getting all behind!' And laughing at his own joke he said, 'It wouldn't do for a dancer to be all behind, not that you're all behind, you've got quite a nice little figure really.'

Joanie tried to edge away, but Stanley Vernon would not be sidetracked, 'Come on darlin,' you may as well be nice to me, it will do your career no end of good,' and he made his move.

She wanted nothing to do with this, or him. But the next half hour was full of disgust, shame and terror for her. No career was worth that depth of humiliation but she would not let him destroy her. When it was all over, Joanie gathered her kimono round her, tears running down her face.

'Silly girl,' said Mr Vernon, 'you liked it really and you'll always remember your first time.' Collecting up the bottle and glasses, he lurched out of the room.

Joanie shuddered with a disgust that shook all of her body. When all was quiet, she made her way to the bathroom and ran the hot water, but when she saw the blood on her kimono she was violently sick. She scrubbed herself as if she was muddy and when her *no-friend-at-all* Barbara came in later, she stayed facing the wall with the bedclothes pulled up to her neck, saying nothing. She never ever wore the kimono again. The next day at rehearsal Mr Vernon put Joanie in the solo spot while Barbara and Sylvia nudged each other and winked.

When they went on stage the next night, the performers were not to know that there was an agent in the audience. Brenda Collinges had come especially to see and hear the tenor, but she saw the rest of the show and in the brown-haired girl in the dance troupe, she liked what she saw.

Unannounced, Brenda came to the draughty corner that served as the girls' dressing room, 'Great show, kids!' she said. Some of the girls sniggered. Who was this old bat? Brenda fearlessly made her way over to Joanie who was brushing her hair, and started a few enquiries, 'Are you under contract?' Brenda asked. Joanie was not sure. 'Has Mr Vernon got your parents' permission for you to be working these hours?'

Joanie's whole story about how she had joined the troupe came out under the influence of a thoughtful and knowledgeable listener. Brenda Collinges looked grim. She had met people like Mr Vernon before. She had a long talk with Joanie, and said that she could offer her work then and there entertaining people in factories doing war work.

Joanie thought it sounded marvellous, 'But Mr Vernon might not let me go,' Joanie voiced her fears.

Brenda said that she would deal with Mr Vernon, and deal with him she did. But not before informing the other girls that they were not being paid enough. Before she went, Brenda had a further talk with Joanie, 'Yes, you have talent, but that alone is not enough. To become professional you must work hard, take singing lessons, learn how to breathe properly and so on. But we can work out your lessons between engagements, because of course you will need to work!'

Brenda came to meet Joanie on Saturday night as she finished off the week in Stanley Vernon's troupe. She arranged new lodgings for her and on the following Monday, she began work in the chorus of a weekly show.

There were rehearsals in the mornings, singing lessons some afternoons and performances in the evenings. It was similar to the shows that she had done with *Vernon's Variety Sparklers*, but there was a different feel to it. 'You are on the way up,' she told herself. But it was to be another twelve months before things really changed, when Brenda got Joanie a spot with the famous *B.B.C.* Radio *Workers' Playtime* concerts.

Playing in the canteens of factories which were doing war work, *Workers' Playtime* was a wildly popular radio show. It featured people with great voice or musical talent; comedians, pianists, singers, bird imitators and actors doing playlets. If you were in *Workers' Playtime* you were somebody! 'Now Joanie, you are *truly* on your way up!' she thought.

Regardless of being well down on the bill she was elated because, 'talent will rise,' she told herself, 'and being the top of the bill will do for me!'

Joanie's voice had greatly improved with the training, so much so that she did more singing than dancing; and sometimes, if they needed an extra girl, she helped out with other acts in the show. 'All good experience and no Mr Vernon!' she thought happily to herself.

Sometimes, Joanie thought about her family but was sure that she had been right to leave home to make her way on the stage and surely her Mum and Dad would see that now? So it was with something of a shock that she had met up with Mary while doing that munitions factory show in the Midlands. But Mary had not only been hostile but had called her a selfish cow! And Joanie felt that she was completely misunderstood.

When she was seventeen and a half and would have been preparing for call-up in the women's services or munitions work, Brenda found a way to get Joanie on to the *E.N.S.A.* show (humorously nicknamed *Every Night Something Awful*). The work involved visiting various army camps and entertaining the troops. It enabled her to brush shoulders with the really famous British stars of the radio, stage and screen, watch how they worked, and it was something that she really enjoyed. In imitation of Vera Lynn, the *Forces Sweetheart*, Joanie soon adopted the name *Forces Songbird*, and attracted quite a following. There had even been talk of her making a record.

Then some overseas engagements became available, and instead Joanie found herself entertaining the troops as part of a concert party in North Africa, looked after by a young officer called Charles.

It was during that trip that she had suddenly met her brother George in the desert and heard of her eldest brother Billy's death. Then it had slowly begun to dawn on her how much her parents were grieving.

Saying goodbye to George had been a wrench for her but then her concert party had gone to Cairo. There she had buried herself in the work and the adulation that it brought her.

When the *E.N.S.A.* party returned again to England, there followed more touring of the camps and then engagements in gradually-liberated France and then back again to England, where she performed at the music hall in Hull.

It was Brenda, her mentor, who suggested to Joanie that she should try now to broaden her horizons by doing more in the field of dramatics and Brenda arranged for Joanie to audition for a place in a repertory theatre.

Her audition successful, Joanie was accepted for a new repertory company called *Reed Marsh Theatre.* There she was given small parts and learned to put her hand to such chores as were expected of minor members of the company. It irked her ambitious streak to have to do menial work, but she desperately needed the experience that the company provided, more than she even admitted to herself.

Joanie felt that she was capable of playing a proper leading role right there and then but - oh - the competition between people in the acting field!

Reed Marsh Theatre's leading lady was Drina Summers. She had striking features and never let anyone forget it - especially the new upstart, Joanie.

The leading man, Peter Winchester was not particularly handsome but had a large stage presence and the sound and timbre of his voice did things for Joanie, just as surely as it did for the ladies in the audience.

One afternoon before the show, Joanie knocked on the door of Drina's dressing room.

'Come in,' she called and when Joanie entered, there sat Drina with no clothes on.

'Oh, it's you,' she said on seeing Joanie, 'I was expecting Peter, but he wouldn't need to knock.' Watching the expression on Joanie's face, she said, 'Don't look so shocked Darling! We've played enough bedroom scenes, Peter and I! But it's the best kind of acting when the audience think it's real, and we know, don't we?'

Joanie, astounded by such behaviour, smiled weakly, made an excuse and left the room, but in the corridor, she met Peter clad in a dressing gown. He stopped when he saw Joanie who stammered out, 'Drina's expecting you!'

'Of course,' said Peter smiling, 'I told her to have the kettle on.'

Joanie wanted to say that the kettle was all she would have on, but held her tongue instead.

Although put on her guard by this incident, as the weeks went by and Peter gave her acting lessons and better parts, she was so thrilled to have such tuition from the illustrious actor that Joanie began to relax, and as she let her guard down, began to fall in love with her mentor.

In the background, Drina watched events, saw the signs, and seethed with jealousy, often making spiteful remarks about newcomers to the company. But, since Peter was the producer as well as the leading man, he always had the last word and Joanie was blissfully happy. As they increasingly worked together, the parts that he played with her offstage became intimate and very personal. Star-struck and feeling that she was in a romantic Hollywood film Joanie allowed herself to be wooed and gave herself to him freely without truly understanding why.

One night before the show, she walked down the corridor to Peter's room to ask his advice on a scene and to hear that delightfully resonant voice speaking just to her. As she passed the dressing room of another cast member, she overheard two people talking and the door was sufficiently ajar for her to hear her name and the names of two others. Stopping in the corridor, she listened to the conversation for a minute before quickly retreating to the nearby toilet and closing the door behind her. Joanie was struck by what she had heard: Peter was in a long term relationship with *both* Drina *and* Troy Harding - another male actor from the group - while Joanie, like many others before her, was merely regarded as light entertainment. Joanie shook as nausea overwhelmed her. She had wanted Peter to make love to her again, indeed she was planning it with the hope of winning herself a deeper, more secure place in his affections. Competition with other women she could deal with, but not with another man.

As Joanie left the toilet white-faced, Drina came pattering down the corridor. Observing Joanie's stricken demeanour closely and seeing the look on her face, Drina guessed what had happened, as it had happened with other girls before her.

She smiled maliciously, 'I could have told you Peter swings both ways, but I thought you would find out soon enough. Quite the little prude, aren't you, Serena?'

Joanie hurried back to the dressing room she shared with other less exalted members of the cast, her mind in a complete turmoil. What was she to do? She had been going to tell Peter that she was probably pregnant. She did not want a baby, Lord, no! And with the gossip stunningly confirmed by Drina's own words, she felt such revulsion that she did not want him either. But what was she going to do?

Joanie, had unlike Jenny, knowingly cut herself off from normal contact with her own family. Did she not believe that her career was more important than any relationship, including her baby? How then could she go back to Ada's Terrace and ask them to help her? Her own shame and pride would stand in the way of her doing so. No, going home was not an option. How she imagined Nanna Shushkin would crow, 'Fancy the clever one getting caught like that! You would think, at her age, *clever clogs* would have known better.'

After some days, Drina, who never missed anything, drew her to one side, 'You're pregnant, aren't you?'

Joanie nodded dumbly. How many of the company had noticed?

'Well, what are you going to do about it? Does Peter know?' Joanie shook her head.

'Peter's a dreamer, he would have expected you to take care of things. And don't think you're the first star-crazed idiot, to fall into that trap. Peter doesn't want a family, I should know - I, who have to mother him!'

Again Joanie shook her head.

Drina sighed with exasperation, 'I can get you some pills, we'll have to say you've got flu for a few days,' she offered.

Joanie tried to thank her.

'Don't thank me!' was the answer, 'It will cost you.'

'How much?' Joanie stammered, painfully aware that saving was not a strong point in her make-up.

Drina named a sum that, with the money due to her in wages, Joanie could just about manage to get by.

'And another thing,' Drina went on, 'it's about time you were looking for another part somewhere else. You're getting stale here, and I'm not about to stand by and see you get parts that should be mine!'

Stunned by the whole turn of events, Joanie nodded her acquiescence. Yes, that's what she needed: a fresh start. She would get in touch with Brenda and see what was about. Already she almost - almost felt better.

If there was one week that Joanie preferred to draw a veil over, it was that week. She took the abortion pills and felt ill with such a pain that she had never ever imagined before. The human life within her came to an end, and the cupboard door that she had tried to close on her conscience did not always stay shut. More tears were shed by Joanie than ever had been in the whole of her life. But Drina kept her part of the bargain and told everyone that Joanie had flu.

Two of the girls in the company came to see her with flowers and magazines, for Joanie was popular with the other girls, always ready to help them with make-up, or learning their lines.

'Drina is like the cat that got the cream now that you're away,' they told her.

Picking her words carefully, Joanie said that Drina had been very kind and helpful.

'She would be!' was the other girls' cynical opinion.

At the end of the week, Joanie rang Brenda Collinges, hoping to make an appointment for an interview with her, but instead, a strange, male voice answered the telephone. She soon learned that Brenda had retired and the agency was now run by John Fielding.

'Serena Waters, yes, that was it,' and, 'would you ring back, say in a week's time?'

A week later, Joanie caught the train to London and went to see John Fielding. It seemed strange to sit in the office without Brenda's cheerful personality there and unnerving that Brenda had not let her know.

John Fielding was a man in his forties, dark-haired and tall. 'My dear Miss Waters,' he greeted her, when his secretary ushered her in, 'do sit down. I've been talking to Brenda about you, since you were her protégé, and she has told me all about you.' He sifted through the papers in front of him. 'Brenda said that song and dance were your strong points, but that she had recommended you for a place in repertory theatre to help you to widen your experience.'

Joanie nodded, 'Yes, I've had ten months there.'

'But you really preferred the other work? There is one thing coming up that you might like to audition for.'

Joanie leant forward in her chair, this sounded promising.

'Edward Taylor is bringing his musical show across from America. The principals are coming over to England to start the show off and I could get you an audition for chorus work, and possibly understudying... Who knows where it may lead?' he said encouragingly.

'Yes please!' Joanie whispered. She could do it, she knew she could. She found her voice and said, 'The songs from the show are already hits, the music is full of good, catchy tunes and the words flow naturally. And if I get the job of understudy then my next big chance may come!'

John Fielding gently reminded her that first she had to pass the audition, but he liked the enthusiasm that Joanie exuded and agreed with Brenda that Joanie would go far.

Happily, *Reed Marsh Theatre* had begun to seem a long way off already to Joanie, but the lessons remained and human life had become more precious to her.

The audition was fixed for the second Thursday in May, and the show was to open in London in the middle of June.

Joanie had, with a strong sense of relief, already finished at *Reed Marsh Theatre, a*nd so on the second Thursday in May, she went for the audition, and was one of the many hopeful girls selected.

True there had been a little leaving party for Serena, with presents, flowers, perfume, even a travelling clock.

At the party, Peter had made a speech, 'We all know that Serena will go far.'

Drina had a half smile on her lips, and Joanie knew that the other girl was thinking, 'but not far enough!'

Somehow, Joanie did not care, because she was on the way up, she just knew it!

CHAPTER EIGHTEEN

Mr Brabham from *Home Farm* was a frequent visitor now to neighbouring *Bann's Farm* and to Annie and Eliza. He would make the excuse that he must call round to see Jackie and give him his orders for the next day. He was always happy to accept the gracious offer of a cup of tea and a piece of cake. For Eliza, it was easy to see that the real attraction for Charlie Brabham was Emma's sister, Annie; she now had an admirer!

For Annie herself, she liked the gruff farmer rather much, but she said to herself that nothing could come of it, 'at our ages indeed!'

Of course being a farmer, Charlie Brabham was not a man to be easily deterred, not least in his courtship. His visits grew a little longer and Annie's feelings for him shone brightly through her eyes.

One night as Annie was seeing him out, he took her hand, 'I truly love you and want to marry you, if you'll have me.'

Annie was pleased beyond words, but worried. Clinging to his hand, she said, 'Please give me time to think about it. A week is all I need.' Agreeing to her request, he left her to think about his earnest proposal. Annie had some very practical questions in her mind. What would Emma and Sam think, and what about Eliza?

When approached by Annie on the matter of Charlie Brabham's proposal, Eliza was tickled pink! Clasping her hands together, she rocked back and forward where she sat, in her joyful merriment. 'Of course! Why not? Anyone could see that he's keen on you,' she said with her eyes sparkling, and then after a thought she said with puzzlement, 'you're not worrying about me are you?'

Smiling, with a hand on her arm, Annie swiftly reassured her, 'Charlie says there's room for us all at the farmhouse. He wants you to come as well. Could you do with the move and upheaval?' Eliza was sure that she could and began happily rocking again.

When Sam joined Emma for her weekly visit, Annie, with a blush on her face, hesitatingly told them also about Charlie's proposal. Sam's face radiated a fond and happy grin which stretched from ear to ear. He instantly reached out and hugged his dear sister-in-law.

Emma was slower on the uptake, but as the seconds ticked by, she became amazingly and happily surprised and the more she thought about it, the more attractive it became. For now, Annie had Eliza for company and they did get on so well together, but Eliza was getting on in years and there would come a day when she would not be there. More than just family and friends, what Annie needed was a good husband! After all, her dear Annie, with Charlie Brabham, would be loved and cared for by a good and honest man; no longer would she be left on her own in years to come. That would be wonderful! Emma hugged her sister Annie and together they danced around the room as if they had springs in their heels!

At the end of the week, Annie sent Jackie with a message to Charlie, asking him to come round to the house. Tactfully, Eliza, Sam and Emma remained in the living room while Annie and Charlie met with each other in the kitchen.

Charlie took his courage in both hands and said, 'I believe that you have an answer for me?'

Hesitatingly, Annie said, 'I've been thinking about your proposal and I have asked if anyone would be hurt. The answer is: no one will be hurt and - yes - I love you too, with all my heart!' With cuddles, kisses and the murmurs of true love, they became engaged and drifted into the living room to spread the good news, to the merriment of all, additionally supported by a glass or two of long-treasured sherry to toast the engaged couple.

And there was more good news on the way as Ivan had been home on leave just after Christmas and Jenny was expecting another baby. Houses were now being awarded to needy people on a points scheme taking into account such factors as being without hot running water, or having a baby on the way and so it led to Jenny qualifying for one of the delightful new *prefabs*.

When she received the offer in the post she burst into tears. Tears of happiness shed at such good fortune. Then she laughed and smiled until her face ached. Going with the news to No. 7, Jenny hugged Emma while begging her to come and see them often. Unfortunately, the *prefab* was quite a distance from Ada's

Terrace and so it felt to Emma like it was causing a geographical split in the family. Everyone had grown so used to Derek trotting in and out to bring his latest school drawing to show them.

Moving preparations took days, as they do, but later in the week while making her farewells on the way to *prefab-land*, Jenny again reassured Emma that she and Derek were going to be frequent visitors to Ada's Terrace. Moreover, as there was the new baby's arrival to be planned for, would Emma be able to lend Jenny a hand?

'Just try keeping me away!' said Emma with a tearful grin.

There did not seem to be much chance of Emma and Sam moving anywhere else as yet, although there were rumbles at the council meetings about the need for slum clearances to be made.

But Emma and many others like her clearly did not think of their homes as slum dwellings. After all, they were clean and well-kept houses. All the same, it would be so nice to have a beautiful new bathroom and to have hot water on tap throughout the house!

In the next few weeks, Annie began spending a lot of time in making preparations at *Home Farm* which was to be their own new marital home. Charlie, the proud fiancé, knowing his limitations, had given her a free hand in arranging the rooms and decorating them. He handed over his clothing coupons so that Annie could get some material for curtains and bed linen, and also money to buy them. After all, nothing was too good for his Annie! After talking it over with Emma and Sam, Annie had considered putting *Bann's Farm* along with its land up for sale and sharing the financial proceeds with them. She felt it was only fair, since Bert had left the house to her, that Emma, her own sister, should have her share too.

Sam and Emma, in turn, argued that Annie had given so much of her life to caring for her parents that it was proper for her to inherit.

Charlie, the new source of finance, then surprised them all by saying that he wanted to buy it! *Bann's Farm* and its land adjoined his farm and he would have it valued and give them a fair price for it; any furniture or belongings that Annie wanted to take with her when she married could be moved up to *Home Farm* but Annie could continue sharing a room with Eliza until the wedding. In truth, as the day of the wedding approached,

Charlie and Annie were so happy that nothing could cloud their joy.

Rationing was still as severe as ever though and Emma was not able to get any little extras now that she no longer worked at the shop.

'We don't need a cake and all that palaver,' said Annie, 'it's not as if we were a young couple just starting out.' But Charlie killed a pig, and somehow after doing a deal with the local baker, there was a lovely iced sponge cake as the centrepiece on the table. Also adorning the table were some of the breadcakes which the village baker was particularly noted for making, along with a large, succulent pork pie.

Mary had come over for the occasion with young David, and Emma was just delighted to have them staying with her and Sam at Ada's Terrace. Jenny and Derek spent a lot of time with them too. David and Derek, the two little boys, got on quite well together. They were like the terrible twins and whatever mischief one did not think of, the other one certainly did!

Annie had a happy shopping trip with Emma and joyfully bought a pale-blue, two-piece suit for the big day.

Eliza chose to wear her smart and trusty navy-flowered dress and navy straw hat, 'I don't need a new outfit,' she declared. Age however was slowly creeping up on her and she just had not got the strength to make the journey into town to go shopping.

It was a cool but sunny day when Charlie and Annie became man and wife together in the lovely, little village church of Redtoft; he kissed his bride and his face turned bright pink with happiness, and in turn, she clung to his arm while her eyes brimmed with the tears of so much happiness.

Although it was intended to be a relatively low-key social occasion, no one was too surprised when most of the villagers turned out to wish them well. Annie loved community life and was well known to be always ready to help in any way that she could in village events. Charlie too was a well-respected member within the farming community and loved the village. When the bride and groom left the church porch, they walked through a flurry of flying confetti. Flowers were joyfully thrown at them in hearty celebration of their marriage.

After a pleasing and amicable wedding feast meal with all the family, Charlie and Sam strolled around the farmyard in companionable fashion.

'I'll take care of Annie and Eliza,' promised Charlie, 'and there's a home here for Jackie for as long as he wants one, though if the girls in the village have their way, he'll be wed before long!'

Sam nodded his approval; he knew that Charlie was a good man and had all the family's best interests at heart.

Leaving the village with an aura of happiness and contentment, Sam and family made their way back on the bus to Ada's Terrace.

Meanwhile Annie, still feeling a little strange but contented, drew the curtains in her new home and put the kettle on.

Charlie and Jackie had already been out to do the rounds of the farmyard, making sure everything was secure. Everyone retired for the night and the farmer and his wife began their honeymoon in their newly shared home.

All over the country, a new craze for housing had begun. People were so desperate for homes to live in that they were taking over disused army camps and moving in. This was so, despite the fact that even essential services such as running water and electricity had been cut off and the old huts were cheerless. People felt that they needed homes in order to survive, and if the council could not help them, then they would help themselves.

The little house at *Bann's Farm* where Annie, Bert and Eliza had lived, stood empty and forlorn in the daylight. So much had happened there, happy times with Bert, and happy times also when Emma and the family came to visit.

One evening, as Annie and Charlie took their evening stroll round the two farms, they saw a drift of smoke coming from the *Bann's Farm* chimney, and found that they too had squatters, at least for a little while.

As time went on, Annie blossomed well as the wife of Charlie Brabham. Jackie still worked on the farm and had a girlfriend called Freda, who lived in the village and there were plans for an engagement at Christmas.

The weeks rolled by, and soon it was time for Jenny to have her baby. Quietly confident, Jenny planned to have the baby at her new home. Greta Smith the midwife was already booked, and very graciously, Emma had agreed to come and look after Jenny as well.

And so it was that, when the time came, Jenny sent her neighbour's lad, Jimmy, with a note to Emma, to say that she had started in labour.

Jenny's neighbours, Ethel and Fred were good, kind-hearted people who were only too happy to look after Derek when he came out of school. In fact Ethel was bubbling up with excitement over the expected new baby, and this helped to keep Jenny buoyed up too.

Amidst such happiness, Ethel's grandma was quick to try and burst their bubble, since she was never one to look on the bright side. 'You won't be laughing in a little while,' she said, 'young mums have it so easy these days. Now when I had my bains...' she carried on enthusiastically grumbling, almost as if she might have thought that grumbling was a command of God!

Fortuitously, Emma arrived at Ivan and Jenny's little house at the same time as the midwife, who was there to examine Jenny. After checking that the labour was going well, Greta smiled encouragingly and to everyone's peace and contentment, pronounced herself satisfied with the way things were progressing, 'an' I 'ave another call that I gotta make an' I'll be back soon.'

Jenny Hawkins could not help but draw a contrast between how things had gone with Derek's birth and the way that this one was happening. The pall of sadness from Billy's death had been eased considerably, Jenny herself was well-nourished and the baby was full term.

How glad Jenny was to be able to grip Emma's hand at the same time as the strong pains of labour gripped her! At a quarter to eight, the long-awaited baby girl entered the world crying noisily, causing Emma to say, 'Well, there's nothing wrong with her lungs!' Feeling the joy of having brought a new baby to the birth, Jenny - when she held the baby close for the first time - shed a few tears of relief and contentment.

Later, a subdued Derek was allowed in to see and admire his new sister.

'What shall we call her?' Jenny asked her small son.

'Susan's my friend at school,' he said, 'can our baby be called Susan?'

Jenny said, 'That will be lovely!' and so the new baby was called Susan.

Emma bustled about getting her grandson Derek ready for bed and Ethel made the tea and took away the washing.

With all the excitement going on, no one had much sleep that night apart from Derek who, *sleeping the sleep of the just*, proved to be no bother to anyone. Wonders would never cease!

Jimmy, who ran the errands for the Terrace, was dispatched with a note for Sam to let him know that he now had an honorary granddaughter, called Susan, and that Emma would not be home that night. All was well.

Ethel saw that Derek got to school the next day along with her own brood, and Emma saw to the usual household tasks.

Jenny was very popular with all her neighbours and there was no shortage of visitors who came to view and admire the new arrival. Of course Emma could not miss the chance to offer a cup of tea to the visitors and to have a good gossip; naturally there was so much to comment on that nothing got done very quickly at all!

Fortunately after the delivery, Jenny regained her strength much more quickly this time. There was so much for her to look forward to; not least the introducing of newly arrived daughter Susan, to proud father, Ivan. Jenny and Derek, on tenterhooks, were counting the days until he arrived.

Emma spent a hectic ten days caring for Jenny and Derek, and admiringly cuddling her new, honorary granddaughter, but it was still with a sigh of relief that she arrived back at Merton Street and turned into Ada's Terrace. She felt that, at last, she was home and could rest!

'Oh!' sighed Emma, when Sam came home that evening, 'It is good to be home again and to sleep in my own bed. I'm getting too old for these shenanigans!'

Sam said, 'Don't you believe it - you're a bonny lass and no mistake! And you look as young as ever.' With that he kissed her boldly on the lips and ruffled her hair delightedly, saying, 'I well remember our honeymoon...'

'Don't you go getting ideas,' Emma, with a mock pout, archly teased him, 'I can do without you getting amorous - at least for the next ten seconds!'

How good it was to snuggle up in his welcoming arms once more.

CHAPTER NINETEEN

Social upheaval which broke up relationships during the war and the direness of war in itself, both caused psychological wounds which often had lasting effects. Sadly, George had experienced both such kinds of wounds, so that he was determined not to love again or get married.

His first love had been Daphne, who had betrayed him and found love elsewhere, and his second was Boon Phi. He had felt sure that she would be his wife and the mother of his children, but now she was dead and he felt lost and empty inside.

Based in Rangoon, he was, fortunately, away from the threatening jungle noises that reminded him of the nights spent undercover in the wild Burmese jungle. Still he remembered those nights of uncertainty and deadly danger while on patrol with his troop. The big moon, in the patches of clear jungle sky had not changed, but for him it felt like everything else in his life had changed and so much of the colour and vibrancy had gone.

George remembered again and again, the village long hut where he and his fellow soldiers had laid the bodies; grieving because they were not even able to give the victims a decent burial. Now, if he could go back there, he was not even sure he would be able to find the clearing. He knew he could not go back and that he needed time for his wounds to heal.

His family had no idea of these torments. They could only wait - however impatiently - for George to come back home.

It was in March that George, on board ship, saw the White Cliffs of Dover and wept like a child at this homecoming to his native shores and his subsequent landing back in England.

Then he was sent on to a camp in York where the demobilisation centre awaited him as the first step back to civilian life.

When Emma, in relief, finally had her first glimpse of him, she was dismayed at how thin her oldest surviving son had become and tried her best to feed him up; it was a long time before George felt really able to enjoy his food or have anything like a normal appetite.

Sam and Emma, so glad to have him safe home and with them again, encouraged him to rest and not be in a hurry to get back to work. For a few weeks he did do just that.

The woodyard where he used to work had been destroyed in the bombing raids, so it meant that, when the time came, he would be looking for a completely new job. Sam was very keen that George should come on to the docks with him. Consequently he enlisted the help of Tim Rollings, the Union representative. He was very sympathetic to the cause of brave soldiers returning to their civilian lives and who were seeking work.

In the meantime, in order to recover, George spent a lot of time alone. He brought his fishing gear out of the shed and would go off on a day's fishing by himself.

Unlike the weather in Burma, the winter at the end of 1946 and the beginning of 1947 was very severe, with so very much frost and snow.

It was as if the winter were compounding the misery of all the people who were in short supply of all the good things that made for warmth, food and comfort. For George, it symbolised the cold comfort of his broken heart, but he took consolation from the fact that the weather would change.

Eventually winter relented and spring arrived, blossoming into an early summer and people were at last able to enjoy the sun again.

There was a particularly warm welcome at *Home Farm* for George whenever he visited there and he liked to sit and spend time with his Aunt Annie and his new Uncle Charlie.

Eliza also was thrilled to welcome George back into the fold and made no bones about telling him so! Although George did not speak of what was troubling him, Grandma Eliza sensed his sorrow, and George, reassured, could feel her unspoken sympathy. Some of his loneliness began to slip away because of her care for him.

Jackie was overjoyed to have his big brother home, and was able to go fishing with George a few times. But there seemed to be an invisible barrier of awful sorrow holding George apart from everyone else.

George wanted to find his old self again. How long it might take, he did not know.

To his relief, he was eventually accepted by the *Dock Labour Board* and went off to work on the docks with Sam. Because of the good years that George had worked in the woodyard before the outbreak of war, he went to work on unloading wood and often worked on wooden pit props. He did not join in the scramble to be on the wagons, the harder job of loading up the strops in the hold, or on the dockside. The men loading up were happy if the pit props were wet, so that they would slide along more easily when they put their hand-hooks into them to load them into the thick, lifting strops. By contrast, those who had to carry them much preferred the wooden pit props to be dry so that they would not be so heavy. There was just no pleasing everybody!

But for George it was as if he was a driven man. It felt as though, by hard physical work, he might erase the images that haunted him by night in dreams and nightmares.

Emma would often hear him tossing and turning, sometimes calling out, but George never opened up enough to say what it was that tormented him. He did not want to admit that offloading to someone might make him feel out of control and vulnerable.

Emma remembered painfully the words from the popular *World War One* soldiers' song: *Oh, we'll never tell them.*

Sometimes George felt the need to get up early to make a pot of tea and watch the dawn come up. Once or twice, Emma joined him but George did not want to talk apart from apologising for disturbing his Mum.

'It's alright son,' she would say, 'you're home now, you can do as you like.' But inwardly she wept for the cheery lad that had vanished. She also knew that he needed to get things said in order to recover from all that he had been through.

'All because of the ruddy war,' she said to herself, 'on top of all the rationing and shortages, what's it done to our family?' She knew the simple answer, 'It's caused us blasted disruption!' Billy was gone, Joanie was off to goodness knows where, and then there were the wartime romances: Huh! Daphne had left George when you would have thought their relationship was solid, and as Emma thought it all through, there popped up in her memory her own relationship with the American; she quickly banished it to the back of her mind as something that she preferred not to think about.

There was no shortage of work on the docks because business was booming. The docks were so full of shipping, that it was said that just by walking over all the decks of the packed timber ships you could get across the dock!

One particular Sunday had been a lovely, warm day and George had been out fishing with Jackie and had returned with him to *Home Farm* to have tea with Annie, Charlie and Grandma Eliza.

Later, on his return to Ada's Terrace, he found his mother and father getting ready to go out for the evening.

'Come with us, son,' Emma coaxed, 'we're going to the club for an hour or so.'

Momentarily, George hesitated, but seeing the pleading in Emma's eyes, he agreed, 'Alright Mam! You go ahead and get a seat, I'll just get washed and changed.'

It was crowded in the *Working Men's Club*; it had been a good week for work and now folks were coming in to let their hair down, so to speak. The beer flowed freely, the one-armed bandit machine rattled away in the corner, while the artist entertained.

First a female singer entertained the audience, resplendent in a gorgeously sequinned dress. Her performance was followed by a raucous comedian who could easily match the earthy humour of the noisy audience. Between groups of artists there was the half hour set aside for bingo and the raffle.

The concert room was hushed as, pens poised, the club members waited for the bingo numbers to be called out. However, there seemed to be some unexpected kind of delay in the proceedings. This interruption was angrily greeted with echoing whistles and catcalls; then a group of men walked on to the stage.

Iggy Soanes, the compère, took up the microphone, 'Ladies and Gentlemen, pardon me for this break in the bingo but the Docks Board Manager has some serious news for you now.' He handed the microphone over to the Docks Board Manager, Dick Thompson, while Henry Baird the Chief Port Labour Officer stood in support beside him.

'I've got to tell you men,' began Dick Thompson, 'that there is a serious fire in the dock. The ship, the *Esmeralda*, is on fire. The Fire Brigade is there on station but we, here and now, are making an appeal for as many of you as possible to go and help offload her cargo of pit props. Come on lads! It's salvage money - more than you can get tomorrow morning in a normal way.'

He glanced around to see what effect his words had brought about and then handed the microphone back to Iggy before going off with Henry Baird. They continued urgently onwards to do a round of the pubs and clubs that night, calling out the men. The dockworkers responded quickly by dashing home to get changed out of their best clothing and into their work clothes.

Sam and George headed home for the same reason, 'Stay for the bingo!' they urged Emma. She would have company to walk home with and it was not dark at night. She would be safe.

But as dockers, Sam, George and their workmates would not be safe until the work was done. Nothing daunted, they rushed off to face danger and to rescue the timber off the *Esmeralda*.

By the time Sam and George got to the dock, it was dark. Men were milling around among the tangle of hoses that snaked across the ground in every direction. The ship's fire had started in the boiler room and the firemen were struggling to contain it. Flames were shooting from the ship's funnel. It was like one of those pictures of *Hades* with shadowy figures silhouetted against the falling darkness amidst shouts, orders and curses as people got in each other's way, in their desperate need to clear out as much cargo as possible.

The dock workers experienced the choking smell of smoke and showers of sparks and steam from the burning ship. They began with real determination to work at unloading the mining pit props from the ship with the help of dockside cranes. For them, it was not just humdrum daily work: if the cargo became furiously alight, then the ship could not be saved and would sink in the muddy waters of the dock. A foreman was frantically trying to organise railway wagons shunted by a steam engine, to come alongside the quay in order to get the unloaded cargo away from the fire danger area.

Sam and George were on deck with several other workers and Bill Honeyman when there was a shout for everyone to get off the vessel which was starting to list badly. Bill, who had more to drink than was good for him, had climbed on top of some of the props and was balancing precariously while swaying about.

George reached up to Bill to give him a helping hand down from the props when the ship rolled and the pile of timber slipped and came crashing down on George, trapping him by his feet.

Pain, like acid lightning, raced through his body. He knew that if the ship turned over only a miracle would save him. He asked for the lesser miracle of the ship not turning over and got what he had asked for.

The evacuated dockers rushed back on board as quickly as they could. With willing hands, the men urgently attempted to lift the props off George, all the while mindful of the danger on board that could so swiftly produce more casualties. George was carried off the ship and taken to hospital, with his father anxiously alongside him.

The work to rescue the ship and its cargo continued on the dockside; the ship was stabilised; then more shouts were heard and a hasty departure of dockers occurred again as the ship rolled once more. By the early hours of the morning the blaze was under control, the ship was rescued, and eventually the fire crews were able to leave. This left the dockers able to push on with the unloading, but the ship reeked of burnt wood for days afterwards.

Sam anxiously waited at the hospital while George was assessed by the doctors on call. The time seemed to crawl by and he wondered if Emma had got home safely. She could not know what had happened to George, and Sam knew that she would wait up for him with a hot drink.

A nurse came along and told him that his son had been taken off to be X-rayed, 'Don't worry Mr Walters, we'll take care of him.' They were as good as their word.

The dawn came up clear and bright with wisps of smoke lazily drifting over the dock and all the while there was the wafting smell of charred wood spreading across the city.

Sam had gone home as it was getting light; Emma had heard him and had come downstairs to hear the news. Sam was able to tell her that one of George's ankles was badly crushed and bruised, and that they could go and see him in the *Infirmary* at visiting time.

Although shocked and upset by the news, Emma, like the good mother that she was, had soon put together pyjamas and shaving gear to bring to her injured son.

At work the men, generous-hearted, had organised a whip round for George and presented Sam with the proceeds. George was not a lazy worker and had always been popular with his workmates: he was well known for pulling his weight and not shirking. The men clearly appreciated this in him.

Tim Rollings had a word with Sam, 'Don't you worry about them expenses for your lad!' he said heartily, 'The Union will take care of things and I'll visit George in hospital.'

Sam passed on the good news when he returned home that afternoon.

Emma was pleased but fretted over George, 'I 'ave to be glad that the Union will take up the fight for compensation for George, but suppose he won't be able to walk again? What kind of life would that be for a young man?'

Emma was naturally upset to see the state of George when she and Sam went to see him later that afternoon. There he was laid back on the pillows, his face looking tired and drawn. The nurses had set up a kind of protective cage to keep the bedclothes off his feet and lower legs. No fishing expeditions for George for yet awhile!

'What did the doctor have to say?' Emma was anxious to know. But the strong pain relief medicine had taken its effect and George was too *woozy* to be able to tell them much. The Sister came along to have a word with them to cheer them up, but at this stage there was really not a lot that she could tell them.

Emma faltered, with distress for her son written all over her face, 'He will be able to walk again, won't he?'

All that the Sister would say was, 'The consultant says it's too early yet to really know how much damage there actually is, so we don't know how long it will take to heal. We need to be patient'.

Afterwards, back at Ada's Terrace, Emma began to practise patience in the midst of her impatience for her son's recovery. She did this while mechanically working through the household tasks, before hurrying off to the hospital whenever visiting hours allowed. It gave her time to reflect on how much she loved all her children and how fortunate the family was to have George back with them after all that he had been through in the war.

Lapsing into her broadest dialect, she asked her Maker to 'give 'im his feet and legs back please, proper like,' and gave thanks for, 'bringing 'im back to us.'

Emma felt a lifting of her burden.

Sam, back at work, continued on with his part in unloading the *Esmeralda*. With some repairs, she would sail again, but Sam longed for his son to walk again.

Bill Honeyman, aware that his careless actions could mean the loss of his job, especially if George complained to the Union, was one of George's hospital visitors. 'I don't know what came over me,' he quavered. Sitting by the hospital bedside, Bill kept apologising for causing the log pile to come crashing down on George.

After ten minutes of listening to this, George, his eyes ablaze with ferocious intensity though not malice, turned to Bill and said, 'You did the wrong thing and got me hurt but I've forgiven you. Take it from me that I've said so!'

Bill was truly grateful for what George had done for him and gave his handshake upon it.

After he had gone, Sam and Emma arrived and heard the news. She ranted, 'I don't know how he had face enough to come! Our George could have been killed by his daft carrying on.'

Sam patted her arm comfortingly, 'Bill is genuinely upset. He knows it was the drink that made him act like that.'

'Then,' she said, 'he should have known better and not lost his senses over a pint of beer!'

Sam was silent. Bill knew that he should not have been so silly, but it was rather easy to see that in hindsight. Every man who turned out that night to do the work was needed, and most of them had had a drink or two. Some, admittedly, more than others. But all the men were keen to take the opportunity to earn extra money when they had the chance and to take part in the rescue.

On her visits to the hospital, Emma noticed a very pretty, little dark-haired nurse who was usually around, and was always eager to fulfil any reasonable requests that George came up with.

'She seems a nice lass,' Emma remarked to George.

'They're all very good,' said George, skilfully avoiding any implications, 'but they aren't allowed to have a lot to say to us and they're always kept busy; Sister Marchant sees to that.'

Emma had, however, noticed that George's interested eyes had a habit of following the Nurse as she went about her duties. The Nurse's caring attitude seemed to lift his spirits.

The days went by far more slowly for George than for his workmates. He had never, since getting the flu as a child, been so inactive. On the ward, George had a wheelchair now and wheeled himself over to the bedside of another patient to spend time chatting, until Sister Marchant ordered him back to his own bed space. 'You'll make the ward look untidy!' she stormed, 'How much time do you think my nurses have to waste on tidying up after you?'

He smiled quietly to himself and thought of her as a good candidate for the role of Sergeant Major!

One of George's ankles, injured in the accident, was still in plaster. It would take some time to heal. Emma aired her concern over its mending to the little Nurse.

'I can see that you're a good mother, Mrs Walters, but don't worry, we'll take good care of him,' she promised.

But as Sister Marchant was keeping a stern eye on every staff member, there was not much time for Emma to pass on any further comments.

All the same, on her many visits, Emma was always looking out for *George's Little Nurse*, as she had dubbed her.

George's Auntie Annie, when she was able, came through to visit the hospital to cheer him up and Jackie and Freda did so on some weekends. These visits of normality definitely helped to relieve the tedium for George.

Jackie, on his visits chatted away about fishing, work on the farm, rabbits, and indeed anything that he thought would interest George. 'I saw a kestrel on me way 'ere. So beautiful it was and hovering patiently on the wind.'

Jackie also told George at first hand, how Grandma Eliza, who was eighty-one now, was frail and shaky and almost unable to collect the eggs and do the little tasks she had once so enjoyed.

Charlie Brabham had become a great favourite of hers and spent time talking about farm affairs, markets and prices with her. She had also taken a liking to Freda, Jackie's girlfriend who lived in the village, saying, 'The lass has a good head on her shoulders.' Eliza's own shoulders were thin and stooped, but if willpower had anything to do with it, she said she would definitely be there for Jackie's wedding!

While Grandma Eliza was not actually up to the hospital journey, she kept up with George's news and every week wrote a letter to him. In doing so, she significantly helped in keeping his spirits up and he appreciated her in that kindness.

Jenny had also managed to visit once or twice with her new baby. She could never forget that in the early days of her living in Ada's Terrace with Sam and Emma, when all was strange and new, George had been so very kind to her. He was like a brother to her.

Days passed, and the good news came that George was going to be discharged from hospital and would be able to come home! He had learned to manage fairly well on his crutches and would be able to continue his treatment as an outpatient, with transport provided.

In Ada's Terrace, this happy news sent Emma into an urgent flurry of cleaning and moving furniture.

Sam was cheerful and could not stop smiling: he commented, 'Good old George will be so glad to get home that he wouldn't notice if you had cobwebs for curtains!' and he was not far wrong!

When the happy day came, Emma had the pleasure of collecting George in a taxi. She had also brought a big box of chocolates at George's request to give to Sister Marchant.

Receiving the chocolates with a smile, the Sister gave George a list of *Recovery Time Instructions* and a list of dates and times for physiotherapy and doctor's appointments.

George leaned forward and gave that stern lady a peck on the cheek causing her to blush and for once to have no sharp retort to make.

'Nurse Smith!' she called to the little dark-haired Nurse, 'Carry Mr Walters' bag downstairs for him, and look sharp!'

Nurse Smith picked the bag up from the bed and Emma could have sworn there was a twinkle in the Sister's eyes.

'Well!' thought the martinet, 'It's up to you now lad!' As she watched George go, she knew that he had been one of her easier patients, always polite and following the consultant's instructions about medication and exercise. 'It's always so much easier,' she said to herself, 'with someone who will help themselves!'

Emma pushed George to the ward lift in a wheelchair while the Nurse held the doors.

George, carrying his crutches seemed strangely tongue-tied.

Emma broke the silence by thanking her for all her help and care, and the taxi driver helped George to get into the front seat of the cab.

The seconds were ticking away and George's heart was beating loudly.

'Take good care of yourself!' the Nurse said to George.

Now it seemed that George was realising that he might not see the Nurse again, as he had no more reason - ever - to go up on to that ward. 'Just a minute!' he said, panic setting in now, 'Would you like to come to tea on Sunday?'

The Nurse, suspended between apprehension and delight, looked hopefully at Emma for confirmation.

Emma almost chortled with happiness, 'You'll be very welcome.'

The Nurse smiled broadly, 'Yes, I'd love to come!'

'But you haven't got my address!' George was despairing while the taxi driver grew impatient.

'It's alright!' said the Nurse, 'We'll have it in the files. See you on Sunday then.' And she meant it.

Goodbyes were echoed as the taxi drove away and Nurse Smith wheeled the chair back to the ward. 'He's invited me to tea on Sunday,' she whispered to another of her friends on duty.

Hearing that, Sister Marchant nodded contentedly to herself, and smiled. Then, thinking that it would not do for these girls to think she was getting soft, she barked, 'Nurse Smith, see to Mr Brown's covers, they are untidy!'

In the taxi, George queried, 'You're sure you don't mind, Mam?'

Emma laughed, 'Of course I don't. She certainly seems a very kind and caring girl. I've only ever heard her called Nurse Smith. What's her first name?'

'It's Valerie,' George informed her, resting back in the cab. 'It will,' he thought to himself, 'be *so* good to be home again and also to have the prospect of a teatime visitor!' His pulse raced a little faster at the thought and he pictured her face again, with pleasure.

Once they were back at Ada's Terrace, with the help of his crutches George hobbled indoors.

'Home at last!' he said thankfully, sitting down in the armchair. Looking round, he thought how small and cosy the house seemed compared with the hospital ward.

Emma was visibly fretting, 'How will you cope with the stairs?' she asked.

'Ah Mam!' he said reassuringly, 'It won't be the first time I've slept on the couch.'

Mollified, Emma bustled round, making tea and plumping up the cushions behind his back. 'I expect you can do with forty winks,' she suggested.

But he was happily settled with the paper although more tired than he liked to admit.

Sam was eager to see his son back home again, and untypically for his work schedule, came home at lunchtime.

In the evening, more visitors came to see him; this time it was Jackie and his new girlfriend Freda who cycled over specially in order to celebrate his return.

It was a happy household that gathered there, with so much news to catch up on.

Beyond any doubt, when Valerie, full of hope and some small trepidation, finally knocked on the door of No. 7 Ada's Terrace, George, in answering the door, felt as if all his Christmases had come at once! There was Valerie, on George's first Sunday home, faithfully keeping her promise to come.

At that moment, hope rose within him: with the first sight of her dear, sweet face, he knew in his heart that something special, very special, was going to come out of this, for both of them.

So it was that Valerie became a frequent, welcome visitor and was soon willing to help the family who had so appreciated her caring for George. Her merry laugh, as the saying goes, *warmed the cockles of their hearts.*

Her own home was in a village out on the Yorkshire Wolds and was not easy to get to on her days off. Soon she began to look on the Walters family as an extension of her own family.

Indeed, her cheerful readiness to help them when they needed it, became a blessed byword in the Terrace.

Naturally, to the delight of George and Valerie, Sunday teas together became a prized and regular event. They provided a safe haven in which they could gradually get to know and trust each other's character. George and Valerie were now *going out together* and very much in love. The love-light that they saw in each other's eyes was a wonder to behold. So much searching for the right person and now they had found each other. They even took to washing up the pots, pans and dishes in the kitchen because it gave them the privacy in which to give each other romantic hugs and kisses.

It seemed such a long time of waiting for George to return to normal health. He was impatient to get on with his life. Inactivity was not an ambition that he longed to have; rather his disability was a trial that just had to be endured; and he felt that it would not be long now before he would be working again. However, in the hospital Physiotherapy Department, when George pressed them for times and results in his recovery, no one would commit themselves.

At last, he was given an appointment to see the specialist who was responsible for his case. When they met, the great man put on his spectacles, looked at the X-rays and then made thoughtful noises as he studied the case notes. Clearing his throat sententiously and looking at George over the top of his spectacles, he said, 'Mr Walters, you find walking difficult, I believe?'

'Yes,' George nodded.

'Well, you may find there is a little improvement, but there will always be a certain degree of lameness, as the accident has left one of your legs shorter than the other.'

For some time, George had had his own suspicions about this, but he had *hoped against hope* that the consultant would offer a different view, but he did not. He would be on the sick list for several more weeks, and what then?

An unaccustomed depression struck him and an anger against his own body. He wanted to work!

Valerie tried to cheer him up, but the mood that had struck George and hung over him was like a black cloud, testing their togetherness.

In a moment of despair he said, 'You'd be much better finding some young chap who's fit and can look after you properly!' reducing her to tears at the thought. George ended up comforting her, 'I don't want to lose you,' he admitted.

'You're not ill,' she said while drying her tears and his, 'just a bit lame, but think of some of those that you've seen in hospital, and some who've come home from the war and are far worse off than you!'

George was thoughtfully silent for a little while, but he knew that Valerie was right.

Tim Rollings came to see George again and had a long talk with him and when Valerie saw him the next time, he was in a much happier frame of mind. The black cloud had departed and he could face her again. 'Mr Rollings says I can retrain as a *tallyman* on the docks,' George greeted her, 'I'll be able to work again - subject to a medical. It's a responsible job!'

Valerie gleefully hugged him, eyes shining bright, 'You see, what did I tell you? I knew you'd be alright!' Their togetherness, at last, had passed the test.

On returning home from work, Sam too welcomed his son's great good news and beaming joyfully said to him, 'You've got a proper career lad and it's a well-paid job too! I'm so proud of you and nobody's going to shoot at you!'

Sam rejoiced in knowing that his son had a practical turn of mind; good powers of concentration along with the ability to train solidly for the job and do well at it. Also Sam knew very well, as of long experience of dock work that the job did not require hard, physical labour so much as honesty, integrity, good ability with numbers and an observant eye for detail.

As he thought about it, Sam was really moved and said to George, 'You've got what it takes lad, to be a real good tallyman. You'll keep 'em straight!'

Emma, joining in the celebrations said, 'Well I never! The first *tallyman* in the family - think of that!' She knew that the job was actually a promotion, in terms of dock work, but Emma thought to herself that she would much rather do without a *Bill Honeyman promotion* for her children on any day of the week!

When Jenny came with the children later in the day, she found the household was definitely in a party mood!

A few days later, Mr Rollings, the Union representative came to see George. He asked for details of the treatment which George was due to have and about his recovery. Accepting a cup of tea gladly, he asked, 'How do you manage the stairs?'

'Well, I often sleep down here,' George informed him, 'but if I go up there, it's mostly on my bottom, so it isn't easy.'

'You would, perhaps, like somewhere more modern, I expect?' Mr Rollings remarked to Emma.

'Yes, I often think so,' said Emma, 'but the housing people say that we are well down the list.'

'The trouble is,' said George, 'that Mam cleans and polishes this place and keeps it like a palace; they don't see how hard she works.'

The very next week, a letter came in the post, offering George's mother, father and himself a *prefab* that was not so far from where Jenny was now living.

Overcome with gratitude and happiness, Emma did not know if she was on her head or her heels. She just had to sit down with a cup of tea in order to recover her composure.

Composure did not come easily with the first cup of tea and she found herself throwing her apron over her head and bawling with tears of happiness. By the third cup of tea, she could say that she would definitely recover from so much good fortune at some time in the near future!

'It's Mr Rollings' doing,' said George. 'I know that he's a good man in his job, all the men speak well of him and he has comrades on the council.' It also had not hurt that the *Esmeralda's* fire and his own accident had been well reported in the local paper.

Needless to say, there was so much to do to prepare for the move, but happy willing hands, provided by Jackie and Freda in their spare time, along with other kind helpers, all helped things move along nicely.

Now the day drew closer for Sam, Emma and George to be moving out of dear old Ada's Terrace.

That Saturday morning, Emma had been with Jenny to measure up the new house for such things as curtains and floor coverings.

People still found that most things were rationed, or in short supply, and shopping could be a frustrating experience, so practising the pooling of coupons and dockets was still an essential art at such times.

In the afternoon, Valerie joined Jenny and Emma on their expedition into town. The trio, full of merriment, laughed and joked their way round the shops together while supporting Emma in buying things for her new house.

When Emma returned home later that day, Sam had prepared the teatime meal for her and was reading the paper. After eating, they sat together in front of the fire and enjoyed watching the play of the flames amongst the coals. With George out with Valerie, it was delightful to be *Sam and Emma together* in the warm quietness of their own home.

Moving home is one of the tough experiences of life and Emma was suddenly quiet and extra alert, assailed by fear about the future while being engrossed in thinking about the new *prefab* home. Would they miss the old comforts of their long-time home in the Terrace? 'Supposing that I don't like it there, in the *prefab*?' she whispered to Sam, who hugged her tight. 'It'll be alright lass,' he said with a reassuring grin. You'll see - you mark my words! Think how often you've wished for good hot water on tap, a posh bathroom worth having and all those nice things!'

Emma did think, and in her mind she had a flashback picture of how her old neighbour Lily Hawkins - face flushed with excitement - had stood in Emma's kitchen with the council letter that was offering the Hawkins family a new house! Emma felt strengthened and heartened at the memory of Lil's good fortune. She felt that she could and would make the move into their own new home. If only both families could have made the move together but a preserving Providence had kept them from both sharing the same ending. Emma happily recalled the good times with her old friend and became quietly determined that both Derek and Susan would know all about their Grandma Lil, who would have loved them so.

It was early September when the *big moving day* came. Some old furniture was contentedly given away, while Eliza insisted generously that she would be treating them to some item or other that Emma would like for the new house.

Emma wandered through the old terraced house that had been their home for so long, with its memories of marriage, work, war, the raising of children, happy times and sad.

Emma's vision blurred with tears as she sat among the brand new packing cases that were waiting stoically for the removal van. She got up and looked around the house again, saying a final farewell to the rooms that she knew and loved so well, tears streaming down her face in rivulets.

There was so much to be said goodbye to: she had already lost Billy, Daisy and Lil. It was this special house that she and Sam had moved into as newly-weds; in this house they had raised all their children and watched them grow up.

Emma knew she only had a limited time for her reflections, because Jenny would be waiting for them at the new house.

Picking up a package from the top of one of the cases, Emma hugged it to herself. Without unwrapping it, she knew well what it was: the picture within the package evoked memories of their son Billy leaving to join the *Royal Air Force*. Sam and Emma would never forget Billy, the boy who grew to be a man, amidst the arguments and laughter.

Then there were the girls, quarrelling one minute, sharing a joke the next, and Joanie so sure that she would be an actress. All her dreams had been centred on that ambition. 'Selfish in a way,' Emma thought, 'but she has proved that, at least, she could achieve something with her life.'

Emma had sent a change of address note to the last address they had from Joanie, but nothing had ever returned to let them know that she was aware of her parents' move or even that she cared at all.

Emma stepped out into the little backyard where one of the old tin baths still hung on its nail on the wall. She banged on it with her fist and it rattled against the wall, 'Well, we won't need you anymore!' she said.

The tin bath evoked memories of Jackie's bath time battle games, of warships and of getting drenched. More memories of Lily Hawkins and her growing kids; of their own house full of her growing kids and finally of the community that had been in Ada's Terrace.

She wept and sobbed again for times of sadness and happiness in and around the home that they had loved. 'Goodbye Ada's Terrace!' she shouted. It was as a farewell to an old friend. Sadness, joy and fulfilment showed strongly in her face, amidst the tears.

'Emma!' It was her dear Sam calling her. Time to go. On to new things. Taking the memories with her. Slowly she went through the house and out of the door to where Sam was waiting.

'Come on, lass!' he spoke. Sam put his arm round her as Emma closed the door. She looked back, as she knew she must.

The curtainless windows stared blankly. Without the family it was an empty shell. And as they were driven away in a friend's car, she thought of one of Eliza's homilies: *the eyes are the windows of the soul*, but sadly now the house at Ada's Terrace was empty. Nobody was living there anymore. But the memories had not died.

The journey passed quickly and then the car stopped. This new beginning was, for her, like being able to open a beautiful gift box full of lovely presents.

Here they were at the new house with the family waiting to greet them, and Emma exclaimed, 'Oh! I can see George and Valerie waving engagement rings and...' she faltered with joy, 'there's Joanie with a big bouquet of flowers!'

She kissed Sam and got out of the car to the adventure of her new life. Old houses or new, *Life goes on!*

Glossary

Albert: A watch chain with a bar at one end for attaching to a buttonhole.

Bain: Hull Dialect for child.

Billet: A place, or a civilian's house where soldiers are lodged temporarily.

Blue bulb: Blackout light bulbs.

Bobby Dazzler: Someone striking or attractive.

Clinker built: is a method of boat building where the edges of hull planks overlap

Clydesdale: A horse of a heavy, powerful breed, used for pulling heavy loads.

Coble: is a type of open traditional fishing boat which developed on the North East coast of England. The southern-most examples occur around Hull.

Colostrum: The first secretion from the mammary glands after giving birth, rich in antibodies.

Commando: A soldier specially trained for carrying out raids.

Embarkation leave: A short period of leave before the troops went abroad.

Fourses: A snack eaten at around four o'clock in the afternoon.

Gurkha: A member of any of several peoples of Nepal noted for their military prowess.

Hades: The King of the Underworld in Greek mythology.

Kasbah: The citadel of a North African city.

Land Girl: A woman doing farm work, especially during the Second World War.

Left-footer: Young beginner.

Lloyd Loom chair: Wicker chair.

Matinee coat: A baby's short coat.

Pathé newsreel: Invented by *Pathé,* the first newsreels shown in theatres prior to a feature film.

Pig Club: Joint ownership of a pig by a number of families.

Privy: Outside toilet.

Reserved occupation: an occupation considered important

enough to render the person exempt from military service.

Slipper Baths: A bath with one high end to lean against and the other end covered over.

Squeeze Box: An accordion or concertina.

Very Lights: Illumination in trench warfare at night in the form of brilliant white flares which are shot into the sky.

W.A.A.F: Women's Auxiliary Air Force.

Wetting the baby's head: Celebrate the birth of a baby by having an alcoholic drink.

Wren: The Women's Royal Naval Service or *W.R.N.S.* popularly and officially known as the *Wrens.*

Zeppelin: A large German rigid airship of the early 20th century, filled with hydrogen, cylindrical in shape and fitted with motorised propellers.

Bibliography

Hull Daily Mail: Back numbers from the History Library
A Century of Hull: by David Gerrard
Hull Dockland: by Michael Thompson
Report and Enquiry into the Major Ports of Great Britain World War II: Wikipedia
History of Hull: www.informationbritain.co.uk
British 14th Army Soldiers in Burma: ww2.wwarii.com
Fourteenth Army (United Kingdom): Wikipedia
The Hull Blitz - 1940 Raids: www.heroesofhull.co.uk
Rationing in the United Kingdom: Wikipedia
George V: Wikipedia
Edward VIII Abdication Crisis: Wikipedia
Queen Elizabeth The Queen Mother: Wikipedia
Siege of Hull (1643): Wikipedia
The Forgotten Army - General William Slim's 14th Army in Burma: www.bbc.co.uk
The Terrible suffering and extraordinary courage of British WW2 soldiers fighting the Japanese in the Burmese Jungle: Christopher Hudson
East Yorkshire Regiment: Wikipedia
British Enter Rangoon: www.bbc.co.uk
West Yorkshire Regiment: www.bbc.co.uk
Bill Slim & his forgotten 14th Army: www.lookandlearn.com
Pte Mervyn Basil Tooke 4th Battalion East Yorkshire Regiment: www.wartimememoriesproject.com
East Yorkshire Regiment in WW2: www.nam.ac.uk
The Prince of Wales's Own Regiment of Yorkshire: www.pwoyorkshire.co.uk
Hull Blitz: Wikipedia
Burma: www.wolftree.freeserve.co.uk/Burma/Burma.html
Not the Image but Reality: British POW Experiences In Italian and German Camps by P Liddle & I Whitehead: ww2talk.com/forums
The History Place Timeline of Events 1941-1945: www.historyplace.com
How the GI influx shaped Britain's view of Americans: Melissa Hogenboom BBC News

The War in Burma 1942 to 1945: archive.iwm.org.uk
Z Force Burma: Wikipedia
The Battle of the Atlantic The U-boat peril by Dr G Sheffield
North African Campaign Timeline: Wikipedia
P.O.W. Free Men in Europe: www.anzacpow.com
Called to the Colours by Norman Wood: bbc.co.uk
Operation Brevity World War II Database: ww2db.com
The Battle of El Alamein: www.historylearningsite.co.uk
Reserved Occupations: www.funtrivia.com
Engagements 1942: www.desertrats.org.uk/battles
7th Armoured Division (United Kingdom): Wikipedia
www.warlinks.com/armour/11_hussars/index.php
First Encounter: 11th Hussars in North Africa: bbc.co.uk
Gen. Montgomery's Eighth Army by J Myers: bbc.co.uk
www.temehu.com/Cities_sites/WorldWarTwo.htm
Rifle Brigade (Prince Consort's Own): Wikipedia
Operation Brevity Order of Battle: Wikipedia
Brief History of the British 7th Armoured Brigade:
        www.desertrats.org.uk
Rommel and the Afrika Korps: www.military.com
Brief History of the Desert Rats: www.flamesofwar.com
Siege of Tobruk: Wikipedia
North Africa: www.history.co.uk
Operation Battleaxe: Wikipedia
The Second World War in France: 1939-1945 Wikipedia
Sid's Dunkirk Story: ww2 The People's War
Blitzkrieg 1940: www.eyewitnesstohistory.com
Battle of Britain: Wikipedia
The Italian Invasion of Egypt: ww2today.com
Italy invades Egypt: bbc.co.uk/history
British Navy in the Mediterranean: naval-history.net/ww2
Guide to Hull dialect: BBC Local Humberside
        www.bbc.co.uk
British Expeditionary Force (WW2): Wikipedia
BEF Memories: Douglas Gough www.bbc.co.uk
1914-1918.invisionzone.com/forums
The 7th Indian Infantry Division: www.burmastar.org.uk
The Second Battalion East Yorkshire 1939-1945:
        eastyorkshireregiment.blogspot.co.uk

Please address all correspondence by email to:
office@frismeck.com

35446147R00151

Made in the USA
Charleston, SC
10 November 2014